# MEADOWSIDE

*A dual timeline ghost story*

By

# Kate Winters

Copyright © Kate Winters 2024
This book is sold subject to the condition that it shall not, by way of trade or otherwise, be lent, resold, hired out, or otherwise circulated without the publisher's prior consent in any form of binding or cover other than that in which it is published and without a similar condition including this condition being imposed on the subsequent publisher.
The moral right of Kate Winters has been asserted.
ISBN: 9798340895790

This is a work of fiction. Names, characters, businesses, organizations, places, events and incidents either are the product of the author's imagination or are used fictitiously. Any resemblance to actual persons, living or dead, events, or locales is entirely coincidental.

*For Joseph.*

*Thank you for your strength, determination, and positivity through the most challenging of times. You have been amazing, courageous, and uncomplaining. I couldn't be prouder of you. You are a force to be reckoned with, and I'm so proud to be your mum. I just can't wait to see what the future will bring to you and to walk beside you on your journey. Shine on, my crazy diamond!*

# CONTENTS

| | |
|---|---|
| ACKNOWLEDGMENTS | i |
| PROLOGUE | 1 |
| CHAPTER 1 | 6 |
| CHAPTER 2 | 24 |
| CHAPTER 3 | 44 |
| CHAPTER 4 | 53 |
| CHAPTER 5 | 79 |
| CHAPTER 6 | 101 |
| CHAPTER 7 | 125 |
| CHAPTER 8 | 141 |
| CHAPTER 9 | 159 |
| CHAPTER 10 | 179 |
| CHAPTER 11 | 208 |
| CHAPTER 12 | 231 |
| CHAPTER 13 | 245 |
| CHAPTER 14 | 256 |
| CHAPTER 15 | 269 |
| CHAPTER 16 | 287 |
| CHAPTER 17 | 305 |
| CHAPTER 18 | 329 |
| EPILOGUE | 342 |
| ABOUT THE AUTHOR | 349 |

# ACKNOWLEDGEMENTS

With huge thanks to my husband, Den, for the reading, amendments, and unwavering support, I couldn't have done it without you!
Thanks also to Ali and Julie for the encouragement and ongoing support, Ben for your endless belief in me, and all the advice and enthusiasm.
Special thanks to Jo Griffiths for all your hard work on the manuscript and support.
Thanks also to my Mum and Dad, who always knew I could do it and helped me believe in myself. I am blessed with very supportive friends and family, and I would like to thank them all for their outstanding support, encouragement, and sharing of social media posts!
Last but not least, I would like to thank everyone who has read, reviewed, and shared my work and has come along with me on this most exciting journey.
I am hugely grateful for every one of you.

# Prologue

## December 2002

Matilda Grey stood at the window, watching the winter shadows steal across the sky, extinguishing the last rays of the feeble December sun, plunging the meadow into darkness. In the black glass, she could see her reflection and was reminded of how the declining year represented her decaying life, for she, too, was in the deep winter of her existence, her light growing consistently dimmer to make way for the young and the new.

Her reflection showed an old lady, frail and small, who had outlived her time due to her sheer determination not to die. A long and troubled life was etched into her face, the lines drawn by tragedy and the relentless passing of time. Her eyes stared back at her, their gaze accusatory and critical, causing her to flinch and turn away from the window.

She hobbled painfully across the large room towards an armchair close to the blazing fire. She lowered herself cautiously into the chair, hearing the creaking of her crumbling bones and her breaths coming in short, laboured gasps.

*Something has to change,* she told herself, recognising that she no longer had the luxury of time being on her side and feeling, with a sharp stab of regret, that she had allowed things to drift for far too long. She sighed wearily, gazing into the cheerful, dancing flames, remembering that she had chosen to do nothing when time stretched forever into the distance.

The fire spat suddenly. Matilda stared at a flickering ember that burned and then died on the tiled hearth, remembering a long time ago when a letter had arrived. Letters were a rare event, for she had nobody in her life who would write to her, yet this one had landed on the doormat in a white envelope, her name written on it in block capitals.

The letter had stayed on the hall table for many months. Now and again, she would pick it up, gaze at it, and then put it back, hoping that it would somehow disappear of its own accord, and she would no longer need to think or worry about it. Ultimately, she grew tired of wondering what it could contain and reasoned that as she knew nobody, its contents could not be of much importance.

She had taken the letter to her bedroom, sitting on the side of the bed as she quickly scanned the handwritten words. It was from a man called David Lewis, who lived in Cambridge. The letter explained that he was trying to research his family tree and believed that he could be related to Matilda. The letter was polite, asking for any further information that she might have.

Upon reading the letter, her first thought was that David Lewis had made a mistake, for Matilda was related to just one person: her sister. Neither of them had married or had children, which made any genetic connection to this man impossible. She decided to ignore the letter, but something made her keep it, replacing it back inside the envelope and storing it for years in the top drawer of her bedside cabinet.

Despite her conviction that David Lewis could not be a relation of hers, she still thought about the letter, occasionally taking it out of the drawer and re-reading it. Sometimes it would make her feel a melancholy sadness; it would have been nice to have had another relation apart from her sister, but she always came to the same conclusion that it was best left alone, for pursuing this would bring nothing but disappointment.

Several years later, Matilda was struck by a thought that made her question her belief that there were no further relatives. She remembered that when she was a very young child, a man and a woman had come to the house, and the man had been introduced as her father's brother. The woman was his wife and had an infant child sitting on her knee. For the life of her, no matter how hard she tried, she could not recall the names of either visitor, nor that of the child. All she could remember was her father saying that they had never been close as brothers, and as far as she knew, her uncle and his wife had never revisited.

If David Lewis was related to her, then he must be the progeny of her uncle. At the time when the letter arrived, and for many years after, Matilda had been fit and healthy; old age wasn't a worry or a concern. Being alone in the world with Kitty was a situation she was accustomed to, but as time passed, she realised that old age was approaching fast. The fact that she was now ancient, with an elderly sister, was now a concern of the utmost importance.

Her thoughts returned to the present, to her troubles and worries. While she sat in the quiet room, she heard familiar footsteps along the corridor of the upstairs landing, then the opening and slamming shut of a door. At that moment, Kitty was in the children's room, a small anteroom that led off from the larger drawing room. The door was open, a soft glow of light spilling out of it into the darkened room where Matilda sat.

She gazed up at the ceiling, thankful that the footsteps and scurrying movements from the upper floor had stopped, at least for the time being. She shook her head sadly. Life was a strange business; time rushes forward, changing everything in its path, and yet amid its destructions and alterations, it chooses to leave some things untouched with no rhyme or reason.

The thought reminded her of her sister, Kitty. The years had aged her but had left her mind childlike. Matilda was in two minds as to which of them was worse off, she herself, who was plagued with the memories of the past, or Kitty who remembered only what she wanted to, blissfully forgetting most of the things that could cause her distress. She remembered long summers spent in the meadow, the Christmases around the fire, the harvests spent in the fields. It was an enviable symptom of whatever undiagnosed ailment had touched her mind, leaving her a very old lady with the simple understanding of a child.

As the years progressed, Matilda became acutely aware of the decline in her own health. The most minor tasks now exhausted her, and the burden of the past and the care of her sister rested heavily on her frail shoulders. One day soon, she would die. The time would come when she could no longer fight against the spectre of death, too weak to struggle for the next breath, and then, for the first time in her entire life, she would leave Meadowside, abandoning her sister to fend for herself, all alone in a house where the past would not stay silent.

She worried constantly about leaving Kitty, but she was also worried about the house itself. After she and Kitty were dead and gone, what would become of Meadowside and the ghosts that whispered from the past?

Matilda had spent countless nights trying to find a solution. She only had three options, and none of them would be easy. She could pay for a nurse to come to Meadowside to help them, but that would still leave Meadowside without a caretaker, and there would be no certainty that whoever she employed would stay and look after Kitty if Matilda died first.

The next option was the one that she had thought about the most. Somewhere out in the world, there was an heir. His name might be David Lewis. If she could find him, perhaps he would be willing to take on the responsibility for herself and Kitty in exchange for being named Matilda's heir in an official will. This option appeared to be the most sensible, mainly because it would solve all of her problems in one fell swoop, and if David Lewis turned out to be the right sort of person, then it could work very well indeed.

The third option caused a cold shiver to run down her spine. She could kill Kitty. Of course, there would be no violence involved, for this would be a mercy killing, a way to be sure that her beloved sister would never be left alone. It would save her from ever having to mourn Matilda's death, for hadn't they both mourned enough in their lifetimes, and it would prevent the unthinkable terror Kitty would feel on finding herself completely alone. Although this would be kinder to Kitty than the alternative, Matilda knew deep in her heart that she couldn't do it, for if life had taught her anything, it was that two wrongs could never make a right.

# Chapter 1

## February 2003

I had always hated the beginning of the year. There seemed little point in winter once Christmas was over and the tinsel and lights packed away. January and February always appeared to be a time of waiting and expectation, waiting for the days to grow longer, for the first bluebells of spring, anticipating a small sign of optimism in the gradual lightening of the sky.

That February was a difficult one for me. I had made no New Year resolutions, having concluded that they served no purpose other than to depress me at the end of the year when nothing had changed apart from the fact that I had taken another journey around the sun but had achieved nothing. We were only in the second month of the year, and my discontent and disillusionment grew stronger by the day, dragging me down. I was stuck in a rut so deep that I could barely see the light of day, let alone figure out how to change things.

Retrospectively, I can see that I was simply tired of myself, of my indecision and inability to find inspiration. I was terminally bored, working full time in a job that brought little satisfaction for a salary that barely covered my bills. The thought that I was wasting the best years of my life squirmed constantly in my mind, merging with the knowledge that I was ill-equipped to do anything about it.

I had a university education and a first-class honours degree but had never found my passion. I had studied history, which I enjoyed but ultimately led to nowhere. I didn't want to be a teacher or an historian or to work in a museum; in fact, there was nothing that I wanted to do.

I had drifted into my job in a bookshop after seeing an advert sellotaped to the large bay window. It wasn't what I had wanted all those years ago, and it certainly wasn't what I wanted twelve years later at the age of thirty-six.

For many years, I felt I was waiting for something, just marking time while I anticipated this momentous event. Still, nothing happened, nothing changed, until a freezing cold, innocuous day in February when suddenly it did.

I remember that morning well and can visualise myself wandering around my small, terraced home with little expectation of the day ahead. I had not slept well, spending the night tossing and turning and then getting up far earlier than I needed to, feeling grumpy and out of sorts. At the same time, I envisaged yet another day standing at the counter, answering the same old questions, tidying up the books that customers seemed incapable of returning to where they had found them.

The doorbell rang dead on 8 am, a strange, urgent sound that penetrated rudely into the only quiet time I would get before returning home that evening. I frowned as I deposited my empty cereal bowl into the sink, wondering who could be at the door this early. It was too early for the postman, and everyone I was acquainted with would know that I was just about to leave for work.

I opened the door to a man on the pavement wearing a dark blue navy suit, shiny black shoes, and a patterned tie. He was tall, dark-haired, and was carrying a briefcase.

"Amber Lewis?" He inquired, looking me up and down as if I wasn't who he expected to see.

"Can I help you?" I snapped, glancing down at my watch to drive home the point that I didn't have time to talk to strange men on my doorstep when I should have been halfway to work.

"My name is Nathaniel Trent. I have some business to conduct with you." He glanced over his shoulder as a group of mothers walking their children to school, passed behind him. "It might be best if we talked inside."

"Business? What kind of business? I have to go to work."

"I work for Johnson and Baxter's solicitors and need to speak to you urgently."

I glanced down at the business card he thrust into my hand with a sinking heart. None of this was making any sense at all, and my fractious brain told me that it could not lead to anything good.

"Is someone suing me?" I asked defensively, racking my brain, trying to come up with a reason that would bring a solicitor to my door.

He shook his head, his dark eyes sincere. "I am not here to deliver bad news, Miss Lewis, in fact, quite the opposite."

I frowned, my interest growing. "This business of yours better be worth me getting sacked." I glanced at my wristwatch, realising that I couldn't make it on time now anyway. "This will be the second time I've been late for work this week, and it's only Tuesday! You'd better come in, I suppose."

I stood aside as he stepped into the narrow hallway. "Straight ahead," I directed him down the passageway, growing increasingly intrigued. "Do you want a cup of coffee, or something?"

"That would be lovely." He sat at the table, placing his briefcase on the chair beside him.

I busied myself filling up the kettle, clattering in the cupboards for clean mugs, spooning instant coffee into a matching pair, feeling slightly agitated. I turned around suddenly.

"You're making me nervous," I said, louder than I had intended, "you are sitting there with your briefcase, knowing this big thing, while I don't have the first clue as to what is going on."

"Sit down," he suggested, "leave the coffee, and I will tell you what has brought me here today."

"Has somebody died?" I dried my hands on a tea towel,

abandoned the coffee cups, and sat opposite him.

"Nobody has died, Miss Lewis, at least not yet."

"Not yet? What the hell is that supposed to mean?"

He lifted his gaze from his briefcase and smiled enigmatically. "I will start at the beginning, and by the end, you will fully understand why I am here and why the matter is so pressing."

"Okay," I agreed, shifting my weight in the chair, consumed with curiosity.

"At the beginning of January, I was called to a house called Meadowside, situated in the Cambridgeshire Fens. My client, the elderly lady who lives there, is called Matilda Grey. Does that name mean anything to you at all?"

"No," I replied after a moment of thought, "should it mean something to me?"

"Never mind," he continued. "Matilda Grey is one hundred and two years old. She was born in the house, Meadowside, in 1902 and has lived there for her entire life. She lives there with her sister, Kitty, who is also extremely elderly. Matilda is now very frail. Her sister is charming, but a little strange. I am not a doctor, so I wouldn't presume to know what ails her, but she may have some learning difficulties. Matilda has cared for her for most of her life."

"I see," I uttered, not seeing at all and wishing that he would hurry up and get to the point.

Nathaniel Trent placed his folded arms on the tabletop and leaned forwards, his eyes suddenly solemn. "Several years ago, well, about thirty-four years ago to be more precise, Matilda Grey received a letter from a man who believed he could have been related to the sisters. The letter explained that he had been doing some research; it seemed he was having difficulty completing his family tree, but some inquiries he made had led him to Matilda Grey. He was asking her for information about her family. Matilda ignored the letter because she could not see how this man could possibly have been related to her, and it was many years later that she remembered that her father had a brother who was married and had at least one child."

"I still don't understand," I said, still feeling confused. "I told you that I don't know this Matilda Grey. I have never heard of her."

Nathaniel smiled slightly. "The name of the man who sent Matilda the letter was David Lewis."

I stared at him, completely shocked.

"David Lewis? That...that was my father's name."

"Matilda instructed me to find David Lewis at the beginning of the year. I found him on a census, living with his wife, Sally Lewis, at the address in Cambridge that I believe was your childhood home and where your mother still resides. A further search informed me that unfortunately, and very sadly, your father, David Lewis, died young."

"That is right," I whispered, "it was a motorbike accident."

"I'm very sorry." He inclined his head, waited a suitable amount of time, and then continued. "I informed Matilda of the tragedy. She was upset because she regretted her decision not to reply to your father's letter, and by the time she had remembered that she had an uncle, too much time had passed, and it was too late."

I felt shaken that the reason for Nathaniel Trent's visit was to do with my father. I was barely three years old when he died, and I only had vague and hazy memories of him.

"I told Matilda that David Lewis had a daughter, and although he had tragically passed away, there was a direct relative of his still alive, and she then instructed me to find you."

"Goodness," I uttered, not knowing what else to say and still not fully understanding the exact reason behind Nathaniel's visit. He took a deep breath.

"As I have explained, Matilda Grey is very old, and her life is nearing its end. She would like to die in peace, with her affairs tied up and in order. She is so worried about what will happen to her sister if she were to die first, and what would become of her home, Meadowside, that peace in her final months is not possible.

"Matilda believes that Kitty would not cope with being alone, nor would she cope with being moved into residential care. Neither of the sisters have ever lived anywhere other than Meadowside, neither of them married, they have no family apart from each other. There are no children, no heirs."

"That is sad," I mused, "it must be extremely challenging for them."

"It is," Nathaniel nodded. "Matilda can no longer manage the house; she can barely look after herself, let alone Kitty. She is dying, Miss Lewis, and terrified that she will pass away before the future for Kitty and the house are settled."

"I can understand that" I said, "it must be an awful worry for her and a tough thing to have to deal with at her age."

Nathaniel gazed at me for a long time as if trying to make an assessment or judgement on me.

"Now it is time to tell you why I have come to see you today. You are the only relative Matilda and Kitty have, connected to them through their father's brother, as he was the only member of the Grey family who ever had a child. The truth of the matter is that Matilda is not at all concerned about how you are related to her, and it has been almost impossible for me to find out. She does not know, or can't remember, the first name of her uncle and has very few memories or details about her family apart from those closest to her, and they have all now died. Matilda wants more than anything else to have an heir to Meadowside, and it doesn't matter to her how fragile that link is or how distant the connection; she just wants somebody to leave the house to."

Nathaniel's words floated around me in the air while my brain struggled to make sense of them. Surely, he didn't mean what I thought he meant, for that would be too ridiculous to contemplate seriously.

I stared at him in abject bewilderment, my mouth opening and shutting as if it wanted to say something but could not articulate the words. A slow smile lifted the corners of his lips, as if he was, in some way, enjoying my confusion.

"I can see that this has come as a massive shock to you, as well it might. I don't know what's happening inside your head now but let me clarify: Matilda Grey wants to bequeath her house, Meadowside, and her considerable fortune to you, lock, stock and barrel. Edward Grey's will states quite clearly that the house, his money and all of his belongings would go to his wife on his death, and when she dies then everything was to be shared equally between his living children when they came of age."

My brain stopped functioning as I stared at him as if he was speaking a foreign language. I had heard the words that he had said, but I couldn't believe that they could be true.

"Of course, there are some conditions."

"Conditions?" I reiterated stupidly.

"Yes, depending on your circumstances, they may be difficult. It is Matilda's wish that you go to Meadowside straight away, at your earliest convenience. She would like you to move into the house and look after her and her sister for the rest of their lives, and in return, she will leave Meadowside and her money to you in her will."

Again, I sat silently as his words slowly dripped into my brain.

"She wants to leave her house and her money to me: a complete stranger?"

"There is nobody else, Miss Lewis. Matilda explained to me that this is the only solution that solves all her problems. Kitty would not be left alone if Matilda died first, which considering her age and state of health, is highly likely, both of them would be looked after, and Meadowside would have an heir instead of being taken by the government or left to fall to ruin."

For a moment, it felt as if the world had stopped turning. My brain buzzed with questions, but I was too overwhelmed to speak.

"I'll make us that coffee, shall I?" Nathaniel stood up and walked to the kettle. "Do you take milk and sugar?"

"Just black, please." I sat at the table trying to assimilate the momentous news Nathaniel had brought, my heart palpitating and my stomach churning. "What's she like, this Matilda Grey?"

Nathaniel brought the mugs over to the table and resumed his seat. "She's remarkable. Very old fashioned, of course. She, Kitty and the house seem trapped in the past. I have the impression that, at one time, Matilda Grey was a woman to be reckoned with. Even now, despite her great age, there is something defiantly stubborn about her, a kind of stoic resilience.

"The thing that I find most incredible is that they have lived together in Meadowside every single day and night of their existence. They are highly reclusive; as far as I understand, they have never been anywhere apart from the house and its immediate vicinity.

"The house is literally like walking back in time, full of furniture that seems to be from the early 1900s. It is a large, solid family home situated by the side of a wildflower meadow, with the fen stretching behind it as far as the eye can see. It is a beautiful building which will require some renovation and updating.

"As it turns out, Matilda's father, Edward Grey, was wealthy. He was an academic, a renowned ornithologist, author and artist. Due to the rest of his children having passed away, Matilda, as the eldest of the two surviving sisters, is his sole heir."

My heart flipped in my chest. "How much money are we talking about?" I felt embarrassed asking the question, but my curiosity was too great not to ask.

"A great deal," he replied, not in the least offended. "Matilda and Kitty have lived quiet, isolated lives and have not needed to spend much of their father's wealth, mainly it has just stayed in the bank, accumulating interest and growing by the year. " He scratched the side of his face thoughtfully. "In fact, I don't think Matilda is aware of how much money she has. She needs so little, and I think she would probably find it quite overwhelming to know that she has at least a couple of million sitting in the bank."

"A couple of million?" I gasped; my eyes wide.

"At least that," Nathaniel grinned.

"I just can't take it in," I muttered, "it seems so unreal, like a dream. Things like this don't happen to people like me; they just don't."

Nathaniel smiled as he leaned back in his chair. "Everybody says that when their luck changes, but the truth of the matter is that things like this are happening to people every day. It's a huge opportunity, a chance that will probably never come your way again, so I would advise you to think very carefully about your next move. The question for you is, do you want to live in Fenland, in the absolute back of beyond, to look after two old ladies you have never met?"

I stared at him in astonishment and then burst out laughing.

"What's so funny?"

I got a grip of myself and bit my lip. "I'm sorry, it's just that I think it's hysterical that you think I have anything to consider or to think about. I work in a tiny bookshop, for goodness' sake, and I can barely afford to live. There is no contest, nothing to agonise over or to weigh up. I will take Matilda Grey's offer and am delighted to do so. I will care for her and her sister, making them as comfortable and as happy as I can."

Nathaniel smiled broadly and then covered his relief with a cough. He folded his arms and breathed out a long sigh.

"I am thrilled to hear this, but nowhere near as happy as Matilda will be when I tell her, she will be ecstatic."

"Are there any other conditions that I should be aware of? For instance, will I have to live at Meadowside for the rest of my life, like Matilda has done?"

"There are no other conditions. Matilda and I have discussed this, and it appears she does not wish to dictate your entire life or where you live after she and Kitty have gone. She is of the firm opinion, however, that you will fall in love with Meadowside and will want to stay. She thinks that you will feel the past that your ancestors have lived there and that the house will become as much a part of you as it is a part of her."

He snapped open the lock on his briefcase and took out a plain, white envelope. He slid it across the table towards me.

"Now that you have agreed to Matilda's proposal, I can give you this. It is a letter that she wrote when I visited to tell her that your father, David Lewis, had died but that his daughter was still alive. She gave me strict instructions that I was only to give it to you if you agreed to comply with her wishes."

I picked it up and opened it quickly. The thin, single piece of paper inside smelled strong of something akin to rosewater. The spidery writing was small and cramped, the author's age visible in the shaky script.

*Dear Amber (*I read)

*I am so delighted that you will be coming to Meadowside. I am waiting for you, and the house is too, for both of us have a story to tell that belongs as much to you now as it does to me. It is my family's story, but even more than that, it is the story of Meadowside, the past, and the secrets that have remained unknown for over eight decades. Please come soon; my time is running out, and I cannot, will not die until my story is told.*

*Sincere best wishes*

*Matilda Grey*

I glanced up at Nathaniel. "What do you make of this?" I pushed the letter towards him. "It all sounds rather mysterious."

"You must remember how old Matilda is. I suspect that the story she is talking about is just as she says: the story of her family and her childhood at Meadowside. What old lady doesn't want someone living to know about her past? I'm sure it's nothing as dramatic as she has made it sound."

He inserted the letter back into the envelope and handed it back to me.

"I think you and Matilda will get on well, and this won't be the last you see of me."

I raised my eyebrows.

"Matilda has asked me to stay in her employ, requesting that I put myself at your disposal whenever you need anything, day or night."

I must have looked aghast, for he quickly added, "don't worry, I am being very well paid to be at your beck and call. Matilda wants me to be around to ensure that the will is executed smoothly. When the time comes, I will be there to deal with any legal snags. When do you think you'll be ready to go to Meadowside? The sooner we move you into the house, the better, so that the will can be finalised, and Matilda's mind put to rest."

"Well, I must tell my mother what's happening; explain it all to her." I laughed excitedly, "this will blow her mind! I think it will be fine for me to leave the shop immediately, this time of year is always quiet, so I can't see any problems. I will need to give a month's notice on the house; it's rented, but I won't have to stay here as long as I pay the rent for the month."

I glanced around the small, cramped kitchen. "It shouldn't take me long to pack up. Anything I want to keep can go into storage for now. I think I could be ready to leave by the middle of next week. Do you think that would be soon enough for Matilda?"

Nathaniel rubbed his hands together delightedly. "She'll be over the moon. How's this for a plan? I will come and pick you up next Wednesday morning and drive you, and any belongings you wish to take, to Meadowside, and then I'll be able to introduce you to Matilda and Kitty?"

I nodded distractedly, suddenly anxious to talk to my mother and tell her about this most unexpected development in my life. As if reading my thoughts, Nathaniel stood up.

"I will see you next Wednesday then. Shall we say about ten o'clock?"

"That would be great, thank you."

I walked with him to the door and watched as he drove away. When his car was out of sight, I returned to the kitchen and resumed my seat at the table. The news that Nathaniel had brought was exhilarating, if it were true. He had seemed genuine and trustworthy, and not the kind of person who could possibly be a liar or a con man, but still, these people were clever, and I needed to be certain.

After a few moments of hesitation, I phoned the number on the business card that he had given me. The phone was answered by a woman, who announced the name of the company and asked how she could help.

"I was wondering if I could speak to Nathaniel Trent," I said nervously. "My name is Amber Lewis."

"Unfortunately, Mr Trent is out of the office at the moment. He had an early appointment, if you hold the line for a second I'll check his diary to see when he is due back." The line went silent for a short while and then the woman returned. "According to his diary he had an appointment with you, Miss Lewis."

I smiled with relief. "That is right." I suddenly felt foolish, "he came round to see me first thing this morning, but to be honest, the reason for his visit has thrown me into a bit of a spin. I just wanted to make sure that he was genuine."

"Of course," the woman replied swiftly, "I would do the same in your position. If it helps at all I have also spoken to Miss Grey on the telephone, to make appointments for Mr Trent to go and see her. She is not good on the phone; I don't expect she uses it very often. I can tell you that she is desperate to meet you. She sounds like a lovely old lady."

"That is very helpful," I sighed, "and thank you, you have really put my mind at rest."

As soon as I hung up I phoned work and informed them that I would be leaving. After a short discussion my boss wished me well, said how sad he was to see me go and agreed that I wouldn't have to work any notice, and that was the beginning of my new life, and my commitment to the mysterious Matilda Grey and her house, Meadowside.

\*

The streets of Cambridge were typically busy, teeming with people who were all having an ordinary day, on their way to work meetings, lecture halls, or just trying to get their shopping done so that they could escape the icy rain and the bustle of the city in the shortest amount of time.

Everything around me seemed unreal and strangely unfamiliar. My leaden legs walked an accustomed route, and yet it was like I had never walked it before. I felt distinctly removed from everything, as if in a dream state, as I struggled with the acknowledgement that everything was suddenly altered, and due to that, I was also no longer the same.

I surmised that this feeling of contradiction must be expected from a person whose entire life had been turned upside down out of the blue, like the hand of fate reaching from the unknown or a bolt of lightning intent on bringing about change. I was grateful for the transformation that was taking place and wholeheartedly accepted it, but at the same time, the speed and craziness of it had unsettled me. To my mind, it appeared as if a line had been drawn underneath the past, telling me that what was over and done with could not be revisited, and there I was, standing on the precipice of the future with no reference to what it would bring or what it looked like.

Standing on the front path of my childhood home, I took a deep breath, my feelings a concoction of excitement, apprehension, and shock. I knocked on the door and waited.

"Amber!" My mother was surprised to see me standing there, her expression instantly confused. "What are you doing here? Why aren't you at work? Are you ill?"

"I'm fine, Mum. I didn't go to work this morning. Something has happened."

"What's happened?"

"It's nothing bad, nothing to worry about." I walked past her into the hallway and then headed towards the kitchen. "It's nothing to worry about," I reiterated, anxious to put her mind at rest, "but it is something extraordinary."

We sat down opposite each other at the pine kitchen table.

"What's going on, Amber? What is this thing that has happened?"

"Well," I began, trying to put my tangled thoughts in order. "Do you remember Dad trying to find out more about his family?"

She looked surprised at the question. She frowned and shook her head, but then an expression of realisation entered her eyes. "I remember him mentioning something about it, and how he wished that he knew more about his family. As far as I remember, he got nowhere with it and was disappointed. I encouraged him to keep trying, but then the accident happened, and I never thought about it again."

"When he was researching, he wrote to a woman called Matilda Grey. Apparently, he told her that his inquiries suggested that he was somehow related to her."

"I don't remember him mentioning that."

"That's not surprising, Mum, because Matilda never replied. As far as she was concerned, she had no living relatives apart from her sister. Neither of them married, nor had children, so she couldn't see how there could be any connection to Dad."

My mother frowned, appearing even more confused. "How do you know about all of this, Amber?"

"This morning, I had a visit from a solicitor working for Matilda Grey, the lady that Dad wrote to. She instructed him to try to track down Dad, of course, he discovered that Dad had died, but then he found me. Years after receiving Dad's letter, Matilda Grey suddenly remembered that she had an uncle on her father's side of the family and that he had at least one child, so she concluded that must have been the connection that Dad found all of those years ago."

"I see," my mother was shaking her head, "but why has she sent this solicitor to find out about your dad? Honestly, Amber, he must have written that letter about thirty-five years ago."

Matilda Grey is one hundred and two years old. She is now very frail and unwell. She wants me to go and live with her and her sister in their house in Fenland to look after them. She is worried about what will happen to her sister if she dies first and what will become of her home, Meadowside."

My mother grimaced as she digested my words. "That is quite a big ask, Amber, expecting you to uproot yourself to live with a couple of old ladies you've never met."

"According to Nathaniel Trent – he's the solicitor who came round, Matilda thinks that we could be related. He said that she's not even bothered about how we could be related or how tenuous the link; she just wants some peace of mind in the final months of her life."

"Are you seriously considering this, Amber? It's not up to you to bring peace of mind to an old lady you don't even know."

"There's more to it than that, Mum." I felt excitement rising within me, a heady sensation of euphoria. "Matilda Grey wants me to go to Meadowside, look after her and her sister for the rest of their lives, and in return, she will leave me the house and a great deal of money in her will."

A long silence settled in the room, during which I watched a series of expressions pass over my mother's face as she tried to take in the news.

"What?" She eventually said, "she's saying that she will leave her house and money to a person who may or may not be related to her, a person she has never even met?"

"That's about the size of it. The two sisters have lived in the same house for their entire lives. They have outlived all their family, are living in the Fens alone, and are not managing very well. If you think about it, my moving to Meadowside solves all of Matilda's problems, she has nobody to leave her house and money to, and probably thinks that I am her last chance to find peace of mind. If I am there to care for them, and to care for her sister after Matilda's death, and to stop Meadowside falling into ruin, then maybe it could be the best outcome for all concerned."

"What about this solicitor?" She folded her arms, her expression sceptical. "Are you certain that he's the real deal and not some charlatan taking advantage of two old ladies, and you into the bargain?"

I shook my head firmly. "No. I checked him out before I came here. He works for Baxter and Johnson's in the city. He seemed decent and invested in doing his best for Matilda Grey. He's coming next Wednesday to take me to Meadowside, and from then on, I will just have to see how it goes."

"Well, it sounds like you've made up your mind."

"I have; look, Mum, I could be related to them. Dad thought so, and in a way, it feels that he, somehow, had a hand in this. He was the one who wrote to Matilda in the first place."

"Amber, if this works out for you, then I will be delighted, over the moon, in fact. If you are related to this old lady, then it is right that you should benefit from her will, and if they are related to you and your father, then it would be what he would want for you. Looking after two very elderly ladies is not going to be a walk in the park though; it's going to be hard work, tiring work. Are you prepared for that?"

I sighed. "I realise that it's not going to be easy, but I am going to do my best for them Mum. Ultimately, it was an easy decision, especially as my life in Cambridge is hardly a roaring success. It will be a new beginning, a new life."

"I'm very happy for you, Amber. You deserve this, and Matilda Grey couldn't have a better person looking after her."

"Thanks, Mum." I smiled warmly. "I will take good care of them both. After all, whatever I must do to make Matilda's life easier will be nothing compared to what she will be doing for me, for us. Maybe you could come to live at Meadowside, too?"

She laughed and shook her head decisively. "I couldn't leave your Granny. She's used to me popping in and out of the home most days, and I wouldn't move her, not when she's settled in so well."

"How is Granny, I haven't seen her for a few weeks?"

My mother stood up and filled the kettle at the sink. "She's fine, very well, in fact." She returned to the table as she waited for the kettle to boil. "I won't tell her too much about all of this, just that you've got a new job. She would only worry if I told her the complete truth. She wouldn't understand; can't say that I really understand it myself."

"It will be okay, Mum," I leaned across the table and patted her hand reassuringly, "and Fenland is less than an hour away. I'll still be able to visit you, and Granny, and you'll be able to drive over and see me whenever you want."

*

The following days were strange. I packed up my belongings and transferred my furniture to a storage facility on the edge of the city.

The smaller possessions I had gathered over the years were wrapped, placed in a box, and stored at the back of my mother's garage. Within a few days, my little cottage was empty, except for a few boxes I was taking with me, and three large suitcases lined up in the hallway.

Several times a day, I was struck by the enormity of what was happening to me and the fact that I was about to give up everything I knew to move to a house that I had never seen, to live with people I had never met. Sometimes I was excited by the prospect of change and the unknown, while at other times, I was fearful and anxious.

As the day I was going to move to Meadowside approached, I became increasingly worried that something about Matilda Grey's proposal didn't seem right, and I found myself time and again returning to the short note she had written to me. It seemed to me that there were hidden meanings behind the words, a suggestion of something being amiss.

*...it is the story of Meadowside, the past, and the secrets that have remained unknown for more than eight decades.*

What did those words mean, and why would she write them to me when she appeared so anxious for me to go to Meadowside? I didn't know for sure at that time, but I had a niggling suspicion that there was more to Matilda Grey than either myself or Nathaniel Trent had realised, and there was more to the house itself. Despite myself, I found that I was becoming intrigued and concerned in equal measure, for the more that I read the note, the clearer I could see that there was something a little bit sinister in the words Matilda Grey had written. She could have written anything to me, perhaps told me a little about herself and her sister, but she had chosen not to and had instead written words that seemed laden with mystery and warning.

I repeatedly reminded myself that Matilda was ancient; not many people lived to her age, and maybe that brought a particular notion, a craving for the past. It was hard to imagine what secrets an old woman who had lived in the same house for her entire life and, by all accounts knew hardly anybody, could have to tell. Then, I would become fascinated that the two sisters had lived such isolated lives. It surely wasn't normal for people to die in the house they were born in or to isolate themselves to the extent that they barely knew anybody, which begged the question as to why this had happened. Was it just that they weren't sociable people, or was there a reason behind it?

I resolved to try and put such thoughts to the back of my mind as there was no point in speculating, deciding that it was best just to wait and see what I made of Matilda Grey once I had actually met her.

# Chapter 2

As arranged, Nathaniel arrived to pick me up just before ten o'clock. I had phoned him to let him know that I had already handed my keys back to the letting agent and would be staying the night at my mother's.

"Here he is," I turned from the window and quickly hugged my mother, "I will phone you and will see you soon."

We dragged my heavy suitcases on to the pavement, along with the two boxes that contained my most precious items, things that I couldn't live without.

Nathaniel loaded the boxes and suitcases into the boot of his black estate car. I introduced him to my mother, and then we left, driving down the quiet avenue to join the city's busier roads.

"How are you feeling?" Nathaniel slowed down to join a queue of traffic at a roundabout. "Today's quite a big day for you."

"I don't really know how I feel," I replied honestly. "Everything has happened so quickly, and I haven't had the time to properly process it; however, I am really looking forward to meeting Matilda and Kitty."

"They are very excited to meet you too. It is going to be quite a change for you. Meadowside is very remote. When I said it was in the middle of nowhere, I wasn't joking."

"I'm sure I'll manage," I uttered.

I had always loved to visit the countryside and mainly chose to holiday in wild and isolated places. Still, I was always happy to return to my cottage, situated within a few minutes' walk of the restaurants, shops, and pubs. I was now wondering how I would fare living so far away from essential services.

I chased all troubling thoughts from my mind and asked Nathaniel to tell me more about Matilda Grey.

"I saw her yesterday, she looked very well, a lot better than the first few times I met with her. I think knowing that you had agreed to move to Meadowside has relieved her of a great deal of worry."

"And Kitty?"

Nathaniel laughed. "What can I say about Kitty? She's very endearing, but, my goodness, she talks so much rubbish, some of it almost impossible to make sense of. Matilda is always hushing her, telling her to stop 'jabbering,' as she puts it. Yesterday, while I was at the house, Kitty was standing at the window, muttering something about somebody being outside and how she wished they'd come in from the cold. Matilda ordered her away from the window and told her to find something useful to do. Poor Kitty just wandered away, muttering to herself."

"Who was she talking about?"

"Well, according to Matilda, she wasn't referring to anybody, and when I went over to the window, there was definitely nobody there. Matilda explained that Kitty was prone to episodes of daydreaming and that they were best ignored as they had been happening since she was a young child."

Out of the window, the landscape slowly changed. The houses and other buildings became sparser, the land flatter, and the skies wider.

"There's something so enigmatic and courageous about Matilda, which is strange considering the life she has led, locked inside Meadowside. According to a handful of locals I have spoken to, Matilda and Kitty are completely unknown in the nearby village. They have a cleaner who goes in two or three times a week, a woman called Beth Marsden. Beth told me that she tries to keep an eye on them, but Matilda has refused all offers of further help, even though it was obvious that she wasn't coping. She even refused to let Beth call for a doctor when she became so unwell that Beth was worried that she wouldn't last until the end of the week. We both think that Matilda is frightened that people will interfere or that professionals would try to take Kitty away and put her in a home, and that is why she keeps everybody at arm's length."

"I suppose if Matilda had become too ill to look after Kitty, then that is exactly what would have happened, especially as they have no family to advocate for them."

Nathaniel flicked on the indicator and remained silent while negotiating a busy junction. "That is why Matilda is so happy that you're going to be there. It's such a huge weight off her mind."

We turned off a main road and were now travelling towards the village. Large, flat fields stretched to the horizon on either side of the car. There were few trees or hedges, hardly any landmarks apart from the occasional barn or farmhouse. The sky ahead was leaden with rain, and huge clouds formed dark, shifting shapes, their reflections skimming the featureless landscape like shadowy ghosts.

I shifted my weight in the leather seat, feeling that there was something mysterious and ancient about the landscape we were travelling through, an air of history and permanence, of things that had remained unchanged for centuries. The road itself was a modern addition, but it was very easy to imagine a time when it wasn't there at all.

The village was fairly spread out, consisting mainly of a broad main street, a shop, a church, a pub, and a small café. There were few people about, just an old lady walking a small black and white dog and a teenage boy pushing a bicycle that appeared to have suffered a puncture.

We drove straight through the village and out the other side, taking a sharp left-hand turn into a narrow, bumpy road.

"Do you see that cluster of trees in the distance?"

I followed his gaze as the first drops of rain hit the windscreen.

"That's where Meadowside is, just beyond those trees. Matilda's father planted them to protect the house from the elements; it can get very windy out on the fen, and even with the trees, gales and storms can still batter the house."

The car eventually turned off the road onto a poorly maintained track and headed across the fen at a snail's pace, Nathaniel expertly avoiding most of the potholes.

We drove to the front of the house and parked on a pathway that seemed to continue forever into the distance. The trees Matilda's father had planted were mainly on the other side of the path and behind the house, their huge winter branches reaching high above the roofline. The trees provided a layer of protection to the house but also separated Meadowside's land from the fen surrounding it. A low wall marked the boundary at the front of the house. To the side was a double wooden gate with large patches of peeling white paint. Beyond the gate a driveway swept up the side of the house, creating a passageway with the side wall of the house and a single storey barn-like construction.

I scrambled out of the car and gazed up at the building.

"I wasn't expecting this," I gasped, although I didn't really know what I was expecting.

"It's amazing, isn't it?" Nathaniel grinned as he shut the car door.

"It's beautiful. I wasn't expecting it to be quite this big."

"Matilda's father, Edward Grey, bought the house in 1894. At one time Meadowside was a bustling home, with a large, young family living in it. It was built in the arts and craft style, which makes it rare in this area."

The house was built from mellow brick. The front of the building was made interesting by leaded light square bay windows. A solid wooden door stood centrally, protected by a porch with a pitched roof.

I wanted to stand there for longer, taking in the house, but a movement in the nearest window had caught my attention. An elderly lady stood there, her face close to the glass.

"Kitty," Nathaniel explained and then took me by the arm and steered me towards the front door. "She's been consumed with excitement ever since she was told you were coming to the house."

He stopped walking as we approached the porch. "Don't forget that Kitty and Matilda aren't used to strangers and have been severely isolated for a very long time, and due to this, they may come across as a little..." he ran his fingers through his hair, trying to find the right words, "odd, or even a little eccentric."

Nathaniel opened the door with a turn of the wrought iron handle, and we stepped into a large hallway. A substantial wooden staircase with carved spindles and an ornate newel post dominated the room. The floor was tiled with decorative Victorian tiles and the walls were wood panelled from floor to ceiling. An old grandfather clock ticked into the silence, its tinkling chimes sounding every half an hour, day and night.

"Wow!" I gasped, my eyes sweeping across the room. "This place is incredible."

Nathaniel smiled at my reaction just as a door opened at the back of the hall, and an elderly woman with rapid, ungainly movements walked in.

She was as tall as me, her back straight, with silver hair worn in a thick braid.

"Kitty," Nathaniel stepped towards her, his eyes shining fondly. "Look, I have brought Amber, just as I promised."

"Hello, Kitty. I have been looking forward to meeting you."

The woman was wearing a three-quarter length skirt made from a thick, mottled blue material, a white blouse, and a baby blue cardigan hung from her shoulders. Her violet-coloured eyes regarded me boldly, looking me up and down, and then as if satisfied by what she saw, she took hold of my hand.

"Tilly is in the drawing room," she whispered, "she's got a terrible headache."

"Kitty! They don't want to spend the rest of the day in the hall listening to you jabbering on about nothing. Bring them in!"

The voice from the room that Kitty had just left sounded irritable and strained. Kitty rolled her eyes to the ceiling and led me towards the open door.

The room beyond was large. Three tall, narrow windows took up most of the far wall. A collection of deep armchairs and a two seated sofa were arranged around a carved wooden fireplace, where a blazing fire emitted soporific heat.

In a high backed, winged chair, an elderly woman sat, her hands folded on the top of her tweed skirt. She was smaller than her sister, thinner and much frailer.

"It's good to see you again, Matilda." Nathaniel sat on the sofa and gestured to me to sit beside him. "As you can see, I have brought Amber."

The woman turned her head slightly and fixed me with dark, steady eyes. "Amber," she smiled, inclining her head towards me. "I am so happy that you have come."

"I am very happy to be here," I replied, my attention constantly drawn to Kitty, who was walking around the room, flitting from one piece of furniture to another, like a butterfly trying to decide where to land. "Meadowside is such a beautiful house."

"Kitty and I are very fortunate to have spent our entire lives here," her voice was quiet, feeble in the large room. "The house has looked after us far better than we have looked after it."

The room that we were in was well furnished, but everything was old fashioned and tired. The fabric of the furniture was faded and threadbare in places, but I could tell that the house was full of treasures. Two heavily engraved silver candlesticks stood on the mantlepiece. A china cabinet with glass doors was full of ornaments and ancient bits and pieces, while a large gold framed mirror hung above the fireplace.

The curtains at the three floor to ceiling windows were made from a heavy brocade, their golden colours now sun-faded and less vibrant than they had once been, but they still appeared sumptuous and in keeping with the rest of the room. I was struck by the fact that it was likely that the room hadn't changed in all the years that the sisters had lived there. I imagined that the ornaments had been placed by their mother, when they had still been children, the angles of the furniture, also decided by her.

My eyes were drawn to a couple of paintings that hung on the wall. I stood up and went to view them more closely. One depicted a magnificent Fenland sunset with a field of golden wheat sweeping into the distance beneath a fiery red sky. The second painting was of a group of four girls, sitting in a field and surrounded by flowers. It was a glorious scene of innocence. The girls were all smiling and happy, and yet the painting had instilled a melancholy feeling within me, that in that moment was difficult to understand.

Matilda had been watching me closely and as I returned to the sofa she said, "my father was an artist; those are his paintings. He was also an ornithologist, so you will find several of his bird paintings around the house. The books that he wrote are also in the library. He was a very accomplished man."

Nathaniel stood up just as I resumed my seat. "I'll make us some tea, shall I? Kitty, maybe you can help me to find where everything is kept in the kitchen."

Once they had left the room and the door closed behind them, I leaned towards Matilda. "Kitty has an extraordinary amount of energy for a woman of her age."

"Indeed," Matilda agreed with a stiff nod of her head. "she has always been the same. I suppose that you have noticed that Kitty is a bit strange. She can't read or write, not even simple words. My father used to despair over what would become of her. The rest of us learned quickly, and all of us could read and write by the time we were five or six. Kitty was never interested in her lessons, preferring to run around the place like a whirlwind, daydreaming her life away." She shrugged her narrow shoulders. "It didn't matter in the end, for Kitty has never needed to know anything, or learn anything, or even encounter the real world."

I wanted to ask questions, to discover why Matilda had locked them away in Meadowside. Was it just to protect Kitty from a world that wouldn't understand her?

"I am so glad that you have come, Amber. Kitty is independent in some ways, she can wash and dress herself, but she is absent minded and can't be trusted not to forget that she has a saucepan on the range, or that she has put a pie in the oven. I have needed to watch and supervise her most of the time, for if I didn't, it is highly likely that she would have burned the house down long ago.

"She is not always easy to look after, it is not that she is difficult in nature, but she is exhausting. My health has deteriorated to such an extent that I can't watch her constantly, like I used to do. I am tired, and every day is a struggle to get through, and every morning when I wake up, I am slightly surprised to still be in the land of the living, and I am painfully conscious of the fact that one day soon, I shan't wake up at all."

"Have you seen a doctor, Matilda? Maybe there is something that can be done."

She laughed dismissively. "Doctors can't turn back the years, my dear. I am ill and weak simply because I have outlived my time and should have been dead years ago. Pain, breathlessness, constant struggle, that is what life is like when you are just too stubborn to give up and die."

I leaned back against the cushions. Matilda had closed her eyes, fighting against sleep. Her thin, blue veined hands were trembling as they lay in her lap. Her body suddenly jolted as if prodded by a frightening dream. She opened her eyes and for a second appeared confused, perhaps forgetting who I was or why I was there.

"I will look after Kitty, please don't be worried about her." I spoke decisively, my voice portraying the determination of my conviction. "I will look after you, too, and will take on whatever needs doing in the house. You have nothing to worry about anymore."

A slight smile lifted the corner of her lips, momentarily lighting up her eyes.

"If only that were true," she said quietly, as if talking to herself. "I can't tell you how happy I was when Nathaniel told me he had found you, somebody who could be a relative of ours, and then, as soon as you walked through the door, I knew that there was no doubt that you are related to us."

I raised my eyebrows, a confused expression on my face. "How could you know that?"

"You were attracted to my father's painting. Perhaps you didn't have the time to study it in detail, go and take another look and tell me what you see."

I immediately stood up and returned to the painting. "There are four young girls, one of them is older, perhaps an older teenager, and the other three are younger. Oh, my goodness," I gasped, "I can see it now."

"Her name was Emma," Matilda said from the other side of the room. "She was my sister, older than me by some eight or nine years. I loved her very much."

I stared with mute astonishment at the painting. The eldest sister in the painting, Emma, looked exactly like me. Her hair was golden blonde, where mine was a chestnut brown, but the features of her face were like looking at my own reflection, even down to the curve of her cheek and the shape of her eyebrows.

Feeling slightly shaken I returned to my seat, wondering if there was any possibility that I could not be related to somebody who looked so alarmingly like me?

"Emma, I think, got her blonde hair from my father's side of the family, Issy too, and as you are likely to come from that side of the family, then it would make sense that there would be a resemblance between you and a few members of my family."

"I can't believe it," I whispered, really not expecting to find a strong family resemblance on my first day at Meadowside.

"As soon as I saw you, I saw Emma. I think you are a little taller, and your hair much darker, and yet the resemblance is uncanny."

The shock of seeing Emma in the painting was slowly beginning to recede. Instead of feeling alarmed by the resemblance, I was starting to feel a sense of place, a feeling of belonging. Where I had been slightly uneasy about accepting Matilda's inheritance, I now felt such a strong connection, that it suddenly felt right and fitting.

"What happened to Emma?" I spoke cautiously, wanting desperately to know, but not wanting to upset Matilda.

"Amber," she began, her eyes misting with tears, "the story of Meadowside, my story, is an extremely tragic one. This old house has seen more distress and upset than most. I will tell you all about it and I promise you that I will not die until I have related to you the entire story of my past and this house. I promise you."

I nodded my head, taken aback by the passion in her voice, feeling the spark of curiosity growing ever stronger within me. It was obvious that the telling of her story was of utmost importance to her, and for the first time, but not the last, I ignored a niggling worry that Matilda's story was in fact, the very reason I was there.

\*

Nathaniel left at four-thirty. The wintry sun had faded quickly, plunging the outside of the house into a darkness that I had rarely experienced before.

"You've got my number?" I nodded my reply. "Phone me if you need anything. I'll come back in a day or two and will bring your car, you'll need it living out here. I'll drive it over and I'll go back to Cambridge on the train. Do you think you'll be okay?"

"Of course, I will," I laughed, while inside I couldn't help but wish that he wasn't leaving, that I wouldn't be left in the middle of the dark fen, with two strange old ladies who I could not quite make head nor tail of.

I was shown to my room later by Kitty. It was larger than I had been expecting and was situated close to the top of the stairs, with a window that overlooked the front aspect of the house, with another window set into the side wall. I went to the side window and gazed out into the vast darkness.

"You can see the meadow from that window," Kitty informed me, "at least, you can when it's not dark. That is why the house is called Meadowside. It's not much in the winter, but just you wait until you see it in the summertime."

Kitty went to sit on the brass framed, double bed and watched as I walked around the room. It was furnished with a large, four doored wardrobe which stood against the longest wall. A dressing table stood in front of the window, and two small armchairs were positioned by the other one.

The walls were covered in a delicate floral wallpaper, and the thick curtains were made from a deep pink velvet. It was a very feminine room, which made me wonder if it once belonged to one of the girls in the painting.

"Why don't you show me your room, Kitty? I can leave my unpacking until later."

She stood up from the bed and I followed her out onto the landing.

"That's Tilly's room." She pointed to a closed door and then opened the one beside it. "This one is mine."

I stepped into a room that been completely untouched by time.

"Has this always been your bedroom, Kitty?"

She shook her head. "We used to share a room; I moved in here when I was about fifteen years old."

"You and Matilda used to share a room?"

"All of us shared a room, all of us younger ones."

"That must have been nice," I said, looking around. "I never had any brothers or sisters. You've got a lovely room now though, right next door to Matilda."

Kitty's bedroom was slightly smaller than mine, and if my bearings served me right, she would have a clear view over the meadow. There were two wooden bookcases standing against the wall, but the shelves only housed a couple of books, most of the space was taken up with the items a child would have collected throughout their childhood: dolls, stuffed animal toys, ornaments of little china dogs and rabbits, painted pebbles, and little wooden boxes standing one on top of the other.

The bed that stood between the two windows was covered by a beautiful, quilted bedspread. "Did you mother make this for you?"

"Oh no," Kitty replied, sitting down on the bed and gently stroking the material. "My mother hated sewing. Emma made it for me, for my birthday, when I was little."

I glanced down at the quilt, noticing that the colours had faded, the edges frayed.

"Emma was very clever," I spoke gently, "it must have taken her a very long time to make."

"She was always making us things. She loved us very much, and we loved her."

I watched as the strange child-woman stood up and walked over to the window.

"I wish she would come inside," she muttered, as if she was alone in the room.

I went to stand next to her, gazing out into the darkness. Silver droplets of rain were trickling down the black glass, and in the distance, I could see the shadows of the trees moving in the wind.

"There's nobody out there, Kitty, it's raining and pitch dark."

"She doesn't like the dark, or the rain. She likes the sunshine and the flowers, but she does still come in the winter, sometimes, probably just to make sure that we are still here."

I really wanted to question her about who could be standing outside of the house in the freezing darkness and pouring rain, but I thought better of it. A despondent sadness had come over my strange companion, and I didn't want to risk making her sadness deeper or upsetting her in any way.

"Shall we go and find Matilda?" I suggested brightly, and almost immediately her sadness evaporated, and we walked together out onto the landing. She hesitated outside her bedroom door, her eyes glancing worriedly towards the far end of the landing corridor.

"Are there more bedrooms up there?" I asked.

She suddenly took hold of my hand and gripped it tightly. "We don't go down there, Amber," she whispered beneath her breath, as if frightened that someone other than me would hear her words. "We never go down there."

"Why on Earth not?" I was confused, baffled by her statement.

"We just don't," she replied firmly.

"Okay," I laughed to cover my bewilderment, "let's go downstairs and find something to cook for dinner."

The kitchen was a large, oblong shaped room at the back of the house, accessed through the middle of three doors situated in the back wall of the hall. There were no fitted units or shiny work surfaces, instead the various cupboards and cabinets were made from old pine, each one with a thick, wooden work surface. An old fashioned, black range cooker stood in an alcove, which could have once been a fireplace, and looked as if it could have been at least as old as Matilda herself.

At the other end of the kitchen was a long, pine table surrounded by a hotch-potch of mismatched chairs. The tabletop was scarred and dented, the wood smooth and mellow through many years of use. A huge built-in dresser stretched the entire length of the wall, while the opposite wall was entirely occupied by a bank of leaded light windows, the small square glass panes all reflecting the amber light from several lamps that stood on a deep wooden bench that jutted out from under the windows, the five or six shelves beneath it, housing pots and pans, mixing bowls and other essential kitchen items, were hidden behind blue and white checked curtains.

There was something very relaxed and comfortable about the room. There was plenty of space for more furniture, perhaps a couple of comfortable chairs by the range cooker would be nice, or at the back of the room, where beyond the table a small, black leaded fireplace stood.

There was not much food in the fridge, or in any of the cupboards, but I found some eggs and ended up making us all omelettes. When we had eaten, I washed the plates up by hand in the deep, butlers sink, leaving them to drain on a wooden rack that stood to the side of the sink.

I dried my hands on a tea towel and then hung it on the rail of the cooker. Standing in the doorway I looked back into the room and wondered if, when the house was legally mine, I would be tempted to have a modern kitchen fitted. I couldn't imagine how it would look, and feared that stark, modern units and conveniences would steal the soul out of the room and ruin the peaceful atmosphere and cosiness.

I returned to the living room. Matilda had fallen asleep in her chair. The fire had burned down, but the room was comfortably warm and still gently lit by the glowing embers. In the distance I could hear Kitty muttering to herself. I walked towards the sound and found her in the strange little room that led from the far end of the lounge. It was furnished like another sitting room. Two deep red sofas faced each other across a coffee table. An ornate tiled fireplace stood empty between two windows; the brocade curtains a similar colour to the sofas. The room was half panelled in dark wood, and above the panelling a dark red, embossed wallpaper gave the room a slightly claustrophobic feel.

Kitty was sitting on one of the sofas, a tangle of green wool in her lap.

"Did this used to be your father's study?"

She shook her head. "He only ever worked in the library; it was his favourite place. This is the children's room." Her fingers worked constantly, trying to remove the tangles and knots from the wool. "This is where we used to come to do our sewing and Emma would read us stories in here before bedtime. She used to teach us how to embroider, make samples and knit, but I was never any good at any of it, so she used to give me the wool that the others had made a mess of, and I would untangle it and wind it back up into a tidy ball. Emma said that I was the best wool detangler that she had ever met, and it was a skill in itself."

"The children's room," I whispered, glancing around at the glass fronted cabinets that were full of childish memento's, such as pinecones, unusual shaped sticks, dried flowers and the skeletons of a few unfortunate small mammals. I stood up to take a closer look.

"Emma used to put our treasures inside the cabinets to keep them safe, things that we brought home to her from our walks. The flowers were Issy's, she loved flowers, and look," she pointed to a piece of yellowed paper propped up against the back of one of the cabinets, "that is Issy's painting of a butterfly. She loved butterflies almost as much as she loved flowers."

She returned to her seat, picking up the tangle of wool. "I have made more of a mess, "she sighed, "it was just a little bit tangled, and now look at it."

"Would you like me to help you with that?"

She threw the ball roughly in my direction as I sat down on the opposite sofa.

"Are you planning to make something with it, Kitty?"

"I thought I could make a scarf out of it, but I'm not very good at making things. I never have been. Issy was very clever like that. Father used to say that she would grow up to become a great artist."

I glanced towards her as my fingers tried to locate the end of the wool and was about to ask her about her sister Issy, when a strange and sudden noise coming from one of the windows almost made me jump out of my skin.

"What the hell was that?" I leapt to my feet, the ball of wool falling to the floor. "It sounded like somebody was knocking on the window."

Kitty bit her lip, her eyes worried and fearful. I went to the window and yanked back the curtains but could see nothing in the darkness.

"Did you hear somebody knocking on the window, Kitty?"

Kitty stood, shuffling her weight from one foot to the other. Her whole demeanour had altered, she appeared frightened and anxious, and for a moment I thought she was about to burst into tears.

"She won't come in," her voice sounded wretched, miserable.

"Who is it Kitty? Who won't come in?"

"Kitty!"

I swung around at the sound of the harsh voice. Matilda was standing in the doorway, leaning heavily on her stick.

"We heard a noise at the window," I explained hurriedly, "for all the world it sounded as if someone was knocking on the glass."

"At this time of night?" She questioned, "who would be outside the window in the dark, in the freezing cold and the rain? It was just the wind."

She fixed her brown eyes on my face, her sharp gaze unfaltering. "There are many noises to be heard in a house like this, Amber, and if you take my advice you will simply ignore them all, they are nothing other than the creaking and grumbling of an old building."

Matilda then turned her attention to her sister. "Kitty, go to the kitchen and warm up some milk for yourself, and for goodness' sake, don't leave it to boil over."

Kitty shuffled across the room, head bowed, squeezing past Matilda in the doorway.

"You mustn't pay any mind to the silly things that Kitty tells you. She doesn't mean anything by it, but her head is full of nonsense, and she will insist on saying the first ridiculous thing that enters her head. It is just the way she is, the way she's always been."

I brushed the strands of wool from my jeans and the front of my jumper. The woman who stood before me now suddenly seemed even frailer than before. Her face was pale, and the iron-grey hair that had been neatly arranged into a bun, was now falling in wispy tendrils around her face.

"You look very tired, Matilda, shall I help you to bed?"

"That would be very kind," she said with a weary sigh. "I wish I could manage myself better, but I simply can't."

"You don't need to worry about that anymore, Matilda, that is why I am here, to help you in any way that I can."

We made slow progress towards the stairs. She held onto my arm, also relying on her walking stick, but still I could feel her body trembling at the sheer effort it took just to walk. When we were halfway up the stairs she needed a break, leaning against the banister, her breaths coming in short, painful rasps. It was a complete mystery to me how she had managed up until then. She was so frail and weak that it was a miracle that she hadn't fallen before now.

"Do you think it might be a good idea if we made a lovely

bedroom for you in one of the downstairs rooms? There's a bathroom downstairs, isn't there?"

Matilda gave the idea some consideration. "I suppose it would make sense," she agreed, "it would certainly be a relief."

"How have you managed to get up and down the stairs up until now?"

"It's surprising what one can achieve when there's no other option. I had to do it, so I did."

We began to walk again, each step causing her pain and a huge amount of effort.

"There is a bathroom downstairs," she panted, leaning heavily against the wall close to her room. "Thank goodness that I listened to Beth a few years ago and agreed to have it installed in a room off the hall that has never really had any purpose, well, not for a very long time, at least. My father used it to store his art equipment, and my brother used to fill it with fishing rods and nets."

"You had a brother? I thought, for some reason, that yours was a family of girls."

"Yes, I had a brother, but he died just before the first war, when I was still a child. His name was Jack."

We walked into her bedroom, and I flicked the light switch. The room was large, and like all of the other rooms, was furnished in an old fashioned but comfortable style. I turned on the bedside lamp and closed the curtains. Matilda sat on the side of the bed, her feet not even touching the floor.

"This room used to belong to my parents." She took a nightdress from beneath one of the pillows. "It has an ensuite, can you believe? The room was just a dressing room, but I had it turned into a bathroom in the early 1970's, long before ensuite bathrooms were popular. It was just the right size for a bathroom. Kitty uses it during the night, the other bathroom is at the far end of the landing, a long way for her to go in the dark."

"Kitty was telling me that she doesn't like going to the other end of the corridor."

From the other side of the room, I saw Matilda's back straighten. "We don't go down there," she said firmly, "it's where our childhood bedroom is, and my brother's and Emma's room, there are just too many sad memories that upset Kitty. She has a lot of fears, most of them imagined, like a child believing that a monster lives in the wardrobe."

"I understand," I replied unconvincingly, because I didn't understand at all. Kitty had lived in the house for her entire life, what could she be so frightened of?

As I tidied around the room, putting Matilda's clothes in an old-fashioned wicker basket that stood in the corner, and her shoes in the wardrobe, I wondered about Kitty. She seemed to be far more capable than she was given credit for. She did appear to be forgetful, distracted, and certainly said the strangest of things, but was the real reason behind this caused by the fact that she had so little experience of life? Could it be that being so protected and knowing hardly anybody apart from her sister, had caused her imagination to run riot?

I helped Matilda to put on a long, flannelette nightdress, and once she was settled in bed, I turned to leave.

"I hope you will sleep well, Matilda. Would you like me to switch the lights off?"

"Just the big one, thank you, Amber."

"I'll sort out moving you into a downstairs room tomorrow, and remember, I am just down the corridor if you need anything in the night."

I turned off the ceiling light and opened the door.

"Thank you for coming, Amber. Having you here is already making a difference."

"It's my pleasure to be here. I am the one who should be thanking you, for inviting me here, for giving me the opportunity to get to know you and Kitty, and for trusting me with the future of Meadowside."

"I will sleep well tonight, knowing that you are here, and tomorrow I will begin to tell my story."

I closed the door quietly and stood for a while on the landing, wondering what the story Matilda was so determined to tell me, could possibly be about.

Kitty had taken herself to her room. I knocked on the door, but when I opened it, she was already in bed.

"I've just come to say goodnight, Kitty."

She patted the side of the bed and I sat down.

"You could read me a story, if you wanted to."

I smiled at the childlike request, remembering that she was unable to read for herself. I glanced around but could only see a couple of children's book in the bookcase.

"Could you read this?" She took a book from beneath her pillow, an old copy of The Tale of Squirrel Nutkin, one of the first books published by Beatrix potter in the early 1900s.

"You have good taste," I remarked, "I had the entire collection of Beatrix Potter books when I was a child."

"Emma bought it for my birthday when I was little, she read it to me every night."

"Has anybody read it to you since then?"

She shook her head. "Remembering Emma makes Tilly sad. I haven't heard the story for a very long time."

She gazed at me thoughtfully for a while, and I thought she was going to remark on my resemblance to Emma, but she didn't and instead grabbed hold of my hand.

"Do you know where the dead people go, Amber?"

I was taken aback by such a strange question. "That is very difficult to answer, Kitty, for nobody really knows."

"Seraphina knew, she told me that the souls go to the quiet places."

"The quiet places?" I repeated, a blank expression on my face.

"Seraphina said that they don't go far away from us, not far away at all."

A cold shiver ran down my spine. "Was Seraphina one of your sisters?"

She shook her head.

"A friend?"

"I don't think anybody really knew who she was, not for sure. She was lovely though, and she knew such things, such wonderful things."

"I see," I shook my head as I picked up the book, disentangling her hand from mine and placing it on top of the bedspread, as I began to read.

Half an hour later I crept out of Kitty's bedroom, having decided to lock up the house and have an early night. It had been a long, strange day and I was feeling unusually tired. Tomorrow was promising to be busy with organising Matilda's move to a downstairs room, and generally trying to get used to my new environment and circumstances. An early night would do me the world of good.

# Chapter 3

I ran down the stairs, checked that the fires had burned down and were safe. I turned the lights off one by one and locked all the external doors. The electricity in the house had not been well designed, for as far as I could tell there was no light switch in the hall that operated the light on the landing, the only switch being on the wall at the top of the stairs, which meant that I would have to walk up in the dark, which was not only unnerving, but also dangerous.

I was halfway up the stairs when I was unexpectedly assailed by an almost paralysing sense of doom. My feet stopped moving as a coldness swept over my skin. I grabbed the banister rail to steady myself, as I tried to understand what this peculiar feeling was and where it had come from.

As I stood there, I wondered if I was ill, for my head began to ache and a heavy sensation of nausea was churning in my stomach. I was freezing cold, frightened and confused, knowing that something strange and unusual was happening around me, but unable to place it or put a name to it.

Gradually I became convinced that there was something or somebody standing at the top of the stairs, blocking my way. I squinted into the darkness, it appeared to be moving, as if shadows were passing through it, as if it was alive with something inexplicable and dangerous.

I felt extremely vulnerable, as if something could happen at any moment that I wouldn't be able to predict or save myself from. My heart was hammering in my chest, reverberating inside my head, causing my bewilderment and fear to grow. I was breathing heavily, the air was thick and choking, the darkness pressing in on me, suffocating and filling my entire body with panic.

Grabbing hold of the bannister I slowly lowered myself onto one of the steps. The sense that I could be pushed down the stairs was strong, and I felt a lot safer sitting down. The air around me was crackling with energy, I could feel it stirring the hairs on my arms and the back of my neck, moving through my hair like cold, ghostly fingers. The darkness buzzed with malice, and while I sat there, terrified, I was aware that there was an intelligence behind this incomprehensible experience, something deliberately trying to petrify and control.

This was my first day at Meadowside, and already something was trying to make me leave. I fought with myself to overcome the feeling of intense fear, inherently knowing that I needed to be strong and courageous, that whatever was threatening me could not win. Instinctively I understood that to retreat, or to show weakness, would be a fatal error. I needed to stand up to it, go into battle and win.

I pulled myself up to a standing position, breathing slowly and steadily to calm myself, and then with a measure of composure that surprised me, I walked boldly and confidently towards the landing and the weirdly pulsating darkness.

When I reached the top of the stairs, I fumbled with the handle of my bedroom door. When I finally managed to open it, I stumbled into the room and closed the door firmly behind me, quickly switching on the light and walking almost drunkenly to the bed.

Sitting on the edge of the bed I tried to make some sense of what had happened to me. I was confused, but slowly began to realise that there was no sense at all to be found in the experience, no matter how hard I thought about it, it remained impossible to explain.

Later, as I lay in bed, my fear and panic slowly receding, I did what most people would do, I tried to apply logic to an illogical situation. Although I had never experienced anything remotely like what I had endured that night, I felt the need to somehow understand it. I was tired, it had been a long day spent in a new environment. Even though I was usually a level-headed person, had I allowed myself to become overwhelmed by my new circumstances, overwrought even?

Both Nathaniel and Matilda had warned me against paying too much attention to Kitty's strange ramblings. Could it be that I had unconsciously allowed Kitty's talk of quiet places, of somebody being outside of the house and dead people, to ignite my imagination? Perhaps I was even more tired than I thought. This must have been it, because the only other explanation was too fantastical to even contemplate.

\*

I fell asleep in the early hours of the morning, but I slept fitfully, tossing and turning, and awoke feeling groggy. It was early when I got out of bed. When I opened the curtains, it was still dark outside, with a waning moon still shining brightly in the sky. Shivering I pulled on my dressing gown and plunged my feet into my slippers. A couple of towels were draped over one of the armchairs, I took them and my wash bag, out onto the landing.

I looked towards the end of the corridor. There was a bathroom down there, but I was disinclined to go looking for it, fearful of inspiring any further nonsense and imaginings. Instead, I went downstairs, and found the bathroom that Matilda had told me about the night before. I found it easily, tucked between the underside of the staircase and the dining room. It was surprisingly spacious with a large, modern shower cubicle and a corner bath.

Later I sat at the dressing table in my room, gazing at my reflection in the mirror, immediately seeing again my resemblance to Emma, the girl in the painting. How very strange it was to know that my genetic makeup had been influenced by a family that I never knew existed.

I blasted my stubbornly curly hair with the hairdryer and then piled it all on top of my head in a loose bun, straight away, long curling tendrils escaped and fell around my face. For a while I stared at my reflection. The fact that I looked like a Grey family member was pleasing to me, making me feel that I belonged at Meadowside, that I had a right to be there. The fact that it also connected me to the father I had barely known, was an added bonus.

The sky beyond the window was growing lighter. The rain had died away to be replaced by a murky drizzle. The daylight had brought me some relief. In the cold light of the morning, my experience of the night before seemed vaguely ridiculous, me getting myself into a state over nothing, just a few random feelings that I had allowed to get out of control. I hadn't seen anything, or heard anything, I had just, because I was tired and a little overwhelmed by the responsibility I had taken on, been spooked by Kitty's strange topics of conversation. I had been an idiot, and I was determined that it wouldn't happen again.

I helped Matilda to get up and dressed at about eight-thirty, and then accompanied her on the slow, painful decent down the stairs.

"I was thinking that we could make the dining room into a bedroom for you. It's right next door to the bathroom, so it would make sense. We don't really need the dining room, not when there's such a lovely area to eat in the kitchen. What do you think?"

"Whatever you think is for the best," she said, fully resigned to the idea of moving downstairs. "I will certainly be glad not to have to struggle up and down these confounded stairs twice a day."

We went to the drawing room, and I settled her in her chair next to the fire. I placed a blanket over her knees and left her to go and see if Kitty was awake. I knocked on her bedroom door and opened it, finding her fully dressed, standing by the window.

"Good morning, Kitty," I said brightly, moving around the room picking up discarded items of clothes and a pair of brown, lace-up shoes. "You really shouldn't leave things on the floor like this, it would be so easy for you to trip and fall over."

I straightened up and gazed at her back as she continued to stand at the window, for a moment wondering if she had heard me, or was even aware of my presence.

"She still isn't here," she said distractedly, half to herself, as she turned away from the window and went to the bed, pulling the blankets and bedspread over the pillows.

"Never mind," I replied dismissively, deciding that it was probably best to humour Kitty and her daydreams. "Maybe she will be there tomorrow."

"It will be spring soon," she smoothed down the bedspread with her hands, "she'll be here every day then, and all through the summer."

"Excellent," I said, folding up a cardigan and putting it into the chest of drawers. "I can't wait to see the meadow in the springtime."

Kitty walked easily down the stairs. It seemed that she didn't suffer with the painful arthritis of her sister, or the breathlessness and fatigue.

We went to the kitchen. The only thing that I could find to make for breakfast was porridge, there was no bread, and only one egg left after yesterday's omelettes. I would need to get some groceries from somewhere, and I also needed to figure out how to get Matilda's bed down to the dining room.

Kitty was wondering around the kitchen as I poured the oats into a saucepan.

"Do you know many people in the village, Kitty?"

"I only know Beth; she lives in the village. I'm not allowed to go there, so I don't know anybody else."

"What do you mean, you're not allowed?"

"Tilly doesn't want me going to the village, neither of us have been there for years, not since we were young."

I turned my attention back to the porridge, thinking that perhaps Matilda believed that Kitty wouldn't be safe going to the village alone, and at that moment in time I didn't know either of them well enough to make a judgement.

"I need to move Matilda downstairs," I said, changing the subject. "The stairs are too difficult for her to manage, and it would be awful if she fell. I need to find somebody who can help me."

Kitty's eyes suddenly lit up. "Nathaniel would help you."

"I'm sure he would," I said, laughing at her enthusiasm, "if I asked him, but he'll be busy with his job. I was hoping to find someone local."

She shrugged her shoulders and looked disappointed.

"Nathaniel will be visiting soon, he said that he would bring my car over."

I took the porridge off the heat and began to spoon it into bowls.

"Maybe it would be better to just order a new bed, have it delivered and leave her old bed where it is." I was thinking out loud, feeling that as Matilda was so frail, a new, modern bed might be more comfortable for her. "the main thing is that I remove any possibility of Matilda falling down the stairs, they are too dangerous for her now."

"Oh yes," Kitty came and stood close to me, the expression in her eyes worried. "The stairs are very dangerous. There was that time, a long time ago. I don't know what happened, but it was terrible."

I turned towards her, wondering what we were talking about now.

"Did somebody fall down the stairs, Kitty?" She stared back at me, her eyes veiled and troubled.

"I don't know," she muttered, as if she couldn't understand why I had asked the question.

I made a pot of tea and set the table, and then went to get Matilda. As I walked from the kitchen towards the drawing room, I wondered what Kitty had been referring to. I was beginning to understand that the old lady spoke sometimes of snatches of memories that she was then unable to place. I paid no attention to what she had said, forgot about it, and didn't think of it again for several months.

Matilda was sitting patiently in her chair when I entered the room.

"You could have your breakfast here, if you prefer, but personally I think that a little walk to the kitchen would be good for you."

I took her walking stick from its resting place next to the fireplace and handed it to her, helped her to stand and walked beside her towards the door.

"I was thinking that it might be a good idea to order you a new bed, instead of trying to bring yours down from upstairs. Did you know that there are adjustable beds now, where you can comfortably sit up, or raise the bottom if you have achy legs?"

"I didn't know that" she said, already slightly out of breath, focusing intently on putting one foot in front of the other.

"Are you happy for me to order one for you?"

"Yes, if that's what you think I need, and you're right, it would be a difficult job getting my bed down the stairs."

I nodded my head, satisfied and feeling happy that it seemed that Matilda was going to be an easy patient, willing to go along with whatever I suggested.

After breakfast I walked Matilda back to her chair beside the fire and returned to the kitchen. Kitty was still sitting where I had left her, staring absently into space, fiddling with the hem of her cardigan. Suddenly a shrill ringing sound caused both of us to jump.

"It's the telephone," Kitty grimaced, her hands over her ears. "It's in the library, it hardly ever rings, and I don't know how to use it, so you will have to answer it."

I ran to the library, thinking that the noise sounded more like a fire alarm than a telephone. Sitting down in the curved back chair at the desk, I picked up the cumbersome receiver.

"Hello," I said.

"Morning, Amber, it's Nathaniel. I just thought I'd give you a ring to see how your first night went."

Straight away a vision of me sitting huddled and terrified on the stairs came to my mind, but I quickly banished it away.

"I'm okay, thanks, everything is going well. Matilda needs quite a lot of help. I've no idea how she's been managing up until now, especially getting up and down the stairs, it's a miracle she hasn't fallen. I'm going to spend today trying to find a new bed for her so that she can sleep downstairs. I thought that an adjustable bed would be ideal for her."

"I can organise that for you. Where will you put her if she moves downstairs?"

"The dining room would be the best place, it's a bit on the large side for a bedroom, but then I thought that, sooner or later, she would probably need to be cared for in one room, and the dining room has more than enough space for another bed, if I ever need to stay down there with her."

"Sounds like a good plan," he said approvingly. "Is there a lot of furniture to be cleared out?"

"There is," I grimaced at the thought of it, "and I haven't even thought about where to put it all."

"Don't worry about it. I'll send some men round to move it out into the barn, it's watertight, so it should be fine out there, and I'll order an adjustable bed and have it delivered to the house."

"That would be amazing, thank you. Make sure you order a top of the range bed, it's important that Matilda is comfortable."

"I will, and I'll be over tomorrow with your car, if that's okay?"

"That will be brilliant. I'll see you tomorrow."

I returned to the kitchen expecting Kitty to still be there, but she wasn't, in fact I couldn't find her anywhere. I checked the drawing room to see if she was with Matilda, but Matilda had been dozing, waking up just as I entered the room.

"Nathaniel is going to sort out a new bed for you and is also going to employ some local men to move the furniture out of the dining room and into the barn. He thinks it will be fine out there."

She smiled fondly. "He's a good boy, after all, he found you and brought you here."

I laughed at her calling Nathaniel a boy, when he must have been in his late thirties at least.

Matilda straightened her back, placed her feet squarely on the floor, and made a move to stand up. "We need to make a start, Amber. Will you take me to the children's room?"

"I can't find Kitty," I said as I helped her to stand.

"She'll be out in the garden, or perhaps in the meadow. It's her routine to take herself off for a walk after breakfast, weather permitting. She knows that she's only to walk in the meadow, or out on the fen track, she would never go to the village on her own."

Once we reached the children's room, Matilda sat down in one of the armchairs. I hurriedly lit the fire and then sat opposite her, wondering why she had felt the need to move from one room to another, especially as it was so painful and difficult for her.

"Meadowside used to be such a happy house," she said wistfully. "A home filled with love and laughter. My parents were kind, good people. Perhaps they were a little spoilt, a little capricious, but good, nonetheless.

"When I was a child, Amber, I thought that life only consisted of love, security and happiness. I didn't know that life could change, and I don't think that my parents knew it either, not really, for when the bad times came, they were both knocked off their feet, and changed into people I could barely recognise. I did not know that there was such a thing as tragedy, and that, in a lifetime, it could visit you again and again. In one way or another, it touches us all. I was so innocent, so closely protected, until, one day in 1913 when everything changed.

# Chapter 4
# Meadowside 1913

Matilda remembered that freezing winter's day well. It was the end of December, a day that dawned the same as any other, and yet it was a momentous day, that would set into action a chain of events that would change the Grey family forever.

Her brother, Jack, had always been a reckless boy, raucous and loud, with a quick wit and no sense of obligation or responsibility. He spent most of his life in his father's library, standing before the large desk, his head bowed in feigned contrition, being admonished for one misdemeanour after another. At twenty-five years of age, he was a constant source of worry to his parents, enraging his father with his lack of ambition and devil-may-care attitude to life. Eleanor and Edward Grey wanted nothing more than to see their eldest child settled into a noble profession, married to a steady young woman, possibly the daughter of one of the wealthier local farmers, making his way in the world. Instead, their son was uninterested in taking life seriously, spending his time on mischief making, or risking life and limb in his endeavours to gain the respect of his peers, or catch the eye of one of the village girls.

Edward Grey was of the opinion, that with the best will in the world, he and his wife had managed to spoil the boy. He was so irresistibly charming, so amusing and handsome, but he was the only boy in a large family, adored by his sisters, and loved far too much by his mother.

"I did not raise you to be a layabout," Edward could often be heard yelling from the library, his angry voice reaching every room of the house. "You are a disgrace to the family, gallivanting around, doing nothing but creating havoc and mayhem. You should have a steady job, you are no longer a child, but a young man who should be making his own way in the world, getting a home of your own, getting married and having a family, building some substance behind you. I have a mind to cut you off without a penny, oh yes, that would bring you up smart, wouldn't it?"

Jack would stand before his father's desk with an expression of contrition fixed to his face, while his father puffed furiously on his pipe, sending clouds of fragrant smoke into the air.

"Yes, indeed, I have half a mind to stop your allowance, that would bring an end to your gallop! Maybe you wouldn't be quite so intent on womanising and wanton behaviour if you were paying for it yourself."

The rest of the family were accustomed to hearing their father's raging voice floating into every corner of Meadowside. Often, they would sit on the stairs, their heads resting on the bannisters, listening to their father's bellowed lectures, wincing at the harshness of his words.

Eventually, Jack would saunter out of the library, hands plunged into his trouser pockets, a cigarette dangling from his lips, as if nothing had happened. His sisters would gather round him. Matilda would always be the first at his side, barging the others out of the way.

"Have you been banished, Jack?"

He would laugh, ruffling her hair. "No chance of that happening, little Tilly, no chance at all."

"But I heard Father say..."

"What Father says, and what Father does, are two different things," he would crouch down and gaze into Matilda's eyes. "I'm not going anywhere without you, Tilly. I wouldn't survive a single day without you, you are the beat of my heart, the twinkle in my eyes, the sunshine in my summer sky!"

"You are an idiot, Jack," Emma would try to keep her voice stern but would always end up laughing. "One of these days you will push your luck too far."

"I always land on my feet, Emmie, you know that."

"Maybe if Father stood by his words and actually punished you for your disgraceful behaviour, then the rest of us in this house could have a bit of peace."

Jack would roll his eyes to the ceiling at the words of the eldest of his sisters. "You are a stick in the mud, Martha. Maybe if you smiled every now and again you would find yourself a husband who would take you away from Meadowside, no man wants a nagging woman as a wife."

Martha would fold her arms and stamp her foot in anger. "No respectable woman would take you for a husband," she would retaliate, "not with the reputation you have. You are a disgrace to the family name."

"Oh, Martha," Jack would laughingly shake his head, "are you ever going to relax and learn that life is to be lived? You're so uptight and rigid. If I were you I would start worrying about my own future and leave me to sort out mine."

It was a day between Christmas and New Year. The winter had been particularly harsh and bitterly cold, and the flooded fields had frozen solid, prompting the fen skaters to busily start planning races and competitions. Jack had left the house early in the afternoon, his skates hanging around his neck, the customary cigarette clamped between his lips.

"Are you going to come and watch me win later, Tilly?"

Matilda was digging up potatoes from the vegetable garden, one of her last chores of the day. She straightened her back and grinned cheekily.

"How do you know you're going to win? You might not."

Jack laughed as he ground the stub of his cigarette into the ground with the heel of his boot. "Of course, I will win. I always win. Do you want to come and watch me, or not?"

Matilda nodded her head with excitement.

"Good. You will be my lucky mascot, Tilly. I will come back for you at three o'clock. Wait for me by the gate and make sure that you wrap up warm. We're in for more snow later, I'm sure."

Matilda walked with him to the top of the meadow, then watched as he ambled towards the woods in the distance, that provided a short cut to the village. When he reached the bottom of the meadow, he turned and waved. She waved back, until he disappeared into the woods and out of sight.

At three o'clock, Matilda was sitting on the gate, which gave her a view both over the meadow and down the track that led to the village. Jack could take either route, but at least she would be able to see him in the distance and run to meet him. She was wearing her new hat, gloves and scarf that had been made by her sister, Emma, and given to her as a Christmas present, but she was still cold, just sitting still, waiting.

By 3.45 it was beginning to get dark, and above her in the shadowy sky a flock of geese squawked and shrieked, flying low after spending the day foraging in the farmers' fields.

At 4.30 she jumped down from the gate and stamped her feet on the frozen ground. It was now pitch dark and she was freezing cold, shivering in the winter wind, feeling the first snowflakes fall against her skin.

She could no longer see the meadow, or the trees at the boundary. She supposed that Jack had been delayed at the village inn, had drunk too much ale and had forgotten all about their arrangement. Feeling disappointed, and a little bit cross, she was just about to return to the house when a strange movement in the distance caught her eye.

She walked away from the gate and out onto the track, giving herself a much clearer view of the meadow. She could see a row of bobbing lights, snaking from the wooded boundary at the bottom of the meadow, and then the lights changed direction and began to head towards the house. The moving lights looked peaceful, strangely beautiful in the darkness, lighting up the night like the elemental beings that lived so vividly in the imaginations of her two younger sisters.

Shaking her head, it dawned on her that something was not right. Her heart began to beat fast and erratically, causing her breath to catch in her throat, as she slowly realised that the lights were in fact, lanterns, that were being held aloft by at least a dozen men, and they were heading straight for her.

Floating on the frosty air she could hear the low murmuring of voices and could now see that the shadows of the men were walked beside a horse drawn cart.

As they neared the top of the meadow, she started to walk towards them, but a man at the front, leading the horse, held up his hand.

"Don't come any closer, Tilly," he ordered, his voice harsh and commanding. "Go back to the house and fetch your father."

"Why?" She asked fearfully. "What has happened?"

"Do as I have asked, Tilly." He spoke sharply, causing her to turn and run back towards the house.

She found her father in the hallway, making his way from the drawing room to the library. "Tilly! Is the devil himself after you? You almost knocked me clean off my feet."

"Teddy Johnson from the village told me to come and get you." She was breathing heavily, fighting back tears. "There are men from the village outside, they have a cart with them. Something has happened, Father, something bad I think."

Her father nodded his head and seemed not to be in any hurry to step out into the cold night air, or to discover what news had brought the men to his door. He stared at Matilda for a long time, and then, confoundingly, he took his pipe from his pocket, slowly struck a match, and puffed three or four times, the smoke billowing around him, filling the air with the sweet, spicy aroma that Matilda was so accustomed to.

Eventually he said, "Did the men tell you why they have come, Tilly?"

She shook her head, her eyes wide with fright.

"I see," he uttered, his voice taut with anxiety. "You stay here, stay in the house."

As her father closed the front door behind him, Matilda ran towards it, placing her ear against the wood, closing her eyes in concentration. She could hear muffled, mumbled voices, all speaking at once. She then heard the voice of her father, one loud exclamation, and then she could hear nothing else.

"Matilda?" The sudden voice of her mother behind her, caused her to jump away from the door and turn around. "What on Earth are you doing?"

"Something has happened," she whispered fretfully, tears falling down her cheeks and dripping off her chin. "Men from the village have come with a cart."

"A cart?" Eleanor Grey repeated blankly. "Why?"

"I don't know," Matilda cried, "they walked up from the woods carrying lanterns. They said that I was to come inside and fetch Father. He is out there with them now."

Her mother rapidly blinked her eyes, slowly shaking her head.

"Was your brother with them?"

"I didn't see him," Matilda said, "I don't think he was with them."

"It will be something or nothing," her mother uttered dismissively, "it's probably that brother of yours, up to no good again. Your father will handle it."

It seemed that Eleanor Grey then changed her mind about leaving her husband to deal with the situation outside. She walked to the mirror hanging above the bureau and stared at her reflection for a long time, before patting down a stray tendril of greying hair, and walking towards the front door.

Matilda followed, pressing herself close to her mother's side.

Her father and the group of men were in deep conversation. One of the men coughed and nodded his head in their direction.

Her father sighed heavily. "Eleanor, take Tilly back into the house. I will be in directly."

Her mother shook her head, her arms held stiffly at her sides, her skin bleached of all colour. "Is it our Jack?" She asked tremulously, her voice shrill with the beginning of hysteria.

Matilda watched in stark disbelief as her father slowly, and reluctantly nodded his head. "It was an accident, Eleanor," he said, almost emotionlessly, as he tried to keep his own shock and grief in check. "He was skating. He fell. He didn't suffer."

"Dead the moment his head hit the ice," said a voice from the crowd. "I am sincerely sorry for your loss."

Eleanor looked at the man who had spoken, as if he had lost his mind.

"The stupid boy was trying to break a record," Edward put his arm around his wife, his voice now breaking with emotion. "He was skating too fast; he made a mistake and fell awkwardly. There was nothing that anybody could do to save him."

Matilda watched as her mother took several steps backwards, for a moment it looked as if she was going to fall to the ground, and then she began to scream.

The cold, strident, sound of her mother's screams, the sight of her beating her fists against her father's chest, would stay with Matilda for the rest of her life.

"How many times did we warn him?" She screeched, her mouth gaping wide with anguish. "Why would he never listen to us?"

"I know, I know," her father replied, taking her mother by the shoulders and turning her around, and with his arm around her waist he guided her back towards the house.

"Edward, I won't be able to bear it," her mother sobbed, "it can't be true, can it? Not our boy, not our Jack. What are we to do, Edward?"

"I don't know, my love. I really don't know."

The front door closed behind them. In their shock and grief, they had inadvertently left their young daughter, standing on the driveway, in the freezing cold and all alone. To Matilda it seemed that time had stopped turning, as if she wasn't real, as if nothing was real. It can't be true, she told herself repeatedly, young people don't die, and Jack was so full of energy, and anyway, he was too much of an expert skater to have made a silly mistake, whoever was inside the cart was not her brother, it couldn't be. Jack would be at the inn, drinking and laughing with his friends. He would arrive home singing in the early hours, causing his bleary-eyed father to come out onto the landing to threaten him with yet another lecture in the library first thing the following morning, a lecture that Jack wouldn't attend due to his headache and the fact that he had spent most of the day in bed.

She glanced towards the group of men, who were huddled close together, shaking their heads and muttering how it was a waste of a young life, and how things could have been different if only he had taken heed of their warnings.

While the men were engaged in hushed conversation, Matilda approached the cart, and while nobody was looking in her direction, she clambered onboard.

She saw her brother's boots sticking out from beneath a rough, grey blanket. He was lying on someone's old door, his hands folded across his chest. She crawled along the side of the makeshift stretcher until she was level with his head. His eyes were half open, as if desperately trying to see something for the last time.

The figure lying there, so still, was her brother and the realisation hit her in the chest like a bullet from a gun. Even then, as the truth was slowly turning into reality, she still half expected him to leap up and grab hold of her, laughing at the shock he had given her, teasing her about how easy she was to fool, but he didn't move, he remained unnaturally still and silent, his blind eyes staring at her, his freezing hand heavy and limp in hers.

"Tilly, love."

The sound of the male voice startled her. She turned her head and saw Jed Carter, one of the smallholders from the village, making his way down the side of the cart to reach her. She smiled wanly, glad that it was he who had come, for he was her friend, an elderly man who lived on the outskirts of the village who allowed her to climb on his haystacks and brought her lemonade that he had made himself.

He sat down beside her on the hard, draughty, wooden floor of the cart.

"This isn't a sight for a young girl like you, you should have stayed in the house as you were told."

Matilda exhaled a shuddering sigh. "It can't be true," she cried, feeling a pain begin in her heart that she was certain would be there for the rest of her life.

"It is true, Tilly. I was there when it happened, and I can tell you beyond a shadow of a doubt, that Jack has gone."

The tears fell harder, feeling hot against her frozen skin.

The old man leaned his back against the side of the cart and shook his head. "I think he'd been at the inn, Tilly, with all the other young fellows. Seemed to me that they'd all had a skinful of ale, messing about they were, acting like lunatics. Jack was in the first race. I told him that he was in no fit state, that he should go home and sleep it off, but he wouldn't listen. He told me that he was going to skate in the first race and then he was going back to Meadowside to collect you. He said that the cold walk home would sober him up quick enough."

He removed his cap and ran his fingers through his sparse hair.

"I was waiting by the gate," Matilda sobbed, "I thought he'd forgotten about me."

"He hadn't forgotten, Tilly. Anyway, everything that happened after that is a bit of a blur. It looked like a straightforward fall; he was travelling at speed when he suddenly lost his balance. He was way out in front, we waited for him to get up, but he didn't move, and then the other racers were all huddled around him. I went over to see what all the fuss was about, thinking he'd broken a bone, but he was just lying there, and it was obvious that he had gone."

"What will happen to him now, Jed?"

The old man sighed. "How old are you now, Tilly?"

"Twelve," she sniffed.

"You're not a little girl anymore, you're becoming a young woman. You know that they will take Jack away and bury him in a grave in the churchyard? You know that don't you?"

She nodded her head miserably. She did know that, on some level, and had listened to the Reverend Cashman droning on for hours about the good souls going to Heaven, and the bad burning forever in Hell. She had never understood it really or wasn't interested enough to give the Reverend her full attention, allowing her mind to wander off, while he preached his sermon on hellfire and retribution.

"That is not your Jack lying there, that's just his body. His soul, the most important part of him, has already gone."

Jed Carter felt sad that this conversation was even happening. He glanced down at the bowed head of his young companion. He had known her since the day she was born, for he had been employed by Edward Grey to maintain the garden at Meadowside for the past twenty years. He had always thought that she was fortunate to live in such an environment as Meadowside, for it had seemed to him that the Grey family had been uniquely blessed with happiness and abundance, which was unusual and envied in the village and surrounding area.

Matilda, he was certain, had never experienced loss before. She was so innocent of the sadness that existed in the world, and quite oblivious to the hardship and struggle of others, the illness and deaths, that occurred in the village almost daily. Her life was full of softness, love and joy, so it came as no wonder to him that the shock of Jack's death would have affected her so profoundly.

"It's not fair," he heard her cry. "Young people shouldn't die."

"You are right there, Tilly, it isn't fair. I am an old man, and death has visited me many times, and it is always a difficult thing to go through, and it is never fair, but I can promise you one thing, and that is that you will not feel like this forever."

"I won't ever see him again?" She felt as if her heart was breaking.

"I want him to come back."

"Of course, you do, but you know as well as I do that he can't come back. He's in Heaven now, and there's no coming back from there."

She rested her head against the sleeve of his jacket, it smelled strongly of tobacco and horses.

"You need to be brave, Tilly."

"I can't be brave without Jack; I don't know how. What do I have to do?"

"Well, the first thing you must do, and this is the bravest thing of all, is to let him go, Tilly. You must be strong, just like he would want you to be. You can talk to him still, you can love him just as much, but you must let him go."

"I can't," Matilda cried pitifully, "I just can't."

Jed Carter blinked away the tears that were clouding his pale eyes.

"Yes, you can, Tilly. Do it for him, let him be free and on his way. If I could take this away from you, I would. If there was anything I could do, then I would do it, but there isn't. The only thing I can do is to pass onto you the things I have learned, the things that you are too young to know, and I want you to listen carefully and do what I say."

Matilda lifted her head and gazed into his eyes, she then nodded her head, wiping away her tears with the end of her scarf.

"When things like this happen, you must be kind to yourself, you have to give yourself time to grieve, and then move on with your life. Of course, I don't mean that you must forget, but just to let things be, to accept that there is nothing you can do to change what has happened. Keeping hold of Jack is not going to bring him back. Like I said, he has long gone and is beyond it all now, but if you don't let him go you will be hurting yourself, and Jack really wouldn't want that." He patted her arm gently. "Now, let go of Jack's hand and let him be in peace."

Matilda closed her eyes for a moment, knowing deep in her heart that Jed Carter was speaking the truth. Jack had gone, and she had to, somehow, learn to come to terms with his death, and accept the cold, harsh truth of it. When she opened her eyes, she looked at Jack's face.

He looked peaceful, with a half-smile lingering on his lips, as if his death hadn't been as painful for him as it was proving to be for her.

She placed his hand back on his chest and whispered, "goodbye, Jack. I'll never forget you."

Jed carter sighed with relief. For a young girl Matilda had handled the heart-breaking situation as well as could be expected in the circumstances.

"Good girl, Tilly. There are going to be sad and difficult times ahead, but all you must do is get through them one day at a time. Now then," he stood up, taking Matilda by the hand and pulling her to her feet. "Let's get you out of this cold, and back inside the house with your family."

\*

It was six months later, and Matilda still thought about Jack several times a day, sometimes it was difficult to believe that he was no longer there, but she didn't cry at his memory as often as before and would regularly find herself laughing as she recalled a joke he had told, or a prank he had played on her. Jed Carter had been right, the passing of time had lessened her pain and dulled the edges of her grief, even if it hadn't taken it away completely.

It was different for her parents. Her mother had entered a period of deep shock, withdrawing into her own world, becoming increasingly distant and aloof, her own all-consuming grief making her blind to the grief of her family. She spent her time alone, either restlessly pacing the floor, or lost in long episodes of bitter weeping. While the passing of time was helping Matilda to heal, it had not blessed her mother with its therapeutic hand, for Eleanor Grey had travelled so far into the darkness of her loss, that she couldn't find her way out again.

Her father too had become quiet and withdrawn, his abject misery stooping his shoulders, and making him appear, sometimes, like a very old man. His appearance had grown gaunt and haggard, and he had taken to spending all day in the library, drinking whiskey, as if forgetting that behind the locked door were five living daughters who needed him.

The care of the three younger girls, Matilda, Kitty and Isabel, had fallen to the second eldest daughter, Emma. She made sure that the children were well fed and clean, she read them stories every night, played with them, listened to their troubles and worries, and just like their mother used to do, she ensured that they were loved and protected.

It was in the early summer, when Matilda left the house soon after breakfast, to take a walk in the meadow, with no shadow of forewarning that, once again, her family and Meadowside were about to be altered by an event that could not have been predicted.

The wildflower meadow was in full bloom as she walked down the mown pathway that led away from the house and towards the woods. She sat for a while on a wooden bench that her father had made two summers ago, feeling the sun's warmth on her face, and watching the busy insects that hovered about the flowers, swarming like clouds of dust, their merry chirping and buzzing filling the scented air with the sounds of summer.

It was at times like this that she missed Jack the most: the quiet times when she was alone, when she couldn't help but wonder what he would be doing in the very moment, if he had lived. She closed her eyes, and instantly a vision of him was etched into her mind as she saw him sauntering to the village to meet his friends, hands in his pickets, whistling a merry tune, without a care in the world. At other times she imagined him inside the house, or in the garden, playing a game of blind man's bluff with the youngest of his sisters.

She stood up and walked as far as the woods, grateful for the canopy of the trees that shielded her from the already scorching heat of the sun. She had hoped that she would come across some of her village friends playing there, so that she could spend a carefree hour in a game of hide and seek among the tress, or cops and robbers, but on that day the woods were silent, her friends probably having decided to play by the river instead. Despite the early hour, the morning was already uncomfortably warm, and Matilda made the decision not to walk to the river in search of her friends, but to instead return to the house.

She walked back to the meadow and was halfway along the pathway when she looked up and saw all four of her sisters standing by the gate, waving their arms in the air to get her attention. Her two eldest sisters, Martha and Emma, were standing close together in animated conversation, while the younger two, Isabel and Kitty, were jumping up and down in either excitement or agitation.

Matilda quickened her pace, holding her straw hat in place with one hand as she began to run towards the house.

As she approached them her eldest sister glared at her angrily.

"Where have you been?" She demanded, her hands on her hips. "We have been searching everywhere for you."

"You couldn't have searched very far then; I was only in the meadow."

"You were not in the meadow when we looked," Martha continued angrily. "While you have been gallivanting all over the countryside, something has happened, as if we needed anything else!"

Matilda felt her stomach twist into anxious knots. "Has somebody else died?" She asked fretfully.

"Of course, nobody has died, you stupid child, and from now on you are not to go off on your own without telling us where you're going. There are dangerous people about, evil people."

Emma stepped forwards, pushing Martha out of her way.

"Nothing terrible has happened, Tilly, it really isn't anything to worry about," she said, her voice soft and reassuring. "We just wanted you to be at home, so that we knew you were alright."

"Why wouldn't I be alright?" Matilda asked, but her voice was drowned out by Martha.

"Not something to worry about! Of course, it's something to worry about. We have no idea who this child is. We don't know the first thing about her." Martha sniffed disapprovingly, her eyes dark with anger. "The only thing we know about her is that she's a vagabond. She could be anyone for all we know, a dangerous thief, or she could murder us all in our beds and, as for you," she took a swipe at Matilda, "we could have done without having to scour the village looking for you. There are bad people about, they could have taken you away from Meadowside and done all sorts of horrible things to you."

"Martha!" It was so out of character for Emma to be angry, or to shout, that the sound of her voice caused Matilda to visibly jump. "There is absolutely no need for that." She bent down and retrieved Matilda's sun hat from the ground, dusting it off and placing it back on her head. She turned towards Martha. "Don't you think we have enough on our plates without you making everything a hundred times worse."

Martha folded her arms and scowled. "This will bring us nothing but shame and trouble. This child will bring about the ruination of Meadowside and this family. One day, in the future, you will all look back and see that I was right."

"Enough, Martha!" Emma's voice was low and dangerous.

Martha then glared from one to the other of them, turned on her heel and stomped angrily back to the house.

"What is she talking about, Emma? What child?"

Emma placed her hands on Matilda's shoulders and spoke calmly. "We have a visitor, Tilly, a little girl who is probably going to be staying here with us for a while."

"A little girl?" Matilda frowned, "but who is she? Where has she come from?"

"That is all that you need to know for the time being. She is just a little girl who has nowhere else to go. Now then," she smiled brightly, as if she didn't have a worry in the world, as if nothing out of the ordinary had occurred. "I need you to take care of Kitty and Issy."

At that moment her youngest sister, Issy, came to her side and took hold of her hand. "I was the one who found her, Tilly," she said, full of self-importance.

Emma sighed. "Now, listen to me, Issy and Kitty, you are to go into the garden with Tilly, you can play there, but you are to stay there, do you understand? You are not to wander off, not even to the meadow, stay in the garden until I come to find you."

The three girls watched Emma as she returned to the house. They then walked up the driveway that led up the side and towards the garden.

"You must tell me what happened, Issy."

Her youngest sister blew the blonde fringe out of her eyes and shook her head gravely. "It's a sorry state of affairs, Tilly, a sorry state of affairs indeed."

Matilda would have burst out laughing if the circumstances hadn't been so serious, knowing that her little sister was repeating words she had heard her father use to describe the situation.

They walked to the far end of the garden and sat on a bench, facing away from the house, looking out on to the fen and the shimmering fields in the distance. Kitty was playing on the rope swing that Jack had made for them two summers ago, and was happily swinging herself around, head tipped back as she watched the spinning branches of the trees.

Matilda turned to Issy, hoping that she could trust her four-year-old sister to tell her the truth of what had happened, with no embellishments or added drama. Despite the fact that Issy had a keen intelligence and a vocabulary far beyond her years, she did have a tendency to add her own details to make the facts more interesting.

"Who is this girl who has suddenly arrived. You must tell me everything and don't leave anything out."

"She's very pretty," Issy commented, tucking her fair hair behind her ears.

Matilda tutted irritably. "I don't care how pretty she is! Who is she?"

"I was at the front of the house," Issy began quietly, her tone of voice heavy with the importance of her story. "I was waiting for you to come back from your walk. I went out onto the track and that is when I saw it."

Matilda turned to her when she stopped speaking, and impatiently nudged her in the ribs. "Saw what, Issy? What did you see, for goodness' sake!"

"It was a gypsy caravan, Tilly, painted all over with flowers and leaves and being pulled by a big black and white horse. The caravan stopped outside of the house and then an old man climbed down, he lifted a little girl out and stood her on the track."

"Then what happened," Matilda asked breathlessly.

The old man came up to me, he had twinkly eyes, and looked kind, so I wasn't at all afraid. He told me to take the girl to Father, and that she belonged to us now. He said there was a note in her pocket and to make sure that Father read it."

Matilda frowned, staring at her sister in bewilderment. "Are you sure that he said that she belongs to us? Were those his exact words?"

Issy brushed her hair back from her face, blinked several times, as if trying to remember what she had been told, word for word, and then she nodded her head firmly. "That is what he said, Tilly."

"That can't be true!" Matilda leapt to her feet, wishing that Emma would come and feeling cross that she had been excluded from whatever was going on in the house. "How could it be true? It doesn't make any sense."

Matilda sat down again. "What happened next, Issy?"

"I took her into the house. She was crying, but I told her that we would look after her. I took her to Father in the library."

"What did Father do? What did he say?"

"He read the note and said that there must be some mistake. He said it was a very sorry business indeed, and then he called for Mother. Martha and Emma came too, and then Father marched me out of the library and closed the door."

There followed a short silence, while Matilda tried to figure out where this child had come from, and why she had ended up at Meadowside.

"None of this makes any sense at all, Issy. A gypsy caravan, and a young girl just being left here for no reason. I don't understand it. Is that all you know, Issy?"

Issy bit her lip anxiously and seemed to be struggling not to cry.

"I could hear Mother. She sounded ever so upset, and I heard Father say..."

"Issy! For goodness' sake, what did he say?"

"He said that if this girl was Jack's child, then they had a duty of care." She nodded her head, satisfied that she had remembered the exact words used. "She must stay here, that is what he said."

Matilda gasped loudly. She didn't know what she was expecting to hear, but it certainly wasn't that. Jack's child! How could that even be possible? It was more likely that the gypsies simply didn't want the girl and had just abandoned her at Meadowside to be shot of her, to make her somebody else's problem.

"Mother was screaming and crying," Issy continued tearfully, "and said that she wouldn't have a gypsy child in the house, that she wouldn't stand for it. She said that the little girl had nothing to do with Jack, and that it was all a lie."

Matilda stood up in a daze. Her legs felt leaden as she walked away from the bench to where the garden boundary met the rougher grass of the fen. In her mind a blurry memory was forming, creating bright and detailed images of a day long ago. She had been very young, about four years old, and Jack had taken her to the fields at harvest time, to see the brightly painted gypsy caravans out on the fen, and to watch the harvest being gathered in. The fields had been full of strangers, travelling people who had come to assist with the harvest, and would then be gone, not to be seen for another year.

She remembered that she could hear fiddle music playing in the distance, and how fascinated she had been with the women's colourful clothes and bright, silver jewellery. Her mother had warned her to stay away from the strangers, telling her that they were not like them, that they were dangerous.

She had told Jack about her mother's warning and he had laughed, telling her that the gypsies were just people, and were no more dangerous than they were.

"They just choose to live a different life, Tilly, that is all. They prefer to travel around, seeing new places, rather than staying in one place, and there is nothing wrong with that."

Matilda had spent an enjoyable afternoon playing with the village children, while their parents worked out in the fields. Late in the day, as the sultry orange sun began to slip steadily towards the horizon, she saw Jack in the distance. He was walking back from the caravans, a beautiful gypsy girl holding his hand and laughing at his side. She ran towards them, but as soon as they caught sight of her, the girl turned abruptly and walked quickly in the opposite direction. She could recall a few details about the girl, and that was probably because she had the most beautiful hair that Matilda had ever seen. It was very long and wildly curly and was the exact colour as the sun that was rapidly descending the arc of the sky.

She turned back to Issy, who had remained sitting on the bench, idly swinging her bare legs back and forth.

"What does this girl look like?"

"She's taller than me, older, I think, maybe she's between you and Kitty. She has very blue eyes, bluer than mine even, and she has red hair, loads of it, all falling down her back."

Matilda felt her heart flip in her chest. She knew for a fact that Jack had once had a girlfriend and that she belonged to the travelling community. The red hair connection could indicate that she could be the mother of this unexpected visitor, but did it mean that Jack was her father?

Jack would have been only sixteen years old at the time, and the gypsy girl had been around the same age. The more she thought about it, the more convinced she was that the new arrival at Meadowside was Jack's child. Why else would the gypsies have left her with them? They must have believed that she was Jack's daughter, for they could just as easily left her at the workhouse, or an orphanage somewhere.

Matilda's next quandary was what to do with this information. Should she tell her parents that she had seen Jack with a flame haired gypsy girl all of those years ago or could telling them make the entire situation worse.

*

An hour later Emma came into the garden. The girls immediately ran to her side, but she refused to answer any of their questions, insisting that their father would inform them of anything that they needed to know.

Issy was walking by Matilda's side as they made their way back to the house. "I don't think she can be Jack's child," she whispered beneath her breath. "Jack wasn't married, so he couldn't have had a baby, could he?"

Matilda stopped walking and gazed down at her little sister. She had always believed that two people had to be married in a church before they could have a child, and she knew for a fact that Jack had never married anyone, but she had, on a few occasions, overheard whispered conversations between her two eldest sisters about a young woman in the village who had a baby boy when she hadn't been married. As Matilda understood it, the young woman and the baby had been banished from her parents' house, and the village, and had never been seen nor heard of again.

Martha had been enraged by the event, as if it affected her personally, saying in hushed tones that the woman was a complete disgrace and fully deserved the life she had coming to her. Emma had remained quiet, but also appeared shocked by the young girl's predicament. This made Matilda think that she had some kind of a duty to protect Jack's good name. She didn't want her parents, or her sisters, to think badly of him.

Emma led them to the drawing room. Their parents were sitting stiffly, side by side on the chaise lounge. Martha, stony faced, was seated in an armchair nearby, her hands clenched into tight fists in her lap.

Standing in front of the fireplace, like an exhibition in a museum, stood the girl, her head bowed, shoulders slumped, and her arms tightly pressed to her sides. As soon as Matilda caught sight of her, she knew beyond any doubt that she was the child of the gypsy girl. It was almost like looking at the same person, the resemblance was uncanny.

"Girls," Edward Grey began, his quiet voice sounding strained. "This child has been brought to us because, unfortunately, both of her parents are dead. She is an orphan." He coughed awkwardly, as if not quite knowing what to say next. "She will be staying with us, here at Meadowside, until we have made some enquiries. Her name is Seraphina."

Matilda repeated the name several times inside her head. She had never heard it before, or any other name like it. She viewed the girl covertly, as she stood with her wild, curly hair falling over her face, her eyes intently focused on the rug.

Her first observation was that the girl was wearing strange clothes, a multicoloured dress that reached to her ankles, and heavy brown boots that her father would have described as 'clodhoppers'. She looked extremely uncomfortable and out of place, as if she would have rather been anywhere other than where she was. Matilda felt a stab of pity for her inside her chest. How awful it must be to be dumped amongst strangers, far away from everyone and everything that you knew. How frightening it must be.

Matilda walked towards her. "My name is Matilda, but most people call me Tilly, you can too, if you like. These are my sisters, Issy and Kitty."

The girl lifted her head slowly and gazed at Matilda through a curtain of tumbling red hair. She had the most startling blue eyes that Matilda had ever seen, and a smattering of freckles across her cheeks and the bridge of her nose.

The girl stared at Matilda unflinchingly, making her feel quite flustered and bemused. She wondered if she had dirt on her face, or if their visitor had taken an instant dislike to her. All around them the room was completely silent. Matilda frowned as the young girl continued to study her in detail, almost as if looking into her soul.

Matilda had seen something in those clear blue eyes. She thought at first it was anger, or defiance, but then concluded that she had made a mistake, it was something else, something mysterious and disconcerting, and although she tried, she could not put a name to it.

"Take Seraphina to your room, Tilly. A bed has already been moved in there for her, she will share with you, Kitty and Issy, for the time being. She has just arrived with the clothes she is standing up in, perhaps you could find some of yours, or Kitty's, that would fit."

Matilda turned to face her parents. Her father's expression was haggard, his eyes deeply concerned, but she saw him smile towards Seraphina, as if he had at least appreciated the situation the poor girl had found herself in.

Eleanor Grey's expression was stony and cold. Her back was ramrod straight, her chin jutting out in a display of haughty disgust. Matilda was saddened by her mother's demeanour, for this was not the woman she knew and loved, this was someone greatly altered, changed by tragedy beyond all recognition.

"Surely, she can use one of the attic rooms, Edward? I'm not sure that...well, I don't think that it's entirely appropriate that she should..." Her voice trailed off, not quite sure how much she could say while the child was standing just feet away from her.

"We can't put a ten-year old child in the attic on her own, Eleanor. Anyway, it is best that she gets to know the girls."

Eleanor Grey pressed her lips into a thin line of disapproval but said no more.

Matilda took a step towards Seraphina and smiled at her encouragingly. "I'll show you our bedroom," she said, taking Seraphina by the arm and gently steering her towards the door, closely followed by Kitty and Issy.

The four girls walked in silence across the hall. When they reached the top of the stairs Matilda noticed that Kitty wasn't with them. She turned around and sighed irritably.

"Kitty, are you coming with us, or not?"

Kitty was standing at the foot of the stairs, not at all sure that she was happy with the prospect of this strange looking girl living in her home and sleeping in her bedroom. The drawing room door was shut, but even so, she could still hear the angry, raised voices, seeping out into the hallway, rumbling like a distant thunderstorm.

Kitty, at six years old, was the quiet one of the family, lacking Matilda's determination and Issy's intelligence, she was often overlooked and forgotten about. Even at her young age, she often felt misunderstood and underestimated by her family, because even though she tried hard, she was simply unable to do the things that the other children could.

Her father had made it his business to teach all of his children to read, write and to understand mathematics. He taught them history, geography and biology, as well as the history of art and the French language.

Jack had never been interested in his lessons but had managed to learn to read and write to a high standard, despite his apathy. However, all of his daughters, with the exception of Kitty, had been quick and eager to learn, with his youngest, Issy, showing great promise, due to her advanced reading ability and vocabulary.

Kitty had been different and was subjected to extra hours in the library with her father, who tried, with great patience, to teach her the simplest of things, until eventually he had no other choice but to admit defeat and to accept the fact that, for a reason he couldn't quite understand, Kitty was simply unable to learn, and his lessons, despite his patience, were achieving nothing, other than turning the child into an anxious, nervous wreck.

A fresh bout of shouting could be heard coming from the drawing room, and reluctantly Kitty walked up the stairs, catching up with the other girls inside their bedroom. Four single beds now stood in a line against the long wide wall of the room, when there had only been three that morning. She went to hers and sat despondently, folding her arms in sulky protest.

Matilda went to the wardrobes that were lined up against the opposite wall and began pulling out dresses and cardigans, placing them on a pile on the rocking chair in the corner.

"These should fit you," she said, "I grew out of them last summer and as you're nearly as tall as me, they should be fine. Would you like to try them on?"

Seraphina was standing stiffly on the large, circular rug in the middle of the room, fiddling distractedly with the frayed hem of her cardigan. She remained silent, with no signs that she had even heard Matilda.

"Maybe she can't speak," Issy offered, looking at Seraphina with a perplexed expression. "Maybe she's been stuck dumb by a gypsy curse."

"That is the most ridiculous thing I've ever heard" Matilda rolled her eyes to the ceiling. "Of course, she can speak, she just doesn't want to, or maybe she's just shy, some people are."

At that moment Kitty suddenly jumped off the bed and ran towards Seraphina, sliding to a halt in front of her, almost knocking her off her feet.

"What are you doing, Kitty? Sit back down on your bed and don't you dare move until I tell you to. Why are you always so stupid?"

Seraphina lifted her head and turned to face Matilda. "She's not stupid," she said, moving her gaze to Kitty. "You're not stupid, are you? You just know other things, different things."

Kitty stared at her wide eyed. She wasn't quite sure that she knew anything at all but was happy enough to nod her head in enthusiastic agreement.

"What does she know?" Issy asked innocently. "She can't read or write. Can you Kitty?"

Kitty shook her head, lowering her eyes as if ashamed.

"There are things that you learn, and things that you feel, and then there are things that can't be taught, and those are the things that Kitty knows."

The three girls stared at Seraphina as if she were the fount of all knowledge, but also because they had never heard anyone speak in such a way before. They had only ever heard the local accent, but Seraphina spoke in the accent of her mother and grandparents, with a slight Irish lilt, and the inflections of the other regions they had visited.

"How can you learn things that can't be taught?" Issy asked indignantly. "I'm sure that I don't know anything that I haven't been taught."

"Of course, you do," Seraphina smiled, "you were born knowing things that you've forgotten."

"What sort of things?" Issy frowned.

Matilda wasn't sure where this conversation was going, and in truth had been completely bewildered by it. One thing she was certain of was that her mother wouldn't like it, for it had an air of the unknown about it, a tinge of things that shouldn't be spoken about.

"You will be alright here," Matilda said loudly, instantly dispelling the awe and fascination displayed by her younger sisters. "We will look after you, and although you are not our sister, you will become like one, and we will love you just as much as we love each other."

"I don't want another sister," Kitty wailed from the other side of the room, "I already have far too many!"

Seraphina suddenly laughed, Matilda quickly joining in.

"Kitty," Matilda giggled, shaking her head. "We can always rely on you to say the first silly thing that pops into your head. You can never have too many sisters, that is a known fact, and now that we have another one we should be grateful."

"I suppose," Kitty reluctantly agreed, "but I hope she isn't bossy like Martha, we don't want another one like her!"

"I won't be bossy, Kitty. I promise."

"That's settled then," Matilda nodded her head, satisfied. "The four of us will be the best of friends, and sisters together."

"Yes!" Issy jumped up and down, clapping her hands together.

"I've never had a sister, or a brother, there was only me and my grandparents."

"Well, now you've got us, Seraphina. Emma will look after you, like she looks after us, the only one you must be careful of is Martha. She's not the same as the rest of us at all, she's always grumpy and miserable, we really don't know what's the matter with her."

Matilda watched as Seraphina wandered over to the pile of clothes and began holding them up against her. She didn't look at all like Jack, for as she had already discovered, she looked exactly like her mother. She stared at her while her attention was taken up by the half dozen dresses that Matilda had donated. Seraphina was tall for her age, and Jack had been over six feet, but there was no other physical resemblance, and Matilda couldn't help thinking that life at Meadowside would have been a lot easier for the new member of the family if she had looked like Jack.

# Chapter 5

## Meadowside 2003

Matilda stopped speaking. She had grown tired, her voice becoming increasingly weak.

"Do you believe that Seraphina was Jack's daughter?" I asked, already anxious to hear the rest of the story and to discover what became of Matilda's family.

"I think it is highly likely," she spoke quietly, her frail voice hardly audible in the large room. "He would have been very young, far too young to be a father. I don't even know if he was aware of Seraphina's existence, or what had happened between him and her mother. Maybe he did know about her but kept it a secret. She was born years before his death, but her mother died when she was a baby, and it's possible that the family never returned to the fens after that. Seraphina was the image of her mother, and that, in the end, brought about her downfall."

"Her downfall?" I queried, frowning at the use of the word.

"She didn't look like any of us. The resemblance to her mother was so strong that nobody could see Jack in her at all. I think that if she had looked more like him, then her life at Meadowside would have been significantly easier. My parents would have loved her, accepted and protected her, and everything would have been different. Instead of that, nobody was sure if she was related to us or not."

"They didn't accept her?"

"They tolerated her," Matilda admitted sadly. "My father insisted that she stayed in the house and was brought up alongside myself, Issy and Kitty, due to the chance that she could be Jack's daughter, their granddaughter. My mother mostly ignored her as if she barely existed, but after a while my father began to warm to her, in fact, I think he grew to love her very much. Myself, Kitty and Issy all adorned her, and of course, Emma loved her, but my mother and Martha, especially Martha, viewed her with deep suspicion."

"You never told anybody that you had seen Jack with Seraphina's mother?"

"I was a child," she replied defensively, staring me straight in the eye. "I didn't know what to do for the best. I thought that if I had said anything it could make things even worse, so I decided to leave it well alone. I believe that, perhaps my mother would have preferred not to know, because then she wouldn't have to face the shame of an illegitimate grandchild, or to confront the fact that Jack was far from the innocent boy she believed him to be. I decided to remain silent, and told nobody, not even Seraphina herself."

She stared into the gently flickering flames of the fire. "I think that I did the wrong thing. I should have told my parents, but most of all, I should have told Seraphina. She needed somewhere to belong, people to belong to, and I kept that chance away from her."

"You were so young, Matilda, and thought that you were doing the right thing. It must have been quite a burden for you to carry for all these years."

"I often think to myself that things might have turned out differently if I had spoken out about what I had seen." She lifted her eyes to mine; they were dark with sorrow and glittering with memories. "The story has only just begun, Amber, there is so much more left to be told."

"You were so young when Jack took you to the harvest, only a baby really. Are you certain of what you saw?"

She inclined her head decisively. "I know what I saw, and even to this day I can remember it clearly. I think it was the distinctive appearance of the gypsy girl, her flaming red hair, the colourful clothing, and the fact that Jack had appeared so happy and relaxed in her company, that has made it stick so firmly in my mind."

Remembering the past in such vivid detail had tired Matilda. I walked back with her to the larger living room and settled her into her chair, placing her blanket over her knees, and helping her to lift her legs onto a footstall.

"Would you like a cup of tea?"

"That would be lovely, Amber. Thank you."

I was halfway to the door when I stopped and turned back to her.

"Why did you want to move to the children's room, Matilda? We could have just stayed here."

Considering how walking even a short distance was painful and arduous for her, I was surprised that she wanted to go to the effort of changing location, when staying put would have been the easiest option, and just as comfortable.

"I have my reasons," she replied testily, her tone of voice not conducive to further questioning. "One day soon you will understand."

I left the room feeling confused, wondering what it was that Matilda was so desperate for me to understand. She had spoken with deep emotion and love about her family and the house itself, and yet, beneath it all I had detected something dark and mysterious.

I made Matilda her cup of tea, placing it within her reach and then went to the dining room. It was a large space, with a long, highly polished table, surrounded by carved chairs, upholstered in a rich burgundy fabric. A dresser stood against a wall, reminiscent of the 1920s, with a speckled oval mirror standing on top of it. The shelves and the deep cupboards within it housed quite a collection of high-quality dinner services and crystal glasses, with the drawers being full of tarnished silver cutlery and serving utensils.

My heart was lifted by the beauty of the items I had found, and with only a little imagination I was able to see the room at Christmas, a huge, decorated tree in the corner, the table set, crystal glasses catching the light from the fire and the candles, and the beautiful fireplace adorned with holly from the garden.

It was easy to imagine Matilda there, with her family, in the days before Jack's death, all sitting around the table on Christmas day. In my mind's eyes I saw little Issy, just as Matilda had described her, her blue eyes shining with excitement. I could see Emma and Kitty, Matilda and her parents, one at each end of the table, her father carving the turkey, her mother holding aloft a glass of wine, her beloved Jack at her side. Martha was there too, scowling slightly, not quite able to join in the festivities with the rest of her family, finding it all frivolous and unnecessary.

I could hear the noise, the chatter of excited young voices, the raucous laughter as Jack told a joke. It was dark and cold beyond the leaded-light windows, but the room was warm and full of flickering light.

I was suddenly jolted back to the present, for a moment having the feeling that I had travelled back in time and had witnessed a Christmas of long ago, as an unseen observer standing in the corner of the room.

Matilda's descriptions of her family and her early life back in the early 1900s had ignited my imagination, making the old occupants of the house feel so real, and I was suddenly desperate to know what had become of them all, and what had taken place to leave Matilda and Kitty alone in Meadowside from such a young age.

I turned and saw that Kitty had walked into the room.

"Did you enjoy your walk?" I asked her.

She lifted her arms to shoulder height and then let them drop back to her sides. "Still no sign of her," she sighed wretchedly.

"I'm sorry," I replied, sympathetically, having decided that the best way to manage Kitty's strange ramblings, was to just go along with them. I changed the subject. "I need to clear out all the items from the dresser so that we can move it out into the barn. You can help if you would like to."

She nodded her head distractedly. "I feel so much happier when she's here."

"Shall we make ourselves a cup of tea before we start work in here?"

She smiled brightly, and I was struck by how quickly her mood could change.

"Also, we need to go into the village and get some shopping. You can come with me. I haven't got my car back yet, so we'll have to walk, but I'm sure it will do us good."

"I'm not allowed to go to the village," Kitty stated.

"I think you're not allowed to go on your own. I'm sure it will be fine if you're with me."

"Beth usually does the shopping for us; she could do it."

"Is Beth here?"

"Yes, she's in the kitchen, cleaning the stove."

I headed for the kitchen with Kitty following close behind me. When I entered the room, Beth Marsden was on her knees, cleaning the inside of the old range cooker. She jumped to her feet as soon as she saw me.

"You must be Amber," she smiled, wiping her hand on her jeans before holding it out towards me.

"And you must be Beth." We shook hands formally.

"Kitty has been telling me all about you and the fact that you are planning to move Matilda into the dining room. Such a good idea."

"She just can't manage the stairs," I explained, "and there's no need for her to be struggling so much when we have a room on the ground floor with a bathroom right next to it."

"I have spent a lot of time worrying about these two living out here all on their own, and the stairs have definitely been one of my biggest concerns." She nodded her head towards Kitty, "I don't think she'd know what to do if there was an emergency with Matilda. I've tried to teach her several times to use the phone, but I'm not sure that she would think to use it if she needed to."

She pulled out a chair and sat at the table. "I can't tell you how relieved I was when I heard that you were coming. They need someone here twenty-four hours a day. Matilda is over a hundred years old, and Kitty's not that far behind her. The situation couldn't have continued for much longer."

I filled the kettle and switched it on. "Kitty and I are going to have a cup of tea before we start to empty out the dresser in the dining room. Nathaniel is arranging for a couple of men to come and move the furniture into the barn and is also ordering a new bed for Matilda. Would you like a cup of tea, Beth? Or a coffee?"

"Tea will be fine thanks. Anyway, I don't think you've got any coffee." She grinned. "Kitty has taken quite a shine to Nathaniel, which I have to say is a good sign, despite her...her differences, she is actually a very astute judge of character."

I poured the boiling water into the old-fashioned teapot and brought it over to the table.

"I can't say that I blame her for liking Nathaniel, he is rather gorgeous," Beth continued, "if I wasn't a proper grown up with a husband and a couple of kids, I would be after him myself!"

I laughed as I took some cups out of the dresser cupboard. "He's exactly the kind of man my mother would choose for me, the sort of man she's been nagging me for years to find."

"Well," Beth poured the tea into the cups, "as it turns out, he has found you! Seriously though, he's a nice chap, and I have to say that he's gone over and above to help Matilda and Kitty. I really liked him on the couple of occasions I have run into him."

Beth Marsden was a woman about the same age as me, with short dark hair and a quick smile. I was already warming to her, and had the feeling that, in time, we could become good friends.

"I'm not allowed in the village, am I Beth?"

"No, Kitty, you're not."

I raised my eyebrows questioningly.

"It's the cars," Beth explained, "Kitty hasn't been to the village since she was a teenager. In those days, especially around here, there was no traffic, apart from the horse variety. She wouldn't be safe, and Matilda has no desire to go into the village at all. I think both of them would be overwhelmed at the changes that have taken place."

Kitty stood up from the table again, abandoning her tea, and wandered out to the garden through the kitchen door.

"It's extraordinary," I frowned, feeling genuinely bewildered, "that they have barely left the house for all these years. I can't understand why. It's almost as if they have been hiding from something. How on Earth have they managed?"

"There has always been a shop in the village," Beth explained. "They used to deliver groceries to Meadowside every week, leaving the shopping bags in the porch and they were paid monthly by the solicitors that Nathaniel works for. I remember the old shopkeeper well, his name was Mr Harrison, a lovely old chap, he told me once that he'd been delivering groceries to Meadowside for more than fifty years and had never once set eyes on either of the sisters."

"How did you come to be working here?"

"Mr Harrison, the shopkeeper, was retiring and was worried about Matilda and Kitty starving to death, so he contacted the solicitors who paid him every month, telling them that he was retiring, and that the new shopkeeper wasn't interested in doing home deliveries, and suggested me as somebody who could possibly help. He knew that I kept an eye on a couple of other elderly residents of the village, doing their cleaning and shopping, things like that, and the next thing I knew, it was all settled. Matilda was struggling with the housework, and needed some help, and agreed to me coming twice a week."

Kitty drifted back into the kitchen, but only sat down for a few minutes before she was off again.

"She never stays still, does she?" I said, gazing at Kitty's retreating back.

"She's remarkable for her age," Beth commented, "she never complains of any aches and pains, and is still very active, it must be incredibly rare for a woman in her nineties."

"She says some very strange things," I muttered.

"Indeed, she does!" Beth smiled knowingly, "I think it must be a learning disability, or whatever it is that's a little amiss with her. She can't read or write at all and has a complete fixation on things that aren't there. Honestly, if you were a person easily influenced, then you'd be beside yourself with terror at some of the things she comes out with, somebody being out in the meadow who won't come inside and then she has the tendency to come out with some baffling one-liners."

Beth quickly changed the subject as Kitty re-entered the room. She leaned on her elbows and smiled at me encouragingly. "You're doing a great job. I'll help you to clear out the dining room, if you like." She glanced to where Kitty was frantically searching for something in a drawer. "I'm really happy that Matilda won't have to struggle up and down those stairs, the thought of her falling has literally given me nightmares."

Kitty suddenly turned away from the dresser, shutting the drawer quickly, whatever she was looking for now forgotten.

"The stairs," she whispered, a look of real fear in her eyes. "They are dangerous, very dangerous."

Beth leaned towards me and said beneath her breath, "You see what I mean? If you were to question her she wouldn't even remember what she had said."

"You don't need to worry about the stairs, Kitty, you are quite capable and safe going up and down them. It is Matilda we are worried about, but we are going to move her downstairs soon. Do you remember that I told you all about that?"

Kitty scratched her forehead, her head to one side as she gazed at me searchingly, as if trying to recall something to mind. She then shrugged her shoulders.

"Like I said, I will help you sort out the dining room." Beth stood up and gathered the teacups and took them over to the sink. "I'll go and get the shopping this morning, if you'd like to make a list of what you need. Shall I get some packing boxes and bubble wrap while I'm out?"

"That would be brilliant, thanks, Beth."

"I'll just do some dusting in the library and then I'll pop out to the shops."

"I'll make a shopping list now."

I went over to the dresser and found a notepad and pen in one of the drawers. Sitting back at the table I watched as Kitty drifted past, following Beth to the library. I wrote a few items on the list, then placing the pen on top of the notepad, I went to a large cupboard in the working area of the kitchen, which was used as a pantry, and looked inside. There was a packet of sugar, a box of rolled oats and a few tins of soup, but not much else.

Returning to the table I sat down again. I went to pick up the pen to add items to the list, only to find that it wasn't where I had left it. Thinking that it might have rolled on to the floor, I looked under the table, moving all of the chairs out of the way, but there was no sign of it. I walked back to the cupboard, even though I was certain that I had left the pen resting on top of the notepad. It was not beyond possibility that I had absently picked it up and had taken it to the cupboard with me. It wasn't there.

Frowning, I left the kitchen and went to the library. Beth and Kitty were both there, Beth flicking a duster over the desk and polishing the brass lamp that stood on the shiny wood. Kitty was sitting in an armchair near to the bookshelves.

"Kitty, did you take the pen I was using in the kitchen?"

She shook her head, with Beth informing me that Kitty had been with her since they had both left the kitchen.

"Well, that's bizarre. I was writing a shopping list and was just checking what we had in the food cupboard, and when I returned to the table the pen was gone, vanished into thin air."

"Here's another one," Beth took a biro from the top of the desk and handed it to me.

That was the first incidence that I experienced of items going missing or being moved, but it was far from the last. The disappearance and movement of objects became a part of my daily life at Meadowside, and annoying and frustrating as it was, I very quickly became used to it. It was inconvenient, and drove me crazy, at times making me question my sanity.

After giving the shopping list to Beth, I went to check on Matilda, who was awake and staring dreamily into the fire. I sat in the chair opposite, and as I did so, I became aware of a strange sound coming from the ceiling. I glanced upwards, straining my ears to hear more clearly, for all the world it sounded like footsteps, someone walking slowly and deliberately up and down the landing.

"Can you hear that noise, Matilda?"

"It must be Kitty," she replied quickly, lifting her eyes momentarily to the ceiling.

"She's in the library with Beth."

At that moment a loud slamming noise caused me to almost jump out of my skin. It sounded exactly like a door slamming shut.

"I think I'll go and investigate."

"It will be nothing," Matilda said quietly, "the wind probably, like I told you before, old houses can be noisy sometimes."

I could have easily accepted the odd creaking of floorboards, or the rumbling of pipes, but not footsteps or randomly slamming doors.

The library door was standing open as I walked through the hall, and I could clearly see that both Kitty and Beth were inside. Walking up the stairs I wondered if a window had been left open, which could account for the slamming of a door, and perhaps the footsteps had just been the house creaking and groaning with age, but even then, I didn't really believe either of these explanations, and was troubled by the feeling that there was somebody else living in the house, somebody that I hadn't been told about.

I got a grip of myself at the top of the stairs, conscious of the fact that I mustn't let ridiculous notions and thoughts take root. There was nobody else living in Meadowside, just me, Kitty and Matilda. Who else could there possibly be?

I glanced quickly into Matilda and Kitty's rooms, and into my own. The windows were all shut. The doors all closed. I then walked to the far end of the corridor. There was a door straight in front of me and two others on either side of the passageway. All of them were shut.

The house was suddenly deathly still, as if it had taken a huge breath and was now watching and waiting. I began to feel flustered, triggered by something I couldn't see or understand, while at the same time feeling stupid for allowing myself to be rattled by something was, after all, just a feeling.

I stood there for a long time, staring at the closed door in front of me. The air around me was crackling with foreboding, a silent warning, an unspoken threat. I could feel danger in the air, and instinct telling me that I didn't know what I was dealing with and should retreat and leave well alone.

Again, I struggled to get control over myself, to think pragmatically, but my thoughts were so confused and erratic that I could barely make any sense of them. Eventually, I decided that I needed to confront whatever was going on, and whatever was causing it, despite my terror, I had to stand strong and firm, mainly, I believed, to convince myself that all the strangeness was nothing but my own imagination.

I tried each door in turn. One of them would have been the bathroom, and the other four, bedrooms. All the doors were locked, and I wondered why this should be. The house was quite big, with several bedrooms to accommodate Matilda's large family. I thought that perhaps she had decided to lock the rooms that were no longer in use, but why would she lock the bathroom?

Standing at the door, directly opposite me, at the very end of the corridor, I suddenly became inexplicably convinced that there was somebody behind it. I could hear nothing, but all around me the air was turning colder, the atmosphere increasingly tense.

I approached the door slowly. "Is there somebody in there?" I whispered into the wood, feeling ridiculous and wondering if I was losing my mind. There was nobody in the room, I kept telling myself. How could there be?

I stepped back from the door. This part of the house seemed to be infused with dark menace, as if something or someone was imprinted into the air, into the darkness itself. I was being watched; I could sense it. I could feel hidden eyes boring into me, causing the hair on my arms to prickle and stand on end.

It was not like me to be sensitive, or easily spooked. I was not even a believer in the paranormal, but there was something strange about this house, and its occupants, something so outside of my experience that I couldn't even name it.

My behaviour was curious to me. How easily I had surrendered to my own imagination, giving it power, almost inviting it to run away with itself. All I had experienced were strange feelings and sensations, and surely, they could have come from nowhere else, apart from my own brain.

"There is nothing here," I whispered into the thick, dense air. "It's just an old house, and I have to get used to it."

I walked back to the stairs, and the further away I walked from the end of the corridor, the lighter the atmosphere became. I was halfway between the landing and the hall when I suddenly stopped dead in my tracks. The pen that I had been using in the kitchen was now on one of the steps of the staircase. It was standing upright. I was immediately struck by how unnatural it looked, standing on its pointed nib, defying every law of gravity that I had ever been taught. It hadn't been there when I had walked up the stairs. There was no way that I wouldn't have seen it. Frowning with bewilderment, I bent to pick it up, but when my hand was just about to grasp it, it was suddenly snatched up, thrown into the air and hurled at the wall at the bottom of the stairs.

I stared down at the pen where it had landed, my entire body trembling with fear. The pen hadn't moved of its own volition. Something, somebody, had picked it up and had thrown it at the wall. The pen had flown through the air. I saw it with my own eyes, and I couldn't even begin to comprehend how it had happened.

I picked the pen up and tucked it into the back pocket of my jeans, just as Beth and Kitty came out of the library.

"Are you okay, Amber?"

I nodded my head towards Beth. "Has Kitty been with you for the entire time you were in the library?"

"Yes," Beth confirmed, appearing surprised at the question. "She was dusting the books. That's what she usually does while I'm working in the library. Are you sure everything's okay? You look awfully pale."

"I'm fine," I laughed, but it sounded forced and awkward. "It's just that I found the pen that I lost earlier, it was on the stairs. It wasn't there when I walked up the stairs, I am sure that it wasn't, but that is where I found it."

"That's very strange," Beth commented, "I wonder how it got there? It wasn't Kitty, she was most definitely with me, and it's entirely unlikely that Matilda would have been able to get up the stairs to put it there, and anyway, why would she want to?"

"Why would anybody want to?" I muttered.

"Maybe you put it in your pocket, and it fell out while you were walking up the stairs?"

"Perhaps," I replied, knowing full well that the pen had been nowhere near my pocket.

A few minutes later Beth left the house with the shopping list, and I returned to Matilda in the drawing room.

"Was it Kitty who was slamming the doors upstairs?" She spoke in a disinterested way.

"Kitty was with Beth in the library." I watched Matilda carefully; her face gave nothing away. "I am sure that I heard footsteps though, and a slamming door."

"Did you find anything when you went off to investigate?"

I shook my head.

"There you go then, it was just creaking floorboards and a door caught in a draught, just as I thought."

I laughed humourlessly, "it's almost like there's somebody else living in the house."

I observed her reaction to my words and thought that I saw a flash of alarm in her eyes. She smiled slightly, her hands restlessly stroking the blanket on her knee, as if it were a fractious kitten.

"I will tell you more of the story tomorrow, Amber." She lifted her head, her eyes meeting mine, her gaze direct and unflinching. "When I have finished you will have a better understanding of the house, and why things are as they are, as they have always been."

"I have never had to understand a house before." I uttered, wanting to press her further, to make her skip through her story so that I could completely understand its relevance.

It was very early days for me at Meadowside, but already, even though I tried to deny it to myself, I knew that there was something very wrong in the house.

"You have to be patient, Amber." Matilda said enigmatically, as if reading my thoughts.

*

Beth, Kitty and I spent the entire afternoon packing up the countless precious items from the dresser, wrapping each individual piece in bubble wrap and placing them into boxes.

Late in the afternoon I phoned Nathaniel, who informed me that that he was planning to drive my car over the next day.

"That's really good of you, thank you."

"Well, it's imperative that you have your car: you'll soon feel very isolated without it. Anyway, how are things going at Meadowside?"

I hesitated for a moment, deciding that I couldn't really tell him about all the weirdness that was going on. He would only think I was hysterical or losing the plot.

"Everything's fine," I lied. "I have met Beth. She helped Kitty and me to pack up everything from the dining room. We got on really well, and I think we could end up being friends."

"That's great," he sounded pleased, "and you're getting used to Kitty and Matilda?"

"Well," I laughed, "I'm certainly trying to get used to them; it's a bit easier said than done, to be honest. Matilda is telling me about her childhood in the house. Did you know that she had a brother who died young?"

"Yes, Matilda has mentioned him on a few occasions."

"I bet you didn't know that he had an illegitimate daughter called Seraphina, and that she came to live at the house after he died?"

"No, I didn't know that. Wow, that must have been quite a thing back in the early 1900s."

"It really must have been, and not all the family accepted her as Jack's daughter, and back then there was no way of finding out for certain. It must have been very difficult for the whole family, but especially Seraphina. The younger children loved her though, and even made her an honorary sister."

"Matilda hasn't mentioned any of this to me. She did tell me that her brother died in an accident when he was in his twenties, but she has barely mentioned the rest of her family."

"So you don't know what happened to Matilda and Kitty's sisters?"

"I don't think anything happened to them. I have always assumed that they just passed away. It's unusual to be as long lived as Matilda and Kitty, and I think that they have naturally outlived the rest of their family."

"I suppose so," I agreed thoughtfully, "but they've lived here alone for so long, the rest of their family must have died quite young."

"Life was so different back then; people could die from illnesses and accidents that are easily treatable now. Maybe, even Jack could have been saved if there had been an air ambulance available."

"Yes, possibly," I agreed.

"By the way, I have ordered Matilda's bed, a top of the range model. It cost an arm and a leg, but she can easily afford it, and you can't put a price on comfort at her age. It will be delivered next Monday, and I have arranged for a couple of men from Ely to move the furniture and boxes out to the barn on Saturday morning. Does all that suit you?"

"That all sounds perfect, and thanks so much for sorting it all out."

"My pleasure," he replied smoothly. "Anytime I can help with anything, just let me know. I'll be over tomorrow with your car, probably around lunchtime."

After speaking with Nathaniel, I went to the kitchen and began to make the shepherd's pie we were having for dinner. Beth had completely replenished the pantry cupboard and the fridge and had left just before I phoned Nathaniel. I was grateful for the help she had given me, both with the shopping and the packing up of the dining room.

Kitty came and sat at the table, appearing bored and listless. She had been a great help to Beth and me that afternoon, and I had been surprised how being occupied had calmed her down and stopped her endless wandering.

"Would you like to help me to make the dinner, Kitty?"

She glanced at me in surprise.

"I'm sure you can take the cabbage off the stalks," I continued, encouragingly.

I demonstrated to her what needed doing, and she just got on with it, putting the dark green leaves in a colander, and the stalks into a pile on the chopping board. She worked diligently and seemed to enjoy being useful.

"Has nobody ever taught you to cook, Kitty?"

"Emma used to teach us, but then Matilda always did the cooking, and all I did was get in the way."

I frowned sadly at the fact that nobody had ever seen any potential in Kitty. Despite the strange things that she said, she appeared to be more competent than I had at first realised, and I was beginning to wonder if her difficulties had been caused by being isolated with Matilda in Meadowside for so long, rather than any diagnosable condition.

"I'm so glad you have come, Amber. I'm feeling less lonely now. Tilly is not good company these days."

"Matilda is not at all well, Kitty."

Once again, I was struck by Kitty's remarkable good health. She was still tall, her back straight, and there were only a few signs of frailty. She was physically strong, able to walk without stiffness or pain, and, I had been informed by Matilda, she had never seen a doctor in her entire life, simply because she had never been ill.

"You are a remarkable woman," I said warmly, "I have never met anybody like you before."

She looked up and smiled but seemed bewildered by my comment. "That's a very nice thing for you to say, Amber, but it isn't true. I don't know the things that other people do."

"Kitty, maybe you know things that other people don't. Just because people can learn things from books and teachers, doesn't really make them clever, especially when they only know the things that can be taught."

She nodded her head in agreement. "That's what Seraphina used to say. She didn't know a lot about subjects and lessons, but she knew things that other people hadn't even thought of."

I turned around sharply. I hadn't heard Kitty talk about Seraphina before. "She sounds very interesting." I dropped the last of the potatoes into a saucepan of water and dried my hands on a towel.

"Oh, she was. Some say that travelling people can sometimes have special knowledge and gifts. Seraphina knew things. Tilly used to say that she had the sight."

"The sight?" I whispered.

"She could see into the future and talk to the dead."

"Goodness!" I breathed, "do you think she really could?"

Kitty shrugged. "She could see the quiet places."

"The quiet places?"

"They are where the spirits go after their bodies have died, they are the places where all the knowledge lives and there is nothing there apart from quietness and peace, that's what Seraphina told me."

Kitty became lost in her memories, while I tried to make sense of what she had told me. It was obvious that both Kitty and Matilda, as children, had believed in the old conviction that some women from the gypsy communities had mystical powers, that they could tell people's fortunes and see into the future.

"Do you believe that Seraphina could see the future, Kitty?"

"Oh yes," she nodded her head, "I believe that she could. It wasn't frightening though, because Seraphina was so kind to everybody, and even though Martha was always horrid to her, she never said anything bad about her. She never said anything bad about anybody."

Gradually I became aware of a creaking of the floorboards above my head, the muffled steps of feet on the landing carpet, the groaning of a door hinge, and then the careless slamming of the door.

"Did you hear that, Kitty?"

She stood up and went to the stove and began frantically stirring the minced beef and onions.

"It sounded like footsteps," I pressed, "you must have heard it."

"It's probably her," she said, her entire body stiffening.

"Seraphina?"

She shook her head. "The other one."

"What other one? Who are you talking about?"

Kitty laid down the wooden spoon very deliberately on the stove top. "If we don't bother her, Amber, then she won't bother us."

"Kitty," I sighed, a shiver running down the entire length of my spine. "I really don't know what you're talking about."

"She should have gone to the quiet places, Amber, but she didn't. She just stayed here."

My blood froze in my veins. "Who stayed here? Who is it?"

Kitty slowly took a couple of steps away from the stove, and then she turned and left the room without uttering another word.

The conversation with Kitty had chilled me to the bone. When I put together what she had said and the handful of strange events that I had experienced, it pointed to the eerie conclusion that there was somebody else in the house.

I went over to the stove and removed the saucepan from the heat and walked quickly to the drawing room. Matilda was sitting there, an open book on her knee.

"Matilda," I began, a quiver in my voice, "I am going to ask you again, and I would appreciate it if you just told me the truth. Is there somebody living in the house that you haven't told me about?"

She lifted her head slowly, her expression completely unreadable.

"I will tell you the truth, Amber. The truth is in the story that I am telling you, but you will not understand it if I tell it to you all out of order."

"You could just answer my question, Matilda."

"What use would that be? If I answered your question now, would it make any difference, and would you even stay?"

I sat down on the sofa opposite her. "I wouldn't leave you and Kitty here without help. If there is a problem in the house, wouldn't it be better if we just sorted it out?"

She sighed and closed her eyes as if exhausted. "Not all problems can be sorted out."

I had only been in the house for a matter of days and already I was feeling weary of this strange cat and mouse game being played out between Matilda and myself.

"I had a very strange experience on the landing earlier, when I went to investigate the footsteps that both of us heard."

Her hands began to pluck fretfully at the pages of the book on her lap. "It is the past, Amber, that is all."

"The past?" I laughed humourlessly. "The past doesn't move things, Matilda, or threaten people on the landing. It doesn't wait for Kitty in the meadow or knock on the windows at night. The past does not turn the air to ice or make the shadows move."

"You have to trust me, Amber."

"Are you and Kitty safe here, Matilda? Am I safe here?"

There was a long, strained pause. "The truth is, that I really don't know. You being here seems to have awoken something in the house, something that has been quiet for a long time."

I sighed almost irritably. "You are talking in riddles, Matilda. What has been quiet for a long time? What are you talking about?"

"The past, Amber." She laughed bitterly. "You can never escape it, you can never outrun it, sooner or later it will catch up with you."

It was on the tip of my tongue to ask her straight out if the house was haunted, but the question seemed so absurd, and I was also worried what I would do with that information. Would I really be able to stay if I knew for certain that there was a malevolent spirit roaming the house? I think, in retrospect, that I didn't ask the question at that point because I already knew the answer and wasn't ready for it to be confirmed.

I slept very badly that night, with the feeling that the darkness was pressing in around me. Outside a noisy storm battered the house, rattling the windows while the wind roared and screeched like a wild animal.

The storm had died down by the early hours of the morning, but still sleep eluded me. I was just considering if I were brave enough to go downstairs in the dark and make myself a cup of tea, when I heard a quiet rapping at the door.

Instantly my heart began to race with fear. I switched on the bedside lamp as the knocking came again, reminding myself that if there was a ghost in the house then it was highly unlikely that it would knock on the door to gain entry to my room. Surely it would just walk straight through the wall and then do whatever it pleased.

I grabbed my dressing gown from the foot of the bed, put my feet into my slippers and opened the door to find Matilda standing there, wearing a thick dressing gown and a shawl around her shoulders.

"I can't sleep," she whispered, an expression of apology on her face.

"Me neither," I replied, "I've been awake for most of the night. Shall we go downstairs, and I'll make us some tea?"

She took my arm, and we began to walk slowly down the stairs.

"You won't have to do this for much longer. Your new bed is arriving on Monday, and your room will be ready for you on Monday night."

"I will be very relieved," she said as we stepped into the hall. "Shall we go to the children's room. You can light the fire and it will warm up quickly."

She sat in her usual armchair, watching as I lit the fire. When I had finished, I stood up from my kneeling position, and went to make the tea.

Returning to the room I placed Matilda's cup on a nearby side table and switched on a couple of lamps, then sat in the chair opposite her.

"This is such a lovely room," I commented, grateful for the cheery warmth of the fire.

"It reminds me so much of the past," she sighed wistfully, "when I come in here it is almost like nothing has changed."

"Do you think about the past a lot, Matilda?"

"The past is where I live, Amber, nearly all the time. It is all that I have left now."

"You have Kitty," I reminded her, "and now you have me."

She smiled, wrapping her shawl tighter around her frail shoulders. "I think that when you grow as old as me, what you have lost becomes more important, and I have lost a lot. I always thought that one day, I would understand. I believed that wisdom accompanies old age, and that sagacity would enlighten me as to why things had to be as they were, but that has never happened, Amber, and I find myself as baffled by the events of my life now, as I was then."

"Not everything can be understood," I struggled to find something pertinent to say. "Maybe, we are just not meant to understand it all."

"Then what is the point?" Her voice cracked with emotion. "War, tragedy, loss and pain, why do they exist at all if we are never to understand?"

"I don't know, Matilda. I only wish that I did, but maybe the events of our life make us into the person we will become."

"Or perhaps they take the person we would have become away, the potential of a different life, the joy and the laughter, the peace. You are right though, Amber, my life has made me into the person that I am, made me live the life that I have lived."

She fell silent as if hypnotised by the fire's dancing flames. "It is times like this that I miss Seraphina the most," she said eventually. "She had so much wisdom for one so young, so much compassion and love. She had been ripped away from everything that she knew and loved, and yet she never allowed it to change her. She might have hoped to be welcomed into Meadowside with open arms, but my parents were too grief stricken to give her what she needed, and then there was Martha."

"Martha?" I leaned forward expectantly, hoping that I was about to hear what had happened in Matilda's life that had caused her to hide herself away, hoping that I was going to hear about, and would finally understand, Meadowside and all of its secrets.

"Martha was suspicious of everybody and was particularly suspicious of Seraphina. I, and my other sisters loved her, she was so beautiful, with such a caring nature, we all adored her, but Martha only saw how she was different to us and became convinced that the only reason Seraphina had come to Meadowside, was to cause harm and mischief. She was very frightened of her, believing her to have powers that she didn't possess, believing her to be a witch who had cursed my family with tragedy and pain."

# Chapter 6

# Meadowside 1914

Matilda was disappointed that Seraphina did not settle into the household as expected. For weeks after her arrival, she continued to escape the attentions of Matilda, Kitty and Issy, preferring to spend most of the day alone, either out on the fen, or hiding in the meadow or the woods.

"I don't think Seraphina likes us very much," Issy said at breakfast one morning. "She leaves the house every morning before we are even awake."

"I wouldn't worry about that child if I were you, Issy." Martha sniffed, her face a picture of disgust. "It's a good thing if she doesn't like you. She shouldn't even be here and should have been marched off to the workhouse on the day she arrived. That is where the likes of her belong, not living with decent, God-fearing people like us. She will bring us nothing but trouble, you mark my words."

Matilda glared angrily at her eldest sister. "Those are horrible things to say about Seraphina."

"She's not right in the head," Martha ranted, ignoring Matilda's protest, "all this unchristian talk about quiet places and the like, she is nothing more than a witch, and we will rue the day she ever set foot in this house."

"She has been raised differently, that is all, Martha." Emma threw her sister a warning look, "and accusing a child of being a witch is horrible, not to mention downright dangerous. She is no more a witch than either you or I, she is just a little girl, who is actually very sweet, if you would only give her a chance, and apart from that, she is family."

"She is no more related to us than she is to the King himself!" Martha scoffed nastily. "She doesn't even look like us, especially not with that ungodly red hair!"

Matilda loved all of her family, but she was regularly reminded of the fact that she didn't actually like Martha very much.

The kitchen fell silent. Matilda ate her boiled eggs, scowling at Martha every time their eyes met.

A few days after Seraphina had arrived, Matilda had been passing the open windows of the drawing room, on her way to collect the eggs from the chicken coup, when she overheard a conversation taking place between her parents.

"What are we going to do about the child?" Her father's voice sounded weary, weighed down with worries and cares. "If she is indeed Jack's daughter, then she has a right to be here."

"She is not Jack's daughter," her mother retorted angrily, her voice shrill and strained. "Jack wouldn't have...not with a gypsy girl, Edward."

She heard her father sigh loudly and impatiently.

"Eleanor, you know as well as I do that Jack wasn't a saint, especially where young women were concerned. There is no reason why this child couldn't be his, and the people who left her here were absolutely convinced. In the letter, given to me, and written by her grandfather, it said in black and white that Jack was her father, that her mother had died soon after giving birth, and that he and his wife were not able to take care of her properly on account of their advancing age. He explained that neither of them was in good health and were greatly worried about what would happen to Seraphina when they passed away."

A long silence ensued, and Matilda was about to walk away when she heard her mother sob.

"If only I could know for certain, then maybe I could learn to love her, but the opinion of an elderly gypsy couple is just not enough. I believe that they left her here simply because they didn't want her, maybe she is a difficult child and was too much trouble for them."

"Eleanor," Edward Grey spoke crossly, as if losing his patience. "If that had been the case then they could have left her anywhere, there are orphanages and workhouses. Why would they have brought her here specifically?"

"If only I could see something of Jack in her, in her eyes or the way that she smiles, but there is nothing, and surely you must think that strange? If she really was Jack's daughter, wouldn't we know? Wouldn't we feel something? Wouldn't we see him every time we looked at her?"

"We can't dismiss her from the house, Eleanor. I will not allow that to happen. What would become of her? None of this is her fault, she is the innocent one in this sorry mess, and apart from that, Emma and the younger girls would never forgive us if we sent her away. There is a possibility that she is Jack's daughter, our granddaughter, and all the while that possibility exists, then she stays here, and will be brought up alongside Matilda, Kitty and Issy."

"I think you're making a mistake, Edward. She doesn't belong here, she is too different from us, and I don't think she'll be a good influence on our girls."

Eleanor Grey surrendered to another bout of weeping. "Don't you think if she really was Jack's daughter that I wouldn't be delighted to have her here, to see the only connection that we have left to our son walking around Meadowside? It would be like having a part of him back. We have been tricked, Edward, our grief used against us by a couple of fraudsters."

"What would you have me do, Eleanor? Shall I take her to the workhouse? We cannot know the truth, we probably never will, but there is a chance, just a chance that she is our granddaughter, and for that reason we will keep her here and give her the opportunity of a good life."

Matilda walked into the garden swinging her egg basket back and forth. While listening to her parents' conversation she had been in two minds about going to them and telling them that she had seen Jack with Seraphina's mother, but something held her back. Would confessing what she had seen make her mother accept Seraphina, or would she be so distressed by the illegitimacy of her grandchild, that it would make the situation worse? It was so confusing, but the fact that Seraphina was safe and would be staying at Meadowside helped her to decide that silence was the best policy, for the time being at least.

Her thoughts were brought back to the kitchen and the present by the grating sound of Martha's voice. "I don't know what Father is thinking of, allowing a stranger to come and live with us. I know one thing though, I don't have to like the gypsy brat, or accept her, or have anything to do with her, and all I'm saying is to be careful, you three." She nodded her head towards Matilda. "We could all be murdered in our beds! One day soon that conniving little madam will prove who she really is, and when she does you will thank me for warning you about her. Are you listening to me?"

"Do you have to keep yelling?" Matilda replied irritably. "None of us are deaf!"

"No," Martha snarled, "but there's none as deaf as those who refuse to listen. Just don't expect me to do anything to save you when she curses you with bad luck and misfortune."

"She wouldn't curse me," Matilda retaliated, "if she was going to curse anyone, it would be you!"

"She wouldn't dare," Martha stood up abruptly and with such force that her chair toppled over. "You had better warn her, Tilly, that if any harm comes my way, I will see her hang for it."

Martha stomped out of the kitchen, slamming the door violently behind her. Emma, who had been washing the breakfast dishes at the sink, came to the table and sat down opposite her young sisters.

"Why do you always let her get to you, Tilly? Whatever she says, whatever she does, you always rise to the bait."

"Why is she always so horrible? I hate her."

"You don't hate her, Tilly, you are just angry with her, and they are two different things."

"She thinks she's so holy and good, but she isn't. She is the worst person I have ever met. I wish that she had died instead of Jack, nobody would have missed her."

"I wish she had died too." Issy flicked her fringe out of her eyes. "Maybe we could ask God to give Jack back to us, and take Martha instead?"

Emma smiled, "that isn't quite how it works, Issy, and Tilly, that isn't a very kind thing to say. Wishing somebody dead is wicked, and Martha can't help the way that she is. She wasn't blessed with happiness, and I think she finds life difficult, for some reason. Maybe we should all just feel sorry for her."

Emma collected the teacups and the remaining breakfast plates from the table and took them to the sink. "What are you three going to be doing today?"

Issy immediately ran to her side. "I'm going to help you with the washing, Emma."

"I'm going to help too," Kitty jumped up from her chair and also ran to her sisters side.

"That just leaves you, Tilly? Do you have any plans?"

"I think I'll just go for a walk, see if I can find Seraphina."

Emma nodded, "bring her back to the house if you find her, it's going to be very hot today. Don't stay out long and remember to wear your hat."

Matilda left the house and wandered to the top of the meadow, scanning the expanse of gently swaying grass and multicoloured flowers. Even though it was early in the day, the sun was already blisteringly hot, the sky above shimmering with heat. She couldn't see any sign of Seraphina, but only momentarily considered walking as far as the woods to see if she could find her there, it was far too hot, and she was already feeling uncomfortable.

As she walked back towards the house, she found her thoughts turning to Jack. She longed for things to be the way they used to be, for her parents to play with them, like they used to. She missed the laughter and constant feeling of being loved and safe. It was not uncommon for days to pass without her even setting eyes on her mother, who spent her time in her bedroom or ensconced in the smaller living room, situated at the front of the house. It appeared that she had no interest whatsoever in her living children, for whenever Matilda did come across her in the house, she was distant and remote, and acted as if she couldn't get away from her daughter quickly enough.

Emma had stepped up to the plate when Eleanor Grey spiralled into a decline of never-ending grief and did everything that she could to be the mother her sisters so desperately needed. She did her very best for the younger children in the family, comforting them day and night after Jack's death, spending most of her time with them, ensuring that they had everything they needed. Matilda was hugely grateful for this. She had always loved Emma for her kindness and gentleness and admired her quiet sense of duty and the way that she never complained, but despite all of this, Matilda couldn't rid herself of the anger that she felt towards both of her parents, but particularly her mother.

"To lose a child is the worst thing that could happen to a parent," Emma tried patiently to explain in the days and weeks following Jack's death, "and, Mother and Father have lost many children."

Emma and her three younger sisters had all been in the children's room. She had been reading to them, the room illuminated by the amber glowing lamps and the flickering firelight. Matilda had been lying flat on her back, as she listened to Emma reading from Oliver Twist.

She manoeuvred herself into a seated position. It had been Issy who had asked why her mother never tucked her into bed like she used to, why her parents never joined them for meals, and why it was left to Emma to read them their evening stories.

"Many children?" Matilda had questioned.

"Yes, Tilly," Emma closed the book and rested it on the arm of her chair. "That is why there is such a large age gap between you and me. There were other children, other babies, that either died before they were born, or soon afterwards."

Matilda did a quick calculation in her head, there were six years between her and Emma, and she had, on occasions, wondered why that was, but had always assumed that it was just the way things had turned out, and had never imagined that there was a reason behind it.

"How can a baby die before its even born?" Matilda was shocked at this possibility. She was no longer naïve enough to believe that young people couldn't die, she had learned that lesson due to what had happened to Jack, but babies? How could that possibly be?

"Sometimes babies do die before they are born, Tilly, while they are still growing in their mothers' body. It could be that the baby is sick, or has something wrong with it, and sometimes everything can seem fine, and then the baby is born dead."

"Oh no," Issy cried, climbing onto Emma's knee, tears gleaming in her wide, blue eyes. "Poor babies."

"What you need to understand, girls, and the reason I am telling you this, is that Mother and Father have lost more than just Jack, there were other children, some of them living a day or two, and some of them not living at all. It made Mother very sad for a long time, and then Tilly came along, healthy and strong, and then Kitty, and last of all, Issy and between you, you all you made her happy again."

"So, Mother and Father are sad now, but if they had another baby, they would be happy again?"

"Mother is too old to be having babies now, Tilly. What I'm trying to say is that Mother and Father's grief over losing Jack is greater than ours. We all know how painful it was for each one of us, we all miss Jack terribly, it is heart-breaking and difficult, but the grief of a parents goes even deeper, and lasts much longer, and we all must be patient. It is my belief that Mother, and Father will grieve for years, but they will, eventually, come out the other side of it."

"It's not fair!" Issy wailed as Emma held her tightly.

"No, it isn't, but it is what sometimes happens, it is part of life."

"I wonder if they were brothers or sisters?" Matilda asked, feeling the need to know, the need to form a connection to these children that she had never met, and knew nothing of, until that day.

"Well," Emma began, with a sigh, "we don't know about the ones who died before they were born, but the two that I remember, who lived for a short while, were a boy called Michael, and a girl called Clementine. They were both born too early, they were so small that they couldn't possibly have lived, but even though they were with us for such a short time, Mother loved them desperately, and Father did too."

"They are angels now," Issy whispered, wiping away her tears with the hem of her dress.

"That is right, Issy, they are angels, in Heaven, with Jack."

Kitty moved from where she had been sitting on the sofa and joined Matilda on the floor. "I feel so sad for them, Tilly, for the babies that died before they had even lived at all."

Matilda put her arm around her strange sister. Sometimes it was difficult to know how Kitty felt about things, or what she knew, and quite often she believed that Kitty just copied the feelings and emotions of the people around her. She would cry, if they were crying, and would be happy if they were smiling.

"Are Michael and Clementine buried in the graveyard, Emma?"

"They are, Tilly. They are both buried close to the path, not far from the big elm tree."

Matilda thought of all the times she had visited Jack's grave and had placed flowers she had gathered from the garden and the meadow, never knowing that the churchyard was also the resting place of another brother, and a sister called Clementine.

"I will make them some daisy chains for their headstones," Issy announced solemnly. "They would like that, wouldn't they Emma?"

"I'm sure they would like that very much, Issy."

After leaving the meadow Matilda walked to the far end of the garden. There was no fence separating the garden from the fen beyond it, her father didn't want anything to diminish the views that stretched for miles. In the winter they watched the flocks of geese flying low over the darkening landscape, and in the summer, they admired the sunsets, staying outside until it was dark so that they see the shooting stars and the silver glow of the moon.

She sat on the bench, removing her sun hat and fanning her face with it. In the far distance she could see people in the golden fields, but as far as she could tell from this distance, none of them were Seraphina.

"Hello there, Tilly."

Matilda was startled to hear the voice, believing that she was in the garden alone. She turned and smiled when she saw that the voice belonged to Jed Carter, who was pushing a wheelbarrow full of weeds towards her.

"Do you mind if I join you for a few minutes? It's so hot already, it's going to be a scorcher of a day."

Matilda shuffled further up the bench to make room for him to sit down.

"You were miles away. What were you thinking so deeply about?"

"Seraphina," Matilda sighed, "she keeps running off and leaving me behind. I don't think she even wants to be friends."

Jed removed his cap and wiped the sweat from this forehead. "Aye, well that little girl has a lot to come to terms with. It can't be easy for her, Tilly."

"She should be happy," Matilda folded her arms and frowned sullenly. "We're all running circles around her, making sure she's not lonely, making sure that she has everything that she needs, making sure we include her in everything. I don't think she cares about us at all, why else would she keep disappearing all the time, making us all worried about her?"

"If there's one thing that I have learned in this life, is that you can't make another person happy, they can only do that for themselves."

He took his pipe from his pocket, stuffed the bowl with tobacco that he stored in a small, leather pouch. "The only person who can make Seraphina happy, is Seraphina herself, and anyway, how do you know that she isn't happy?"

"Because she keeps going off on her own, she hardly ever speaks and never plays with us, or spends any time with us."

Jed struck a match and puffed enthusiastically on his pipe. "It is highly likely that she is sad, Tilly. She lost her mother when she was a baby, she never knew her father, and now she has lost her grandparents too. She has arrived at Meadowside from off the road, living a nomadic life, and placed in a family that she doesn't know, expected to be a person she's never been before. I think it's fair to say that she probably doesn't know how to do it, or how to be, and is just trying to figure it all out."

"Poor Seraphina," Matilda said after a long silence, during which she tried to put herself in Seraphina's position. She knew for a fact that she would literally fall to pieces if she was taken away from her family and Meadowside. "I didn't think about all of that."

"Of course, you didn't," Jed laughed softly, "you're but a child. It would be difficult for you to place yourself in Seraphina's position, that's a skill that you learn as you grow older."

"Life is hard, isn't it Jed? It's not all about getting up in the morning, breathing and eating, it's more about figuring things out and understanding them."

"It certainly can be hard, but life is full of contrasts, Tilly. Happy times, sad times, laughter and tears. We learn from the bad times, and rejoice and find joy in the good, and all of it is life, a gift that we are lucky to have, despite all of its trials and tribulations." He patted her gently on the arm, "the good times will come back soon, for you and Seraphina, you just need to be patient for a little while longer."

"My parents haven't accepted Seraphina, not properly, and neither has Martha. In fact, I think that Martha hates the sight of her, because she doesn't look like Jack."

Jed Carter stared out into the distance. "Well, that's because she's the spitting image of her mother. The resemblance to Katerina is so strong, but maybe she'll grow to look more like Jack when she's older."

"Katerina?" Matilda glanced up at him, frowning. "Was that Seraphina's mother's name? Did you know her?"

"I knew her as well as it's possible to know the travelling people. They are just as suspicious of us as some people are of them, and they often have good reason to not trust us settled folk."

"What was she like, Jed?" Matilda asked breathlessly, straightening her back, ready to pay attention.

Jed scratched the side of his face thoughtfully. "She was beautiful, right enough, with long red hair and eyes the colour of a summer sky. She was also clever, as bright as a button. Every year she would arrive with her parents, Seraphina's grandparents. I remember her as a baby, with her curly hair and rosy cheeks, and every year that she came, she had grown a little bit more. She was born with the sight, a gift that some travelling women have."

"The sight?" Matilda whispered.

"She could gaze into the flames of a fire and see images of the future. She could heal the sick thanks to her potions of flowers and herbs. People would queue up outside her caravan to have their ailments cured by her little glass bottles, or to see what their futures held. She was very wise for such a young woman. The villagers didn't mind hearing their fortunes or taking one of her potions to heal their rheumatics, but they were wary of her, scared of her even, and none of them would admit going to see her, it would all be done under the cover of night, because, at the end of the day, they believed they were committing a mortal sin by just being in her company."

"Were they committing a mortal sin, Jed?"

He gazed down at Matilda and laughed, shaking his head. "Of course, they weren't. She was helping them with ingredients freely found growing on the land, things that had been put there by God himself. How anyone could think that using nature's bounty to heal the sick is sinful, is beyond me. In my opinion, nobody was committing a sin of any kind, let alone a mortal one."

He sighed as he watched a flock of starlings swoop and dance in the sky like a swarm of hornets. "People are suspicious of things they don't understand, it's just ignorance really, but you have to remember that young wives were being hanged for less in the past."

Matilda glanced up sharply. "You mean, witches?"

"Indeed," Jed inclined his head and lowered his voice. "There was a time, and not so very long ago, where women like Katerina would have been hanged as a witch on the evidence of a few whispers. It was a very dangerous time to be a woman, especially a woman like Katerina."

There followed a long silence, during which Matilda carefully ruminated on Jed's words. In her mind's eye she saw Katerina again, walking by her brother's side, her hair blowing in the gentle breeze.

"Could Seraphina have inherited her mother's gift, like she inherited her red hair?"

Jed nodded his head thoughtfully. "It does tend to run in families, passed down from mother to daughter. Seraphina's grandmother had it too, so it is likely that Seraphina has the gift also."

"That could be it," Matilda bit her lip thoughtfully, "that really could be it."

"What are we talking about now, Tilly?" He asked, a hint of amusement in his eyes.

"Seraphina says strange things, and sometimes I think that she knows things, things that she doesn't talk about."

"I wouldn't be surprised; she is Katerina's daughter after all. Like I said, Tilly, it will take time for her to adjust to her new circumstances, but she is young and soon your family and Meadowside will replace what she once had, and she will settle down and will become more like you and your sisters."

The two sat in companionable silence for a while. Matilda was not convinced that Seraphina would ever change, and in a way, she didn't want her to. She liked the fact that she was different, with an air of quiet confidence that was sometimes disconcerting in one so young. She didn't want to change who Seraphina was, she just wanted her to become a part of the family and to spend more of her time with them.

Matilda had several worries on her mind, the aloofness of her parents, and the way that Martha had taken against Seraphina, were two of them, but recently another, new concern had begun to also trouble her.

"Martha says there's a war coming," she said, knowing that there was no better person than Jed Carter to put her mind at rest in relation to Martha's outlandish and hysterical claims. "She says that the fen will be crawling with Germans by the end of the year."

Jed chuckled dismissively. "Well, Martha is right on one count, it is growing increasingly likely that there will be a war, but the Germans won't come here. Hopefully, something can be done to avoid a war, but if not, then it will be fought in Europe." The old man shook his head sorrowfully. "You mustn't worry about it, Tilly, it will not affect you, and now that your Jack is no longer with us, it shouldn't affect your family either."

Seeing Matilda's confused expression, he continued, "if he had lived, then Jack would probably have been recruited, eventually. Already I have heard of young men in the village talking about the great adventure they will have, it's almost as if they are rooting for a war, just so they can go and fight and experience something different."

Again, he shook his head, his eyes darkening with sorrow. "They don't understand what they are wishing for, they have no idea. They are fools, too young to have any sense, and already they are saying that it will be over by Christmas and that they will all return home as heroes. They will soon regret their stupidity and their reckless youth, for war is a nasty, painful, deadly business. Jack would have been there with them, counting down the days until he could volunteer, most likely getting himself blown to bits for the privilege."

Jed stood up and returned to his wheelbarrow while Matilda watched as Emma came out of the back of the house, carrying a huge basket of gleaming white sheets. Issy was skipping along at her side, swinging the peg bag back and forth. Emma placed the basket on the grass and Issy passed her the pegs, one by one.

As she watched Emma working diligently in the scorching heat, she wondered if she was happy in the role she had so readily inherited from her mother. She did seem to be, but surely, she had hopes and dreams of her own. She might like to fall in love and get married, have a family, but what chance would she have for any of that while being tied down, washing, cooking and cleaning for them all.

Matilda felt a stab of guilt and resolved to do more to help Emma from now on and thought that the other one who could help was Martha, but then Martha helping anyone would be nothing short of a miracle. Matilda did not know what Martha did with herself all day, but she certainly did nothing to help Emma, just expecting her meals to be cooked and her washing cleaned and left folded on her bed once a week.

As much as Seraphina was an enigma to Matilda, she understood her eldest sister even less. Martha was a total mystery to everyone, mainly avoided by the younger members of the family. Her opinions and feelings, if she had any, were mostly ignored. The only person who had any insight into Martha was Emma, who despite often feeling irritated by her sister's prickly nature, was always kind and tolerant towards her.

Emma believed that far from being cold and harsh, Martha was, in fact, the opposite and had a theory as to why she was so difficult and irascible.

"She is damaged," she tried to explain to Matilda after, yet another argument inspired by Martha's criticisms and sharp tongue. "She wasn't always this way, in fact, there was a time when we were children that she reminded me of you."

"Me?" Matilda was horrified, dismayed that her beloved Emma could ever see a resemblance between her and Martha.

Emma had laughed. "She used to be so clever, probably the cleverest of us all. We used to spend our days, pretty much as you do now, playing in the meadow or walking on the fen, sometimes Jack would come with us, but mostly it was just Martha and me. These were the days before you were born, Tilly, but they were difficult times for Mother and Father. Remember I told you about the babies that had died before you were born? Martha and I were so excited when Mother gave birth to a little sister, she allowed us to name her, and Martha wanted to call her Clementine. For a few days we helped to care for the baby, forgetting that just a year before there had been another baby who we had loved and cared for, who we had named Michael."

Matilda nodded her head, remembering well the conversation when Emma had told them about the brother and sister who had died.

"Well, as you know, little Clementine didn't survive, and it had an altering effect on Martha. She became angry and distant, and I think during that time, when she was still so young, she decided not to love anybody else ever again. When you were born, she behaved as if you didn't even exist, and the same with Kitty and Issy, she couldn't love you because she was frightened of losing you too, and despite you being healthy and strong, she is still frightened. So, you see Tilly, Martha isn't cold and without feelings, the trouble is that she feels things too much, too deeply."

Matilda was astonished by this insight into Martha, and for a short while her feelings of animosity towards her lessened, but then Martha continued in her moodiness and argumentative ways, and Matilda began to react once again, until her feelings returned to how they had been before.

Matilda watched the sheets billowing in the gentle breeze, believing that it would only be half an hour before they would dry in the heat and Emma and Issy would be back to take them down from the line. Kitty did not return back to the house with her sisters but walked over to join Matilda on the bench.

They both watched Jed as he resumed his work in the garden, ripping the weeds from the hard, parched ground.

"It's too hot," Kitty said, her face flushed and with a new crop of freckles blooming across the bridge of her nose.

"There will be a storm," Matilda announced confidently, "there always is when it gets this hot, and then it will cool down for a while."

"I don't want there to be a storm, they scare me."

"Storms are just nature, Kitty. They are nothing more than noises, rain and light, there is nothing really to be frightened of."

"If there's a storm tonight, can I come into your bed, Tilly?"

"If you have to," Matilda said then smiled kindly. "Of course, you can, Kitty, and I will read you a story to help you go to sleep."

Kitty stood up from the bench and walked a short distance out onto the fen. She was now six years old, and Matilda had become increasingly aware of things not being quite right with her. She was nowhere near as astute and clever as Issy, who was only four years old. Issy could read entire books, while Kitty still had a great deal of difficulty remembering the alphabet or how to write her own name."

Kitty had a lovely, sweet nature, and was very similar to Issy in that way. The pair of them inhabited a vibrant world of make believe, populated by fairies, elves and dragons. They would spent all day long playing together in the meadow, if it was summertime, or in the barn if the weather was bad.

Matilda was sure that Issy would grow and develop and would cease to believe in fairies and magic kingdoms, she would leave Kitty far behind, lonely and lost without her playmate, for Matilda was certain that Kitty would never change, and could, in some ways at least, remain childlike forever.

Kitty drifted back to the bench. "I can't see Seraphina out on the fen," she said as she sat down. "Maybe she's gone to the village, she likes seeing the horses."

"Does she?" Matilda was surprised, believing that Seraphina was desperate to get away from people, and yet she was happy to go to the village, which was teeming with them, while avoiding all the inhabitants of the house.

"Oh yes, she loves the horses, they used to pull her caravan and she misses them."

As the girls walked back towards the house, Matilda was struck by how Seraphina was afforded more freedom than she was, even though she was older. At that moment in time nobody knew where she was, she may return to the house in the afternoon, or she may not, sometimes staying out until bedtime. This was not allowed for the other children in the family, Emma always wanted to know where they were going, and there was no way she would allow them to be out on their own after dark.

Matilda's frustration with Seraphina continued for several weeks. War was declared in early August, and many of Jed Carter's predictions came to pass. Life continued very much in the same way that it had always done. Shortly after the declaration was made, the call for volunteer soldiers was announced, and already, just as Jed had told her that they would, the young men of the village left in droves, leaving their mothers broken hearted, and younger boys, old men and women to work in the fields and put food on their tables.

It was the middle of September, when Matilda, whiling away an hour or two in the library with a book, was alerted to loud and excited voices coming from the hall. She abandoned her book on the arm of her chair and walked towards the door, with a niggling feeling of concern.

"I cannot believe the bare faced cheek of that girl!" Martha was iridescent with anger, a grimace of disgust on her face. "Where did she even get two shillings and sixpence from? That is what I want to know. A whole half-crown!"

"What's going on?" Matilda went to where her sisters were standing in a huddle, close to the open front door.

"It's Seraphina," Emma had an amused glint in her eyes, a soft smile on her lips. "Apparently, she has bought a horse."

"A horse?" Matilda gasped, manoeuvring both Kitty and Issy out of the way so that she could get access to the front door. Sure enough, Seraphina was standing outside the house, holding onto the reins of a huge black horse.

At that moment Edward Grey came from the back of the hallway, and at the same time, disturbed by the noise and excited chatter, Eleanor Grey came down the stairs, an expression of alarm on her face.

"What is all this noise?" Edward Grey bellowed testily. "Can't a man have five minutes of peace in his own house?"

Emma stepped forwards, but before she could open her mouth, Martha barged her out of the way.

"It is that child, Father. She has been out of the house all day, getting up to goodness knows what, since before we were awake this morning, and now she has come home with a horse."

Martha was standing with both hands on her hips, her eyes glittering with malevolence. "She bought it from Matty Holbrook in the village for two shillings and sixpence. If I were you Father, I would force her to take it back."

"A horse?" Eleanor Grey was aghast, "a horse, here at Meadowside?"

"Yes, Mother, a horse." Martha snapped impatiently. "I am assuming that she didn't ask permission before taking it upon herself to bring a horse here. What I want to know is where she got that money from? I wouldn't put it past her to have stolen it from right under our noses."

"Get out of the way, Martha," Edward Grey strode towards the door, "let me see the blasted animal at least."

"This will be it," Martha gave a self-satisfied smile. "She will be out of Meadowside and on her way to the workhouse before this day has ended."

The small group huddled around the doorway, watching as a short conversation took place between Seraphina and their father. A few minutes later he walked back to his family.

"The horse is staying," he informed them, his voice loud and firm. "We will make space for it in the barn. Seraphina knows how to look after it, so it won't be any trouble for anyone else."

"No, Edward," Eleanor stepped towards her husband, her expression determined. "She can't keep it here, it's unsanitary."

"Don't be ridiculous, Eleanor, it's not going to be living in the blasted house."

"Where did she get the money from?" Martha looked at her father with disgust, feeling that he had allowed himself to be manipulated and had let the gypsy girl get the better of him.

"Her grandparents gave it to her all that time ago. Apparently it was all the money they had in the world, and she has held on to it ever since." He viewed his wife and eldest daughter scathingly, his eyes moving from one to the other. "It's not going to kill either of you to let the child know a little bit of happiness, it isn't going to kill any of us. The horse is staying, and that is my final word on the subject."

*

After his conversation with Seraphina, Edward Grey had gone out to the barn, clearing a large corner area, and then had gone to the village to order hay and straw to be delivered to the house as soon as possible.

When he returned he found Seraphina in the barn, busily sweeping the cleared area in readiness for the straw bedding to be laid.

"He'll be the most comfortable horse in all of Cambridgeshire," he remarked approvingly. "What is his name?"

Seraphina shyly shook her head; this was a question that she had omitted to ask Matty Holbrook before paying for the horse.

"We will need to think of one then. Do you have any ideas?" Edward smiled kindly, conscious that he had made little effort to get to know Seraphina and had left her care entirely up to Emma. He realised now that he had been remiss and was anxious to make amends. "He is a fine specimen, Seraphina. It is obvious that you know a thing or two about horses. Maybe we could get a cart to attach him to, then you girls could take him on trips to the village?"

Seraphina went to where the horse was tethered to a large iron ring attached to the barn wall. Almost immediately the horse lowered his head and began to snuffle her shoulder.

"Merlin," she said suddenly, as if the horse had told her himself. "His name is Merlin."

Edward smiled broadly. "The magician who protected King Arthur. A splendid choice."

"My grandfather was telling me the story of King Arthur and his knights the evening before he left me here."

There was a long silence during which Edward busied himself, kicking away a lump of wood and needlessly moving objects from one place to another.

"I am sorry, Seraphina," he uttered softly. "I am sorry that your grandparents felt that they were too old and ill to look after you, and I am sorry that your mother died."

He sat down on the cold earthen floor, leaning his back against the rough barn wall. "I know what it's like to lose people that we love. My son, my son Jack, he had an accident and died. It was sudden, a terrible shock. He was so alive, so vital, and then he was gone, almost as if he had never existed, as if he'd never been here at all."

Seraphina sat beside him, a few feet away. "My grandparents told me that he was my father."

"Yes," Edward sighed, "that is certainly what they believed, and it is what they wrote in the note that they left in your pocket." He turned slightly towards her. "Can you remember your mother telling you anything about your father?"

Seraphina shook her head. "My mother died when I was a baby, not long after I was born, but my grandmother told me about him."

"Really? What did she tell you?"

"She said that he lived in a house on the outskirts of the village here. She said that he wasn't one of us, but that he had the heart of our people. She told me that he had fair hair, the same colour as the cornfields in the summertime and that he was good and kind and that he loved my mother very much."

"Did she know how he died? Did she tell you that?"

"I don't think she knew exactly how he died, she was told that it was an accident, but nothing more. It was someone that she met on the road who told her about it, and then she told me. She was very sad about it, and so was I."

Edward smiled and nodded his head. "He was a very fine young man, a little bit wild, and always up to mischief, but he had a good heart. Did your grandmother tell you if your father knew about you? I am sure that Jack would have wanted to do the right thing by you, if he had known that he had a child."

"I don't know," Seraphina lowered her eyes, "I was born in Yorkshire, and then my mother died soon after that, and I travelled around with my grandparents, but I don't think we ever came here. I don't think that my father knew about me, Mr Grey. Maybe, if my mother had lived, she would have wanted to come back here, find him and tell him about me, but I don't think that ever happened."

"I don't think he knew about you either." Edwards lowered his head until it was almost touching his bent knees. "If only I could speak to him now and lay my eyes on him for one last time, but I can't do that, he has gone so far away from me that I cannot always recall exactly what he looked like, or the sound of his voice. He seems so far beyond my reach."

"He has only gone to the quiet places, Mr Grey, and they are all around us."

"The quiet places?" He questioned, a frown creasing his brow.

"When we die our souls leave our bodies, but sometimes they come back to visit, and when they do they go to the quiet places. I have seen them there, the spirits of the people who have died."

Edward Grey was stunned. He stared at Seraphina, trying to understand what her words meant, and if she could possibly be speaking the truth.

"Have you seen Jack?" His voice rasped in his throat. He swallowed hard. "Have you seen my son?"

She inclined her head slowly and then fixed him with her vivid blue eyes, replying with a steady voice. "I have seen him. He was with my mother."

Edward shook his head in wonderment. "I have never...I have never in my life heard of such things, Seraphina. I can't believe that what you are saying could possibly be the truth."

"What do you think is the truth, Mr Grey? That when we die we are buried in the ground, and all the things that we had, the love that we knew, the joy, the sadness, the suffering, just all goes away? What would be the point in life if that were the truth?"

He turned his head to gaze at this child who had come into his house as a stranger. There was something about her, how she spoke in her quiet voice with such conviction, such knowledge, and how she seemed wise beyond her years.

"Seraphina, I do on occasion, visit the church in the village, not very often nowadays, but sometimes I am drawn to visit. I go there to try and find some peace, in a way I go to try and find Jack, to try to feel his presence, but I never have. I have this feeling, you see, that he is somewhere, that he hasn't just completely ceased to exist, but I can't reach him. Perhaps if I tried harder, believed more strongly, then maybe..." his voice petered out, he turned and smiled at her. "Maybe one can try too hard?"

"They are there, you just have to let yourself be still and quiet and let them come to you."

"And these quiet places that you talk of, where are they?"

"They are everywhere, Mr Grey, quite often I find them when I am outside on my own, but they can also be in houses, the quiet corners and the empty rooms, but mostly, I think, they are a place in my head, a place where I can hear them talking to me and see them as clearly as I am seeing you."

Edward stared hard at her. He knew that there had always been suspicion in the village against the itinerant travellers that came every year to assist with the bring in of the harvest. He had heard talk of fortune telling, curses and miraculous healings of the sick. He was aware of stories revolving around gypsy folk having supernatural gifts, and the ability to know things that other people were unable to understand. He had never believed these rumours, but now he was unsure.

"You have a gift, Seraphina. I expect that you have inherited it from your mother's family, but you must be very careful." He rubbed his eyes wearily, suddenly feeling the need to protect this unusual child from the world, from the people who would not understand her curious ways. "You do know that gifts like yours are dangerous to have, most people will not understand, and you could find yourself in a lot of trouble if you are not careful. People, ignorant people, are terrified by the things they can't understand, as much as they are terrified by people who are different to them. Do you understand what I'm trying to say?"

She nodded her head, for he was not telling her anything that hadn't already been said by her grandmother since she was old enough to understand.

"I will be careful," she promised, her expression serious.

"Good," he smiled, his eyes twinkling. "I must keep you safe, it's the very least that I owe to you, and owe to Jack. We will keep your special gift a secret between you and I, and, needless to say, you must never speak of it in the presence of Mrs Grey, or my eldest daughter, Martha. Now, tell me again of the times that you have seen my Jack. Was he well? Did he appear happy?"

"Oh yes, Mr Grey, he was happy. He was wearing a brown jacket, the pocket was torn and hanging off. Sometimes he has a dog with him, a black and white one, her name is Sky."

Edward bowed his head, feeling tears stinging the back of his eyes. "It was his favourite jacket, and the pocket was almost ripped off when he got it caught on the gate at the front of the house, it was beyond all hope of repair, but he insisted that he was still going to wear it, and he did, despite his mother's protests.

"Sky was my dog, she used to sit beneath my desk while I was working, and then Jack was born, and gradually Sky became his dog." He chuckled to himself as if recalling distant memories. "They say that a dog will choose its master, and Sky chose Jack. They loved each other and were inseparable."

He stared into Seraphina's steady blue eyes. "You are extraordinary," he whispered. "I think it's highly unlikely that any of my daughters would have known about Jack's torn pocket, maybe the older two might just about remember Sky, but why would they have mentioned a dog that has been dead for more than ten years?"

Seraphina stood up and went over to the horse, standing in front of it and stroking its neck. Edward Grey watched her as she whispered gently to the animal, calming the impatient stamping of its feet and the shivering of its muscles, gaining its trust and adoration in just a few words.

Edward did not believe in the supernatural, or at least he never had done, but this girl, with her quiet ways and gentle nature, had convinced him that her gift was genuine. She was so innocent, with an ethereal quality about her, and when he looked into her eyes, trying so hard to see his son, he saw instead truth and honesty, and knowledge so deep that it took his breath away.

"I ask one thing of you, Seraphina." He stood up and went to stand near to the horse. "Next time that you see Jack, tell him I am sorry for all of the times I shouted at him, lambasted him for his misdeeds, punished him for his wildness. He was only trying to become who he needed to be, while I spent so much of our time together trying to turn him into what I needed him to be." He smiled fondly at her, "I regret that we spent so much time with me being angry and him being resentful."

"I think he knows that Mr Grey," she replied. "I think that when we die we can understand everything. My grandmother used to call it seeing the whole picture, for while we are alive we can only see half of it. You will see Jack again, Mr Grey. When you die, when it is your time, he will be the one who will come and take you. You will always be together then."

Edward took a sharp intake of breath and turned away from her so that she would not see the tears in his eyes. He was thankful when a clattering noise came to his ears.

"That will be the hay and straw for Merlin," he said, brushing the dust and cobwebs from his jacket. "Let's unload it and make up his bed for the night."

# Chapter 7

Matilda leaned her head back and closed her eyes for a few moments. The small, blue veined hands trembled slightly as they rested in her lap and her skin had grown pale. I wasn't sure if it was the effort of speaking for such a long time that had exhausted her, or if it was reliving the memories of her childhood, but I had noticed that the telling of her story seemed to deplete her, bringing on a deep fatigue.

"Things got better for a while after Merlin arrived. Seraphina appeared happier and more settled, and my father, although not quite being the same man as he had been before, began to smile again, and to drink less, spending less time behind the locked door of the library."

"Seraphina told you about the conversation she had in the barn with your father?"

"She did, eventually, many years later, and I think her telling him about the things that she saw, the things that she knew, seemed to really help him." Matilda smiled wistfully. "She was very good like that, in tune with other people, and we have to remember that Seraphina was very young, and yet always knew the right things to say in almost any situation."

"She was very sensitive," I mused, "psychic, maybe?"

Matilda shrugged her thin, narrow shoulders. "To this day I don't fully understand what Seraphina was capable of. Martha believed that she could cast spells, use magic to get her own way, and I'm not sure whether this was the truth, or not."

I couldn't help but wish that Matilda wasn't quite so old, that she had more stamina, for I yearned to know more of her story. Up until that point she had revealed nothing that would account for the feeling of disquiet in the house. I was convinced that something of great significance must have occurred to create such a heavy and lingering atmosphere. My impatience to discover the secrets of Meadowside was growing at the same pace as my apprehension, but I knew that it was pointless to ask too many questions, or to push her for answers, for Matilda was determined to tell her story from beginning to end, at her own pace, and I had no other options but to accept this and be patient.

We returned to our beds and even though I was tired, I still found it impossible to fall asleep. My mind was alive with visions from the past and every time I closed my eyes, I could see Matilda as a child, Issy and Kitty playing in the meadow, Seraphina, lonely and somehow adrift, walking through the flat countryside, try to acclimatise herself to a completely new set of circumstances, and a strange new environment.

I could see Emma in the kitchen, Edward Grey in the library, I could even see Jed Carter in the garden, pushing his wheelbarrow or sitting on the bench, that still existed on the edge of the fen. I found it harder to imagine Martha. Matilda had once said that Martha would have been a great beauty, if she hadn't been so difficult and cantankerous. She described her as having fine features, dark hair and piercing eyes that were always on the lookout for something to complain about or criticise.

"She was an uncharitable, irascible person," Matilda had said, a hint of distaste still lingering in her eyes. "I could never understand her harshness. She was cold, temperamental and cruel, and as a child I disliked her with a vengeance."

"And now?" I had asked, "do you still hate her?"

Matilda had stared for a long time into the fire flames, watching them as they danced, creating images from long ago.

"The passage of time changes a lot of things. I suppose, in a way, I understand Martha better than I did as a child. She was bitter, as if life was nothing but a huge disappointment. She was too self-absorbed to realise that she was her own worst enemy, and in the end, was the author of her own downfall."

She then focused her attention back on me, her eyes dark with something dangerous and indefinable. "I have promised to speak the truth Amber, for I feel that I must, and I have to say that despite the passing of time, despite me being so much older and wiser, my feelings towards Martha have not changed."

*

The next few days were extremely busy. Three men arrived on the Saturday morning and removed all of the dining room furniture out of the house and into the barn, covering it with dust sheets. I did not know how it would fare out there, but this wasn't one of my concerns, the most important thing was that Matilda was comfortable and safe. Nathaniel was a frequent visitor, helping Beth and me to clean the dining room from top to bottom in readiness for Matilda's bed being delivered on the Monday. Between the three of us we brought down Matilda's chest of drawers, two bedside tables and lamps, as well as other bits and pieces she would want to have around her.

Nathaniel and Beth were in the kitchen making coffee and some lunch for us all. I walked in carrying two photographs in silver frames that I had found in Matilda's room.

"Look at these," I said, placing them on the table. "I think this is Issy, the youngest of Matilda's sisters."

The photograph depicted a young child, probably around years five or six years old sitting on the gate at the front of the house. She was wearing a light-coloured calf-length dress, a floppy straw hat, and was holding a kitten in her lap. She was smiling brightly, a look of happiness and excitement in her eyes.

Nathaniel and Beth joined me at the table.

"What a beautiful child," Nathaniel picked up the photo, looked at it closely and then passed it to Beth.

"She's sitting on the gate at the end of the drive," Beth commented, "it's amazing to think that it's still there after all of this time."

The second photograph was of four young girls, standing together at the end of the garden, the huge expanse of fen land stretching to the distance behind them.

"This is Matilda, Kitty and Issy," I pointed to each girl in turn, "and this," I said, pointing to the girl on the far right, "this must be Seraphina."

It was a candid photo and seemed to have been taken without the knowledge of the subjects. They were not posing or looking towards the camera, instead they appeared to be deep in conversation. How I wished that the photograph had been taken using a modern camera, in full colour, but instead I had to be satisfied with a blurry, fading image in sepia.

"These must have been taken by Edward Grey," Nathaniel picked up both photographs and viewed them closely. "He included some photographs in the last book that he published. I wonder when these would have been taken?"

"I think, due to the age of the youngest girl, Issy, that it must have been around 1917"

"That would make sense," Nathaniel nodded, "camera technology came on leaps and bounds during the first world war, as people began to appreciate the importance of having a visual record, however, I don't think there would have been many people with access to a camera. Matilda's father must have realised how photographs could be helpful to him in his work, even though taking photographs in those days was not quick or easy, it would have been a lot quicker than painting a scene, or a bird, for him to illustrate his books."

I gazed again at the photographs. They were charming, depicting such happiness and innocence. This was the first image that I had seen of Seraphina, as she wasn't in the painting that hung in the drawing room. Her head was slightly bent towards Kitty, her long curly hair falling forwards, obscuring some of her face. Looking at the image you would never have known that she had red hair, or that her eyes were a vivid blue. Although I loved seeing the photographs, for me, they were nowhere near enough.

After eating a sandwich for lunch, I stood up from the table and took my plate over to the sink. "I think I might go for a walk, "I said, looking out of the kitchen window. "I could really do with some fresh air."

"Yes, go," Beth came over to the sink and turned on the taps, "you haven't been out of the house for days, it would do you good." She glanced towards me mischievously, "in fact, why don't you and Nathaniel both go, I can stay here and keep an eye on Kitty and Matilda. The children are having tea at a friend's house, so I don't have to pick them up from school, so you can take your time."

"That sounds like a plan," said Nathaniel, standing up. "That's if it's okay with you, Amber? I quite understand if you need some time on your own."

"No," I replied quickly, "that's fine. Perhaps we could walk on the fen, or through the meadow to the woods."

"Either sounds good to me." He took his jacket from the back of his chair and I collected my coat and scarf from the hall. We left the house through the front door and headed towards the woods.

It was a bright and sunny day, with a clear blue sky, the remains of the earlier frost still lingering on the edges of the path, and the tips of the long grass.

"So," Nathaniel zipped up his jacket and plunged his hands into the pockets. "How are things going for you?"

"Not too bad at all, still finding my feet though."

"This place must be stunning in the summer." We were halfway down the meadow path. Nathaniel had stopped walking to admire the view, gazing out to where the fen beyond the meadow met the horizon.

"I can't wait to see it," I said, turning my head back towards the house.

"Are you worried about leaving Matilda?" He asked, seeing my hesitation.

"Not really. Beth is used to both Kitty and Matilda and knows very well what they can be like. There's no need for me to be worried."

We continued to walk towards the woods.

"You know that Matilda is telling me all about Meadowside and her family?" He nodded his head. "Well, I'm having a hard time trying to not imagine them still living in the house. I can see them all in my imagination, and just now I was remembering Matilda telling me about the evening her brother died, how she had been waiting for him to come home when she saw a trail of lantern lights moving up through the meadow, towards the house, and it turned out to be some men from the village bringing his body home. Then there is Kitty, and the things that she says, and how she stands at the window for hours on end waiting for somebody. Do you know that neither of them will go to the far end of the landing?" I shuddered involuntarily, "it's all a bit weird, even Matilda's story of the past is strange, a mysterious young girl arriving at the house with powers of foresight, talking about quiet places and such things."

"It sounds fascinating. You must remember that the past that Matilda is telling you about all happened at Meadowside, so it's no wonder that hearing about them all now that you're living there has fired up your imagination. So little has changed in the house over the years, the house is the same now as it would have been then, so it would be easy to imagine past occupants in the rooms."

"I've had so many odd experiences since I arrived at Meadowside."

"Like what?"

"Oh, I don't know," I shook my head, wishing that I hadn't said anything. "Funny feelings, like being watched, or there being someone angry and threatening in the house. Why won't they go to the end of the landing? There must be a reason."

"Have you asked them?"

I threw him a withering glance. "Of course, I have asked them. They won't tell me anything. Kitty fears something. I think she realises that she's scared but can't really remember what of, and Matilda just says that I must be patient and that everything will be revealed in the story that she's telling me. There is nothing I can do to hurry her along; she is determined to tell me it all in chronological order."

Nathaniel was walking silently by my side, his head bowed as if deep in thought. I didn't know if he was taking what I was saying seriously or was just humouring me. At that moment it was important to me that he believed what I was telling him and didn't think that I was just hysterical or overly dramatic.

"Things keep vanishing into thin air, and then reappearing in unlikely places," I continued with an edge of desperation in my voice. "There's something, or somebody that taps on the windows at night, and the house, especially the landing and the stairs, has such a strange atmosphere, as if the building itself is holding on to something from the past."

"What are you trying to tell me, Amber? Do you believe that the house is haunted and that both Kitty and Matilda are aware of the fact, but keeping the truth from you?"

I laughed. "It sounds ridiculous when you put it like that."

He sighed, with a slight, bemused shake of his head. "I think it's just an old house, and they do tend to have strange atmospheres and noises. I think, given a little more time, you will just get used to it."

"That's what Matilda said when we both heard footsteps coming from the landing. At first, she blamed Kitty, but she was in the library with Beth, so it couldn't have been her, then she said it was just the house making noises."

Nathaniel stopped walking and turned to face me. "The only advice I can give you is to try and not get carried away with anything that either of those old ladies say. They are both lovely, and I am very fond of them, but they are both bonkers, extremely old, and have lived a bizarre existence. I think you are allowing them to influence you too much, and Matilda telling you her life story is adding to that. There is no ghost in Meadowside, Amber, do you really think that Kitty and Matilda would have stayed there for all this time if the house was haunted? I don't think so."

It was good to get out of the house for a while, and away from Matilda and Kitty. I felt myself beginning to relax and was now feeling a little bit foolish for talking to Nathaniel about my fears that the house was haunted. Away from Meadowside it all seemed a little bit fanciful and vaguely crazy.

"I'm sorry," I laughed to cover my embarrassment, "of course, you're right, it's just me being an idiot, getting carried away with Matilda's story."

Nathaniel grinned. "No problem. It's all the changes that you've lived through recently, how sudden it all was, so it's not surprising that you've been feeling a bit overwhelmed with it all."

We walked all the way to the village and stopped off at the little coffee shop for some tea and cake.

"We've talked quite enough about me and my overactive imagination, how are things going for you?"

Nathaniel placed a tray on the table, removed his jacket, and placed it on an empty seat next to him, and sat down.

"Not so good, actually."

"Oh," I said, surprised, "is it work?"

"I've just become so bored of it; in fact, I handed in my notice at the beginning of the week."

"I thought you enjoyed your job."

"There was a time that I did, but not so much recently." He laughed sardonically, "I think I'm having a bit of a mid-life crisis; I've just got a hankering for something different." He threw his hands in the air, "don't ask me what though, I really don't know. Being a lawyer suited me when I was younger, but now I'm thinking that there has to be more to life than the four walls of an office."

"Mid-life crisis!" I teased, "surely you're not there yet?"

"The next big milestone in my life is hitting forty, and I'm not married, haven't got a family, I've sacrificed all that for work. I've been far too career orientated, only to realise that it's not what I want anymore. Up until the last year I was content enough, but then I got the notion in my head that life was passing me by. I've had the career success that I was craving, I've got the house and the money, and now I'm wondering what the point of it all is."

I understood Nathaniel's predicament completely and was sympathetic.

"What are you going to do then?"

"I have absolutely no idea," he shrugged, pouring milk from a jug into his teacup. "I suppose I will take some time out to figure out what I want, and hope that inspiration will come along and point me in the right direction."

He poured the tea from the pot into both of our cups, adding sugar to his and stirring it listlessly. "The partners at work have agreed that I can continue to work for Matilda, until she...well, until she dies. They understand that I have made a promise to her, and I'm determined to keep that promise, so I won't be starting anything else until my work with Matilda is complete."

I sipped my tea thoughtfully. Nathaniel was the type of man who should have been snapped up years ago, and was, in truth, exactly the type of man that my mother had been pestering me to find for the past decade.

"I'm sure it will all work out," I said supportively, "and, I do understand because I was in a similar position. In the past I have made so many mistakes with men that it made me feel that I couldn't trust my judgement. Honestly, if there was a shady, cheating, walking nightmare, I would make a beeline for him, and eventually I decided that I was better off on my own. Life wasn't easy, my job was badly paid, and barely covered my living expenses, but it was comfortable and untaxing. I can really understand the need to shake things up and try something new."

When we had finished our drinks and eaten a huge slice of coffee and walnut cake, we left the coffee shop and headed back to the house.

"Is it normal in an inheritance case for you to be employed by the client until they pass away?

We had walked through the woods and out the other side. The evening shadows were just beginning to fall, and the meadow was dark and mysterious, the long, damp grass swaying elegantly in a chilly breeze.

"It's not usual at all, but Matilda hasn't got anyone else to oversee things for her. Usually once a will has been written, that is it, although there is often more work to do once the client has passed away. Matilda's case was unique, in as much as she didn't even have an heir, and so instructed me to find your father, which in turn led me to you."

"Was I difficult to find?"

"Not at all, it was very straightforward. I found your parents' marriage certificate, and your birth certificate, I found you easily enough on the electoral register, but I would have gone to your mother for information if I had run into any difficulties. The letter that your father wrote to Matilda indicated that he had carried out a great deal of research. He seemed pretty sure that he was related to her, but he didn't elaborate on how he had reached this conclusion, or give any details on the research he had done.

"As we know, Matilda declined to respond, and years later remembered about her uncle and his family and decided that was the only way you could be related to her."

When we reached the bench at the side of the pathway, we sat down.

"I have to admit that I wasn't at all comfortable carrying out Matilda's wishes to find you. I tried to persuade her to let me do a proper investigation into her family tree, or even to hire a professional genealogist to help, but she wouldn't hear of it. For her, the whole thing was time sensitive, and who knew how long it would take to complete a thorough investigation. Her fear of dying before her affairs were settled was the driving force behind her trusting that the letter written by your father was the only evidence she needed."

"I'm sure that my dad wouldn't have written to her saying that they were related if he hadn't believed it to be true."

"I don't doubt for a minute that your father believed it was true, but Amber, believing something doesn't actually make it the truth. As far as I was concerned, I could be bringing someone into Matilda's life who wasn't related to her at all."

"I see," I said quietly, not able to deny to myself that this possibility had never dawned on me. "But there's my resemblance to Emma."

"There is that" Nathaniel agreed, "and the resemblance is strong, but could still just be a coincidence. Anyway, none of that really matters, for in the end I began to understand that Matilda just wanted somebody to come into her life and solve her problems. She needed the reassurance that someone would be around for her when her health deteriorated, and to care for Kitty and secure the future of the house. It is my belief that she wouldn't let me investigate further because she simply didn't want to know, and she definitely didn't want the relationship between her, and your father disproved."

I let out a long sigh, suddenly feeling deflated.

"The good thing is," Nathaniel continued, "is that it has all worked out better than I, or even Matilda, could have hoped for. Matilda is getting what she needs, Kitty will be cared for, and Meadowside will have an heir, and at the end of the day, that is all that Matilda was interested in. As far as we are aware, there are no other legitimate heirs, so why not you? There is a good chance that you are related to her in some way, and if she's happy, then that's good enough for me."

I stood up and walked to the far edge of the path, watching the clouds lumbering across the sky. In the distance I could see the first red streaks of the sunset, and the shadows of the birds as they headed back to the woods and their nests.

"Matilda's will has been finalised," Nathaniel came and stood beside me. "It is straightforward and watertight, her intentions as clear as a bell. The house, everything in it and all of her money will go to you on her death, on condition that you continue to take care of Kitty until she also passes away."

"I see," I folded my arms, feeling the chilly breeze blow through my hair. "I want you to know something," I said, my voice being carried away by the falling shadows and the wind. "I would have come and helped Matilda without the promise of the house and the money. I would have come based on the possibility that we are related."

Nathaniel placed his hand gently on my shoulder. "I know that,

Amber. I knew that you were a decent person when I first met you. I knew that Matilda and Kitty would be safe with you, and that I had nothing to worry about."

"Thank you," I said with a smile, before turning and walking back to the house.

*

"Kitty has been fine while you were out, she spent the entire afternoon staring out of the window as usual, and Matilda has been asleep."

Nathaniel had left a few minutes before, in a hurry to get back to Cambridge, and Beth was putting her coat on in the hall.

"Matilda has had a couple of disturbed nights," I explained to her, "that's probably why she's been so tired lately. Thanks for staying with them."

"It was no problem; I just read my book and had a lovely, peaceful time. How did you get on with Nathaniel?"

I rolled my eyes and sighed dramatically. "I got on with him fine, he's a nice man and easy company. We had a nice walk, a bit of a chat, and a cup of tea and cake in the coffee shop. That is all."

"How boring," she joked, wrapping a bright red scarf around her neck.

When Beth had left, I went to check on the sisters, finding Matilda still soundly sleeping in her chair, and Kitty in the children's room, again doing battle with the stubbornly tangled wool.

"I'll be in the kitchen if you want anything, Kitty. You could come and help me to cook the dinner if you feel like it."

She glanced up at me, her eyes full of frustration and impatience. "I need to sort this out," she held the ball of wool out towards me.

"We could always find a craft shop and buy you a nice new ball of wool that isn't all tangled up."

"Oh no," she said, aghast at the suggestion, "I've had this wool for a very long time."

I sighed. "Okay, well I'll just be in the kitchen."

I went straight to the larder cupboard and then to the fridge, trying to figure out what I could cook for dinner. There was chicken in the fridge that needed to be used up. If I had been on my own I would have whipped up a curry or a stir-fry, but the two old ladies had very simple, old-fashioned tastes, so I decided to cook the chicken breast plain, with some vegetables and mashed potatoes.

I took the chicken out of the fridge and was just looking in the larder for the bag of potatoes, when an unexpected noise caused my heart to flip in my chest. I turned abruptly, confused by the sound and not immediately able to identify it.

My eyes quickly scanned the room and then rested on the taps. Somebody had turned them on, and they were now running at full pelt into the sink, the water hitting a discarded plate and a couple of spoons and spewing onto the floor and splattering against the window. I quickly ran and turned the taps off, feeling a deepening sense of unease. The taps were old, stiff and difficult to move. There was no conceivable way that this was something that had happened of its own accord. Somebody must have turned them on, and yet, as I glanced around the kitchen, I was entirely alone.

I gripped on to the edge of the sink and took several deep breaths. I was confused, agitated, and yet again aware of that cold, shadowy presence, freezing the air around me and bringing with it the feeling of threat and foreboding.

When I was sufficiently composed, I strode out of the kitchen and into the drawing room. Matilda was still asleep. I found Kitty in the children's room, where I had left her, still trying to untangle the ball of wool.

"Kitty," I dragged my trembling fingers through my hair, my voice sounding harsh and strained. "Were you just in the kitchen?"

She looked up, puzzled. "No," she sighed, "I've been here doing this." She held up the wool then dropped it with exasperation into her lap. "Why did you think I had been in the kitchen?"

I shook my head. "It doesn't matter."

Returning to the kitchen I walked straight over to the sink, turning the taps on and off to see if there was any way that they could have turned on by themselves, but they required a firm grip and some determined pressure to make them work, and couldn't have been switched on by accident.

I moved around the kitchen quickly, peeling the potatoes and vegetables, cooking the chicken in a frying pan on top of the range. All the while my mind was exhausting itself trying to figure out how this impossible thing had occurred.

As we sat at the kitchen table, fifteen minutes later, Matilda commented that I didn't seem quite like myself and enquired after my health.

I pushed my plate away from me, not feeling at all hungry.

"I'm fine," I replied testily, "but I did have a rather unnerving experience while making the dinner. I was looking in the larder cupboard, and while my back was turned somebody came into the kitchen and turned the taps on. I turned around as soon as I heard the noise, to find that there was nobody there. I was completely alone."

Matilda picked up her knife and fork but said nothing.

"Has this ever happened before?"

"No," she said quietly, avoiding my eyes, "I don't believe that it has, are you sure it wasn't..."

"Kitty was in the children's room," I interjected, "and anyway, there's no way that she could have come into the kitchen, turned on the taps, and returned to the children's room in a matter of seconds! It definitely wasn't Kitty."

"I was untangling my wood, Tilly."

"You've been untangling that wool since 1953, Kitty!" Matilda snapped, obviously irritated. "I can't understand your fascination with it."

I placed my knife and fork on my undisturbed plate, placed my folded arms on the table and leaned towards Matilda.

"Objects vanishing into thin air and reappearing in strange places, you two refusing to go to the end of the landing, not even to use the bathroom, sudden freezing blasts of air, inexplicable footsteps, weird feelings of being watched, and now taps turning themselves on. You wouldn't be able to blame me, Matilda, for thinking that Meadowside might have a resident ghost."

"She won't bother you, Amber, as long as you don't bother her."

"Kitty!" Matilda seemed to slump in her chair, "what have I told you about saying these ridiculous things?"

"She won't bother me, if I don't bother her." I frowned towards Kitty and then turned my attention to Matilda. "Who won't bother me, Matilda? Who is it?"

"She stays out of our way, doesn't she, Tilly? She doesn't want to see us, and we don't want to see her, and we all live here together."

My blood turned to ice. "Matilda, what is she talking about?"

Matilda pressed her thin lips together, gripping her knife and fork until her knuckles turned white.

"There is more to Meadowside than I have told you, Amber, but you must trust me, it will all become clear."

"Why can't you just tell me what is going on now?" I pleaded.

"Because you won't understand, Amber. You need to hear about everything that happened, and you might leave if you knew the truth."

I covered my face with my hands. "Are we safe here, Matilda?"

Tears trickled down the parchment skin of her face as her frightened eyes met mine. "I don't know," she uttered wretchedly, "I really don't know."

\*

Kitty went to bed at her usual time, but Matilda, after spending so many hours asleep during the day, was not tired and requested to be taken to the children's room. As was becoming the routine, I drew the curtains, lit the fire, and sat down in the chair opposite her.

"How long have these strange things been happening in the house, Matilda? Were they happening when you were a child?"

"No, not when I was a child, but they have been happening for a very long time, probably for about eighty-two years."

"Eighty-two years!" I gasped. "You have lived with this for all of that time?"

"It comes and goes, sometimes nothing happens for years, and I forget that it ever did, and so does Kitty, and then something will occur out of the blue, the sudden slamming of a door, items being hidden and moved, footsteps that don't belong either to myself or Kitty."

"It has never got any more serious than that?"

She shook her head, "it's annoying more than anything else, annoying and inconvenient."

"I can imagine," I shuddered.

"There have been no occurrences for several years, apart from the sound of footsteps. Nothing else has taken place, until you arrived."

"Matilda, I need to hear this from your own mouth. Is Meadowside haunted?"

She gazed at me for a long time, her expression unreadable. "You won't leave, will you Amber?"

Even as I sat there beside the roaring fire, in the quiet and peaceful room, I knew that leaving, no matter how difficult things became, was never going to be an option. How could I leave Matilda and Kitty alone in the house? How would I ever live with myself knowing how difficult life would be for them both?

I sighed as if resigned to my fate. "I won't leave, Matilda. I made a promise to you and I intend to stand by it. I will be going nowhere."

Matilda inclined her head, as if satisfied, her eyes closing with relief. Before she resumed with her story I had one question to ask her.

"Do you know who it is? The ghost, I mean?"

She lifted her head and gazed at me directly. "Oh, I know who it is, alright," she replied, her voice cold and bitter.

# Chapter 8

## Meadowside 1915

To Matilda's great delight she felt that, in some ways at least, her father had come back to them, not quite the same man that he used to be, but more frequently she was seeing glimpses of his old self returning. He had stepped back into the family, spending less time alone in the library, and taking some pleasure in the trials and tribulations of family life. Eleanor Grey, following the example of her husband, also began to spend more time with her children, sometimes listening to Issy reading out loud, or spending hours trying to teach Kitty some knitting and sewing skills.

In early June Issy's seventh and Kitty's ninth birthday were fast approaching. It occurred to Edward that due to Jack's death, and the melancholy atmosphere that event had brought to the house, there had been no celebrations of any kind. The thought troubled him deeply, for birthdays had always been celebrated at Meadowside, and it had forcibly struck him that his two youngest daughters may not have any memories of their own birthday celebrations, and he felt at pains to rectify this.

Over the following few days, a plan began to form in his mind, and at the end of that week he found Emma, Matilda and Seraphina in the kitchen. Emma was teaching the two younger girls to cook, vital skills for when they grew up and had families of their own. On that particular morning they were learning how to make bread.

"Ah, I have at last found you three girls on your own, without Kitty and Issy." Their father hovered around the kitchen door, just to make sure that the two youngest girls were definitely not present.

"Father!" Emma was surprised, but delighted to see him, for he very rarely entered the kitchen, seeing it very much as a female domain. "Come in," she smiled encouragingly, "sit down at the table and I'll make you a cup of tea. Matilda, clear away the mixing bowls and Seraphina, wipe down the table so that Father doesn't get flour on his jacket."

Edward sat down, watching as the three girls tidied up around him.

"Is everything alright, Father?"

"Everything is splendid, thank you Emma. I was just thinking to myself that little Issy's birthday is next week, and Kitty's the week after, and we should have a celebration for them, you know, like we used to have. What do you think?"

"I think they would like that very much." Emma removed her apron, folded it and placed it on the dresser before sitting down opposite her father. "In fact, I think they would be delighted."

"I will leave the details to you girls, but as we are being blessed with some wonderful summer weather at the moment, I was thinking that we could hold the celebration out in the garden, some cake and a game or two will make for a birthday that the two of them will remember, don't you think?"

"That is a wonderful idea, Father." Emma's face was flushed with happiness, this was all the proof that she needed that things were, slowly but steadily, going back to how they used to be. "I will make the birthday cake, Tilly and Seraphina can help; it will be a good skill for them to learn for the future."

He nodded his approval. "I have been working on a present for them both in the barn, with Merlin keeping me company," he winked towards Seraphina "he doesn't seem to mind me being there, in fact, despite the banging and sawing, he seems to quite like it."

Later that day, Emma, Seraphina and Matilda were again seated at the kitchen table, with Emma writing a list, with suggestions being made by the younger girls.

"The birthday bunting is in the attic," Matilda said, "I remember putting it there. It was the last birthday that we celebrated, which was mine, in September 1912."

"Bring it down, Tilly, and I think that the outside table is up there too. Now then," Emma leaned her elbows on the table, "there is no way that we are going to be able to keep this a secret from Issy and Kitty and we won't be able to keep them out of the house while the arrangements are being made, so I was thinking that it might be for the best if we didn't even try. I will see what Father thinks, but I believe we should tell them what is happening. It will be lovely for them to have something like this to look forward to, rather than trying to make it a big surprise."

"I agree," Matilda said enthusiastically, "those two are everywhere, they'll soon cotton on if we don't tell them."

At that moment Martha walked into the kitchen and demanded to know what was going on, and what they were whispering about.

"We are planning a birthday celebration for Issy and Kitty," Emma explained, "Father believes that it is time for us to start celebrating birthdays again, and I for one wholeheartedly agree with him."

Martha leaned her tall, slender frame against the dresser, her arms folded. "I can't agree," she sniffed disapprovingly. "This is not a time for celebrations of any kind. There's a war going on, in case you've forgotten. Men from the village are being killed and maimed."

Emma sighed wearily. "It's just a small birthday party, Martha. I can't believe that you would want to deny Issy and Kitty that? Of course, we are upset about the war, but that doesn't mean we have to deny ourselves every bit of pleasure that might come our way."

"It's a disgrace. Father is not thinking straight. Those two girls would be better off learning about the sacrifices that others are making for their freedoms, rather than having frivolous parties."

"Oh, do be quiet, Martha!" Matilda wished that she was able to ignore her sister's constant nagging and arguing, like Emma was always advising her to do. It didn't matter what anyone said, or what they did: Martha would always have an opposing view to everybody else.

"Who do you think you're talking to, Miss? How dare you tell me to be quiet!" Martha took a step forwards and punched Matilda hard on her shoulder.

"I am someone who is sick to death of the sound of your sanctimonious, whining voice. You are nothing but a parasite, Martha, sucking the joy out of everything and everyone. Just because you're a miserable shrew, doesn't mean that the rest of us have to be like you."

Martha took another step forwards, but Matilda, anticipating this move, jumped up from her chair and swung around.

"Just you try punching me again, Martha." Matilda braced herself, drawing herself up to her full height. "I am as tall as you now, and twice as strong. Take one more step towards me and I'll slap that smirk from off your face, once and for all."

"You wouldn't dare!" Martha spat; her dark eyes almost black with anger.

"I am not a child anymore, and I am more than a match for you. You can test me if you want to, but I'm warning you, you will come off worse."

Martha's entire body was taut with fury. Two spots of crimson colour had appeared on her cheekbones, and her hands were clenched into fists.

"I will talk to Father," she seethed, her lips drawn back into a snarl. "I will not have you speaking to me like that!"

"The days where you could speak to everybody as you pleased, treat us all as you pleased, and expect us to just tolerate it, are long gone. We are all growing up and see you for what you are: a sad, miserable, nasty bully."

Martha stared at Matilda for a long time, her expression a mixture of shock and rage. Matilda stood her ground, her eyes holding a challenge, her body primed and ready to retaliate.

"Try it, Martha," Matilda goaded, "and see what you get for your trouble."

Martha viewed her younger sister with sneering contempt. "You think you've won," Martha's voice was low and quiet, although barely a whisper her words were loaded with intimidation and threat. "There are more ways than one to skin a cat. I will make you sorry, Tilly, but I will bide my time, just when you think I've forgotten about this, that is when I will strike."

Martha, keeping her back straight and rigid, with her head held high, walked out of the room, slamming the door behind her so violently that it caused the glass panels in the windows to vibrate in their frames.

"You've done it again, Tilly. Instead of ignoring her like I have told you to do countless times, you have antagonised her even further."

"I don't care," Matilda shrugged, "I can't just sit back and let her say what she likes to me, and why should I? I've had enough of her miserable sermons and threats, and I won't be standing for any more of it. If she confronts me again, then she will get back what she deserves."

"Then there will be another war to contend with, and it will be taking place within the walls of Meadowside."

"I'm not good like you, Emma. I haven't got your patience or kindness, and I can't just let her make my life miserable. I don't think she can be right in the head."

Emma smiled indulgently. "You were born with a temper, Tilly, and with a fire in your eyes, and now you need to learn to control it. Ignoring Martha and not reacting to her at all is the best way to have a peaceful life, all you have done is to give her more ammunition to attack you with. Martha is unfortunate, she hasn't been blessed with an easy personality, but we can hardly condemn her for something that isn't her fault."

"You're always making excuses for her," Matilda cried. "She knows what she's doing, she has control over her tongue like everybody else, but she's hellbent on making us all as miserable as she is. I despise her, and I can see no respite in the future, it's not like she's ever going to get married and leave Meadowside. Who on Earth would want her moaning and haranguing him for the rest of his life? No, we are stuck with her forever, and that is the thing I am sorry for."

"I think it's very sad." Emma and Matilda turned their attention towards Seraphina, who had remained completely silent up until then. "I think Martha must be very unhappy to be the way she is. It isn't normal, and it must be caused by her own feelings of unhappiness."

"She thinks you can cast spells, Seraphina." There was an edge of amusement in Matilda's voice, "she's absolutely convinced of it. Maybe you could slip some flower petals or herbs into her tea to improve her mood, or even a vanishing potion!"

Seraphina laughed. "Martha just needs to understand herself better, to figure out why she's so unhappy and do something about it. My Grandmother used to make an elixir that lifted people's moods, but I can't remember the recipe."

"That's a shame," Matilda commented dryly, "so, I suppose there is nothing else to do but put up with Martha the way that she is."

"I'm afraid so," Seraphina smiled.

Martha had gone to the library to find her father, to inform him in no uncertain terms of her thoughts and feelings about having a party in the middle of a war, but the library was empty. It was likely that he had gone to the barn, for he had been spending a lot of time out there recently. Martha would not enter the barn, not with that great black beast of a horse being in there.

She was walking past the kitchen when she heard the muttering of voices coming from within. She pressed her ear against the closed door and listened to every word that was spoken, her anger growing like a tornado inside her chest, growing wilder and stronger with every passing second.

Even though Martha could hear the entire conversation, it was Seraphina's words that stuck in her mind and caused her the most consternation. She heard the girl say that she, Martha, wasn't normal and how she felt sorry for her. She heard her talk about spells and potions. She was breathing heavily as she fought to contain her anger, and then she smiled, knowing that one of these days she would exact her revenge on the gipsy girl, and that day couldn't come soon enough.

*

Eleanor Grey threw herself wholeheartedly into the party preparations, frequently showing her husband and children flickers of the woman and mother she used to be.

The party was to take place in the afternoon. Seraphina had helped to drag the narrow wooden table down two flights of stairs and out into the garden. She found a snowy white tablecloth inside the kitchen dresser, and Matilda strung homemade bunting from the trees and bushes.

Seraphina found Matilda at lunchtime, telling her that she needed to go into the village, glancing around to make sure that the over-exited Issy wasn't in hearing range.

"Why do you need to go to the village?" Matilda asked.

"I need to collect Issy's present. I won't be very long."

"Issy is doing well for presents this year. Did you know that Father has made her a dolls house? It has all the little people inside, and he has made all the furniture himself, she's going to be delighted with it."

"He has made one for Kitty too." Seraphina had seen both of the dolls houses in various stages of completion in the barn while she had been tending to Merlin.

"What present have you got for Issy? Did you make something for her and leave it in the village?"

"No," Seraphina shook her head, stepping closer towards Matilda and lowering her voice. "Mrs Dane's cat has had a litter of kittens, and she agreed to me having two of them in return for me looking after her twins for a few hours so that she could go and visit her sick mother. I have a black one for Issy, and a black and white one for Kitty, which I will collect and give to her when it's her birthday next week."

"What a wonderful idea for a present, Seraphina. The girls, especially Issy, are going to be delighted."

"I asked your father if it would be alright, and he said yes, as long as the girls looked after them properly, and that I supervised them to make sure the kittens are fed and well kept. He said they would be good to catch mice in the barn."

It was a beautiful day with the sun pleasantly warm and not a cloud in the sky. As she busied herself getting ready for the party, Matilda was reminded of days gone by, when celebrations like this were a frequent occurrence. She was humming to herself, realising that this was the happiest she had felt since Jack had died. Her parents were getting better, and the only blot on her happiness was the fact that Jack wasn't there.

Her father came out into the garden to see how the proceedings were coming along. "Splendid," he smiled approvingly, "you girls have done a wonderful job." He looked around the garden and then asked where Seraphina was.

"She's just gone to the village to collect Issy's birthday present."

"Ah, yes, the kitten." Edward winked, then glanced back towards the house. "I think, even though she is up to her elbows in flour helping Emma in the kitchen, that I really should go and inform your mother about Seraphina's present."

He turned and walked back to the house, whistling tunelessly to himself.

Matilda returned to her work for a while and then walked to the meadow to gather some wildflowers for the table. She carried a wicker basket in her hand and walked to the middle of the meadow where the flowers were most abundant. She was thinking about the change that had come over her father and was feeling very glad of it. He appeared to have greatly warmed to Seraphina, often seeking out her company, usually in the barn while she was grooming Merlin, or cleaning the saddle and reins. Her mother was not quite as tolerant of Seraphina as her husband, but did at least maintain a demeanour of politeness, and had begun to include her more frequently in conversations.

With her basket full of flowers, she straightened her back and saw Seraphina emerging from the woods. She set the basket down on the pathway and ran to meet her. As she drew closer, she could see the tiny black kitten being held gently in her hands.

"She's beautiful," Matilda gushed.

"It's a boy," Seraphina informed her, "your father said that I could get the kittens for the girls as long as they were boys as he was not at all keen on having regular litters of kittens being born at Meadowside."

"He is gorgeous," Matilda stroked the top of the kittens silky head with her finger. "Issy is going to love him."

"Let's take him to her now," Seraphina suggested, her eyes shining with excitement. As they walked, she turned to Matilda and asked, "what have you got for Issy as a present?"

"Not much really, just some clothes that I made for her doll, and a little blanket, but unfortunately, they are not very good."

"Well, let's give the kitten to her as a joint present from both of us."

"Really, Seraphina? That would be wonderful. Are you sure?"

"Of course, the most important thing is that Issy will have a kitten to love, and it really doesn't matter which one of us thought of it."

"Thank you, Seraphina," Matilda smiled happily, thinking to herself how kind and thoughtful Seraphina was.

Kitty and Issy were running around the garden, oblivious to the arrival of Matilda and Seraphina. Edward Grey came out of the French doors of the library and strode quickly towards them

"Let me have a look at the little chap," he said. "He's very sweet. I have a feeling he's a born mouser, Seraphina, and will very soon pay for his keep. Are you ready to give him to Issy now?"

"Yes," Seraphina grinned, "but he's not just a present from me, he's from Tilly as well."

Edward smiled and then turned towards the garden. "Isabel," he called at the top of his voice, "come and see the present your sisters have for you."

Issy skipped over, and as she watched her approaching Seraphina felt her eyes fill with tears. Mr Grey had said 'sisters,' giving her the same status as Matilda. It may have been a slip of the tongue, but as far as Seraphina was concerned, it was Mr Grey's way of letting her know that she was a fully-fledged member of the family.

Issy skidded to a halt in front of them, and Seraphina held out her hands.

"Happy birthday, Issy, he's your birthday present from me and Tilly. I hope you like him."

"He is the most beautiful kitten I have ever seen," Issy gasped, holding the tiny creature against her chest. "What's his name?"

"He hasn't got a name yet, Issy. He's your kitten, so it's up to you to name him."

Issy held the kitten up in front of her face and then suddenly smiled. "I know," she grinned, "I'm going to call him Blackjack, because he's black and because Jack really loved kittens."

Everyone fell silent. Matilda glanced quickly at her father, wondering how he would feel about the kitten being named after his dead son. For a moment he appeared taken aback, but then, much to Matilda's relief, he stepped forwards and ruffled Issy's hair.

"What a splendid name, Issy," he smiled indulgently, "Blackjack it is then."

\*

The celebrations began in the middle of the afternoon and continued well into the evening. They played games and the garden was alive with laughter and excitement. Even Martha joined in a little, managing to last several hours without using any barbed insults, or snide remarks.

Late in the evening all the girls went to bed at the same time, Matilda and Seraphina almost having to carry an exhausted Kitty and Issy up the stairs. They had the kitten with them, after Issy had begged for him to be allowed to spend the night on her bed.

"He will be so frightened," she cried, "he is only a baby, and he'll be so scared in the dark, all on his own."

"You are not having an animal in the bed with you, Issy, and I don't want to hear another word about it. It isn't sanitary, or healthy."

Issy turned her tearful eyes away from her mother and ran to her father's side.

"Please, Father," she begged, "please."

Edward Grey gazed down at his youngest daughter. "Your mother said no, Issy," he crouched down in front of her, a twinkle in his eyes, "which surprises me a little, for I know for a fact that when your mother and I were newly married, long before you were born, I bought her a little spaniel puppy called Polly, and for the next twelve years I slept in the bed with a spaniel on my feet!"

"Edward," Eleanor Grey sighed, exasperated. "You are no help at all, that was completely different."

"Come along now, Eleanor, the only difference is that Issy is just a little girl, and you were a fully grown woman, crying and begging me to let the blasted animal sleep on our bed."

"It was because she wouldn't stop whimpering and crying."

"She didn't cry and whimper for twelve years, Eleanor, but she certainly slept on my feet for all of that time!"

Eleanor grimaced as she admitted defeat. "Alright then, Issy, you may take the kitten to bed with you, but I want you all to know," she glanced at her family solemnly, "that it is against my better judgement, and if the kitten gives you fleas, Issy, then it will be entirely the fault of your father."

"Horrible creature," Martha scowled with disgust, "I wouldn't even let it inside the house, let alone in my bed."

Nobody paid any attention to her words at all.

The kitten was a huge hit, and the following week, on Kitty's birthday, the other one arrived, which she christened Timmy. The kittens followed the two girls everywhere they went, but then, four weeks later, both disappeared, much to the distress of the children.

"It's alright," their father insisted, "they are growing up and they have just gone exploring and hunting. They will come back."

The following morning when the girls came down for breakfast, it was to find the two kittens waiting at the back door, miaowing frantically to be let inside and fed.

"I wish I knew where they've been," Issy said, cradling Blackjack on her knee.

"They have been out on the fen all night, or in the meadow, that is what cats do, Issy, you need to get used to it." Emma placed a pitcher of milk in the centre of the table. "The good thing is that they go out all night, having adventures, then every morning they come back to the person who loves them, and also, of course, to be fed."

Issy and Kitty soon realised that having cats for pets meant that they had to allow them their freedom. The cats were no longer interested in sleeping on their beds at night, preferring to prowl the countryside for small prey, but they always returned home in the morning, that is until one morning when one of them didn't.

It was a day in late August. Kitty and Issy came down to the kitchen and immediately went to the back door, to find that only one of the cats had returned, Timmy, but there was no sign at all of Blackjack.

"Don't fret, Issy, he'll be alright," Emma dried the little girl's tears with a handkerchief tucked inside her apron pocket. "He's just having too much fun and has forgotten the time. He will come home when he's hungry."

Issy spent a subdued day, constantly opening and closing the kitchen door, but the cat did not appear. She walked all over the meadow and covered as much of the fen as she could, but she couldn't find a trace of him.

"Where could he be?" Issy was still worried and distressed at bedtime. Emma sat on the side of the bed and tried to settle her fears.

"Issy, this isn't unusual for cats, they can disappear for days at a time, please try not to worry."

"He must be lost," Issy sobbed, "or he might have had an accident."

"I bet anything you like that he will be back tomorrow morning, and if he isn't, then we will organise searches, we will all help you to find him."

Despite her worries and distress, Issy fell asleep quickly, due to the number of miles she had walked that day in search of her pet.

It was usual for Emma and the older girls to spend the evening in the children's room, sewing, reading or just chatting about the events of the day.

"Poor Issy is still distraught about the cat," Emma sat down, wearily rubbing her tired eyes. "I told her that if he wasn't back in the morning that we would all go out and look for him."

"Is she in bed now?"

Emma nodded towards Matilda. "Fast asleep, worried or not, she has exhausted herself by all the walking she has done today. "

"Poor Issy," Seraphina closed the book she had been reading, "I wish she'd believe us when we tell her she has nothing to worry about and that he'll come back when he's ready."

"She won't be happy until he's safely back home," Emma yawned. "If he's not back in the morning we will all go and look for him, just in case he's got himself into trouble. He may have got trapped in an outbuilding, or perhaps taken in by somebody who thought he was a stray."

The following morning there was still no sign of the kitten, which resulted in hysterical crying from Issy.

"I know this is very worrying for you," Emma tried to console her, "but I wish you would believe me when I say that he will come home." She busied herself around the kitchen, boiling the huge kettle on the stove, and setting the table for breakfast. "As soon as we've eaten, we will go and look for him, it doesn't matter how long it takes, we will keep looking until we've found him, and if we don't find him today, then we will look again tomorrow."

Issy wiped the tears from her eyes. "I think he got lost, Emma. He will be so happy when we find him."

As soon as the breakfast dishes were washed, dried and put away, and the kitchen returned to its usual clean and tidy state, the girls all gathered at the front of the house.

"Tilly, you go out on the fen, Seraphina and I will go to the village, and Kitty and Issy can search the meadow and the woods. We'll meet back here in two hours."

They all moved away from the house, in different directions. Matilda walked along the rough pathway that led along the top of the meadow and towards the acres of open fen land. Although she was more than happy to help with the search, she was certain that she would never find the small animal in such a large space, nevertheless, she was determined to try and find the wayward cat, for Issy's sake.

She walked for an hour, now and again walking off the path onto the rough grass, calling the cat's name over and over. Eventually, she concluded that she was wasting her time, even if the cat was out there, it would be unlikely that she would be able to find him while trying to cover so many acres on her own. As she turned around to head back to the house, she fervently hoped that the cat had been found, and they could all return to normal life.

She was the first one to arrive back at the house. She leaned her back against the gate, enjoying the late summer sun on her face and admiring the billowing clouds that floated across the perfectly blue sky.

Hearing voices in the distance she turned and saw Seraphina and Emma walking towards her.

"Any luck?" She called out, feeling disheartened when she saw Seraphina shake her head.

"We looked everywhere we could think of, we even knocked on people's doors and asked them to check their gardens and outbuildings, but nobody has seen him."

Emma had walked to the top of the meadow, shielding her eyes against the sun to see if she could spot Kitty and Issy in the meadow.

"I hope they've found him," she said with an anxious sigh, "there will be no peace in the house if we don't find him today."

The three girls walked to the bench and sat down.

"Don't you think that they should be back by now?" Matilda said fifteen minutes later, standing up and gazing back down the meadow path.

"They've probably lost track of time," Emma said, "you know what the pair of them are like. We'll give them another ten minutes, and then, I suppose, we will have to go and look for them too."

A few minutes later Seraphina pointed into the distance. "There's one of them at least."

Emma stood up and saw Kitty alone, running from the woods. She expected Issy to appear at any moment, but she didn't, and Kitty was now halfway between the woods and the bench. Emma frowned, for there was something unusual and worrying about the way Kitty was running, not her usual slow movements, she was running at full pelt towards them, pushing herself as hard as she could.

"There's something wrong," Emma uttered, her heart sinking in her chest. "Tilly, there's something wrong."

Matilda and Seraphina both jumped up from the bench, and with Emma closely behind them, they ran to meet Kitty on the path.

"Where's Issy?" Seraphina demanded, knowing that Kitty was rarely to be found without her little sister.

Kitty just stood there; her face bleached of all colour. She was crying, her breaths coming in huge, choking sobs, and she was opening and closing her mouth, trying to say something but unable to get the words out.

"Kitty! For goodness' sake, what has happened?" Emma stepped forwards and took the young girl by the shoulders, shaking her roughly. "Where is Issy?"

Kitty lifted her arm and pointed towards the woods, and then, to everyone's horror, she fell to the ground.

"She's fainted!" Seraphina knelt beside Kitty, who lay on the grass, her skin alarmingly white. "She's out cold."

Emma glanced worriedly towards the woods. "Stay with Kitty, Tilly. Seraphina and I will go to the woods and will bring Issy back. I can only think that something has happened to the cat. We will be as quick as we can."

Matilda held Kitty's hand, tapping it sharply as she watched Emma and Seraphina running towards the woods.

"Kitty," she gently shook her, relieved to see her eyes flickering and beginning to open. "You fainted," Matilda informed her, helping the trembling child to sit up, "don't worry, you will be fine in a couple of minutes."

Matilda pulled Kitty to her feet and supported her as they made their way to the bench.

"How are you feeling now?" Matilda sat her sister on the bench, thinking that she looked far from well. She sat down beside her. "Emma and Seraphina have gone to the woods to find Issy, you really shouldn't have left her on her own."

A shadow passed over Kitty's face and her eyes grew dark and frightened. She started to cry again, huge, heaving sobs that shook her entire body.

Matilda put her arms around Kitty's shoulders. "Did you find Blackjack?" She asked gently, believing that Emma's fears about something having befallen the cat was probably right. "Don't cry, Kitty, everything will be alright."

Kitty was shaking her head. "He was up a tree," she sobbed, "I told Issy not to go up there, that we should go home and fell Father, but she wouldn't listen to me. It wasn't my fault, Tilly, I tried to stop her."

Matilda felt a cold hand grip her heart. "What are you trying to say, Kitty? Is Issy stuck up a tree?"

"She climbed very high, Tilly. I told her that she must come down, that it was dangerous, but she didn't hear me. Blackjack jumped to an even higher branch, and Issy stretched out to catch him, and then..." another bout of hysterical crying overwhelmed her, "and then... and then, she fell out of the tree, Tilly. She was so still. I shook her, and yelled at her, but nothing would make her move."

Matilda stared at her sister in horror and then jumped to her feet, pacing backwards and forwards along the path, as if her feet couldn't keep still. "She'll be alright," she whispered over and over, like a chanted mantra. "She's probably just broken a few bones, that is all, it won't be anything worse than that."

Her eyes scanned the meadow, then focused on the line of trees in the distance. "Where are they?" She yelled, "Why are they taking so long?"

Kitty sat slumped on the bench, her shoulders heaving with distraught crying.

"They are coming," Matilda turned towards Kitty. She could see two figures coming out of the woods, Emma and Seraphina. "I don't think they could find Issy. Which tree did she fall out of?"

"The one where we get our conkers in the autumn, the one on the edge of the clearing."

Matilda frowned. Surely they would have found her there, for you couldn't walk in or out of the woods without passing the old chestnut tree.

"Are you sure it was that tree, Kitty?"

Kitty lifted her head; her eyes were red rimmed and dark with misery. "I'm sure," she uttered wretchedly.

"Stay here," Matilda commanded, already walking away quickly towards Emma and Seraphina.

"She's fallen out of the horse chestnut tree," she said as she neared them, but one glance at Emma's face caused her to stop dead in her tracks. The expression that she saw in her sister's eyes made her want to turn around and run away.

"We found her," Emma cried, "there was nothing we could do."

"What?" Matilda screamed, her voice echoing around the meadow, causing a couple of crows squabbling on the path to take flight in alarm. "What do you mean there was nothing you could do? What do you mean, Emma?"

Emma lifted her head slowly; her skin was deathly white and streaked with tears. She took a steadying breath that seemed to shudder throughout her body.

"Issy has died, Tilly. She fell from the tree. We tried to lift her, but she was too heavy, we realised that we couldn't carry her home." Emma swiped the tears from her eyes with the back of her hand. "We had to leave her where we found her."

"No!" Matilda shrieked, falling to the ground. "Not Issy! She will be alright, it will just be a concussion, just you wait and see. Issy is strong, she'll get better."

"Oh Tilly," Emma cried, "if only that were true, but it seems that Issy was killed by the fall. She has hurt her head, and it seems that she died as soon as she hit the ground. I'm sorry, Tilly, I wish I could tell you something else, but I can't, Issy has gone."

"Gone?" Matilda stared at Emma; her eyes full of confusion. "She was only a little girl, a child; she can't just be gone."

"I'm so sorry, Tilly," Seraphina was crying and looked every bit as pale as Emma. She helped Matilda to her feet, and together they walked towards Kitty, who was still sitting frozen in shock on the bench.

# Chapter 9

Retrieving a tissue from the sleeve of my jumper, I dabbed at my eyes, feeling the awful shock and disbelief that must have been felt by Matilda and her family all of those years ago.

"Matilda, your family must have been shattered, completely devastated."

"My family never recovered," she shook her head sadly, speaking quietly, "we missed and mourned Jack when he died, but with Issy the pain was horrific, the loss so agonising, the absence of her in the house was almost impossible for any of us to bear. She was the beating heart of the family, the golden child, the one who always made us smile and brought sunshine and joy to us every day. Meadowside was cold, dark and miserable after her death, and one by one, bit by bit, my family simply fell apart."

Matilda gazed almost longingly into the fire. "I have missed her every day of my life, and even now I can feel the pain of her loss and can't believe she has gone." She laughed humourlessly. "How silly that is, after all of this time, but if things were bad for me, then they were even worse for Kitty."

"Poor Kitty," I sighed, hardly able to stand the thought of the pain that Issy's death must have caused her. "It must have been awful for her to have witnessed Issy's accident."

"Kitty was never the same again. She blamed herself, I think, although it was never her fault. Issy was a headstrong child, if she wanted to do something then she would go right ahead and do it, she would not have listened to Kitty, and nobody, least of all Kitty, would have been able to stop her climbing that tree." Matilda wiped a stray tear from her cheek and looked at me in anguish. "The thing that has caused me the most pain was that when my father and Jed Carter went to bring Issy's body back to the house, the kitten was sitting beside her. Poor Issy didn't think that if the kitten could have climbed up the tree it could have surely climbed down again. The following day Seraphina took both of the kittens into the village and gave them to another little girl. Kitty had lost interest in hers, and I'm afraid that little Blackjack did nothing but remind us that he was the cause of Issy's death."

Another tear trickled down Matilda's cheek. "She must have been so delighted to have found the cat and alarmed that he appeared stuck high up in a tree. She wouldn't have thought twice about going up there after him, it would have been her natural instinct.

"It was a shocking, terrible accident, and it broke the hearts of every one of us. The pain has never really gone away, but over the years I have learned to live with it, but Kitty, who finds it so difficult to learn anything, has never really moved on, and has spent every single day since Issy's death standing at the windows of Meadowside, waiting for her to come home."

I felt the tears stinging the back of my eyes. "That's who she's been waiting for, it's been Issy all along?"

"Kitty withdrew into herself. She barely spoke a word for months after Issy's funeral. The two of them were always together, inseparable, and Kitty became like a shadow of herself, roaming from window to window, waiting for the impossible to happen."

"That is heart-breaking," I dabbed my eyes with my tissue, "and now, more than eighty years on, she is still waiting for her to come back. Poor, poor, Kitty."

"My parents didn't fare much better. My father retreated back into the library, and my mother took to her bed, both of them so consumed by their own grief that they could barely function. In fact, it seemed to me that they were both just waiting for their own deaths to bring about some relief. We could go for several days without setting eyes on either of them, it really was like they had forgotten that we even existed."

*

I found it difficult to sleep that night, my thoughts centred on Matilda's tragic story, and like watching a sad film, or reading a heart-wrenching novel, I had been greatly affected by hearing about Issy's death.

I did manage to snatch a few hours of sleep, but when I awoke the following morning, my heart was heavy with sadness for what the family had endured. I had so often imagined Issy playing in the garden, a golden-haired little girl, as Matilda had described her 'the beating heart' of the family, running around the flower beds, or swaying back and forth on the homemade swing, the remnants of which, miraculously, still dangled precariously from the oak tree.

As soon as I was washed and dressed, I went into Matilda's room to see if she was ready to get up. Usually, I would find her still in bed, but awake, but on that morning she was still sound asleep.

Kitty and I ate our breakfast in the kitchen, and then I returned to Matilda's room and opened the curtains. When I turned from the window it was immediately apparent that Matilda was unwell.

"What's the matter, Matilda? Are you sick?"

I was kneeling on the floor beside the bed. She tried to say something, but she was too weak. She coughed and as she did so I could hear a disquieting rattling noise coming from her chest. "You stay here and rest," I said to her soothingly, "I will be back soon."

I went directly to the library and dialled the number for the doctors surgery in the village, and then phoned Nathaniel, feeling that this was something, as Matilda's solicitor, he should know about.

"Nathaniel, it's me, Amber. I'm just phoning to let you know that Matilda's sick. I've just called the doctor out and he's going to visit in the next hour or so. I thought you should know."

There was a short silence and then he asked, "how sick is she, do you think?"

"She looks terrible, Nathaniel," I ran my fingers anxiously through my hair, "she's got a cough, and a horrible, rattling sound coming from her chest, and I think she's got a temperature."

"That doesn't sound good," he sighed, "but at least the doctor will be there soon. Do you want me to come over?"

"I don't think there's any point, it's not as if there's anything you can do, thanks for offering though. I'll phone you when the doctor's been."

After speaking to Nathaniel, I went to the kitchen to find Kitty. She was still where I had left her, sitting at the table and staring dreamily into a cold, and half empty cup of tea. I explained to her that Matilda was ill and that the doctor was coming to see her.

"Tilly is never ill," she said, a stubborn edge to her voice as if I must be telling her untrue information or making it up.

"Well, she is today. It seems to be her chest; she has a bad cough and a high temperature."

Kitty looked at me appalled; her eyes full of fear.

"The cough?" She uttered anxiously, "like before?"

I frowned, confused. "Has Matilda been ill like this before, Kitty?"

She shook her head, confusing me even further.

"Have you?"

Again, she shook her head, leaving me baffled as to what she could have been referring to. "Well, the doctor will be here soon," I informed her, and hopefully it is just a bad cold."

"The doctor wouldn't come last time, too busy the woman said."

"Who said that the doctor was too busy?"

"His wife. We went to his house, but he couldn't come."

"When was this, Kitty?"

She shrugged her shoulders, and at the moment the back door opened, and Beth came into the kitchen. She placed her handbag on the table, filled the kettle at the sink and went to the dresser to get some clean cups.

"It's a nightmare every morning trying to get my two to school, it's only a ten-minute walk, yet we never manage to get there on time, what with forgotten homework, forgotten lunches, and this morning we were halfway there, only for me to discover that one of them was still wearing his Postman Pat slippers! Do either of you want a cup of tea?"

Kitty suddenly stood up and left the room.

"Was it something I said?" Beth shrugged, "is she alright?"

"Matilda is ill," I informed her with a heavy sigh, "and I think Kitty's worried."

Beth sat down at the table, removing her handbag and placing it on the chair next to her. "What about you? Are you worried?"

I nodded. "I suppose any illness in a person of her age is worrying, it could just be a cold, but she has an awful cough, a temperature and a horrible noise coming from her chest."

"That does sound a bit worrying, Amber. Have you called the doctor?"

"Yes, he'll be here any minute now."

Beth stood up and made us both a cup of tea. When she returned to the table I asked her if she knew if either Matilda or Kitty had ever been ill before with similar symptoms to what Matilda had now.

She frowned. "Neither of them has ever been ill since I have known them. Of course, they have had a few minor colds, but nothing you could actually call an illness."

"That's very strange," I stirred my tea absently, "when I told Kitty that Matilda was ill, she first said that Matilda is never ill, and then, when I explained the symptoms, she started to act weird, as if she was frightened. She said something about the doctor not being able to come before, how he was too busy, but then she clammed up. I was just wondering what she could have been talking about."

Beth shrugged her shoulders. "I have no idea. They weren't even registered with the doctors when I first started coming here, I soon sorted that out, so, she must have been talking about years ago, or maybe it's just one of Kitty's ramblings. Who knows?"

I stood up. "Will you keep an eye on Kitty, and show the doctor up to Matilda's room when he arrives? I'm going to sit with her."

"Of course," Beth said, "don't worry about anything."

I crept into Matilda's room and pulled a chair up to the side of the bed. She was still asleep, her chest wheezing noisily with every breath that she took. She appeared so small lying in the bed, struggling for every breath, and as I sat there I hoped and prayed that Matilda wouldn't die so soon into our relationship. I had barely got to know her, and also, would I ever learn the truth about Meadowside if she died before she was able to tell me?

The doctor arrived ten minutes later, a young man with ruddy cheeks, a quick smile and kind, twinkling eyes.

"How long has she been like this?" He placed his bag at the end of the bed, taking out a stethoscope and a thermometer.

"Only today," I explained anxiously, "she was fine yesterday, a bit tired, but that is quite normal for her, at her age. When I came in this morning she appeared very unwell, so I called you straight away."

He nodded his head. "She's got pneumonia," he took the stethoscope out of his ears and returned it to the bag. "It seems to be in the early stages, but due to her age and frailty, I think it would be for the best if she were treated in hospital. She will need intravenous antibiotics and fluids, so hospital would be the best place for her."

Matilda's eyes were flickering, trying desperately to open. She was agitated, her thin, blue veined hands plucking fretfully at the bedspread, her mouth opening and closing as if trying to speak. It was my belief that she probably wanted to refuse hospital treatment, but I agreed wholeheartedly with the doctor's assessment. Matilda needed to be in hospital, and the sooner she got there, the better.

"I will be back in a minute or two, Matilda," I told her gently, "I'll just see the doctor out and then I'll be straight back."

When we reached the hall, the doctor turned to me and asked if he could use the phone. I showed him into the library, and while he was dialling the number he needed he asked if I was a relative to Matilda.

"Yes, I am, quite a distant relative, but the only one that she has, apart from her sister, who is also very elderly."

"Okay, perhaps you could pack a bag for her, the ambulance won't be long."

He made his telephone call while I waited in the hall. As I walked him to the front door I asked him how long he thought Matilda would be in hospital.

"That will depend on how well she responds to treatment. I anticipate at least a couple of weeks, but it could be several."

I nodded my head, feeling increasingly concerned.

"She is an extremely old woman," the doctor smiled kindly, "you need to prepare yourself for the fact that she might not come through this. She is dangerously ill, and her age and frailty make it even worse, but, having said that, I have seen other very old patients do very well, and go on to live another year or two."

As soon as I had closed the door behind the doctor, I went to find Beth. She was in the smaller front lounge, with Kitty. I stood at the threshold of the room and beckoned her over. She left Kitty standing at the window, and followed me back into the hall, closing the door behind her.

"It's pneumonia," I felt flustered and upset, but tried not to let it show. "The doctor's having her admitted to hospital for intravenous antibiotics and fluids. He thinks she'll be there for a few weeks at least."

"Poor Matilda," Beth whispered, "she's not going to like that one bit."

"No, she really isn't, but hospital is the best place for her while she's so sick. Would you mind going to her room and packing a bag for her? She will need nightdresses, dressing gown and slippers, toiletries and underwear. I want to explain everything to Kitty before the ambulance arrives."

Beth turned immediately and ran up the stairs, while I hesitated at the door of the front sitting room, hoping that Kitty would be able to cope with the news that her sister was being taken to hospital.

Kitty left the window as I entered the room, wringing her hands, the expression in her eyes one of fear and dread. I sat down on the sofa and she came and sat beside me, sitting down stiffly as if she was bracing herself for bad news.

"Kitty," I began carefully, "Matilda is very sick, and the doctor has said that she needs to go to the hospital for a while so that they can give her some medicine that we hope will make her better."

"Is it the Influenza?"

"No, not exactly, she has got an illness called pneumonia, and like I said, she needs special medicine to make her better, medicine that she can only be given in hospital."

"She will get better though?"

The easiest thing would have been to lie to her, to assure her that Matilda would be fully cured and would return to Meadowside, but how would I then explain it to her if this wasn't the case and Matilda died.

"We are all hoping and praying that the medicine will work, but I have to be completely honest with you Kitty, it might not work, and there is a possibility that Matilda might die."

She seemed to slump in the seat next to me, her shoulders sagging and her chin almost resting on her chest.

"We need to think positively, and to trust that Matilda will recover." I patted her hand reassuringly, at the same time trying to reassure myself that the words I had spoken would turn out to be the truth. "In a short while an ambulance is going to come and take Matilda to the hospital, and then later, when she's had time to settle in, we can go and see her."

Beth came into the room. "The ambulance is just down the track; it will be here in a few minutes. Matilda's bag is packed, I've put it by the front door."

I stood up and walked over to where she stood in the doorway. "Can you stay with Kitty?"

"Of course, how did she take the news? Was she okay?"

I shrugged, "who can tell, but she did understand what was happening."

I ran up the stairs to Matilda's room, letting her know that the ambulance was almost here. She opened her eyes and slowly turned her head towards me.

"Don't worry, Amber," she whispered, her voice was so weak and frail that I had to put my ear near her lips to be able to hear her. "I have no intention of dying yet, not until I have told you the rest of my story."

"Don't worry about that now, Matilda, just concentrate on getting yourself better and coming home to Meadowside as soon as possible."

Three firm knocks sounded on the front door.

"That will be the ambulance," I said, on one hand relieved that they were there, but on the other hand, feeling concerned and worried about how Matilda would cope being away from Kitty and Meadowside. "I will come and visit you this afternoon," I spoke quickly, hearing the voices of the male paramedics drifting up the stairs. "Don't worry about Kitty, she'll be fine, and I'll bring her with me when I visit you this afternoon."

The ambulance left quickly. Kitty stood tearfully in the hall, watching as Matilda was stretchered out of the house, and it struck me that this was very likely to be the only time in her entire life that Kitty had been separated from her sister.

"Everything will be okay, Kitty. We will see Matilda this afternoon, and we'll visit her every day until she is back at home."

While Beth took Kitty into the kitchen, I went to the library to update Nathaniel.

"How are things?" He asked cautiously, his voice sounding strained.

"She's been taken to hospital," I informed him. "The doctor thinks that she has pneumonia. I know that I haven't been here for long, Nathaniel, but I can't stand the thought of anything happening to her." I wiped away a tear that was trickling down my cheek. "As you know, Matilda has been telling me the story of her life, and I think that is why I feel that I have known her and Kitty for far longer than I have."

"If it's any comfort to you, I feel exactly the same. Matilda being ill has completely knocked me off my feet today."

"Kitty hardly knows what to do with herself, but I am taking her with me to the hospital this afternoon, hopefully it will put her mind at rest knowing exactly where Matilda is."

"Did you know that Kitty has never been in a car before?"

"What? That's crazy, surely that can't be right."

"Well, that's what she told me," Nathaniel chuckled, "she said that she had seen Beth come and go in a car, and of course, me, but that she'd never actually been in one. I did offer her a spin around the block, but she declined. Mad, isn't it? It makes sense though, the pair of them have barely left the house since they were young."

In the end I gave Kitty the choice whether to come with me to visit Matilda, explaining that it would involve a car journey of about thirty minutes duration.

"I want to see Tilly."

"Have you really never been in a car before, Kitty?"

"No," she replied simply, "Tilly and I have never been anywhere that required us to travel in a car, we have only ever stayed close to Meadowside."

"Well then," I shook my head incredulously, "this is going to be quite an experience for you.

As it turned out, apart from being a little bit apprehensive to begin with, Kitty coped remarkably well with the car journey, and was actually enjoying it by the time we arrived at the hospital. Walking across the carpark towards the large, anonymous building, I was grateful that Nathaniel had brought my car back during his last visit to Meadowside and commented to Kitty that we would have been in a bit of a fix without it.

Kitty was mesmerised by what she saw around her. The hospital was situated on the outskirts of a market town, and she had appeared completely overwhelmed by the number of cars that were on the roads.

"Nobody in the village had a car when we were children," she said, "and then I think the doctor had the first one, but it looked nothing like these cars here."

"While you and Matilda have stayed in Meadowside for all of these years, the world around you has changed, and has progressed enormously."

Matilda's ward was on the ground floor, her room situated directly opposite the nurse's station.

"That isn't Tilly," Kitty stated as soon as we set foot in the room.

"It is her," I walked to the bedside, thinking how tiny Matilda looked in the bed, so fragile and pale. "It's all the tubes and machines. You aren't used to seeing her like this, but you don't need to be frightened about all the equipment; the tube in her arm is giving her the medicine she needs, and the tubes in her nose are giving her oxygen and helping her to breathe."

Matilda stirred as I took hold of her hand, her eyes fluttering open.

"How are you feeling?" I asked. She didn't reply and seemed to be struggling to stay awake. "We won't stay for long; we don't want to tire you."

I placed her hand back on top of the snowy white sheet and turned to Kitty.

"I'm just going to pop outside for a minute to speak to a nurse. You stay here and don't touch anything."

The nurse at the nurse's station looked up as I approached her. "How's she doing?" I asked quietly, "I'm a relative of Matilda's, in fact I live with her. Is she going to be okay?"

"It's early days," the nurse smiled, "but her observations are certainly better than they were when she arrived, so that is a good sign. All I can really tell you is that, at the moment, she is doing as well as can be expected for a woman of her age and seems to be responding to treatment."

"You will phone me if anything happens, won't you? You have my contact details?"

The nurse looked down at a file on the desk. "Miss Lewis?" I nodded my head.

"Then yes, we have your contact details and will phone you if we need to."

Matilda had fallen back to sleep when I returned to the room, with Kitty anxiously standing over her. "I don't think there's much point in us staying any longer, Kitty, Matilda needs to rest, and we need to get something to eat."

It was almost seven o'clock and I was starving, and in the end we had dinner in the hospital canteen. Kitty enjoyed her fish and chips; she had never eaten chips before and was very taken with them. The more time that I spent with Kitty, the more I was reminded of what a terribly small life she had lived. Sometimes it was like trying to explain life on Earth to an alien who had only just arrived in the world.

*

The house was cold and dark when we arrived back, and I wished that I had thought to leave the hall light on. I put my keys on the bureau, removed my coat and then helped Kitty to take hers off. I hung both coats on the coat stand, turned to pick up my keys and put them in my handbag only to find that they were not where I had left them just two minutes before. There was no point in asking Kitty, I would have seen her if she had moved them. In fact, I didn't even mention it to her. The annoying and inconvenient movement of objects had become a regular occurrence that I almost expected as part and parcel of living in the house. The keys would turn up eventually, they always did.

I felt uneasy as we walked into the small, front lounge. I quickly turned on the lamps, pulled the curtains and lit the fire, all the while having the weirdest feeling of being watched, a sensation that caused the hairs to prickle on my arms.

I sat in one of the deep armchairs, thinking to myself that I would ask Nathaniel to get a television for that room. The house was far too quiet, and a television would be a welcome distraction, and would be good for Kitty. Matilda seemed to really enjoy the peace and quiet of the larger sitting room, so it wouldn't be fair to put a television in there, but it shouldn't disturb her in the small room at the front of the house.

Kitty had been to the children's room to retrieve the ball of wool that she was eternally fiddling with. As I watched her patiently turning the wool over and over in her hands, I wished that I knew the name of the condition that affected her, what it was that made her the way she was. A modern diagnosis would certainly be helpful, but unfortunately, would come far too late to be of any benefit to Kitty.

"I haven't got my glasses," she sighed, laying the wool to one side. "I need them if I am ever to find the end of that ball of wool."

"Do you know where they are? I don't think I saw you wearing them at the hospital."

"I think I left them in my room," she moved as if intending to stand up.

"You stay there, Kitty. I'll get them for you."

I jogged up the stairs and was halfway to the landing when something sharp and hard suddenly flew out of the darkness, hitting me square in the chest, to be shortly followed by a tinkling, clattering sound as whatever it was hit the hall tiles.

I stopped dead, staring up into the darkness, thinking that I could see it moving, heaving and swirling, as if something was there, something darker even than the shadows that surrounded it.

I rubbed the spot of my chest where the object had hit, already it was sore, for even though whatever had hit me had been small, it had struck with some speed and force. Objects did not fly out of nowhere of their own accord: it defied all the laws of nature. There was no explanation other than the object having been thrown, deliberately towards me. A cold sweat broke out on my skin as I became convinced that there was something hugely threatening, standing at the top of the stairs, hidden by the shadows but still almost, but not quite, visible.

As I stood there, trembling, stunned and too scared to move, I had the feeling that I was being challenged, mocked even, as if the foreboding presence was amused at my discomfort and was interested to see what I would do, how I would react. The air around me hummed with expectation. Would I run away? Or would I fight?

I took several deep, calming breaths, gathering my wits together, instinctively knowing that I had to, no matter what, keep my composure, and to be stronger and more courageous than I had ever needed to be before, and to keep walking up the stairs regardless.

I walked slowly and stiffly towards the landing, still seeing the half invisible shadow clinging to the wall. When I reached the top, my hand swept across the wall trying to locate the light switch. When I found it, I fumbled to turn it on, and eventually, for no more than a few seconds, the landing was illuminated, and I saw something, for one terrified beat of my heart. It was a face, luminously pale. It was a young woman with dark, furious eyes, long dark hair, with an expression so full of malice that I could feel her rage hit me like a physical force. The light flickered and extinguished almost as soon as I had switched it on, but I had seen her, and she didn't like the fact one little bit. She didn't want to be seen, to be exposed. She liked the darkness for the advantage it gave her.

Again, I switched on the light, and this time it stayed on. The landing was empty, there was nothing there, no spectral figure with hostile eyes, no moving shadows. I walked quickly to Kitty's room, sitting down heavily on the edge of the bed, my heart continuing to thump in my chest, my bloodstream flooded with adrenaline.

"What the hell...?" I clasped my hands tightly together trying to stop them from trembling. I felt confused, my brain trying to make sense of something that seemed inexplicable. What had I seen? If it was what I thought it was, then how?

My time at Meadowside, up until that point, had been plagued by strangeness. Objects disappearing, disembodied footsteps, dark, moving shadows that bled against the walls, and now objects being thrown from out of nowhere. Matilda had strongly intimated that Meadowside was haunted, she had said that she knew the identity of the ghost, but a large part of me, still searched frantically for more logical explanations, and I hadn't fully believed her.

I felt deflated sitting there on the side of Kitty's bed, but was also thinking about how, in the end, the explanation that seemed the most unlikely, the most ludicrous, was the only one that made any sense at all. The house was definitely haunted, but why, and by whom?

I found Kitty's glasses on the windowsill, where she had probably left them earlier in the day when she had been standing at the window, so patiently and determinedly watching over the meadow, waiting. I had never taken this repetitive behaviour seriously until that moment. Matilda had said that Kitty was waiting for Issy to return to the house. I had just seen a ghost on the landing, and was slowly assimilating the fact, that if I could see a ghost, then why couldn't Kitty?

I picked up the glasses and braced myself to step out onto the landing. The long corridor that led to the back of the house was empty, unnervingly silent, but a chilling atmosphere lingered in the air.

With Kitty's glasses in my hand, I ran down the stairs. I switched on the light in the hall and searched the tiled floor for the object that had been thrown at me. It had skidded some distance away and was lying on the other side of the room, close to the wall. I picked it up, examining it closely. It was an old penny, the engravings on it smooth and eroded by time, but I could quite clearly see the date, 1913.

I dropped the coin into the pocket of my jeans and entered the sitting room.

"Here are your glasses, Kitty." I handed them to her and sat down.

"Thank you, Amber," she put the glasses on, they were very old, didn't suit her, and would not have been the right prescription, possibly they had once belonged to another member of the family. I made a mental note to make her an appointment to have her eyes properly tested.

"Kitty," I began carefully, desperate to ask my question in a manner that would not cause her any distress or alarm. "Do you remember your sister, Martha?"

"Oh yes," she replied with a grimace, "I remember her very well indeed. She was horrible to us younger children, she called me an imbecile, but she hated Seraphina the most."

I shuffled myself forwards in my seat, leaning my elbows on my knees.

"Is Martha the reason you won't go to the end of the landing corridor?"

"Martha has been dead for a very long time, Amber, a very long time indeed."

"Yes," I sighed with frustration, "yes, I understand that. Did Matilda ever tell you why you weren't to go to the end of the corridor, or why she locked all the doors down there?"

"She said that I wasn't to go down there so that I didn't upset her, and if I didn't upset her, then she would leave me alone."

"She?" I repeated, an icy chill trickling down my spine. "So, Matilda was talking about an actual person? Kitty, can you think of anybody else, apart from Martha, who Matilda could have been talking about?"

"She's not here because of me, that's what Tilly said. She said that I wasn't to worry about it because none of it was my fault. If I stay away from her, then she'll stay away from me."

"We're talking about Martha, aren't we Kitty?"

She nodded her head, her expression worried and tense.

I leaned back in my chair, feeling suddenly exhausted. "Have you ever seen Martha in the house since she died, Kitty?"

"No, but I've heard her sometimes. She doesn't bother us, and we don't bother her. That's the way it's always been, Amber."

I covered my face with my hands, not wanted Kitty to see the fear and shock in my eyes. What on Earth was I going to do? Matilda had told Kitty that Martha was not there because of her, which must mean that she had stayed in the house after her death, because of Matilda. The only hope that I had to cling on to was that Matilda was able to keep her promise to me, that she wouldn't die until she had to told me the rest of the story of the past, of Meadowside, of herself and the woman who had once been her sister.

\*

Yet again, I slept fitfully that night, and for every other night over the following weeks and months. I was frightened, uneasy and very aware that I needed to proceed with the utmost caution. I had no knowledge of the paranormal, which wasn't surprising considering I had never believed in its existence before coming to Meadowside. How quickly and entirely a person's thinking could be changed by their own lived experience.

For a while I seriously contemplated moving myself and Kitty out of the house into rented accommodation. I would have been able to do that, and it would been by far the easiest and safest option, but ultimately, I decided that nothing would be resolved by me running away, and anyway, it would have caused great distress and confusion for Kitty.

I had been so delighted and overjoyed to learn that I was going to be made the heir of Meadowside, and to be honest, I would not have been happy to give it all up, and to break the promise I made to Matilda.

I thought things through very carefully. At that moment Matilda was safe in the hospital, as far as the situation at Meadowside was concerned at least. Kitty, I believed, was also safe, because as far as I was able to ascertain, the ghost had never harmed her, or even troubled her to any great extent. She stayed away from the far end of the landing because Matilda had instructed her to, rather than due to anything she had experienced herself.

Matilda had spoken about the spiritual activity in the house having been sporadic and intermittent, sometimes not being experienced for years at a time. I wondered what had caused this spike in activity. Was it because I had come to the house and upset the status quo, or was it because Matilda had, hopefully temporarily, left it?

The following morning, I searched the house from top to bottom for my car keys that had vanished the evening before, and the longer that I searched fruitlessly the more frustrated and angrier I became. It was imperative that I found them quickly, I needed them so I could visit Matilda in the hospital later that day, or in case of any other emergency situation that could arise while living alone with a woman in her nineties.

In the kitchen I searched through the dresser drawers and inside all the cupboards.

"Have you lost something, Amber?"

I turned to see Kitty standing in the doorway, still wearing her nightdress and slippers, a thick shawl wrapped around her shoulders.

"My car keys went missing when we returned from the hospital last night." I tried to keep the anger and frustration that I was feeling out of my voice.

"Tilly's belongings are always vanishing too. Once she went to put her outside shoes on and the shoelaces were missing, we searched everywhere for them, and then months later we found them in a tangle on the hall floor, as if they'd always been there, but of course, they hadn't."

"It all seems so childish," I threw my hands in the air with exasperation. "I mean, what is the point in hiding things, what does she gain by doing it?"

"Tilly says it's to remind us that she's still here. She says that she was always an awkward baggage, so why would she be any different now. The belongings always turn up in the end, Amber."

Kitty went to the sink and filled up the kettle, she then took the teapot down from the shelf. "Is this them?" She said, bringing the teapot over to me.

I peered into the teapot and sighed, "yes, that's them. How on Earth did they get in there?"

"It wasn't me," Kitty said quickly. I smiled and reassured her that I knew that it wasn't she who had taken my keys, wondering how often she had been blamed for the mischievous deeds of her long dead sister.

After we had eaten breakfast Kitty became upset by the fact that Matilda was not there. As soon as I had finished tidying up the kitchen I went to phone the hospital to help put Kitty's mind at rest.

"She's had a comfortable night," I said, walking back into the kitchen. "The nurse said that she slept well and is a little bit better than she was yesterday. Visiting hours start at two o'clock, so we can go and see her then."

As soon as I had finished speaking the phone rang.

"That will be Nathaniel," I commented, heading towards the door. "He'll be phoning to see if there's any news about Matilda."

"How's Matilda?" He asked as soon as I answered the call.

"There's no real change. I just spoke to the hospital. The nurse said she had a comfortable night and is doing as well as can be expected, but there's no notable change in her condition yet."

"Is Kitty okay? It must be strange for her not having Matilda there. I don't think they've ever been separated in their entire lives."

"She's alright, missing Matilda, of course, but she seems to be coping quite well."

"And how are you coping?"

"I am worried about Matilda," I said, wishing that Matilda and her health were the only things I had to worry about. I was in two minds about telling him what I had experienced the night before. He would probably think that I was losing the plot. I had already intimated to him that there was something strange about the house and thought that perhaps I could test the waters a little bit further.

"Meadowside is quite a house," I began cautiously. "Last night my car keys went missing, completely vanished into mid-air, and this morning Kitty found them in the teapot of all places."

"Do you think that Kitty might have…"

"It wasn't Kitty," I interjected sharply, "it couldn't have been her, there's no way that I wouldn't have seen her taking them."

"So, what do you think then?"

I sighed, reminded of what a totally ridiculous situation I was living with. "Last night I was walking up the stairs when suddenly something flew out of the darkness and hit me in the chest. It was an old coin. How could that have happened? Kitty was in the front sitting room, and there were only the two of us in the house."

There was a long silence and then Nathaniel said, "do you think that Meadowside has a poltergeist?"

I was struck dumb with surprise for a few moments. "What do you know about poltergeists?" I asked, wondering if he was being serious, or teasing me.

"I don't know anything about them, just that they are a type of paranormal phenomenon that likes to move things around."

"I have no idea," I admitted dejectedly, "but I do know that there is something very weird going on around here." I laughed awkwardly, feeling the need to backtrack in case Nathaniel was given the impression that I was a fantasist, or at best a person who would allow their imagination to get the better of them. "Maybe there is something about Meadowside that is bringing out the fanciful part of me, or perhaps Matilda's story has got inside my head. I really don't know."

"Well, the only thing I can tell you is that I have been to Meadowside on numerous occasions and haven't experienced anything out of the ordinary."

After I put the phone down, I sat at the desk in the library for a while. I hadn't expected Nathaniel to believe me. At least he hadn't laughed at me, but still it was difficult to know what he really thought. The impression he had given me was that he thought it was probably all my imagination, based on the fact that he hadn't experienced anything at the house himself. On face value it was an arrogant way of looking at it, but I didn't feel angry with him, knowing that there would have been a time, not very long ago, where I would have struggled believing my story if it was being told to me by someone else.

# Chapter 10

The following few weeks were busy. Matilda's downstairs bedroom was now complete and would be ready for her to use when she came out of hospital. Kitty and I visited her every day, usually leaving the house straight after lunch and returning late in the afternoon, but sometimes we visited in the early evening instead. The progress that was taking place in Matilda's condition was painfully slow, but she could now sit out in her chair and the nurses had informed me that her appetite was growing, and she had started to take short walks in the corridor.

The house had been quiet, with just the occasional creaking of the floorboards, but still I could not shake off the feeling that I was being watched, monitored even, by something that stayed just out of sight, brushing the edges of my consciousness every now and again, patiently waiting in the shadows.

Due to the absence of any inexplicable activity in the house, I began to relax a little. I settled into Meadowside and began to feel comfortable in the house, to think of it as home and to feel as if I belonged there. Even though the occasional strange event did still occur, a book that I was reading would disappear, and would then return itself to the exact place that I had left it a few hours later, or I would catch sight of a fleeting dark shadow in my peripheral vision, I was quick to dismiss them as nothing of great importance, not understanding at the time that this period of relative tranquillity could not be trusted, and was, in fact, the lull before the storm.

The time passed smoothly, and soon the winter melted away into a glorious spring. My days had fallen into a solid routine. I would usually join Kitty on her morning walk, visiting the woods to see the blooming of the bluebells, or sitting on the bench in the meadow watching as the grass became a richer green and the buds of the flowers getting ready to burst into colour.

All around Meadowside the landscape was changing. The sky became an airy blue, and the trees in the woods began to blossom. In early May the weather suddenly took a turn for the better, the days becoming longer with unseasonably warm sunshine and just a gentle breeze.

"The doctors are so pleased with Matilda's progress that they are thinking of letting her come home. In fact, they think she will be well enough to leave by the weekend. Won't that be marvellous, Kitty?"

We had left the house soon after breakfast for our customary walk. We had strolled as far as the woods and were now heading back to the house across the meadow.

"It will be wonderful," Kitty agreed, but she appeared surprisingly subdued considering the good news we were discussing. "she's been gone such a long time."

Despite the fact that it was barely nine-thirty in the morning, the sun was already high in the sky, and it was pleasantly warm.

"I expect Matilda will be very happy to be back at Meadowside..." I turned to find that Kitty wasn't walking by my side, but was standing several feet away, completely still on the edge of the mown pathway, as if transfixed.

"Kitty? Is everything alright?"

I walked towards her, and she turned to face me as I approached. Her face was beaming with delight, her pale eyes sparkling with excitement. She turned back to gaze out over the meadow; her eyes fixed on a spot in the distance.

"She has come back," she whispered, her voice laden with emotion. "I told you that she would, didn't I, Amber?"

Frowning I followed her gaze. A flock of starlings were swooping and dancing in the sky, and the shimmering sun had turned the distant fields to a warm golden colour. I could see the long grass swaying, the nodding heads of the flowers, and the swarms of insects that hovered like constantly moving clouds over the meadow. I could not, at first, see what had captured Kitty's attention.

At that moment a pair of squabbling rooks landed on the pathway nearby, only to fly off towards the woods a few seconds later. I returned my attention to the meadow, and then with a shocked gasp, I saw something moving in the middle distance, something vague and indistinct, and yet definitely there.

Squinting into the sun I took several steps forwards, hardly able to believe what I was seeing. It was a young child, a little girl, wearing a white summer dress, a straw hat in her hand, leaping and dancing across the meadow, her movements rapid and effortlessly fluid, her pale, golden hair billowing behind her. There was such unbridled joy in the movements of the child, such a blissful innocence, and for a moment the sight of her made me smile, but then, slowly, a coldness passed over my skin, causing the hairs on my arms to stand on end and a freezing shiver to pass down my spine.

"Kitty?" I uttered, knowing without doubt that this was no ordinary child. The way she moved was odd, and she seemed illuminated from within by an ethereal glow that was neither natural nor ordinary.

"She has come back," she reiterated, as if the sight before us was a regular, perfectly normal thing to see.

I nodded my head silently as I watched the child running among the flowers, slightly out of sync with her surroundings, not as defined as she should be, moving at a brisk pace, but at the same time as if in slow motion.

"Can she see us?" I asked, my words catching in my throat.

"She can sometimes, but not always."

"So," I smiled, wiping a tear from my eye, "this is Issy. You have waited a long time to see her."

"I have always worried that one year she simply wouldn't come, that she would have forgotten about me, but she's been coming every year for a long time. I have grown into an old lady, while Issy has stayed just the same, and in the summertime, she plays in the meadow, just like we used to do when we were children together."

"Kitty," I let out a long breath, blinking the tears from my eyes, "this is such a special thing, an incredible thing. I have never seen anything like this in my entire life. I feel so happy, joyful, I suppose."

"That's how Issy was. She brought happiness wherever she went, and we all loved her so desperately. Tilly used to call her the blessing among us, the most beloved of us all."

"Has Matilda ever seen her?"

"I don't think so, but then I don't think that Tilly has ever tried."

I watched as the little girl ran to the top of the meadow, until she was standing with the house behind her, gazing over the slight incline, as she must have done many, many times in her lifetime. I felt energised by what I was seeing, so affected by this little ghost child and her infectious happiness that I could feel something shift and change within me. No wonder that Kitty was so anxious to see her, she had brought a vitality to the meadow, as well as the long, warm months of summer.

"This is incredible," I whispered, as the little girl tipped her head back, turning her face towards the sun, her arms stretched out to the sky. "She is so beautiful, Kitty. She must have been very special."

The vision of the child stayed in the meadow for several minutes, and then she stepped into the long grass and melted away.

"She'll be back tomorrow," Kitty turned and began to walk back to the house.

I stood in the meadow for a few minutes longer, trying to take in what I had seen. I did not know where the child had vanished to, or where she had come from, but I knew in that moment that my entire life would be changed by what I had seen. My belief that death was the end had been completely altered by the time I had spent at Meadowside up until that point.

The only blight on my euphoria as I slowly strolled back to the house was the realisation that if I could see a ghost child in the meadow, then how could I disregard or try to explain away what I had seen and experienced inside the house. A ghost was a ghost, after all, so how could I believe in one, and try to deny the other?

*

"Are you okay? Since coming back from your walk with Kitty, you've been very quiet." Beth was tidying around the kitchen. She folded a wet tea towel in half and laid it on top of the range to dry.

The cup of coffee she had made for me had gone cold. I wondered how much I could tell her about what was going on in the house, how much she would actually want to know. She came and sat down at the table; her expression worried.

"Have you ever seen anything unusual in the meadow, Beth? You've been coming here for a few years now. Have you ever experienced anything, anything at all, that has spooked you, even a little bit?"

She shook her head, baffled by the question. "What sort of thing do you mean?"

"I saw something in the meadow today, and well it seems that the person that Kitty has been waiting for has actually put in an appearance."

"No, Matilda said that…"

"Never mind what Matilda said," I interrupted, "I have actually seen who Kitty has been waiting for. I saw them with my own two eyes, as clear as day."

Beth looked at me, her eyes wide with surprise. "Who was it?" She asked quietly, as if she only half wanted to know.

"It was a ghost, Beth. It was Issy, Kitty and Matilda's youngest sister, the one that fell out of the tree when she was six or seven years old. It was her."

Beth slumped in her chair as if the wind had been knocked out of her. Her face drained of colour. "You actually saw her?"

"I really did, and it was the most remarkable thing that I have ever witnessed. I still can't quite believe it, but I saw her Beth, and not just a fleeting glance, she was in the meadow running around the flowers for more than ten minutes."

She looked at me for a long time, as if assessing if what I had told her could possibly be the truth. "I always thought that Kitty waiting by the window day after day was just part of her condition, you know, the way that she is. I never, not even for a moment, believed, or even considered, that she could have been waiting for a real person."

"Not exactly a real person though. A ghost."

Beth shook her head, completely at a loss to know what to say. "I have always thought that Meadowside was a strange place," she said eventually, "but I just put it down to the strange and weird things that Kitty says, but recently, well I have noticed odd things happening, things that are difficult to explain."

I sat bolt upright, every muscle in my body suddenly tense. "What sort of things?" I asked quietly.

"Vanishing objects mainly. Only this morning I put a small vase on the table and then went out into the garden to pick some roses for Matilda's room, the white ones that she loves have bloomed early this year. I was only gone for a couple of minutes, and when I came back to the kitchen, the vase had disappeared. I know that I put it right here," she patted the tabletop next to her. "Last week it was a letter addressed to Matilda, it was nothing important, just a circular that I intended to throw away. I put it on the bureau in the hall and when I went back to it, a very short time later, there was no sign of it. On both occasions I had been in the house on my own."

"I've had the same things happen. My car keys vanished and then turned up in the teapot. I have had an old coin thrown at me while I was walking up the stairs."

"Do you think it's the little girl you saw in the meadow?"

I shook my head. "I don't know who it is for certain, but I think it could be Kitty and Matilda's older sister, Martha."

"But why would she still be here after all of these years?"

"I don't know, I only wish that I did. I have seen something on the landing, it was a young woman, wearing dark clothes, and the atmosphere she created was utterly terrifying. I believe that it is because of her that Matilda and Kitty won't go to the end of the landing corridor, and why the doors down there are locked, even the bathroom door. I am almost convinced that it is she that moves and hides things."

"Goodness," Beth gazed at me with worry in her eyes. "It all sounds rather sinister and dangerous. Do you think you should even be here, Amber? I mean, is it safe for you to be here?"

"Kitty and Matilda have been here alone for decades; nothing has happened to either of them. I think that the activity in the house has grown more intense since I arrived, and also, I don't think that Martha is happy that Matilda isn't here."

"You seem pretty convinced that this thing on the landing is Martha, but you could be wrong, Amber, supposing it is something even more disturbing and dangerous?"

"Kitty thinks that it is Martha too, and I think that Matilda must know that it is, and having listened to Matilda's story, I can't see anybody else that it could be. Kitty told me that the ghost wasn't here because of her, it was here because of Matilda, and I am sure that all the answers are contained within the story of the past that Matilda is so determined that I must know."

"So, you're planning on staying here? Surely that can't be a good idea; anything could happen. You could be in very real danger, Amber."

"I will be fine," I insisted stubbornly, "I promised Matilda that I would stay, and I absolutely refuse to be chased out of Meadowside by a ghost."

\*

Two days later Kitty and I returned to the house after visiting Matilda in the hospital for the very last time. The following day she was due to be discharged, after being an inpatient for more than two months. Over the past few weeks Matilda had made solid progress and was now able to walk the full length of the hospital corridor with her wheeled walker and had just about returned to her previous level of mobility. She remained frail but was now able to do all the things that she could before her admission, and that was a far better outcome than I could ever have hoped for.

It was late in the afternoon by the time we returned to the house. Kitty went straight to the front room and switched on the newly acquired television, while I went into the kitchen to make dinner.

When I entered the room the first thing that I saw was a casserole dish covered over with a kitchen towel, with a handwritten note resting on top. *I made you and Kitty a fish pie to save you having to cook when you get home from the hospital. Just bung it in the oven for half an hour. Love Beth.*

I smiled gratefully, followed her instructions and returned to the front room, where Kitty was totally engrossed in a loud and frivolous game show. After we had eaten our dinner, I took our plates out to the kitchen. Kitty had been so absorbed in her television program that we decided to eat our dinner off trays and to stay in the cosy room.

As soon as I walked out into the hall, I noticed that it was freezing cold, far colder than it should have been considering the central heating was on and the two radiators in the hall were both hot. I deposited the trays onto the kitchen table and then ran upstairs to my room, grabbed a jumper from the back of one of the armchairs, put it on and then stepped back out onto the landing.

I closed the door behind me, and once again became aware of the numbing coldness. An arctic breeze brushed over my skin, moving through my hair like icy fingers.

"For goodness sake," I hissed angrily, "not again. Why don't you just leave me alone?"

The air around me was instantly drenched with menace, the darkness pulsating before my eyes. There was something slightly luminous advancing towards me from the end of the corridor. It was moving slowly, deliberately, and the closer it came to me the stronger the feeling of peril became.

I wondered what I should do. I could turn and flee down the

stairs, but I intrinsically knew that I had to stand my ground, for the last thing I wanted was to demonstrate weakness or fear, giving her the impression that she had won, and if she could intimidate me once then she could do whatever the hell she wanted.

Turning quickly, I went back to my room, closing the door behind me. I went to the chest of drawers, finding the camcorder that my mother had given to me at Christmas. It was fully charged and ready to go. Switching it on I walked slowly out of the door and back on to the landing.

"Who are you?" I demanded; my voice tremulous. "What do you want?"

I heard no reply. I inched carefully towards the light switch.

"Are you Martha?" I called out, as I reached out my hand and switched on the light. Immediately it started to flicker on and off, and I could hear a strange fizzing noise coming from the socket, as if something was interfering with the electrical supply. I was convinced that the purpose of the flickering light was to disorientate and terrify, and I was stoically determined that it wouldn't succeed.

As I stared fearfully towards the end of the corridor, my blood turned to ice. Something was flying towards me, a dark shape moving at incredible speed, a white face, it's mouth open as if screaming.

I only had a few seconds to think of what I should do. Should I stand my ground or turn around and run before this wild looking, frightening creature, sent me hurling backwards down the stairs. But there was no time to move, for in the blink of an eye the figure was standing right in front of me. The camcorder fell out of my hands and cluttered to the floor.

"I'm not afraid of you," I managed to utter, but my voice, trembling and quiet, betrayed my false confidence.

The figure that stood before me was tall and slender. Her dark hair was loose, falling to her waist. She was young, possibly in her mid-twenties, appearing fuzzy and indistinct in the constantly flickering light. Her eyes glared into mine, and in the dark, dead stare, I saw infinite rage and hatred.

The woman just stood there, staring at me, her head on one side as if trying to make sense of what she was looking at. Her skin was luminous and startlingly white, her eyes as dark as black holes. She stood completely still, her hair lifting and falling in a bizarre breeze that I could not feel.

The air around me felt rarefied, as if it was a living thing pressing in on me, humming in my head, static with electricity.

"What do you want?" I asked again, "there is nothing you can do to me, for I am supposed to be here, and you are not. You are dead, and I'm quite sure that there is somewhere else you should be."

Her face twisted into a snarl of hatred. I braced myself, expecting her to lunge towards me, and due to the fact that I was standing so close to the stairs, I felt vulnerable. To my surprise and utter relief, she stood there staring at me for a while longer, and then simply turned and walked away, blending into the shadows and darkness until she could no longer be seen.

I heaved a spluttering sigh of relief, picked up the camcorder from the floor and staggered unsteadily towards the bannister. Gripping tightly to the smooth, polished wood, I lowered myself onto the stairs, and gave myself a minute or two to let what had just happened sink in.

Feeling weak and strangely detached, I sat there, trembling but also with a sense of pride in myself, for I really had no idea how I had stayed there or how I had stopped myself screaming hysterically. It had been an intimidating, terrifying experience, but now it was over, I thought that in some way, I had won. She had backed down, slinked off into the shadows as if beaten, demonstrating that perhaps she had reached the height of her powers to frighten and terrorise. She had failed in her attempt to chase me out of the house, and I naively believed that she would now realise that she could never win.

Several minutes later, when I was fully calm and composed, I returned to the front room, to find Kitty exactly where I had left her, her game show now coming to an end.

"Would you like a cup of tea, Kitty? Or a hot chocolate perhaps?"

She turned and smiled brightly at me, "a cup of tea please, and Amber, thank you so much for getting the television for me, I do so love watching it."

"That's okay, Kitty, I'm just really glad that you are enjoying it. I'll go and make us some tea."

I switched on all the lights in the kitchen and as I waited for the kettle to boil, I sat at the table and wondered how Kitty and Matilda had been living in the house for so many years, while all the time that ghost creature was upstairs.

My head ached, throbbing with tension as I considered what I should do. Whoever it was haunting Meadowside couldn't stay, whether or not it was Martha, they would have to leave, but how could I make her if she didn't want to? Now that I knew that ghosts were real, I thought about how I couldn't be the only person affected, and how others got rid of them. Were there procedures to follow, places to go for help? If this was happening to me, then it made sense that it must be happening to other people too.

In all honesty I had surprised myself and felt quietly pleased and a little smug that I had stood my ground and hadn't run away screaming. I didn't know that I possessed such resolve or could be quite so courageous in the face of terror; nevertheless, I was not prepared to live in the same house as a vengeful ghost. She would have to go, and I was ready to do whatever it took.

Ten minutes later I handed Kitty her cup of tea, not knowing then that my bravery had only served to make matters a lot worse than they would have been if I had cowered in a corner or had run away, for now she had the measure of me, and knew if she was going to drive me out of Meadowside, she would have to be even more resourceful and twice as terrifying.

Later, I returned to the kitchen with our empty cups. I was holding the mugs in one hand as I opened the kitchen door with the other. I took one step inside the room, switched on the light and immediately dropped the mugs, which splintered on the flagstones, scattering across the ground.

For several moments I was completely paralysed with shock. I pressed my hand tightly against my lips to silence a horrified shriek. The kitchen had been ransacked, as if a tornado had passed through it. Every single drawer and cupboard door were standing open, items from inside them had been removed and placed in bizarre and precarious positions. Plates were standing on their rims, knives and forks miraculously poised on nearly every surface, and in the middle of the table a pile of china teacups stood, like a twisted sculpture, as if glued together.

Dried food items had been scattered across the floor, tea towels hung from the light fittings, chairs had been turned upside down, glasses had been inserted into each other until they formed a tower on the dresser top, and, most horrifically of all, three sharp carving knives had been driven into one of the dresser doors.

I have no idea how long I stood there, frozen to the spot, my shocked and confused brain trying desperately to make sense of the scene before me. I didn't know what to do or what to think. It was impossible to explain. How could inanimate objects have moved themselves, balanced themselves in such weird and insecure positions, opposing all laws of gravity and reason? How could this have all happened within feet of where Kitty and I had been? How could it have taken place without alerting us at all, for it had been done silently, and even that was miraculous in itself.

Suddenly, from a distance, I could hear Kitty calling me.

"Stay where you are, Kitty," I commanded, and the very instant that my voice broke into the silence, everything around me crashed to the ground in an explosion of sound.

The lights began to turn themselves on and off. The dresser doors began to slam shut, one by one, and the drawers, as if mechanically operated, opened and closed themselves repeatedly, while one of them was flung across the room, hitting the opposite wall, the items inside, pens, old keys, a couple of notepads, flew across the room, the drawer itself splintering into jagged shards of wood.

I lifted my eyes to the ceiling at the sound of a low rumbling noise, gradually growing louder. I could feel the floor vibrating beneath my feet, as if the earth was moving, as if the house could crumble and fall in around me.

The adrenaline flooded my veins, causing my heart to beat hard and painfully in my chest, as terror seeped with freezing deliberation throughout my entire body. The noise was deafening, and the constant flickering of the lights was disorientating.

I heard Kitty screaming, a cold, terrified sound that seemed to focus my energy like a jolt of electricity. I ran out into the hallway. She was standing by the open door of the front sitting room, her face white with fear.

"Kitty," I yelled, trying to make my voice audible above the noise that sounded like a storm was taking place inside the house. I didn't know what to do, or where we could go to be safe, but then a thought prodded my mind. "Go to the children's room, Kitty. Go there now, I will join you in a minute."

I ran to the library, my hands shaking violently as I picked up the phone. My call went straight to answerphone.

"Nathaniel," I shrieked into the mouthpiece. "You must come to Meadowside, as soon as you get this message, please come. Kitty and I are in danger."

I replaced the receiver and returned to the hall. The lights were still flickering, and the noise was unbearable, heavy thuds as if the walls were being attacked with a sledgehammer, slamming doors, and underneath it all a human sounding voice, screaming and wailing like a banshee, or a lunatic set loose. As I quickly made my way to the children's room, I wondered how this could be really happening. I had seen things like this in horror films, but had always believed it was fantasy, coming from the fevered imagination of some inspired storyteller, but there was nothing imaginary or fantastical about this: this was actually happening in my own life, and the noise and destruction were devastatingly real.

Kitty was sitting in one of the armchairs. Her body was rocking back and forth, and she was crying with fear. At that moment I had no words of comfort to give to her.

"What is happening?" She asked, eventually.

I sat down in the chair opposite her. "I think it's Martha, I think that she is doing all of this, and Kitty, I think you know it too."

"Martha," she whispered, her eyes still fearful, "she's never done anything like this before."

"I think it's either because I have come to Meadowside, or because Matilda isn't here, I don't really know, but something seems to have upset her."

"She was always upset," Kitty shook her head, "she was always so angry. Tilly said that she had a cold, cruel heart."

"What did you think of her, Kitty? She was your sister, after all."

She shrugged her thin shoulders. "She used to make me sad."

"And Matilda told you that she wasn't here because of you?"

"Yes," Kitty glanced around the room nervously, as if either Matilda or Martha suddenly jumped out of the shadows to berate her. "She told me that Martha was here because of her, that it had nothing to do with me, and that I needn't be worried about it."

I nodded thoughtfully. It was becoming clear that the story of Meadowside was indeed Matilda's story too.

Gradually the activity in the house began to die down. The lights stopped flickering and the bangs and thuds became less frequent and loud, until they could barely be heard at all. Martha, it seemed, was running out of energy.

"There are no photographs of Martha," I observed, looking around the room at the silver photograph frames placed here and there, "and she isn't in your father's painting either."

"She didn't like being photographed or painted. Tilly said it was because she didn't like herself very much, but it was also because she didn't spend much of her time with us. Father got a camera at the beginning of the war, he was fascinated with it, but Martha hated it and even believed that it could steal people's souls."

"I have seen a couple of photographs with Martha in them, but she was always looking down, or away from the camera, surely somewhere in the house there must be an image of her?"

Kitty stood up and went over to a cabinet, returning with three old photographs.

"Tilly won't have pictures of Martha on display in the house," she said, sitting down and handing them to me. "These are the only clear ones that we have, and you can see by Martha's expression that she is none too pleased."

I gazed down at the photographs that depicted a straight-backed young woman, standing stiffly, her hands clasped in front of her. She was staring belligerently straight into the camera, wearing dark, sombre clothes. Her eyes held a slightly aggressive expression. In two of the images her hair was scraped back off her face, but in one of them it hung down, thick and glossy, past her waist. It was this photograph that convinced me that the woman I had seen on the landing, and the woman in the photo, were one and the same.

"Jack used to say that Martha would have been the prettiest one of us all, if she would only smile now and again and do something different with her hair."

"I can see what Jack meant," I said, "she was certainly very striking, if there was a little more softness in her face, then she would have been very beautiful."

I returned the photographs to the drawer. It was very late, and the house was now eerily silent. "I phoned Nathaniel," I said, resuming my seat. "I had to leave a message, he was out somewhere, but he might come over."

I glanced quickly around the room, and through the open door that led to the lounge. "The kitchen is in a terrible state, Martha has caused havoc in there."

"I don't understand it, Amber. The only thing that she's ever done is hide Tilly's belongings, and sometimes we hear her moving about upstairs, but nothing like this."

"I think it's because I have come to the house, she doesn't like it, and also because Matilda isn't here." I thought that the real reason she had wrecked the kitchen was to show me what she was capable of, but I kept that to myself. "What was she like, Kitty? I mean, what was she really like as a person, she couldn't have been difficult all of the time, there must have been a nice side to her?"

"I don't really know what she was like. I wasn't fond of her, but I was very young when she died. I remember her being cross most of the time. She called me nasty names and didn't have any patience with me at all, and, of course, she absolutely loathed Seraphina."

"She doesn't sound very pleasant," I commented.

"None of us could really understand why she was always so horrible, we younger ones just avoided her, but Tilly used to stand up to her, argue with her, especially when she was being mean to me or Seraphina."

"Do you have any photographs of Seraphina?"

Again, she went to the same drawer and returned with a single photograph.

"This is the only clear one we've got of Seraphina. My father took it a few days before Issy's accident."

I gazed down at the face of a young girl, aged about eleven or twelve. She had long curly hair, and a faraway expression in her eyes.

"You can't see it in that picture because it's not in colour, but she had the most beautiful red hair, and the bluest eyes I have ever seen."

"What happened to her, Kitty?"

"I really don't know, maybe I never did know, or maybe I have just forgotten, the only thing I know for sure about Seraphina is that she died," she shrugged sadly, "like they all did, until there was just Tilly and me here at Meadowside on our own."

Kitty's eyes were glistening with tears, so I sought to change the subject.

"Are you looking forward to Matilda coming home tomorrow?"

"Oh yes, the house has felt so strange without her. I have missed her."

I was looking forward to Matilda coming home too, not least because I was growing weary of the daily drive to the hospital to visit her, but as much as I wanted her home, I was worried about how the activity in the house had escalated, and how it would affect her.

The grandfather clock in the hall stuck midnight. "We need to go to bed," I said, standing up and yawning, deciding that Nathaniel wouldn't be coming over that night, and as he hadn't phoned either, I assumed that he hadn't picked up my message. "I'll sort the kitchen out in the morning, before we collect Matilda from the hospital. Do you think you'll be okay in your own room tonight?"

"I'll be fine," Kitty smiled wanly, "she's never come into my room before."

"That's good," we walked towards the hall, "and you know where I am if you become worried about anything in the night."

Later, I lay in bed, staring up at the ceiling, still not able to fully believe what was happening to me. I wished that I could see a way forward, or a solution that would bring about a conclusion to the whole situation, but I could see none, and was beginning to wonder if I was going to be subjected to Martha's wrath for as long as I stayed at Meadowside.

The night passed slowly but uneventfully, with me dozing off every now and again, but not sleeping for more than a few minutes at a time. I got out of bed early, just as the first rays of the morning sun began to creep beneath the curtains, had a quick shower and got dressed.

Half an hour later I entered the kitchen to face the chaos that had been created the evening before. I could not believe that such mess and devastation could have been produced so quickly and silently. It just seemed impossible.

I stepped carefully over broken glass and crockery, strewn cutlery and saucepan lids, and went to the sink to fill the kettle. While it boiled, I ran back upstairs to get a cardigan to wear over my summer dress, and also picked up the camcorder that I had abandoned on a chair. Returning to the kitchen I made myself a black coffee, and took it, along with the camcorder, to the patio outside, sitting in a wooden chair beside a small, circular table. It was a beautiful morning, and despite the early hour it was already warm. A floating ground mist swirled across the fen in the distance, and on the horizon the sun was rapidly rising, casting a mellow orange hue across the landscape.

I drank my coffee, with the camcorder on the table in front of me. I was feeling conflicted about replaying what I may have captured the previous evening, but ultimately my curiosity got the better of me. I was prepared for the likelihood of not having captured anything at all, and as I braced myself before switching the camera on, I was half hoping that would be the case.

At first the small screen was only filled with darkness, and then I could see a mist developing at the end of the corridor, rising and falling as it moved towards me. The mist, that at first was nothing more than a shapeless, swirling mass, began to take on a human form.

I heard my own voice, tremulous but with a distinct note of frustration and anger within it. "Who are you? What do you want?"

It was then that the lights began to flicker on and off, illuminating the landing for a second at a time. "Are you Martha?" I demanded.

A dark shape was hurtling towards me at phenomenal speed, and it stopped dead in front of me. My hands were violently shaking, causing the recording to be blurred and indistinct, and then the camcorder dropped to the floor and all that could be seen was a section of wall and the edge of the bannister, but the audio continued to be recorded.

"What do you want?" I heard myself asking again, my voice ringing in the silence. I was amazed that I had been able to speak at all, and then, just before she turned away and walked back into the shadows, I heard a voice that wasn't mine, a voice that I was certain I hadn't heard the night before.

"Get...out...of...my...house."

The voice was little more than a growl, a hiss, and the sound of it chilled me to the bone. I quickly turned the camera off, placed it back on the table and then pushed it as far away from me as I could.

The voice was shocking, full of malevolence and fury, but I didn't have time to gather my thoughts, or consider what I was going to do, for as soon as I pushed the camera away from me a frantic banging noise began in the distance. My first thoughts caused my heart to skip a beat, and a shiver to pass over my skin. She had come back. She was coming for me. Then I heard my name being called.

I stood up. The voice belonged to Nathaniel.

"Amber," he stood on the doorstep, breathless and panting, as if he'd run all the way from Cambridge. "I only got your message this morning, I came straight away. Are you alright? Is Kitty alright?"

"We are both fine," I reassured him quickly as he stepped past me and into the hall. "Well, at least Kitty is okay but I'm not so sure about me."

"What's going on? You said you were in danger."

"Come with me." I turned and walked towards the kitchen, Nathaniel closely following.

As soon as we entered the kitchen, he stopped dead. "What the hell has happened here? Was it a break in?"

"It was her," I said beneath my breath, frightened that she could be listening from the shadows, ready to pounce.

"Who? Kitty?"

"Of course not, Kitty," I retorted crossly, wondering how he could think, even for a second, that an old woman in her nineties could have caused such destruction. "It was the ghost. It was Martha."

"Martha?" He appeared confused, frowning as he gazed down at me, as if I was speaking a foreign language.

"Yes, Martha," I confirmed tetchily.

"But" he looked around the kitchen, running his fingers through his hair in disbelief, "Amber, what are you trying to tell me?"

"Meadowside is definitely haunted, and I think that the ghost is Martha, Matilda and Kitty's older sister. I have seen her," I said, folding my arms as if to reinforce the truth in my words. "She is here," I whispered, "and not only that, I have proof."

Nathaniel stared at me for a long time, trying to figure out if I had completely lost my mind or if I could be telling the truth.

"I know you thought there was something in the house, but I

believed it was just Matilda's story getting under your skin, and the things that Kitty comes out with. I didn't for a minute believe that you were truly convinced that the house was haunted."

"I haven't really got much choice but to be convinced. I saw her with my own two eyes, and she did all of this," I waved my arm expansively over the smashed glasses and plates. "Kitty and I were in the front lounge, we didn't hear a single thing, not a thing, Nathaniel. She wants me out of the house, and God alone knows how far she'll go, or what she's capable of to bring about her wish. She's deranged, and she hates me."

"Even if this was all true, why would she hate you? If Matilda and Kitty are her sisters, and you are here to help them, then why would she want you to leave? It doesn't make any sense."

"What do you mean, even if this was all true? What do you think happened here?" My voice had risen with anger, as again, I waved my arm to encompass the entire room, kicking a broken plate across the floor. "Do you think that I did all of this myself?"

Nathaniel was looking at me with an expression of utter bewilderment in his eyes. "I don't know what to think, to be honest." He narrowed his eyes. "You said you had proof?"

"I had a run in with Martha on the landing last night, before she did all of this. I filmed the whole thing on my camcorder. I can show it to you, but it would have been better if you'd just believed me without the proof."

He laughed dismissively. "Would you have believed me if the shoe was on the other foot? Of course, you wouldn't, and if you have proof then I want to see it. I just think that there might be another explanation."

I stared up at him for a moment or two, ready to retaliate, ready to be angry, but deep inside I knew that he was right. I would not have believed him.

"You'd better prepare yourself," I warned, walking towards the back door. "My camera is out the back."

We sat at the little round table, and I handed him the camera.

"Really, Nathaniel, you need to prepare yourself for what you are about to see and hear, and also," I continued with a wry smile, "just to make things clear, I am not an expert of special effects or ventriloquism."

He glanced towards me; his eyes full of scepticism. "I'm certain there will be an explanation for what you saw, one that doesn't involve a woman who's been dead for several decades."

At that moment I was feeling exceedingly glad that I had the foresight to use the camera and was almost looking forward to his reaction when he saw the recording. I watched his face closely as his expression quickly changed from nonchalant amusement to abject horror. The colour drained from his skin and his hands, holding the camera, had begun to tremble.

"Are you okay, Nathaniel?" I leaned forward and touched him lightly on the arm.

He looked up with horror and disbelief on his face. "I have never seen anything like this is my life," he uttered incredulously. "You must leave Meadowside, Amber. You and Kitty need to go somewhere safe."

"What?" I gasped, "I can't do that, that would mean that she's won, chased me out of the house as if I didn't have the right to be here. Anyway, Matilda is coming home this afternoon. It would be impossible to care for her properly in a hotel room, or even a rented house, and she's been so looking forward to seeing Meadowside again. No," I folded my arms stubbornly, my expression determined. "If anyone is going to leave this house, then it will be her, not me, and certainly not Matilda and Kitty."

"You can't be serious, Amber," Nathaniel shook his head, leaning towards me. "You can't live here with that...that creature, threatening you. How can you even think of staying here? You are in danger, anything could happen to you, or Kitty and Matilda. You would never forgive yourself if anything happened to either of them."

"Nothing is going to happen to them, Nathaniel. They have been living with this for more than eighty years and nothing has happened to them."

Nathaniel slumped in his chair, defeated. "You must be terrified though?"

"Of course, I am, but that doesn't mean I should leave, it means that I should stay and fight for Matilda and Kitty's right to live here in peace. Martha thinks that I don't belong here, but she's wrong. Matilda invited me, and all the time that Matilda wants me here, then I will stay."

Nathaniel placed the camcorder back on the table and gazed at me earnestly. "So, Matilda knows that the house is haunted?"

"She knows. She tries to hush Kitty when she refers to anything to do with Issy or Martha."

"Issy? Wasn't that the name of one of the younger children in the family?"

"Yes," I smiled tenderly, "Issy was the youngest daughter. She had an accident and died after falling out of a tree. It is Issy who Kitty stands at the window waiting for all winter long, and it is Issy who is too frightened of Martha to enter the house."

Nathaniel looked at me, disbelief still in his eyes.

"Don't look at me like that," I said sharply, "you saw the footage, you know that I'm telling the truth." I sighed as I leaned back in my chair, deciding that there was no point in telling him half of the story and expecting him to understand. "The other day Kitty and I were in the meadow, and I saw Issy, a beautiful little blonde-haired girl, wearing a summer dress, playing among the flowers. She could have been any little girl, perhaps a child from the village, but there was something so ethereal about her, something strange. One second she was in the middle of the meadow, and in the blink of an eye, she was standing at the top."

I smiled at the memory, and desperate for Nathaniel to fully believe me I quickly continued. "It was one of the most wonderful moments of my entire life. I can't explain it, but it was so beautiful and peaceful. The little girl was shining with happiness, and since the day I arrived at Meadowside I have never seen such a delighted, contented expression on Kitty's face. Her sister had come back, the thing she had been waiting for through so many long, dark months, had finally materialised, and her utter joy was infectious."

A tense silence followed, then Nathaniel sighed. "What are you going to do, Amber? Martha, if it is her, can't stay here."

"I don't know," I replied truthfully, wishing that I had a better answer. "Matilda will be back later today, and I am convinced that the answer to all of this lies in the past that she's telling me about. Even when the ambulance was taking her out of the house the only thing that she wanted me to know was that she wouldn't die until she'd told me everything, and, despite how ill she was, and her great age, I believed her. I knew that Matilda would be returning to Meadowside and that I would learn the entire truth about the past."

"I'll make us some coffee," I said, standing up. "Have you had any breakfast?"

"No, I haven't eaten anything, I came over as soon as I picked up your message. I was out last night, it was a late one, rather too much alcohol consumed, I'm afraid."

"I can make you something to eat?"

He shook his head with a grimace. "Just some coffee, please, I'm still feeling a bit worse for wear."

When I returned to the patio Nathaniel was standing on the edge of the lawn, staring out across the garden. I placed the tray down on the table and went to stand beside him.

"Matilda's story is so vivid, it's almost as if I knew all of her family, and that they are still here, alive and active in my imagination. I can clearly see Issy's birthday party taking place right here in the garden. The family had just about started to recover from Jack's death, were picking up the threads of their lives, and then Issy..." My eyes filled up with tears. "Matilda and Kitty have known such a lot of tragedy, all of their family apart from the two of them, have all gone."

"I suppose that is what happens when you live a long life, you lose people along the way."

I glanced up at him. "Matilda and Kitty have lived here alone for more than eighty years, which means that all of the rest of the family must have died young. I keep imagining them throughout the house, especially when I'm in the children's room."

"The children's room," Nathaniel repeated with a small smile, "every time I hear Kitty or Matilda refer to it as that, it sends a shiver down my spine."

"Matilda tells me her story in there, and last night when Martha kicked off, it was where Kitty and I ran to, somehow I knew that little room was sacred, protected, a place where Martha wouldn't enter. I intrinsically knew that we would be safe there."

"I can't believe that this is happening, and to tell you the truth, Amber, I am not at all sure what I should do about it?"

"You don't have to do anything about it, Nathaniel. I can handle it."

He turned round and resumed his seat at the table. "This is it, isn't it?" He uttered, with a deep, dejected sigh. "I have always thought it was odd that Matilda insisted on paying me a weekly wage to stay in her service. Amber will need you, she said, she will need someone to call on for help. I thought she was referring to the time after her death, in case there were any legal hiccups with the will. I was wrong, for now I think that this is what she was talking about. She knew what you were going to have to go through, what you would be dealing with, and she didn't want you to face it on your own."

"I think you might be right," I said quietly after a short silence. I had thought the very same thing myself. "But honestly, Nathaniel, I will be fine, we will all be fine, you don't need to feel responsible for us."

I poured the coffee from the cafetiere and pushed his cup across the table, towards him.

"I will have this," he nodded towards his coffee cup, "and then I will go home, pack a bag and come back later this afternoon."

"You don't need to do that," I protested quickly, "like I said, we will be okay."

"I feel that I have to, Amber, for several reasons, but the two main ones are that I won't get a wink of sleep or a minute of peace worrying about what could be happening here, and secondly, I seem to have inadvertently promised Matilda that I would be here for you, that I would look after you."

"I do not need looking after," I replied irritably.

"I have nothing better to do," he replied firmly, "I've finished my job now and am at a loose end. My plan is to spend my time trying to figure out what I want out of life and I can do that here as well as anywhere."

"Good for you. Do you think you'll continue in law in some way?"

"I don't know," he shrugged, "I only know that there must be more to life than working morning, noon and night, and getting nowhere."

"It sounds like you've made a good decision."

He glanced at his wristwatch. "What time are you picking Matilda up?"

"Around two o'clock."

"I'll stay until then. I'll help you to clear up the mess in the kitchen and will leave when you go and get Matilda. I should be back by five or six."

"Are you sure that you want to do this, Nathaniel?"

"I'm positive. There are plenty of spare bedrooms?"

I laughed teasingly. "There are several at the end of the landing. Unfortunately, one of them seems to be occupied by Martha, but the others are vacant."

He looked up in alarm. I giggled, "don't worry, you can have my room, and I'll move into Matilda's old room. Kitty uses the ensuite bathroom during the night otherwise you could have had Matilda's room."

We continued to chat for a while, when our conversation was suddenly interrupted by a blood curdling scream.

"Beth," I said, jumping to my feet and moving quickly towards the kitchen door.

"What the hell has happened?" Beth was standing in the doorway between the kitchen and the hall, her hands on either side of her face, her eyes wide with shock. "Have we been burgled?"

"We haven't been burgled, come and sit down." I guided her towards the table, picked up one of the upended chairs and pushed her into it. "It was the ghost. It was Martha."

She looked around her, horrified. "She did all of this? I mean, how? Why?"

"I don't know the how's or the why's, I only know that it was her. She is angry, she doesn't want me here. She went completely berserk."

Beth took several deep breaths, trying to calm herself, but even so she still appeared shocked and astonished by the sight before her.

"Is it safe for you to be here, Amber?" She asked me again. "If she could do this, then what could she do to you, or to Matilda or Kitty? Is Kitty alright?"

"She's fine," I assured her. "She understands that it was Martha who did all of this. I think Kitty is very used to having Martha in her life, in one form or another. She just went to bed as normal and didn't seem frightened to be alone in her room, apparently because Martha has never entered her bedroom."

"Is she still in bed?"

The grandfather clock in the hall struck eight as Beth was speaking.

"She had a very late night."

"Well, let's try and get the majority of this cleared up before she comes downstairs." Beth stood up and began to pick up the larger shards of broken crockery. Nathaniel was at the other end of the kitchen retrieving the tea towels that hung from the light fittings and the tops of the dresser doors. "What's he doing here?" Beth whispered behind her hand.

"I called him last night in a bit of a panic, and now, apparently, he's moving in."

"I see," she smiled knowingly, "well, I'm glad that he's going to be here, this is too much for you to handle on your own. The fact that the house is haunted would have me running for the hills. You must be terrified."

"I am a bit," I confessed, "but strangely not as much as you'd expect. To be honest, I feel angry more than anything. Matilda and

Kitty should be spending their last years in peace, not having to go into battle with their dead sister."

"What are you going to do? How are you going to get rid of her?"

"I have no idea. I suppose I am hoping that she will just go of her own accord when she realises that I am staying put, or that somehow, what I need to do will become obvious."

Beth's expression was sceptical. "Aren't there people who could help, like the church or some other kind of professionals who know what they're doing? Suppose she doesn't leave? Suppose things get worse?"

"Then I will cross that bridge if and when I come to it. In the meantime, my focus must be getting Matilda back home and settled, not least so that she can continue with her story of Meadowside. In her own time Matilda will tell me everything that I need to know."

\*

Kitty and I went to the hospital to collect Matilda, finding her in good spirits, but still very frail. She was now in a wheelchair, for although she could walk to the end of the hospital corridor, the effort of doing so wore her out for hours afterwards. She was weak, but despite her age, remained determined to make a full recovery.

I settled her into the front passenger seat of the car, folding her wheelchair and placing it in the boot. Kitty sat in the back; her cheeks flushed with delight at having her sister back again.

"I bet you can't wait to get home," I said as I manoeuvred out of the parking space. "You've been gone a very long time."

"I have missed Meadowside more than I can say," she said, her voice feeble and quiet. "I have never been away from it before, not once since the day I was born."

"That must have been very hard for you and being away from Kitty."

"It certainly wasn't easy," she sighed, "but at the end of the day I had to do what I had to do to get well enough to come home." She turned her head and gazed out of the window and then said, "I trust that everything has been alright in Meadowside while I've been away?"

I knew what she was asking but hadn't expected to be having this conversation so soon after picking her up.

"Mostly," I said, lowering my voice, "but Matilda, I have to tell you that the ghost, Martha, has become a lot more active and troublesome than she was before."

To my astonishment she smiled enigmatically. "So, you have come up against Martha, have you? How did you know for certain that it was her?"

"It had to be her, nothing else made any sense. Who else could it be?"

She nodded her head slowly.

"I need to know what happened, Matilda, and I need to know it quickly. Martha is becoming very difficult to live with, and it can't continue."

"She has never caused any trouble before, mostly we have just ignored her."

I laughed bitterly. "You wouldn't be able to ignore her now. She completely wrecked the kitchen last night. It seems that she isn't happy that I am living in the house, I think she may have also been disturbed by the fact that you had left it."

"Yes," Matilda closed her eyes, suddenly weary, "both of those things would have disturbed her. She never did like strangers coming to the house. She was always so suspicious of everybody, so it makes sense that she wouldn't tolerate you for long."

"She needs to leave," I said firmly, my hands tightly gripping the steering wheel. "It's not fair on you or Kitty, and to tell you the truth, it's not fair on me either."

"I have always thought that she would leave when I did. When I am dead and gone there will be no reason for Martha to be at Meadowside. She will leave when I do. Perhaps there will be a standoff between us when that day comes, or maybe she will just leave quietly, simply because she will no longer have a reason to stay."

Matilda went straight to bed when we arrived back at the house. The car journey, although no longer than half an hour, had tired her.

She slept soundly for several hours, and then got up to have a light meal of boiled eggs and toast.

"Nathaniel is staying here for a while," I informed her as I remade the bed. "He thinks that he needs to be here because of what's been going on with Martha. I've moved into your old room; I hope you don't mind."

"I don't mind at all," she said, looking around her new bedroom with approval, "in fact, I think it's a very good idea. Having the ghosts of my past haunting you cannot be easy, and if having Nathaniel here helps, then I'm all for it."

"Talking about ghosts," I placed the pillows back on the bed. "I saw Issy in the meadow. I know that you thought it was Issy who Kitty had been waiting for, but did you know she could actually see her in the meadow, every summer?"

"I didn't know," Matilda sighed sorrowfully, "darling Issy, she so loved the meadow and the sunshine. You know what Kitty is like, when she kept talking about Issy as if she were still here, I didn't think anything of it. I have never seen Issy myself, so I assumed that Kitty couldn't either."

"I was with Kitty in the meadow, and I saw her. It was a wonderful experience. Kitty said that you have never seen her because you've never tried."

Matilda laughed softly. "Kitty is probably right; I never have tried. When your life has been full of tragedy and distress, you try to forget about it, not bring it all into the present. I suppose it was the only way I knew to get through the days, pretending that the past had never happened at all."

I continued to tidy up around the room, chattering about how I had bought a television for Kitty and how much she loved it.

"I'm feeling much better now, Amber," Matilda said when I had finished. "Would you take me to the children's room? I felt a thrill of excitement, like a child about to get the next instalment of a bedtime story and knowing that very soon I would know all of Meadowside's secrets."

# Chapter 11

## Meadowside 1917 – 1918

After Issy's accident the house fell into a long period of darkness and grieving. As is the way of life, it continued, the grandfather clock in the hall ticking away the minutes, and hours of the long, sad days, while outside the world turned, just like it always had, as if nothing had happened.

The family, not knowing how to cope, dealt with their grief in different ways. Edward Grey slipped back into the library, drawing the curtains against the intrusive sunlight, locking the door, drinking until his distress was numbed, until he could no longer remember the cause of it, while his wife retired to her darkened bedroom, taking sleeping draughts given to her by the doctor, until she was no longer able to function or to think coherently.

In the rest of the house, Emma tried to put aside her own grief to support the younger members of the family. Kitty was inconsolable, sinking into a mute depression that lasted for weeks on end. Matilda and Seraphina sat silently for hours, reeling with shock, all three of them, in their own ways, trying to come to terms with what had happened.

Martha too appeared distressed, although none of the family had witnessed it, for like her parents, she took herself to her bedroom and was rarely seen, so it was a surprise when she suddenly appeared in the kitchen one day, several weeks following Issy's death, her face set into an expression of grotesque rage.

Matilda and Seraphina were sitting at the table, their hearts heavy, neither of them able to think of a single thing that would bring about respite from their pain. Kitty was sitting in the rocking chair beside the range oven, Issy's old ragdoll on her knee, morosely rocking herself back and forth.

Emma was working at the sink when Martha suddenly stormed into the room, agitated and ready for a fight.

"It was her," Martha strode to the centre of her room, her hands clenched into fists, her entire body moving and jerking as if it could barely contain her anger. She pointed a shaky finger at Seraphina, her eyes febrile and glittering with hatred. "This is all her doing. She was the one who gave the kitten to Issy. If she had never come to this house, Issy would still be alive. She has cursed us, I tell you, and all I can do is wonder which one of us will be next."

"Martha," Emma stepped away from the sink, her voice sounding weary and tired.

"She won't be happy until she has killed every last one of us."

"Stop it Martha, stop it right now!" Emma advanced towards her sister; her face flushed with anger. "You are upsetting the girls. Don't you think they are upset enough as it is?"

Martha braced her shoulders, her chin rising with defiance. "They will be even more upset after that evil little madam has killed another one of us. Why can't you see what she is? Are you all completely blind?"

Matilda stared at Martha in astonishment. She looked strange, her face was pale, and her eyes were unnaturally bright and darting all over the room. Her body was twitching, as if she had no control over it. Martha's behaviour was frightening, and there was something so dark and feral about her, that Matilda found herself wondering if this is what madness looked like in a person.

"Don't be ridiculous, Martha," Emma's voice had risen to a tearful scream. "Seraphina was nowhere near Issy when the accident happened, she was actually with me. Your nasty little mind is just trying to cause trouble, when all of us have had enough, more than enough."

For a moment Martha seemed taken aback by the anger in Emma's voice, but then she smirked and narrowed her eyes. "One day you will see that I was right, Emma. Then we will see who shall have the last laugh." She turned her attention to Seraphina, and in a voice low and dangerous, she hissed, "you might have fooled these imbeciles, but you haven't fooled me. I know what you are, and I know that you have been sent to curse us, but you will not win. I will see to that, even if it's with my dying breath, I will see you suffer for what you have done."

To everyone's relief, Martha turned and marched out of the kitchen, slamming the door behind her.

"Don't listen to her, Seraphina," Matilda was holding Seraphina's hand tightly. "We all know that Issy dying had nothing to do with you. You only gave her the kitten to make her happy, it wasn't your fault."

Seraphina stood up, her chair scraping against the flagstone floor. "I want to be on my own," she said, tearfully, walking to the back door and stepping out into the garden.

"That Martha!" Matilda muttered as soon as Seraphina left the room. "What a terrible thing for her to say, accusing Seraphina of harming Issy. It's just not fair that Martha makes her life a misery."

Emma sighed wearily and sat down at the table. "You know that Martha won't listen to me, and Mother and Father can't deal with her either. She's just got this crazy notion stuck in her head about Seraphina, and she won't listen to reason."

"There's something wrong with her, Emma." Matilda lowered her voice, making sure that her words could not be overheard by Kitty, who still sat morosely in the rocking chair. "Martha has always been vindictive and horrid, but this is something else, Emma, it's as if something has taken her over. She's like.... well, she's like a madwoman."

Emma nodded, worried. "She's grieving too, Tilly and doesn't know how to express it in any other way, I'll have a talk to her after she's calmed down and see if I can make her see how damaging her outbursts are to us all, especially Seraphina."

Several days passed, quietly and without incident. Seraphina, who had been spending much more of her time inside the house with Matilda and Kitty, began to leave the house in the early hours of the morning again, usually riding off over the fen on Merlin, and not returning until after dark.

One evening, a fortnight after Martha had made her accusations against Seraphina, things came to a head. Seraphina was trying to enter the house unobserved and to sneak up the stairs to the girl's bedroom, when halfway up the stairs she suddenly found herself being confronted by Martha again.

"Where have you been until this time of night?" Martha was standing at the top of the stairs, her hands on her hips, a malicious expression on her face.

"Nowhere," Seraphina replied quietly, deciding to continue up the stairs in the hope that Martha would step aside and let her pass.

"Nowhere?" Martha queried sarcastically; her eyes narrowed with suspicion. "You have been out of the house for hours, but have been nowhere?"

"Nowhere important," Seraphina corrected.

"One day I will have you banned from this house." Martha looked down on her. "One day my family will see sense, and you will be banished, and I for one, can't wait to see you scuttling back to where you came from."

"I have every right to be here," Seraphina drew herself up to her full height. "Your brother, Jack, was my father."

"You know as well as I do that is not true. My family may have been taken in by your lies, but not me. Your mother was a gipsy witch, and my brother would not have touched her with a barge pole, let alone father a child with her. I have heard you casting your spells and muttering your heathen nonsense. I've seen you gathering herbs for your poisonous concoctions."

"They were for Merlin," Seraphina protested, "he scratched his leg on a fence post."

"I will have that stinking animal shot when you've gone," Martha snarled, "you should never have been allowed to keep it here in the first place."

Seraphina steadied herself with a deep breath. She knew that Martha was deliberately goading her, trying to get her to do or say something that she could use against her.

"Get out of my way, Martha."

Martha smirked down on her, moving slightly so that her body fully blocked the top of the staircase. Seraphina didn't know what to do but felt that surrendering to Martha's bullying would be a mistake. In the end she decided to call her bluff and continued to walk up the stairs towards her. When she neared the top, she pressed herself against the wall and tried to squeeze past her, but as she neared her the older girl suddenly lunged at her, grabbing hold of a handful of her hair, viciously forcing her head to one side.

Seraphina screamed out in pain and shock, struggling desperately to be free of Martha's grasp, to be as far away from her as she could possibly get. The scream brought Matilda and Kitty running into the hall from the children's room, and seconds later Emma arrived from the kitchen. Martha still had hold of Seraphina, who was struggling and kicking her legs to break free.

Eventually, while the others watched in horrified silence, Seraphina was able to kick Martha sharply on the shin, causing her to shriek in pain and release her grip. As soon as she was free Seraphina ran back down the stairs, stopping halfway to check that Martha wasn't chasing her.

"Stay away from her," Martha screeched, "the girl is deranged and has attacked me for no reason. She will cast a spell over us all, stay away from her."

"Don't be stupid, Martha," Matilda stepped forwards, ignoring Emma's warning glance. "You had hold of her by the hair, all of us saw it, and anyway," she glared belligerently up at her oldest sister, "if you really believed that Seraphina was capable of casting spells and curses, then I am sure you would be more careful around her. Seraphina has never harmed any one of us, but you will keep on with your ridiculous accusations. We are all sick to death of you, and if Seraphina was to curse you, then it would be no more than you deserve."

"What did you say?" Martha hissed, her face draining of colour.

"I have said it before, and I will say it again, the only person in this house who is at risk from Seraphina, is you. I would be very careful what you do and what you say around Seraphina from now on." Matilda felt suddenly emboldened, realising that she had managed to get under her sister's skin, and the feeling was exhilarating. "You need to watch your step, Martha, for one of these days Seraphina may decide to exact her revenge on you."

"Tilly," Emma came to her side, shaking her head, warning her that she had gone too far, had said too much, ultimately making the situation considerably worse.

Martha took a step forwards and then let out a high-pitched scream as she stumbled and fell. Seraphina just managed to get out of her way as she tumbled down the stairs, landing with a sickening thud against the wall at the bottom. It wasn't clear what Martha's intentions had been, but it looked as if she was hellbent on attacking Seraphina again. The four girls stood in shocked silence for a moment, looking at each other in horror, until their father, hearing the commotion, came out of the library.

"What is going on here?" He demanded angrily. "All I ask for is a bit of peace and quiet in my own house."

"It's Martha, Father," Emma stated calmly, "she has fallen down the stairs."

"For goodness' sake!" Edward Grey walked to where his eldest daughter lay on her back, one arm flung out to the side, one of her legs trapped beneath her body at a grotesque angle.

"Is she dead?" Matilda asked emotionlessly.

"No, she is not dead," her father replied grumpily. "Martha," he spoke firmly, his voice still sounding angry. He tapped Martha's cheek sharply, until her eyes began to flicker open.

Martha managed to get herself into a seated position, gritting her teeth against the searing pain in her leg, and the throbbing agony of her head. "It was her," she screamed, pointing towards Seraphina. "She looked at me strangely, muttered something beneath her breath, and the next thing I knew I was flying through the air. She didn't even need to touch me, Father!"

"You are speaking utter nonsense, Martha." Edward glanced towards Emma, "she must be delirious. I suppose we will have to ask the doctor to come, I don't like the look of that leg, and it seems that she may have banged her head as well."

"It wasn't anything to do with me," Seraphina uttered miserably.

Edward turned and smiled at her. "Well, of course it wasn't. It's like I said, she's delirious and doesn't know what she's saying."

"It wasn't you, Seraphina. I saw it happen with my own eyes, she was going to hit you and she fell. She got her stupid foot stuck in the hem of her dress. It's her own fault for continuing to wear the longer style. Maybe she has broken her leg, pity it wasn't her neck and we could all be shot of her."

"Matilda!" Edward Grey admonished, "that is a terrible thing to say. I will not have talk like that in this house. Do you understand?"

Matilda nodded her head miserably, feeling the injustice of being yelled at for speaking the truth, and yet Martha, with all her nastiness and lying got away with saying anything she pleased.

Edward heaved Martha to her feet, and with the help of Emma, managed to get her up the stairs and into her bedroom.

Kitty had been silently sitting on one of the high-backed chairs in the hall throughout the entire drama that had taken place, staring into space with Issy's doll clutched tightly to her chest. Matilda glanced towards her and then turned to Seraphina.

"How are you?" She asked quietly, "we hardly see you at all these days."

"I miss Issy," was the simple reply, "it's hard being in the house when she's not here."

"I know, I miss her dreadfully too. I just can't understand it, Issy was only a little girl, she had barely begun to live. She was so important to us all, we all loved her so much. Why did it have to happen? How can it be that Issy had to die, and yet Martha, who nobody would have missed at all, should live? It doesn't seem fair."

Matilda had been thinking a lot about the injustices in life. She knew that it was wrong to wish someone dead but given the opportunity she would have bargained with God to have Issy returned to them, and Martha taken instead.

"It does you no good to think or say things like that, Tilly," Seraphina said, as if reading her mind. "It just makes you feel bad because you know that wishing Martha dead is very wrong." She sighed as she looked into Matilda's sad eyes. "Do you think it's true that the good die young and become angels, and those that are left to live a long life, suffer in their old age?"

Matilda deliberated on the question for a few moments. "I don't know," she whispered eventually, feeling the tears spring to her eyes again. "It doesn't seem all that fair to the ones left behind who have to live without the good people who have died young."

"It isn't fair," Seraphina readily agreed, "and it doesn't make sense to us now, but maybe one day it will."

"You mean when we are grey haired and ancient, crippled with rheumatism, all because we weren't good enough to die young?"

Seraphina burst out laughing. "You are so funny, Tilly. Of course, some good people need to stay in the world to teach other people how to be kind and thoughtful. Maybe that is what we will do when we are old ladies."

"Maybe you will, but not me." Matilda folded her arms as if her mind was decided. "I'm far too angry, too opinionated to be teaching anyone anything." She glanced to where Kitty sat, staring blankly at the wall in front of her. "I can't even teach her to remember her alphabet or write her name."

At that moment Edward Grey came down the stairs. "A sorry affair," he said, half to himself. "It looks like Martha has broken her ankle, and she has a few other bumps and bruises, but I have no doubt that she will live to see another day."

"More's the pity," Matilda mumbled beneath her breath.

Her father stood at the bottom of the stairs; his hands clasped together behind his back. He glanced first towards Matilda and then to Kitty, sighing loudly when his eyes rested on the younger girl. She had been so altered by Issy's death, as had they all. It had been several weeks and, as far as he was aware, Kitty hadn't spoken a single word since the day of the funeral, existing in a bubble of her own creation, and he knew, that yet again, he was not being the father that she or his other children needed, the man who could withstand tragedy and be strong enough to steer his family through it. On that count he was a failure, and the acknowledgement caused him nothing but shame and anguish.

"Emma is taking care of Martha." He turned towards Seraphina, and said quietly, "can you come to the library please, Seraphina, I would like to talk to you."

Matilda watched as they walked across the hall and into the library, her father shutting the door firmly behind them. After a few minutes she walked over to the door and pressed her ear against it, straining to hear what was being said, but it was no use, all she could hear was the droning of her father's voice, but not a word of what he was saying."

"Come on, Kitty," she held out her hand to her sister, who rose stiffly and reluctantly from her chair. "Let's go and make a start on the dinner. I'm sure that Martha will keep Emma very busy for the foreseeable future, so we will have to do everything that we can to help her."

As they walked to the kitchen, past the library door, Matilda again strained her ears trying to detect the reason why her father wanted to speak privately to Seraphina. It seemed such a strange thing for him to do, and she was worried that Martha may have persuaded their father that Seraphina had, after all, been responsible for her fall.

\*

Seraphina stood awkwardly in front of the huge desk, standing in the exact same spot so often occupied by her father years before.

"Do sit down, my dear." Edward Grey spoke kindly, and then seeing the look of apprehension in her eyes, he added quickly, "you do not need to be worried. I know that you were not the cause of Martha falling down the stairs, and I wouldn't, not even for a second, think that you were capable of such a thing."

Seraphina sat down, while Edward watched her closely. What was she now, twelve, maybe thirteen years of age? He gazed at her gently while she settled herself in the chair, thinking what a beautiful child she was with her flame-coloured hair and vibrant blue eyes. She was a quiet girl, self-contained and thoughtful, her movements fluid and elegant. In personality she was nothing like his son, Jack, but as she had grown older, he had started to see glimpses of him in her physical appearance, which he was certain was not just wishful thinking, especially in her facial expressions, and it gladdened him a great deal. In fact, since the day Seraphina had brought the horse, Merlin, to Meadowside, he had felt inexplicably drawn to her, sometimes deliberately seeking out her company, for something about her quiet, kind demeanour simply made him feel better.

The truth was that Seraphina, as fond of her as he was, also disturbed him to the extent that he often found himself worrying about her. She was such an unusual child, and despite the years she had spent at Meadowside, she remained different and strangely aloof. He had spent many hours trying to understand what it was that made her stand out as so obviously unique. Was it simply the circumstances of her birth, into a way of life that was shrouded in mystery, superstition and folklore, that had shaped and influenced her early years? Or was it, as he was beginning to suspect, that the girl had been born with an innate understanding of the human condition, with knowledge and comprehension of things that most people hadn't even considered, let alone sought to learn?

Sometimes he thought he was being fanciful, seeing something in the girl just because he wished it to be true, but he would see her out in the garden, sitting perfectly still, listening intently to something that nobody else could hear, gazing out over the fen for hours at a time, as if there was something out there holding her attention, something that she could see, that was far beyond the sight of his own eyes. While his younger children sought out the company of each other, Seraphina chose to spend a lot of time on her own, an enigma to the rest of the household, and yet so greatly loved by them all.

Edward Grey had heard plenty of talk about the travelling people that periodically visited the fens. The locals were instinctively wary of them, believing that they had mystical powers, and treating them with a grudging respect, possibly because fear so often was the companion to ignorance.

Overall, the villagers were church going people, bound up in their own superstitions, mainly uneducated and vulnerable to the influence of the vicar. They generally believed what he told them to believe, and the vicar had no conscience over condemning those who were different, or who followed an alternative path.

Up until Seraphina's arrival at the house, Edward Grey had never really given the travellers much thought. They worked hard, he knew that much, and would suddenly disappear, as mysteriously as they had arrived, leaving behind a community enthralled by their much-discussed abilities of foresight and healing, and their use of wildflowers and plants found growing freely in the hedgerows.

He glanced now towards Seraphina, who was sitting in the chair opposite him, her hands resting in her lap, perfectly composed, perfectly still.

"I hear that you have been on the receiving end of my eldest daughter's sharp tongue, and I am sorry to hear it."

"I didn't push her," Seraphina replied levelly, "I was nowhere near her, and even if I was, I wouldn't have pushed her down the stairs."

"Of course," he inclined his head gravely, "although Martha is of the opinion that you didn't need to be anywhere near her to be the cause of her accident."

"That is ridiculous." Seraphina said quietly. "How could I have caused her to fall down the stairs without even touching her?"

He smiled at the indignant tone of her voice. "Witchery and magic," he said with a hint of amusement, "according to Martha."

Seraphina quickly fixed her eyes on his face and seeing the amusement in his eyes, she smiled softly.

"You could try standing up to her," he suggested, "giving back as good as you get."

"I think if I did that, I would antagonise her even more. Martha is a very sad, unhappy person. She is blind to all the good things in life and can only see the bad. That is a very sad way to be, if you think about it. The thing is," Seraphina shuffled herself forwards in the chair until she was able to rest her elbows on the desk. "Martha has also lost her brother and one of her sisters. She is grieving too, but I don't think she quite knows how to do it, and it has made her angry and bitter. She needs somebody to blame for Issy's accident, and for how she feels. She can't blame her family. I'm sure that she loves you all, deep down, so instead she blames me, and for that I feel sorry for her."

"Seraphina," he was shaking his head, "Emma has told me that Martha's abuse of you has sometimes verged on the very cruel and vindictive. The fact that you can sit here and not condemn her, is quite remarkable, and your words have quite taken my breath away. Your insight and maturity are astonishing."

Seraphina looked down. "That is how I see it," she said, feeling awkward and uncomfortable with the praise, especially as she was certain that she didn't deserve it. "What is the point in fighting Martha? It will not change the way she feels about me. She is already in pain, Mr Grey, and to cause her any more would just be as cruel as when she tries to hurt me. In the end, the least said the soonest mended. My grandfather taught me that," she explained, a hint of pride in her voice, "and how trying to understand another human being is far better than condemning them."

Edward Grey was listening to her intently, his eyes misty with the emotion that he often felt in her company.

"My grandfather used to say that no one knows the inner

workings of another person, neither do we know their troubles or their fears, therefore it's best to treat others with kindness, even if they don't treat you the same. He said that all human hearts are as fragile as blown glass and taught me to speak carefully so that I would never be the cause of a shattered heart. I try to do that as much as I can, in honour of him."

"Your grandfather sounds like a remarkable man, Seraphina. Was it he who taught you about the quiet places?"

She shook her head. "No, I found them by myself. I was very young, and alone in a field by the side of the road. My grandparents were both busy setting up camp for the night and I had wandered a fair distance away from them, when I suddenly realised that I wasn't alone anymore. I saw a young woman, with hair like mine, smiling at me. It was my mother, and I knew then, even though I was barely four years old, that I would never be alone again.

"I told my grandmother what I had seen. She cried and said that I had seen my mother, and then she told me about the gift that had been passed down through the women in my family, the gift of sight, to sometimes see those that have died, or things that are yet to happen."

"Remarkable," he said, leaning towards her. "I have, of course, heard of such things, but I never really believed it was possible to see the dead. You have made me think differently, and I thank you for that."

For a moment he lowered his head and seemed to be trying to compose himself. "At this moment in time, Seraphina, I am finding life extremely difficult. I do believe that you are in possession of this incredible gift, but I still feel lost and empty without Jack and Issy, even though I know that wherever they are, they are safe and at peace."

Seraphina smiled sadly. "I know how you feel, for I feel the same. Even though I know that my parents, and now my grandparents, and Issy, are all perfectly happy where they are, it doesn't stop me wishing that they were properly here with me, living life with me. All I can say is that Issy and Jack are still with you, but there is a separation as they are not with you in the ways that they were before, and that is hard."

Edward nodded his head and closed his eyes. "You understand me, Seraphina, and sometimes I think that you're the only one that does. I am a man, a husband, a father, I am supposed to be strong, to be the one who knows how to make everyone else feel better, but the loss of Issy has hit me hard, very hard, and I simply do not know what to do."

"My grandfather used to say, when you don't know what to do then do nothing, let time pass and wounds heal, and one day, you will wake up and you will know exactly what to do, and remember, grief is just love wearing different clothes."

Edward lifted his head and stared at the child who sat before him. Sometimes it was impossible to assimilate that she was still so young for she understood things more completely than any adult he had ever met. "You are very wise, Seraphina, far beyond your years, and for the time being I will take your counsel and just let things be and wait for that time when I know what I need to do to move forwards in life."

\*

Several weeks later, Seraphina was walking back to the house down the fen track. The summer had slowly faded into autumn, bringing the first golden hues to the trees, and the whisper of winter was in the air.

As she neared the house, she could see that it was in darkness, apart from a light in Martha's bedroom. Emma would be there, still taking care of her ungrateful sister after her fall down the stairs, even though she knew, as well as everyone else did, that Martha's leg must surely have healed by now.

As she gazed at the house in the distance, the air around her suddenly grew much colder, a breeze picked up the dust and debris from the fen and it swirled all around her, like a mini tornado. Above her the sky grew dark and ominous, as huge rolling clouds billowed across the wide sky towards her. She shivered with a sense of foreboding.

"What is this?" She whispered into the wind, but her senses wouldn't tell her. She stood still, her hair streaming out behind her, her heart growing heavier and more afraid with each beat.

There was something dark approaching Meadowside. Already she could feel the sadness of it, the desperation and hopelessness. It was coming soon, and was warning her, telling her to leave, for her being there would make everything so much worse.

Seraphina trusted so implicitly in her gifts inherited from her mother and grandmother that she even began to make half-hearted plans to leave Meadowside. Her plans were all well and good while they remained in her head, but the thought of acting on them caused her nothing but distress. How could she ever leave Emma, Kitty and Matilda, or Mr Grey, when she loved them all so much? They were the only family that she had now, and the thought of leaving them was more than she could bear. Anyway, she thought to herself, where would she go? How would she survive?

As the weeks passed by, Seraphina's uneasiness grew. A cold, gnawing worry had settled within her, which she couldn't escape from or ignore.

The weeks turned into months, one year ended and another began. The sense of doom that had plagued Seraphina in 1917 ebbed and waned all through the following year, until she had grown used to its company and had almost ceased to notice it.

Life in the house, although not the same as it had been, had improved a little. Kitty had started to speak again, but still spent many hours gazing out of the windows. The girls spoke often about Issy, laughing at her antics and the funny things that she used to say, and slowly the house adopted a new normal.

Martha continued with her campaign of animosity against Seraphina, continuing to blame her for Issy's death and for the constant, although probably imagined, agony in her leg. She had taken to using a wooden crutch on occasion, and even though her injury had only been a minor fracture of her ankle, she referred to herself as disabled, which effectively excused her from any household tasks.

In the early days of January 1918, Kitty and Matilda had gone out for a walk in the early afternoon. This was a habitual activity for them, for Emma believed that Kitty, especially, needed the exercise and fresh air. Seraphina would often accompany them, and they would walk out onto the fen, towards the wide horizon, wrapped up against the blistering cold. On this particular day Seraphina stayed in the house as she was feeling unwell with a headache.

They walked for an hour and a half.

"The fen goes on forever," Kitty commented, "we could walk for ever and never come to the end of it."

Matilda guffawed. "You are an idiot, Kitty! If we continued to walk in this direction, we would eventually come to the town of Ely. Look," she pointed into the distance, "you can see the cathedral on the horizon. A cathedral is a large church, Kitty. The villagers sometimes go there, the women sell the things they have made in the market, and the men trade livestock and drink in the inns."

Kitty, born in Fenland but not to a farming family, knew nothing of towns and markets, and was not even able to imagine it in her mind's eye. She had never been anywhere, and to her the world consisted of Meadowside, the woods, the meadow and the village, and the fact that further afield other places existed was a concept beyond her comprehension.

They turned back to the house, walking into the icy wind, feeling the freezing sting of sleet on their skin.

Kitty was having a hard time adjusting to being the youngest child in the family. She was now ten years old, a child in a house full of adult, or near adult women. She felt like the odd one out, which caused her to mourn the camaraderie she had once shared with Issy.

They knew there was something wrong as soon as they entered the house. Emma was not in the kitchen, and in the distance, they could hear the mumbling of voices. They walked into the hall. Emma and their father were both there. Martha was halfway up the stairs, leaning on her crutch, a self-satisfied, gloating expression on her face.

At first Matilda didn't see Seraphina, but then her father turned around and there she was, lying on the floor, her face deathly white, perfectly still.

"Seraphina!" She screamed, rushing forwards.

"Stay where you are, Tilly," her father's words were loud and urgent, striking fear inside her. "Do not come any closer. Seraphina is very sick. We need you to go to the village and fetch the doctor. Tell him that Seraphina has collapsed, that she is very hot with a fever, and that we can't wake her. Take Kitty with you and be as quick as you can."

Matilda and Kitty, still wearing their outside clothes, left the house through the front door. Darkness was quickly descending, and even though they were not allowed in the woods after dark, Matilda made the decision to ignore the rule, given the gravity of the situation, and the fact that they would reach the doctor's house far quicker if they took this route.

They ran to the entrance of the woods, breathless, their chests aching from the freezing air and the effort of running. Kitty had a stitch and was leaning, doubled over, against a tree, trying to catch her breath.

"Come on, Kitty," Matilda snapped impatiently, "we need to get to the village as soon as possible."

Kitty straightened up slowly, her eyes dark and frightened. "Is Seraphina going to die too?"

"Of course not," Matilda blustered, "the doctor will make her better."

They walked through the trees at a steady pace, thankful that the doctor's house was close to where the path beyond the woods led into the village.

Matilda knocked on the door of the symmetrical, double fronted house, until the doctor's wife appeared, wearing a crossover apron, bouncing a baby on her hip.

"Tilly? Kitty? What can I do for you?"

"Seraphina is sick," Matilda explained hurriedly, "and my father has sent us to fetch Doctor Phillips."

"He is not here, Tilly. I haven't set eyes on him since yesterday morning. There is a fever in the village, and he is run off his feet attending to the sick and the dying."

"Dying?" Matilda gasped, her heart sinking. "People are dying?"

"Yes, my love, they are. It has gone through the village like a wildfire. Mrs Hampton died this afternoon, and Sally Granger this morning. It is taking the young as well as the old. All I can advise you to do is to try and keep Seraphina cool, give her water, if she'll take it. Who is caring for her?"

"Emma and my father."

"Then you and Kitty, and the rest of the household, must stay away from the sick room, and from Emma and your father. Do you understand?"

Matilda morosely nodded her head, took Kitty by the hand and dejectedly led her back down the garden path. Already Kitty was crying, huge sobs that shuddered though her body.

"Seraphina is going to die," she wailed, "like Jack and Issy, and Mrs Hampton and Sally Granger."

"She is not going to die," Matilda firmly insisted, while silently praying that her words would turn out to be the truth.

Their father came down the stairs as soon as they entered the house.

"What news of the doctor?" He asked hopefully, "when is he coming?"

"There's a fever in the village," Matilda stood close to the front door, while her father hovered at the foot of the stairs. "People have died from it, and the doctor is already out tending to the sick. Mrs Philips hasn't seen him at all since yesterday morning."

"I see," his head sunk to his chest. "Emma is with Seraphina now. I will go to the library and will stay there, and Emma will stay with Seraphina. You must not come near either of us until the fever has passed and it is safe."

His worried gaze fell on Matilda. "Tilly, you will need to keep

Emma well fed, and myself and your mother, just leave the food on trays outside the doors and do not enter any of the rooms until I tell you it is safe."

"What about Martha?" Matilda asked scornfully.

"Martha has gone to her room, and will no doubt stay there until the risk of her catching the fever has diminished. It is down to you, Tilly, to take care of Kitty and prepare food for us all. Do you think you could manage that?"

"Yes, Father," she replied, anger rising in her that, even in an emergency, Martha was going to be no help at all.

"We will look after Merlin too." Kitty said flatly, "Seraphina would want us to."

Edward Grey nodded, walking towards the library, skirting the wall to avoid any contact with his daughters. He then went inside and quietly closed the door behind him.

*

Matilda couldn't remember ever feeling quite so tired, her entire body ached with fatigue. She was worried about Seraphina, who, after three full days of being ill, was still showing no signs of recovery.

On the fourth day Matilda left a breakfast tray on the floor outside of the sick room and then knocked lightly on the door.

"Is she any better yet, Emma?"

"Yes, Tilly," Emma's voice sounded weary, but there was not the tone of fear and worry that had been present before. "She can sit up in the bed this morning and has drunk some water. She is sleeping now, but I think she has turned a corner."

The relief that flooded through Matilda was almost overwhelming.

"Am I going to get anything to eat today?"

Matilda turned to see Martha standing in her bedroom doorway, still dressed in her nightclothes, her dark hair hanging loose, giving her a completely different appearance, softer somehow.

"I'll get around to you when I can, but there is also Mother and Father, and Kitty, of course. You could always make your own breakfast; it wouldn't kill you."

"I would if I could, and anyway, if you're feeding everyone else you can feed me too. My foot is particularly painful today."

"There is nothing wrong with your foot, Martha. It was just a minor break and it healed weeks ago." Matilda had half a mind to kick her sister in the other leg but managed to restrain herself. "You are pretending that you're still in pain so that you don't have to do anything to help, and due to your unwillingness to do the simplest of things for yourself, I have put you on the bottom of my list, and due to the way you have treated Seraphina, think yourself lucky that I don't just let you starve to death."

"That girl has brought a plague on this house." Martha whispered.

Matilda turned and walked away, hearing the slamming of Martha's door, and the sound of something heavy being thrown against the wall in a fit of temper.

When she arrived back in the kitchen, she was surprised to find that Kitty wasn't there. She had been left in charge of stirring the porridge, but much to Matilda's annoyance, she had wandered off leaving it unattended, and now it was no more than a gelatinous mess burned to the bottom of the saucepan.

Matilda removed the saucepan from the stove and then went off in search of Kitty, eventually finding her standing as still as a statue at the window of the front sitting room.

"Kitty!" She yelled angrily as she marched into the room. "The porridge is ruined! Don't you think I have enough to do without you making even more work for me? All you had to do was to stir the porridge, but even that simple task seems to be beyond you."

Kitty turned slowly from the window, her face tearstained and miserable, causing Matilda to feel instantly guilty.

"I'm sorry," Matilda went over to her and placed an arm around her shoulders. "I didn't mean to shout at you, it's just that I'm tired, and there's so much that needs to be done. I don't know how Emma keeps up with it all, day in and day out."

"I'm sad, Tilly. I miss Issy."

"We all miss Issy," Matilda replied softly, knowing that even though they were all still gripped in the vice of grief, it was Kitty who was suffering the most. She smiled, "I have some good news though, Seraphina is feeling better today. Emma said that she was able to sit up in the bed and had drunk some water."

Kitty blinked away her tears and smiled briefly. She then turned back to the window.

"Why don't you come and help me to make some more porridge? You can't stand there by the window all day."

"I can't, Tilly, I need to be here when she comes back."

"Oh, Kitty," Matilda closed her eyes and sighed, "she's not going to come back, not today, or tomorrow, or at any other time. Issy has gone, and she isn't able to come back, and you standing by the window all day is not going to change that."

Matilda saw her sister flinch, but then she straightened her shoulders. "She will come back, Tilly. I know that she will."

Matilda frowned as she wondered what they were going to do with Kitty. She couldn't spend her entire life waiting for something that could never happen. After a few minutes Matilda left the room, feeling far older than her years, and yet again, she found herself longing for the past, when Jack was alive, when Issy was still with them, the days when the house was vibrant with noise and laughter, and her parents were so happy and carefree. The house seemed colder now, and she had to accept that, just like Issy, those days were gone and could never return.

*

The following day Seraphina's condition had drastically improved, and although she was still very weak, Emma decided to allow her to get out of bed and to spend some time with Matilda and Kitty in the children's room.

"I was so worried about you," Matilda fussed, making sure that Seraphina was comfortable on the sofa, with a blanket covering her from her feet right up to her chin. "I was so happy to hear that you were getting better. There's a fever in the village, people have actually died, and when we went to fetch the doctor, he couldn't come because there were so many ill people for him to tend to."

"I knew that I was very ill," Seraphina said feebly, laying back against the cushions that Matilda had arranged for her, "but I knew that I wasn't going to die. I knew that it wasn't my time."

Matilda knelt on the floor beside her. "Did Issy die because it was her time, and not because of the accident?"

"Everybody needs a way to die, Tilly, and nobody is born or dies by accident. That is what I believe."

Seraphina closed her eyes and drifted off to sleep and Matilda went to sit in one of the armchairs close to the fire. Kitty was sitting opposite her, a tangled ball of wool in her lap, turning it over and over in her hands. Emma had given her the wool a few weeks previously, and asked her to untangle it, to give her something to do. It seemed to be a soothing activity for Kitty, and at least while she was focused on the wool, she wasn't standing at the window waiting for an impossible miracle to occur.

Matilda stared into the dying fire. The conversations that she had with Seraphina always make her think, usually about things that she had never thought of before. She thought a lot about life now, inspired by the things that Seraphina sometimes said, and she had begun to ponder on the meaning of it all. People lived and then died, and nobody really understood the purpose behind it, but where Seraphina was happy to believe her own philosophy and to live by it, Matilda wanted proven answers, she wanted to know the truth of life and death, for if Seraphina was right, everyone lived their lives following a preordained path that they didn't even know about, they lived their life and died on the day that had been given to them, without ever learning the reasons why they were ever born at all.

It was later that evening when Emma came to see them to let them know that both of their parents were now ill, with very similar symptoms to Seraphina. She stayed standing in the doorway but did not enter the room.

"I will look after them both in the same room, and we will just have to hope and pray that they are both as lucky as Seraphina has been."

Matilda was alarmed to hear about her parents being sick but was also worried about Emma. "You must let me know if there is anything that I can do to help. You must be exhausted after looking after Seraphina."

"I had a long sleep this afternoon and feel quite revived now. You just continue to do what you've been doing. You're doing a wonderful job, Tilly, and I'm very proud of you and the way you have coped."

"I could help you to look after Mother and Father?"

Emma shook her head firmly. "Kitty and Seraphina need you, Tilly, and the risk of you catching it is far too high. Just keep doing what you were doing before, that is the very best help you could be."

An hour later Seraphina stirred from her sleep. Matilda went straight to her side, pouring her a glass of water from the glass pitcher on the side table, and helped to plump up the cushions behind her to make her more comfortable.

"Mother and Father have now both caught the same illness that you have had," she informed her quietly, glancing over her shoulder to make sure that Kitty was occupied and not listening to their conversation.

"Oh no," Seraphina looked distressed, tears springing to her eyes.

"You said that Issy died because it was her time, and that you survived the illness because it wasn't the time for you?"

Seraphina nodded her head, anticipating the question to come.

"What about my parents, Seraphina? Is it their time, or not?"

Seraphina lowered her eyes. "I don't know," she whispered, "honestly Tilly, I don't know."

"You must know," Matilda insisted.

"I don't, Tilly." Seraphina lifted her eyes to Matilda's face. They were dark with fear, and in that instant, Matilda knew that she was lying.

# Chapter 12

Matilda was growing tired, and even though I was desperate for her to continue, I knew that it would be unwise to push her too much.

"Seraphina survived, but what about your parents?"

"Neither of them made it, they both died the following day, within hours of each other." Matilda looked very pale now, as if all the memories and the telling of such a sad part of her story, had completely exhausted her. "I was worried about my mother, she was so thin and fragile, and I wasn't altogether surprised when the fever took her so quickly, but we all thought that my father would pull through. At the time, though, I don't think any of us were fully aware of the problem that he had with alcohol. I think that it weakened him, either that or, after Issy's death, he just didn't have the will to fight it."

"The fever?" I repeated thoughtfully, "do you think it could have been the Spanish flu? Wasn't there a pandemic around the end of the first world war?"

"Yes, I think that is what it was, but of course, we didn't know that at the time, or that it was spreading like wildfire across the world. All I knew was that an illness had broken out in the village, an indiscriminate illness, both the young and the old died, but the worst thing about it was that it favoured the young. Years later I heard that it was being blamed on the soldiers returning home from the war. What a time it was, what a terrible, tragic time."

We sat in silence for a while. Matilda seemed to have withdrawn into her memories and was staring listlessly ahead of her, as if picturing it all in her head. I was thinking about how sad her story was, but how it was a story running through the history of most families who had lived at that time, before the days of advanced medicine and research, when people were at risk of dying from simple illnesses.

"Despite all that had happened up until that point, it was the following few years that were the worst of my life," Matilda suddenly started speaking again, her voice thick with emotion. "I had been such a carefree child, Amber, cossetted and protected." She laughed bitterly. "Before the deaths of Jack and Issy I don't think that I understood that such things could happen, that healthy young people could die. In my mind it was old people that died, in their beds, their lives complete, peacefully and painlessly in their sleep. Nothing else had really occurred to me, and for some reason, I believed that my family, and Meadowside, were divinely blessed, special in some ridiculous, childish way. I thought that life would always stay the same, that happiness and innocence would be my lifelong companions, but I was wrong, so very wrong."

"I am so sorry, Matilda. I can't imagine what it must have been like for you. As you know, I never really knew my father. I was so young when he died that I haven't got any memories of him at all. I never really grieved for him. I have, however, missed him every day of my life, but it is different: you can't grieve for something that you never really had in the first place."

"Seraphina once said to me that grief was just love wearing different clothes," she smiled suddenly, and it lit up her entire face. "She was always saying things like that. She said that love turns to grief when a person dies, but that, at the end of the day, it is the same thing, and you can't have one without the other."

"Goodness," I said with surprise, "that is a very profound thing for a child to say."

At that moment we heard knocking on the front door.

"That will be Nathaniel," I stood up. "Will you be okay here for a short while?"

"I will be fine, thank you Amber," she said, then closed her eyes as her thoughts and memories drifted, yet again, far back into the past.

*

The house became quiet after Nathaniel moved in, as if it was taking stock of yet another change, another person living within it, but the peace was laced with a menace that only I seemed to be aware of, for nobody else had noticed how oppressive the atmosphere was, seething with anticipation and suspense. I knew that despite the warm summer weather, the fragrant air and the fact that the house was busy and distracted, that Martha was still there, disguised by the shadows, watching and waiting.

It appeared to me that her silence was a deliberate ploy to create a false sense of security, while inside me an unbearable tension was growing. She was playing a game of cat and mouse, and I was ever vigilant while waiting for her next move.

I walked through the meadow most days, sometimes with Kitty, and at other times alone. I often saw Issy running through the flowers and twice I had found a bouquet of flowers laying on the bench, as if placed there for me to find. I would take them home, place them in a vase of water, my brain turning itself inside out trying to understand how something so real could have been gathered by a child who had been dead for so many years.

For three weeks the house remained quiet, and almost normal, and I began to wonder if Martha had gone, if she had realised that her actions to drive me out of Meadowside had failed and she had just given up. It was a comforting thought, but still, in the back of my mind, the nagging unease remained.

On a warm August evening, Nathaniel and I walked into the village. Beth had offered to stay at the house with Matilda and Kitty, it was coming to the end of the school holidays and children were staying with her parents for a few days. Her husband was working late, so she was happy to give me a break for a few hours, suggesting that Nathaniel and I visited the village pub.

We walked through the meadow and the woods. I was thinking how strange it was to be walking the exact same route that Matilda and Kitty had taken to the doctor's house all those years ago, and recently I had realised that an old chestnut tree, close to the entrance to the woods, and on the edge of a large clearing, was probably the very tree that Issy had fallen out of. It was strange how so many things had changed since those long-ago days, and yet so many other things had remained completely unaltered by time.

"This is nice," Nathaniel commented as we emerged from the woods and onto the pathway that led to the village. "It's good for you to get out of the house once in a while."

"It's such a beautiful evening," I smiled up at him, "and you're right, it is good for me to get away from the house as often as I can. I must confess that I sometimes find the atmosphere in Meadowside rather oppressive."

"I think that's just the age of the place, and the fact that it's barely changed since the early 1900's. It could be a spectacular home if it was spruced up a bit, modernised and renovated. Is that what you're planning to do?"

I glanced up at him and shrugged my shoulders. "I suppose that is what I would like to do eventually, but before I can even think about that I need all of this with Martha to be sorted out. She's gone quiet, and it's almost worse than when she was rampaging around the place throwing things at the walls. The anticipation of what she might do next is becoming increasingly difficult for me to live with."

"I haven't seen or heard a single thing," he kicked a stone off the path into the overgrown hedge to the side. "Maybe me being in the house has thrown her off course, or maybe she's just left, she tried her best to get you out, it didn't work, so she's just moved on."

"I don't think she's moved on anywhere, Nathaniel, she's still in the room at the end of the corridor, plotting her next move, realising that it has to be even more frightening and devastating than the kitchen drama to make me leave."

We came to the church with its squat tower and sprawling

graveyard.

"Shall we have a look around?" Nathaniel suggested, "as far as I am aware the entire Grey family are buried here."

I followed him through the creaking, wrought iron gate, wondering why I had never thought to do this before. We walked up and down the curving paths until Nathaniel called me over to a row gravestones a little way off the main pathway.

"Here they are," he beckoned, gazing down at the overgrown graves, the headstones covered with moss and green slime. The inscriptions were visible but difficult to read.

"These two little headstones are for Michael and Clementine," I said, pulling the weeds away to make the engraved words easier to read. "These were the babies that died before Matilda was born. This one is Jack, and here is Issy."

I shuddered as I gazed down on the small, narrow grave, hardly able to take in the fact that the body of the little girl who ran through the meadow and left flowers on the bench, was resting beneath my feet.

I moved along the path a little way and found the grave of Edward and Eleanor Grey, buried together after they died on the same day.

There was another grave, standing next to that of Matilda's parents. I walked slowly towards it, certain that it would belong to Martha, and feeling a great deal of trepidation about going anywhere near it.

When I approached the grave, I bent over to read the inscription and my heart sank. "It's Emma," I uttered sadly, "she died just a few days after her parents." I looked up at Nathaniel with tears springing to my eyes. "Matilda and Kitty must have been heartbroken, they loved her so much. It's unbelievable that one family could be put through such tragedy and grief, how on Earth did Matilda and Kitty ever live through it?"

"Sadly, that was what life was like back then. Medical knowledge and science were still in their infancy and people died of things that could be easily cured just a decade later, especially people who lived in such a rural area as this. It's incredibly sad."

I stepped back on the pathway feeling shocked and completely saddened by Emma's death. It just didn't seem fair that after losing their parents, Matilda and Kitty then went on to lose the only other mother figure that they had, while they had both been so young.

"Where's Martha?" I asked suddenly, my eyes scanning the nearby graves. "Surely she must be here somewhere?"

Nathaniel walked off to look at other graves in the vicinity, after a while returning to where I was standing, admitting defeat.

"She doesn't appear to be here," he said, scratching his head in bemusement, "maybe she didn't die in the village, she could have got married and moved away."

"I doubt it," I laughed, "according to Matilda nobody would want her due to her sour nature and how miserable and moany she was. Do you think she could have been cremated?"

Nathaniel shook his head, "it's very unlikely, cremation wasn't common back then and there definitely weren't crematoriums like we have now."

"So where is she? The other one who also isn't here is Seraphina, now, I could believe that she might have left Meadowside and got married, although Matilda has intimated that she also died young."

I made a promise to myself that as soon as I could, I would go to the churchyard and tidy up the graves and clean the headstones, it was the very least I could do.

Later we sat at a corner table in the pub, situated beside a huge, empty fireplace. Nathaniel went to the bar and returned with a pint of bitter and a large glass of white wine.

"I can't understand why Martha's not in the graveyard," I said as soon as he sat down. The fact that we couldn't find Martha's grave was playing on my mind, making me feel uneasy. If we had found her grave it would have settled things in my head. Martha was dead, I had seen her grave, she was safely buried, and if that had happened then it would have brought some kind of a conclusion to Martha's story. We had thoroughly searched, and Martha definitely was not there, and the fact was making my brain overactive with possible scenarios.

I sipped my wine, and then an horrific thought entered my mind. "You don't think...." I laughed and shook my head. "Don't worry," I back tracked quickly, realising that the idea that had popped into my mind was crazy and extreme, "I'm just being paranoid."

"What?" Nathaniel spread out his hands. "Tell me. The fact that Meadowside has a resident ghost is crazy and extreme in itself, nothing that has popped into your head can be crazier and more extreme than that."

"Well," I began, feeling a shudder pass through me. I looked up at him, my eyes worried and fearful, "you don't think that she could still be in the house?"

He let my words sink in for a few moments. "You mean...?"

I nodded my head, "I mean, do you think there is a possibility that she's never been buried, that her body is still in her room at the end of the corridor? Think about it, Nathaniel, that would explain why Matilda told Kitty never to go down there and why the door has been locked for more than eighty years. It would also explain why Martha has never been able to leave, from what I know of her, she would have expected a proper Christian burial."

Nathaniel seemed to be deep in thought for a minute and then he looked up, shaking his head. "I don't think that Matilda and Kitty would have been able to tolerate the smell, apparently a rotting corpse causes a terrible stench. It would explain the locked doors and the fact that Martha has stayed in the house, but it doesn't explain why Matilda would have done such a thing. There is no reason that I can think of why Matilda wouldn't have given Martha a decent burial."

"You're right," I sighed, "which leaves us with the possibility that Martha left Meadowside sometime after the death of her parents. Martha couldn't abide Seraphina living in the house, and now that we know that Emma also died back in 1918, that would have left just Matilda, Kitty, Seraphina and Martha living in Meadowside. Maybe, Seraphina and Matilda got the better of her. Martha was so frightened of Seraphina, due to her belief that she was some kind of a witch, that maybe Seraphina actually scared her away."

"What I can't understand, what I have never been able to get my head around, is why Matilda and Kitty have lived such isolated lives, with barely any contact with the outside world. It must have been a conscious decision, a deliberate choice that Matilda made, but why?"

"Something drastic must have happened," I stared for a moment out of the window, watching a dog walker strolling past, and a couple of teenage boys kicking a football up the road. "I don't know much about ghosts, but I imagine there must be a reason for them. Something must have caused Martha to be grounded inside the house."

I glanced at Nathaniel as he drank his beer. He seemed much more relaxed than he had been before. His dark hair had grown longer, and his casual clothes suited him much better than the sombre work suits he used to wear.

"Are you any closer to deciding what you are going to do after Matilda and Kitty have gone? Do you think you'll stay at the house?" Nathaniel placed his glass onto a cardboard beer mat and looked at me expectantly.

"I haven't really thought that far ahead, to be honest. In a way, in a big way, I want to stay. I love the house, but all the tragedy that has taken place there and the fact that it's haunted, makes it all so much more difficult." I drained my glass and placed it on the table. "It's also very hard to imagine a time when Matilda and Kitty won't be around. The house is so much about them, their lives, their history, their family. I'm not sure that I will ever feel that Meadowside is truly mine."

"I suppose you just need to give it more time," Nathaniel replied wisely. "I would think that redecorating and putting your own stamp on the place might help."

"It's also a very big house for me on my own. I don't know how I would fill the rooms and make the whole house feel like a home, while rattling around there alone. I think you're right though; time will tell in the end."

We just had one drink in the pub and then slowly walked home. It was a beautiful summer's evening, with the shadows of dusk just beginning to fall. When we reached the meadow, I stopped walking for a couple of minutes. The sky was blazing with a magnificent sunset, as the orange ball of the sun rested on the horizon.

"I can't ever imagine wanting to leave this," I said, watching the dark shadows of the birds flying across the fiery sky. "It's magical, isn't it?"

"It certainly is," Nathaniel agreed as we turned and walked back towards the house.

As we reached the top of the meadow he turned to me. "Are you ever going to open up the rooms at the end of the corridor? Are they just bedrooms?"

"Yes, four bedrooms and the bathroom. One of the rooms used to be the children's bedroom, and then there are Jack's and Emma's rooms, and the one right at the end belonged to Martha. I suppose I will open them up at some point, maybe after Matilda and Kitty have both gone."

"Maybe opening up the rooms would encourage Martha to leave?"

"Perhaps, but it could also make things a lot worse, and that really wouldn't be fair on Kitty and Matilda. I was thinking about those rooms recently in relation to me staying at Meadowside and was wondering if I would ever be able to use them. In a way, the room at the end will always be Martha's, in my mind anyway."

Nathaniel lifted the catch on the gate and swung it open. "The past is over and done with, or at least it should be. I'm assuming that the rooms still contain the belongings of the people who used to occupy them, and maybe that is why the house feels so stuck in the past. Maybe, if we cleared out those rooms, decorated them, it would give the house a completely different feel. What do you think?"

"Matilda wouldn't agree to it, and for the time being, at least, Meadowside is still her house. I also think that it would provoke Martha and I don't want Matilda or Kitty upset or disturbed in any way."

"Couldn't we just have a quick look inside them? There must be keys for them somewhere in the house."

"I know that unlocking the doors is something that I will have to do at some point, Nathaniel, but I don't feel that now is the right time."

We entered the house to find that Matilda had gone to bed. Kitty and Beth were in the front room watching the television.

"Everything alright?" I sat down on the sofa next to Beth.

"Fine," she replied, "Matilda was tired and went to bed early, but I suppose that is to be expected after how ill she has been."

"Anyone fancy a cup of tea?" Nathaniel was standing in the doorway.

"Lovely," Beth and I replied in unison.

As soon as Nathaniel had left for the kitchen, I turned towards Beth. "We went to the graveyard," I whispered. Kitty was engrossed in a comedy drama on the television and didn't seem at all interested in our conversation, but Beth, wanting to know more and for us to be able to speak freely, suggested that we go to the kitchen with Nathaniel.

We sat at the kitchen table while Nathaniel stood waiting for the kettle to boil at the other end of the room.

"We found the graves. Jack, Issy, the parents, they were all there, but Emma was there too, which was a bit of a shock, she died the day after her parents, probably from the same illness."

"How awful," Beth was shaking her head sorrowfully. "Didn't Matilda and Kitty rely on Emma quite a lot when their parents fell to pieces after the deaths of Jack and Issy?"

"She was like a mother to them; they must have been utterly devastated."

"It's hard to believe the amount of tragedy that they have lived through, and all in the space of just a few years." Beth seemed to have been greatly affected by the news that after losing Jack and Issy, the sisters went on to lose their parents and Emma as well. "I don't know how they lived through it, if anything ever happened to one of my children, or anyone else that I was close to, I don't think I would know how to cope."

"It really is heart-breaking what they went through. And the saddest thing of all is that Emma and her parents, could have been saved by modern medicine. Although people still die from the flu today, they are at least given a fighting chance with intensive care and drug therapy. It seems that back in the era of the first world war you could quite easily die from an illness that we don't even worry about today."

I stretched my legs out beneath the table and shifted my weight in the wooden chair. "The strange thing is that we couldn't find the graves of Martha or Seraphina. We think that Seraphina may have left Meadowside, probably she got married and had a family of her own, that would easily explain why she's not buried in the same plot as the rest of them, but I am pretty sure that Martha would never have married or moved away."

"That is very odd," Beth frowned. "Where could she be?"

Nathaniel came to join us, placing the mugs of tea on the table.

"It shouldn't be too hard to find out," he pulled out a chair opposite me and sat down. "I could look up births, deaths and marriages on my computer. I have it all set up in the library, but the internet connection here is rubbish."

I had never educated myself on the use of computers. Technology had never been a part of my school education, although I did learn to type. I made the decision there and them to start learning how to use one, especially as they seemed to be here to stay.

"That would be fantastic, Nathaniel, thank you."

"I think I'll go and do it now, see what I can dig up."

"So," Beth leaned towards me across the table as soon as Nathaniel was out of earshot. "How are you two getting on?"

"Fine," I replied dismissively.

"Amber," Beth grinned mischievously, "surely you have noticed that he has a thing for you?"

"No, he's just trying to help, as a friend," I bristled uncomfortably,

"I don't think there's anything more to it than that."

She leaned back in her chair and folded her arms, a knowing expression on her face.

"Do you like him?"

"Of course," I snapped, "what's not to like?"

"I think he's lovely, a decent, good person, and handsome and successful to boot. You could do a lot worse, Amber."

"Now you're sounding like my mother," I laughed and then quickly moved the conversation on to other things, and we went on to discuss how Beth was preparing her children for going back to school after the long summer holiday, and general gossip about the village and the people who lived in it.

An hour later Nathaniel returned to the kitchen.

"What did you find out?" I asked excitedly as soon as he walked through the door.

He eased himself slowly into a chair, frowning dejectedly.

"Nothing," he sighed as if completely bemused. "I found out nothing because there is nothing to find. I found the death records of Jack, Issy, Emma and the parents, but nothing at all for either Martha or Seraphina."

"What does that mean exactly?" Beth asked, her expression confused.

"I think it means that neither Martha nor Seraphina's deaths were properly registered, or that they are impossible to find due to both of them marrying and changing their names, but I also can't find a marriage certificate for either of them when searching with their maiden names."

"That doesn't make sense," I sat upright, trying to figure out what all of this meant. "We know that Martha has died because she's haunting the house, and even if the ghost isn't Martha, she would definitely be dead by now anyway. She was the eldest of the sisters, I think about ten years older than Matilda, which would make her approximately 112 years old by now."

"Maybe Matilda didn't register her death, maybe she didn't know that she had to?" Beth suggested.

"That could have been the case," Nathaniel was nodding his head thoughtfully, "I suppose it would have been Emma who registered all of the other deaths, then Martha would have probably known that she needed to register Emma's death, and maybe Matilda just didn't realise that she needed to do the same for Martha."

"But" I pointed out, "if Martha didn't have a death certificate then how could she have been buried? Isn't it required in order to have a burial?"

"Yes," Nathaniel agreed, "you're absolutely right, although I don't know exactly what the procedure was back in 1918, but I can find out. I'll also have another trawl through the records, I might have missed something."

Later, after Beth had left and Kitty had gone to bed, Nathaniel and I sat in the front lounge, each with a glass of brandy.

"Do you ever feel strange in the house, Nathaniel? As if you're being watched or followed around the place?"

"Kitty follows me practically everywhere," he laughed lightly. "I do know what you mean though, there have been a few occasions where I have been convinced that someone was standing behind me, but when I turn around, there's no one there."

"I feel constantly that I am being watched from the shadows. Sometimes, I can see the darkness moving, as if there's something within it, and all of the time my belongings are vanishing and then turning up in places I couldn't possibly have put them myself. I've had objects thrown at me when I've been walking up or down the stairs, the list is endless, and yet you haven't had a single thing happen to you, apart from the occasional feeling of being watched."

"Maybe I am not as receptive to the paranormal as you are, not as open to it. It could be that you are just more empathetic than me, more sensitive."

"Maybe," I agreed reluctantly, "but I had never experienced anything at all before coming here."

"Then Meadowside has perhaps brought it out in you?"

"Sometimes is seems to me that the house itself is holding so many secrets, as if it's an actual character in Matilda's story. The answers to all of the mysteries of the past are contained within these walls and are all around us."

*

The following morning, I was sitting in the children's room with Matilda. Kitty and Nathaniel had gone for a walk, Nathaniel desperately hoping to catch a glimpse of Issy in the meadow and feeling that he had a much better chance if he had Kitty with him.

Despite the warm weather, Matilda was chilly and asked for her blanket, which I tucked in around her knees.

"Nathaniel and I went to the graveyard last night," I informed her casually. "I was so shocked and upset to see Emma's grave there and the fact that she died in the flu epidemic along with your parents."

"She didn't stand a chance, Amber," her feeble voice caught in her throat. "She looked after everyone, protected me and Kitty, she even protected Martha. She became ill in the early evening of the day our parents died, but she didn't tell anybody. I suppose she could have thought she was just tired, but I think it was because she knew that I would have wanted to look after her, and because that would have put me at risk, she just kept it to herself and went to bed.

"When she didn't come down for breakfast we didn't think anything of it. We knew that she was exhausted and decided to just let her sleep. It was Martha who found her, cold and dead in her bed."

Matilda's eyes had taken on a sad, faraway expression, as if she was living that day, minute by minute. "I don't know what made Martha go into Emma's room, she had stayed well clear of her and my parents during their illness, leaving all the care and nursing to Emma. Perhaps she grew worried as to why she heard no movement coming from Emma's room, I really don't know."

She lifted her eyes and gazed at me for a long time. Eventually she said, "that was the beginning of it, Amber, that was the day when everything began to spiral out of control, and the worst days of my entire life began."

# Chapter 13

## Meadowside 1918

The house was deathly quiet. Matilda, Kitty and Seraphina were in the children's room, the fire was blazing as outside the frigid winter's day pressed against the windows, dark and gloomy, even though was only just after lunchtime.

All three of the girls were in deep shock, each in their own way trying to adsorb the fact that their parents were both dead, along with Jack and Issy. Matilda felt strangely numb, as if no longer able to feel anything at all. In the back of her head was the thought that life was out of her control, that any terrible thing could happen at any time, and there was nothing that she could do about any of it. She felt weakened and vulnerable, as if life wasn't her friend anymore, as if, for some unfathomable reason, it had turned against her.

Seraphina felt desolated by the death of Edward Grey, her grandfather. He had always spoken to her with great kindness, and they had enjoyed several long conversations together. He had provided her with a father figure to go to, she had trusted him, and felt that they had formed a special bond, an unexpected relationship, and now he was gone. Seraphina had known that she would always be safe all the while that Edward Grey was alive, but now her position in the house felt unstable and in jeopardy. Matilda, she knew, would always stand up for her and defend her, but was

Matilda really a match against Martha?

Kitty was sitting on the floor, gazing into the fire. She had been told that her parents were dead, and although the expression in her eyes altered for a fleeting moment, it was unclear how much she had actually taken in.

"Emma really should have something to eat," Seraphina said, interrupting the deep silence in the room. "I know that she must be very tired, but she hasn't eaten anything at all since yesterday morning."

Matilda and Seraphina both turned their heads towards the open door at the sound of a strange noise.

"What was that?" Matilda jumped to her feet, "it sounded like a scream."

The two girls hurriedly left the room, closely followed by Kitty. They stepped into the hall and were halfway to the stairs when Martha suddenly appeared, running down the stairs at breakneck speed.

"Where is that child?" She was screaming, her voice sounding shrill, on the brink of hysteria.

Martha stood for a while at the bottom of the stairs, holding tightly to the bannister post. She was breathing heavily, her entire body heaving with each breath that she took. Her face was bleached of colour, and her dark eyes were gleaming with something hostile and frightening.

"Martha?" Matilda cautiously took a few steps towards her. "What is the matter with you?"

"What is the matter with me, you ask? Well, you are asking the wrong person. Ask her!" She pointed towards Seraphina; her expression full of loathing. "Not content with killing Issy and both of our parents, she has now murdered Emma too."

The room fell completely silent, as if time had shuddered to a halt.

"Emma?" Matilda uttered, feeling the blood draining from her face. "What are you talking about? She's tired, she's just sleeping."

"Do you think I don't know the difference between a sleeping person and a dead one? She is stone cold in her bed, taken some time in the night by the witch." Martha slowly advanced towards Seraphina. "It was you who gave the kitten to Issy, and it was you that went to the village and brought the fever back to the house."

Martha then swung around to face Matilda. "Don't you think it's strange that Mother, Father and now Emma, are all dead, and yet she survived? I warned you all. I told you that she would not stop until all of us are dead. She has cursed us, it's nothing short of murderer, and I will not have her in this house for a second longer."

Martha lunged forwards and grabbed hold of Seraphina by the hair, forcing her to the ground and then dragging her across the tiled floor.

"Martha!" Matilda yelled, grabbing hold of her sister and smashing her body with her clenched fists. "Let go of her."

Martha lashed out with her free hand, causing Matilda to stumble to the floor. "She will leave this house today, and so help me God, if I ever set eyes on her again, I will kill her."

Matilda quickly scrambled to her feet and once again she ran at Martha, kicking her in the legs, punching her, pulling her hair until it fell free of its grips and tumbled around her shoulders. Martha was dragging Seraphina towards the front door and when Matilda realised that she wasn't going to be able to beat her sister into submission, she threw herself against the door.

"Get out of my way!" Martha hissed; her face contorted with fury. "I am in charge here now, as the oldest child of the family still alive, the house is mine, and it will be me who decides who can live in it."

"You can't throw her out of Meadowside," Matilda argued, "where would she go?"

"I don't care about where she goes. I'm sure the workhouse would take her, but she is definitely not staying here."

Pressing her back against the wooden door and spreading her arms, Matilda glowered at Martha, her anger like a burning furnace in her chest.

"Don't you think if Seraphina was capable of cursing people to death, then you would have been the first one to die? She would never hurt Issy, Emma or Mother and Father, but she hates you, just as much as I do."

"You are an evil child," Martha snarled into Seraphina's ear. "See how you have turned my family against me?" She suddenly pushed Seraphina to the ground and advanced towards Matilda. "I wouldn't be surprised if you were a part of the curse, an accomplice, trying to keep Meadowside for yourself."

Matilda braced herself, trying not to react or cry at Martha's words. "If Seraphina leaves, then Kitty and I will leave with her. How would you like that, Martha, having to feed yourself, and live all alone until you die a pathetic, lonely, uncared for, bitter old woman with nobody to pray for you?"

Martha lifted her chin and stared coldly into Matilda's eyes. "You can leave if you want to, but you will not take Kitty. Kitty will stay here with me, and if you even attempt to take her away from this house, I will set the law after you. I am the eldest by far, the heir of Meadowside, and until she comes of age, I am also Kitty's guardian. The law is on my side," she smiled nastily, obviously enjoying the small amount of power that she had over Matilda. "Kitty will stay with me. I'm sure that she will miss you, imbecile that she is. She will probably cry and stop speaking again, and will waste away, and it will be all your fault."

"You are a despicable person, Martha. You are not a normal human being, and I hate you."

"I don't care about your opinion of me, Tilly, now get out of my way."

Martha went to where Seraphina was still lying, on her back on the floor. Seraphina knew that Matilda had done everything she could to prevent Martha from throwing her out of the house. She thought for a moment about what it would be like, how it would feel, to be banished from Meadowside and to never see Matilda or Kitty again. Life would become dangerous and brutal, and now she could see that the only way to prevent this happening to her was to play

Martha at her own game. Martha was frightened of her, she was sure of it, and that was the only ammunition that Seraphina had to use against her. If Martha believed she was a witch, then she would let her believe it.

Martha was standing over her. Seraphina quickly scrambled to her feet, fixing her adversary with her vivid blue eyes.

"You will not lay a hand on me." Seraphina's voice was bold and steady as she kept her eyes fixed on Martha's face. "I don't need to be living in the house to curse you, Martha. I can do that from anywhere in the world. Remember how I threw you down the stairs without even touching you, that was just a warning, Martha, but I am capable of much worse. From now on you will treat me, Kitty and Tilly with respect. You will not threaten us or lay a hand upon any of us ever again."

"You dare to threaten me?" Martha's entire body seemed to twitch with anger. She took several steps towards Seraphina and grabbing her by the shoulders she began to violently shake her, she then raised her hand high into the air and slapped Seraphina full in the face with her open palm.

At that moment Kitty began to scream hysterically, her voice steadily growing louder and shriller.

"Shut her up," Martha demanded. Matilda ran to her younger sister and placed her arms around her, but nothing would quieten her.

Seraphina stood with her hand pressed against the side of her face. She took a couple of minutes to compose herself, to steady her nerves. "I don't think you quite understood me, Martha." She walked slowly and deliberately towards the older girl, her expression one of strength and defiance. "If you come near any of us, if you dare to strike any of us again, I will make your life so miserable that you will rue the day you were born. I will see to it that you will never have another minute of peace, or another night of untroubled sleep, for you will never know when or how I will strike, but believe me, Martha, you will sorely regret antagonising me."

Martha's mouth fell open. For a moment she appeared terrified, and then, without uttering another word, she turned and with her back straight, walked away from them and up the stairs.

"Kitty, for goodness' sake, stop screaming now." Matilda took her sister by the hand and guided her towards the children's room, sitting her down in a chair. Seraphina slowly followed.

"I want Emma," Kitty muttered, "I'm scared, I want Emma."

Matilda sat heavily on the sofa, placed her head in her hands and cried bitterly. How could this really be happening, Jack, Issy, her parents and now Emma. It was shattering and seemed so unreal that the true impact of it all wouldn't be fully realised for a very long time.

"Emma was so good," Matilda wept, "like an angel, and now she is gone. What are we going to do?"

Seraphina blinked away her own tears. "We will carry on," she said firmly, "we will carry on and do exactly what Emma would want us to do. We will be brave; we will look after Kitty, and we will do the very best that we can."

Seraphina sat back in her chair, feeling concerned and worried. She wondered if she had done the right thing in standing up to Martha in the way that she did. In the moment she couldn't think of anything else to do, and in her panic she had deliberately played on Martha's fears and superstitions. It had made Martha retreat. She had scared her, made her feel unsafe and vulnerable in her own home, but she believed she had only bought herself some time, but had not completely solved the issue. Martha would attack her again; she was certain of it.

"She's going to make our lives hell, especially yours, Seraphina." Matilda raised her head and wiped her tears away with the sleeve of her cardigan. "You won't leave me here with her, will you, Seraphina? We could leave together, we could make something of ourselves somewhere else, but I couldn't leave Kitty, and I think Martha is right, I think she does have legal control over her, and probably me as well, but she doesn't care about me, she would happily let me go, and she has no feelings for Kitty either, she's just using her to spite me."

"I won't leave you, Tilly." Seraphina said, "I promise."

\*

Life did continue at Meadowside, but it was a very different life. The house always felt cold, and even when summer came around again, there was no respite from the coldness and emptiness.

Matilda spent a lot of her time in the garden. The house felt so hostile and depressed that she often felt the need to escape.

One scorching day Jed Carter found her sitting quietly on the bench. "How are you, Tilly?" He called out to her, abandoning his hoe against a tree and walking towards her.

"Alright, I suppose, but things are difficult in the house."

He sat down beside her and puffed on his pipe. "Things are bound to be difficult, these are difficult times, not only at Meadowside but the whole world over. Many families in the village are going through what you are going through, having lost children and older folk alike. As if people hadn't suffered enough due to the war, all those young men fighting in the trenches, putting their lives on the line, only to come home and be killed by Influenza, of all things."

"I don't know how to be me anymore, Jed. My parents are gone, and Issy and Emma, I just don't know how anyone can recover from such sadness. I feel lost without them. On top of that we have to put up with Martha, stalking around the house like a lunatic, blaming Seraphina for everything from the deaths to the milk being sour. She can't understand how Seraphina caught the same illness and lived, but everybody else in the house who caught it, died."

"Seraphina was lucky, but a lot of people did survive. Of course, a lot of people didn't, there's no rhyme or reason to it."

"I just don't know how I'm going to tolerate Martha. I would leave Meadowside, but she won't let me take Kitty. It's like she's unhinged, Jed, like a mad woman. She thinks that Seraphina has special powers, that she's a witch. She tried to throw her out of the house, but Seraphina stood up to her, and threatened to use her mystical gifts against her. That scared Martha, and now she just skulks around the place causing a horrible atmosphere in the house, and I really don't know how much longer I can stand it."

"What would you do if you left Meadowside, Tilly? Where would you go?" He glanced down at her with worry etched into his face. "Let me tell you this, Tilly: Martha or no Martha, you would be far better off staying here, where you are at least safe, with food to eat and a bed to sleep in. Life outside Meadowside is hard and can often be dangerous. I'll admit that Martha isn't the easiest person to get along with, but you have to remember that she has suffered all of the losses that you have suffered. She must also be grieving, and maybe just doesn't know how to handle it and is taking it out on you and young Seraphina."

"She just won't be happy until she has driven Seraphina away. I don't understand why she's behaving like this."

"Because she's upset, Tilly, and in mourning. Sometimes people don't act in their right minds when they're grieving. She can't understand why these terrible things have happened, and she needs someone to blame. Remember that Martha might be difficult, but she is still a human being. Do you think trying to understand her, just a little, might help?"

Matilda sighed crossly. "Sometimes I think that she's lost her mind, that she's going mad." Her eyes followed a bee that was hovering above the wildflowers that grew on the edge of the fen. "She keeps herself to herself most of the time, which is a blessing, but whenever we see her she starts off with her accusations. The good thing is that she hasn't tried to throw Seraphina out of the house again, and I think that is just because she is too frightened of her to do anything more than name calling and goading."

"I'm not sure that it was a good idea for Seraphina to encourage Martha to think that she is capable of harming her. It would be better for Martha to see that Seraphina hasn't got these powers, for her to become less fearful of her."

Matilda glanced up at him and shrugged her shoulders. "Seraphina had to do something. Martha was going to throw her out in the freezing weather, and at least it stopped her doing that."

"All of you have been through a terrible time, and it's all still new and raw. Give each other time to heal, be gentle with each other, even Martha."

"I will try," Matilda promised, then worriedly bit her lip. "The thing is, Jed, I need Seraphina. Kitty is walking around all day like a lost soul or standing at the window for hours at a time. If it wasn't for Seraphina keeping me sane, I don't know what I would do. I'm frightened that she will leave, or that Martha will drive her away, or will succeed in killing her."

Jed laughed at Matilda's dramatic words. "Martha won't kill her," he said with confidence, "for if she did she would surely hang for it. Just let time pass by, wait for things to settle down, and you'll see that it will all change, and you'll begin to feel better. After all, you and Kitty are the only family that Martha has left now, and one day she will see that if she wants to keep you, then she will have to change her ways."

*

As the days slowly began to grow shorter, and the winter stole away the flowers in the meadow and turned the ground hard with frost, the house fell into a solid routine. As much as they could, the girls followed Emma's schedule, making sure that the washing was done on a Monday, that bread was baked on a Tuesday, and the household tasks were completed to the exacting standards that Emma had taught them. They ensured that Kitty was in bed by eight and up at seven, they read stories to her and tried their utmost to make her happy, but Kitty had been struck by a relentless, melancholy mood, that saw her spend silent hours idling her life away. It was as if the ending of summer had taken away the short bursts of hope and optimism within her and had replaced it with a despondent depression.

"Maybe we should take her to see a doctor," Seraphina suggested one day. "I know that she's been through an awful lot, but this isn't normal."

Matilda continued to wipe down the kitchen table with a damp cloth. She was also worried about Kitty but believed that the village doctor only saw those with physical ailments, and whatever was wrong with Kitty could not be cured by a pill or a potion.

"It's like she doesn't really understand what has happened." Matilda sat down, rubbing her eyes wearily. "Only this morning she asked for Emma, and then there's all the hours she spends at the window waiting for Issy to come home. It doesn't matter how many times I tell her that they have gone, that they couldn't come back even if they wanted to, but nothing I say to her seems to register."

Matilda remained silent for a while, her head bowed, thinking to herself that her childhood was now over, and she would, somehow, have to take the place of her parents and Emma in the life of her younger sister.

"I don't know how to be a parent to Kitty. She is still so young, and she doesn't understand things in the way that other people do, and I don't know how to help you, and, of course, Martha is the next best thing to useless. I feel that I'm too young myself, that I don't know enough, and it's all too much responsibility."

"You are not doing this on your own, Tilly. I'm here, and between us we'll raise Kitty the best that we can. She will be alright; she will grow up, and so will we, and maybe when she's older she'll understand things better."

Matilda smiled gratefully. "I hope so. Everything feels so strange. Sometimes I feel that I could even be a little bit happy, if it wasn't for Martha. I keep thinking about what the future will be like, next year, the year after, in five years' time. Is Martha still going to be here, lording it over us, making our lives miserable? How are we ever to bear it?"

"We could leave when Kitty is old enough to come with us, without Martha's permission."

"That is years and years away." Matilda replied desperately, "and anyway, why should we leave? Meadowside is as much our home as it is Martha's."

There was something about Martha that caused Matilda to constantly feel uneasy. She was always creeping around the house, trying to stay out of sight, walking in her stockinged feet, always watching and waiting, trying to catch them out doing or saying something that she could berate them for. It made Matilda constantly on edge, unsafe, as if she had to censor every word that she spoke, just in case Martha was hiding, ready to use whatever she overhead to her own advantage.

Matilda tried her hardest to be pragmatic about the losses they had all suffered. Emma and Issy were gone, and they would remain gone whether she was miserable or not. She learned that the only way to move forward in life was to accept that the things she couldn't change must be endured to the best of her ability.

# Chapter 14

It must have been exhausting for Matilda to keep dredging up the distant past over and over, and it certainly did seem to tire her out. I was thinking about how dreadful it all must have been for the three girls that were left and how painful and difficult life must have been.

"At least Martha stopped bothering you and Seraphina," I said.

"She did, for a while, but she remained secretly determined to see the back of Seraphina, not understanding, or considering for a moment, that Kitty and I had lost our parents and three of our siblings, and couldn't lose Seraphina too, but then, Martha never did think about anyone else."

"I just can't understand why she felt the need to be so cruel and difficult. It doesn't really make any sense and seems so unreasonable. You would have thought that the deaths would have brought you all closer together."

Matilda seemed to be deep in thought for a while. "Just like Jed Carter said, we have to remember that Martha suffered the same losses that we did, and for some reason felt the need to blame somebody. I can see now, looking back, that Emma would have been the greatest loss for her, they were close in age and Emma was always so good at appeasing her, making excuses for her, supporting her no matter how nasty and disagreeable she was.

"Emma used to tell us to feel sorry for her, that people couldn't help the personality they were born with, but I never could, and maybe, at the end of the day, that was a fault in me. I disliked Martha and was too young and immature to look behind the spite and anger, to try to see the cause or reason behind her behaviour. The truth is that I never cared enough about her to do that. Emma could see no bad in anyone, and she pitied Martha, stood up for her and pacified her, even when Martha didn't deserve any of it."

I walked with Matilda back to her bedroom and settled her for a rest on the bed. When I went back into the hall, I could feel the atmosphere that Matilda had talked about. It was a heaviness in the air, an inexplicable tingling in the silence.

Beth was just leaving as I entered the kitchen. She had worked hard getting the doors of the dresser fixed, replacing broken items and straightening everything up, to the extent that it now looked as if nothing had happened there.

"Nathaniel has taken Kitty for a ride in the car, now that you're not driving to the hospital every day she is missing getting out and about, he said they would only be a couple of hours."

"That's great," I grinned, knowing how much Kitty had grown to love the daily trips out in the car.

"How is Matilda this morning?"

"She's okay, but very tired, but still, much better than I expected her to be."

After Beth left I went to the dresser, admiring the job that the local carpenter had done on the doors and the broken drawers. I opened one of the cupboards and found a neatly stacked pile of brand-new plates, and on the shelf above were a selection of vases. The sight of the vases inspired me to think about going out into the garden and the meadow to pick some flowers for the house.

I took out two of the vases, and there, right at the back of the cupboard was a bunch of keys, hidden in the corner. As soon as my eyes fell on them, I knew that they were the keys to the locked rooms upstairs.

I reached in and took them out, placed them on the table and sat down, staring at them for several minutes. I had become increasingly curious about the locked rooms since Nathaniel had suggested opening them up. I also felt angry that Matilda had ever felt the need to lock them in the first place, as well as the fact that even now, after all these years, Martha was still controlling her, controlling us all.

Recently I had been wondering how it would all end. Would Martha just leave of her own accord, or would I somehow have to get rid of her, and if that was the case, then how was that outcome going to be accomplished? At that moment in time, we were not utilising the whole house, tiptoeing about, walking on eggshells in order not to offend someone that had no right to be there in the first place.

I so much wanted peace for Matilda and Kitty, and for myself too. Although Matilda was essentially cured of her illness, she was very weak and frail, and even with the best care in the world, it would have been unrealistic to believe that a woman of her age could possibly live for much longer. I wanted her to have a resolution, for the remaining months of her life to be happy ones, without the constant worry over what could happen next.

It was these thoughts that encouraged me to take the keys and open the door to Martha's bedroom, as well as a rising anger at the unfairness of it all, and how Martha was holding the entire household hostage.

My belief that I was stronger than her and that I had far more right to be there than she did, emboldened me with more courage than was, perhaps, sensible. I also knew that once the idea had sparked in my brain it was best to act on it immediately, for who knew how long such naïve bravery would last, or how long it would take me to talk myself out of it.

I stood up quickly, and walked to the centre of the hall, the keys cold and heavy in my hand. I was immediately struck by the familiar feeling of menace that drifted down the stairs towards me. The air around me grew viscous and difficult to breathe, as if Martha, hiding somewhere in the shadows, was fully aware of my intentions and was doing all that she could to deter me.

For a moment I thought about returning the keys to the dresser and occupying myself with something far more mundane and less dangerous, but I reminded myself that I was doing this for Matilda and Kitty and was prepared to be courageous beyond my wildest dreams, for their sakes.

The moment that I set foot on the stairs, an object came flying towards me, hitting me on the shoulder, then falling at my feet. It was a small glass bottle, with an ornate silver top. A perfume bottle, I thought as I stared down at it, and then moved it out of the way to the side of the step, with the toe of my shoe.

I closed my eyes, drew in a long deep breath as a worrying thought entered my head. If she could throw coins and little glass bottles, what else could she throw at me? A heavier item accurately aimed could do a lot more damage, a sharp object, thrown with force, could kill me.

I emptied my brain of such destructive thoughts, reminding myself repeatedly that I had never, in my entire life, heard of a human being that had been killed by a ghost. I continued to walk up the stairs, while all around me the silence fizzed in the air, and the atmosphere grew dense and ominous.

Even though it was late summer, the landing area of the house was dark, it was always dark, the closed doors at the end preventing the light from the bedrooms to illuminate the space.

I could feel the air circulating around me, as if someone had left a window open on a chilly winter's day. It was growing colder by the second, an arctic chill seeping into my bones, causing me to struggle to catch my breath.

My movements became weak and jittery, as if I hadn't eaten for days, but it seemed that nothing would prevent me from reaching the end of the landing, my determination driven by my need to bring an end to this untenable situation that I found myself in. I was also determined to show Martha that, no matter what she did, or how uncomfortable she made me, I would never concede to her bullying and manipulation. I was going to win. There was simply no other option.

I staggered further into the darkness, trembling despite all my efforts to remain calm. A short distance away from the door that I was convinced was Martha's bedroom, I held up the keys in front of my face trying to decide which one of them to try first, when they were suddenly wrenched from my hands and hurled back down the corridor.

At that juncture I seriously considered running away. Something that I hadn't even seen had ripped the keys from out of my hand. My head was spinning with terror. What was I doing, provoking a ghost, dabbling in something that I couldn't even understand? What danger was I putting myself in, and what else could I unwittingly unleash?

I turned and walked back along the corridor, towards the staircase. The keys had travelled a fair distance and were lying close to Kitty's bedroom door. I picked them up, weighing up the consequences of pursuing this crazy stunt, but as I stood there I heard a noise. I turned my head, and saw, to my utter astonishment, the door at the end of the corridor suddenly swing open of its own accord.

This was something I had not bargained for, and for a few moments it completely threw me, perhaps just as it was intended to. It seemed to me that I was being taunted, as if she was testing my courage, and I knew then that to backdown would be a big mistake.

I had expected that I would have to struggle with the lock on the door, that it would be stiff and unyielding after being locked for at least eighty years. The fact that the door had opened, meant that Martha must be inside the room, waiting for me. I assumed that she believed I would turn and run away as fast as I could, and believe me, that is the very thing that I wanted to do.

After a minute of hesitation, I jutted out my chin, braced my shoulders and walked with speed and deliberation towards the open door.

I halted at the threshold of the room, gazing into the murky shadows. The room was large and square with a wood framed double bed standing against the wall, covered with a tattered bedspread, that at some point in its history may have been a deep pink colour.

Two long windows were situated in the wall opposite the door, draped with flimsy, moth eaten curtains, one of which was hanging from the rail by just a few threads.

There was an unpleasant, musty smell, and the air was so thick with dust that it was difficult to breathe freely. Intricate cobwebs trailed from the ceiling to the wooden floor, which was covered in a large, threadbare rug, its unravelled edges reaching out into the room.

A dressing table stood between the two windows with a large oval mirror standing on top of it. The mirror was so mottled and thick with dust that it had become opaque. Two candlesticks in ornate sconces stood on either side of the mirror, swathed in cobwebs and the grime and dust of more than eight decades.

"Are you here?" I asked, my voice barely a whisper.

I heard a thin, bitter laugh, as the skin on the back of my next prickled with apprehension. The laughter seemed to come from everywhere and nowhere, echoing inside the tomb like room and the dead, stagnant air.

"You shouldn't be here," I said, my eyes darting around the darkness trying to locate where the voice had come from. "It's not fair on Kitty and Matilda, and it isn't right."

"You shouldn't be here," said a hissing voice close to my ear, so close in fact that I fancied I could feel an impossible breath against my skin.

I took a couple of steps forwards into the room and the instant that I moved, the door slammed shut behind me. I immediately turned and fumbled with the door handle, but as I had anticipated, the door was jammed.

I turned back to the room. "Where are you?" I glanced quickly around me, but could see nothing apart from the grim dreariness, and the particles of dust that floated around me like minute insects.

"Are you too much of a coward to show yourself?" I felt trapped and claustrophobic, which lit a fire of anger within me. "Of course, you're a coward, only a coward would torment children like you did.

Did it make you feel big and important, that little bit of power that you had? You were a pathetic human being, Martha, but now you're not even that, you are nothing, you are the past, and everyone knows that the past doesn't exist anymore."

All the time that I was talking, my voice bouncing off the dead air like a rubber ball against a wall, I was frantically trying to figure out how I was going to escape, how I was ever going to get out of there.

"Show yourself!" I demanded aggressively, feeling increasingly angry and frustrated.

As soon as my words escaped my lips an object was thrown through the air, tumbling and twisting across the darkened space with speed. I ducked as a silver backed hairbrush slammed onto the door behind me. Straight away another object came flying towards me, this time a book, that struck me in the chest, exuding a choking puff of dust, and then falling to the ground in disintegrated pieces.

At that moment I became aware of a movement in the far corner of the room.

"Is that you?" I asked, straining my eyes to see through the gloom. I glanced towards the windows, tempted to rip the curtains away, but then realised that they were so insubstantial, more holes than material, that they were already letting in the tiny amount of light that they could. The dimness in the room was due to the glass in the windows being so filthy.

The darkness in the corner of the room began to move like dark smoke, and then I could see a vague, shimmering light, that slowly took on a human form. In a matter of seconds, she stood before me, my adversary, my nemesis. I don't know what I had been expecting to see, but it was not this. She was smaller than I expected and appeared younger. Her skin was translucent and ashen, her eyes large and dark. Her hair was pulled back untidily from her elfin face, long tendrils escaping and trailing down her neck. Despite the fact that she looked pitiful and harmless, I could see a stone-cold defiance in her eyes, a dangerous malevolence.

I stood completely still, too scared to move, hardly able to believe what my eyes were showing me and finding it difficult to process the fact that I was standing in front of a ghost. It seemed surreal and dreamlike, and I had to keep reminding myself that I was fully awake, and this was actually happening.

She wore an ankle length, simple black dress, which did nothing but emphasise her startling pallor. The front of the dress had narrow pleats, but that was the only decoration that adorned it. She reminded me of a Victorian woman in deep mourning.

My eyes rested on her face. She was scowling, the heavy dark eyebrows knitted together with anger. Her face appeared fragile, the cheekbones delicately carved. There was no doubt, despite the unflattering dress and the dark hair that was in need of a good brush, that she was, or could have been, unusually beautiful.

"What are you going to do now?" I asked quietly, controlling my voice so that I sounded far more confident than I felt. "Throwing things at me hasn't driven me away, your pathetic display in the kitchen hasn't made me leave, constantly moving and hiding my belongings hasn't worked. I should think that you must be running out of ideas."

She took one step towards me. A cold, bone-chilling smile twisted her lips. She tilted her head fully to one side, her eyes glinting with a flash of amusement. It seemed that she was considering her next move.

My body grew twitchy with anticipation. She was going to do something unexpected, something terrifying, I just knew it. I had to get the better of her right there and then. I had to show her that she couldn't beat me, and that I would not tolerate her presence in the house.

"I think I'll clear all of the rubbish out of here," I spoke as if I was thinking out loud. "I'll redecorate, buy new furniture, perhaps get a carpet to cheer the place up, and new curtains too. Of course, I would have to clean it first, from top to bottom until there isn't a speck of dust left, and when I have done that every trace of you will have been swept away. What will you be staying for then?"

My words had been spoken to diminish her, to make her see that she no longer had a place in the house, but instead of making her weaker, my words seemed to have had the opposite effect.

The air around me began to vibrate with a dull humming sound and then, from nowhere, a freezing blast blew into my face, causing my hair to lift and float around me as if I was submerged in water.

The flimsy material at the window lapped into the room, lifting and falling like waves on a beach. The cobwebs that trailed from the ceiling spun and danced, and the dust and debris of eighty years of neglect, whirled and twisted in the stale air.

"I have one thing to stay for," the harsh, hissing voice whispered in my ear again. "Matilda."

"Matilda?" I repeated, "she is old and sick, what could you possible want with her?"

"Revenge," came the savage reply.

I wanted to challenge her further. The thought that she was harbouring ill intent towards Matilda made the anger ignite within me yet again, but at that moment the front door opened and was then heavily slammed shut. In the distance I could hear the low, rumbling voice of Nathaniel, and the excited chatter of Kitty.

Before I knew what was happening I could feel myself being violently spun around. The door that was now in front of me, swung open, and I was catapulted out of it with considerable force into the corridor, landing in a heap several feet down the landing, as behind me, the bedroom door was slammed shut.

I stayed sitting on the ground, not trusting that my legs would hold me up if I tried to stand. I could hear Nathaniel calling to me, but no matter how hard I tried, I couldn't answer. Eventually he came up the stairs and knocked on my bedroom door, and when I didn't answer he turned and saw me sitting, stunned on the floor.

"Amber! What on Earth are you doing down there? Did you fall over? Are you ill?"

I shook my head and just about managed to scramble unsteadily to my feet.

"You don't look at all well, you're as white as a sheet."

"I'm fine," I assured him, close to tears. "Where's Kitty?"

"She's downstairs somewhere, she's fine. Is Matilda okay?"

"She's having a rest in her room," I placed my hand against the wall to steady myself and took several deep breaths to try and ease my jangling nerves. "I've just had quite an experience," I said breathlessly. "I...I went into Martha's room."

He came towards me and took hold of my arm. "Let's get you downstairs. I'll make us a strong cup of tea and you can tell me about whatever it was that possessed you to go into Martha's room when I wasn't here, when nobody was here apart from Matilda. What on Earth were you thinking of?"

"I just got fed up with it all, the worry and anxiety over what she was going to do next. I suppose I wanted to force something, show her that I wasn't intimidated."

"Do you think it worked?"

I laughed bitterly. "I doubt it very much and if you hadn't come back when you did, then I think I would have been in real trouble."

In the kitchen I sank into a chair while Nathaniel made the tea.

"Tell me exactly what happened." He sat down and stirred a spoonful of sugar into his mug. I recounted my experience in detail, still hardly able to believe that it had happened at all. "What was she like?" He asked, fascinated. "Did she look evil, or demented?"

I thought for a moment and then shook my head. "She looked very angry, and that was the strongest emotion that I picked up on. I was actually taken aback and surprised by her appearance, I was expecting something more substantial, but she was just a waif of a girl, maybe somewhere in her twenties."

"Did she tell you why she was here?"

"She said that it was to do with Matilda, she wants revenge."

"Revenge?" Nathaniel frowned with confusion. "What could Matilda have possibly done to cause that much hatred?"

I shrugged. "I have no idea. In the story Matilda says that Martha was vicious and cruel, ruling over the girls with an iron fist. Matilda retaliated against her several times, and Seraphina did too, but it seems that the reason that Martha is here is all down to Matilda alone."

Nathaniel drummed his fingers impatiently on the tabletop, asking eventually, "why has Martha not got a death certificate?" This is the question that had plagued him the most since he had looked the family up on the internet. He then slowly lifted his eyes to mine, a light of realisation shining within them. "You don't think that Martha could have been murdered?"

"Murdered?" I choked on my tea, spluttering it across the table. "By whom? Matilda?"

"It would explain a lot," he lowered his voice, glancing over his shoulder to make sure that Kitty was not around. "If Martha was murdered, then her death might not have been registered, and if Matilda was the murderer, then it would also explain why Martha is still here and hellbent on revenge."

I laughed in disbelief that he could even think such a thing. "Matilda would never kill anybody," I said with conviction. "She would never have been capable of such a thing."

"Well, not now," he agreed, "but we don't know what she was capable of when she was young. You've already said that she hated Martha, still hates her in fact, maybe she just lost her temper and committed a crime of passion? And what about Seraphina? There is not a single mention of her in any record that I can find."

"So, you think that Matilda killed her too?"

"No, I don't think that at all. It wouldn't make any sense. You said that Matilda loved Seraphina, depended on her, so why would she kill her? We know that Seraphina was born into the travelling community back in the early nineteen hundreds, and maybe they didn't see the need to register births, deaths and marriages, and lived by different rules."

"This is crazy," I ran my hands through my hair in frustration. "Matilda wouldn't have killed Martha, and anyway, if she did, then how did she get away with it? Surely she would have been hanged for it?"

"That is correct," Nathaniel conceded but then gazed at me levelly. "She would have been hanged for it, but only if somebody reported the murder or reported Martha as missing, and who would there have been to do either of those things? Would Seraphina have betrayed Matilda? Would Kitty have had the wherewithal?"

A heavy sensation of dread settled in my chest. Every word that Nathaniel had spoken made sense and appeared to explain everything.

I stood up. "I'm going to speak to Matilda and if she's feeling less tired after her rest, then I will ask her to move the story along. I'm going to insist that she tells me today, how Martha died and what happened to Seraphina."

Nathaniel looked at me pleadingly. "Try to get to the bottom of it, Amber. Meadowside and Matilda herself, need to be at peace."

\*

Half an hour later Matilda and I were sitting in the children's room.

"I have a confession to make," I said after settling her in her armchair and sitting down myself. "I went into Martha's room. I found the keys in the dresser, but in the end, I didn't even need them. The door unlocked and opened by itself."

Matilda at first looked surprised and then shocked. "Why did you do that, Amber?"

"Because of the horrible atmosphere in the house, the constant tension. I wanted it to end for you and Kitty, and for myself. I don't like the feeling that I am being watched and controlled by her."

Matilda inclined her head slightly, as if she understood my reasoning.

"I wanted to force the situation, make it come to a head, finish it."

"Did you succeed?"

"Of course, I didn't," I sighed wearily, "I've probably only made everything worse."

Matilda smiled enigmatically. "Martha never did like being challenged, she just thought that we should live by her rules and be happy about it, accept unquestioningly that she always knew what was for the best. She had an overblown sense of her own authority, without out ever bothering to look into the future to see that children grow up, and that young adults live by their own rules."

"I need to know what happened, Matilda. While I was in Martha's room she said that she was here because of you and mentioned something about revenge."

Matilda sighed. "After all of these years she still believes that she was in the right, that she could do and say whatever she pleased."

"Will you tell me what happened, Matilda? I need to know what became of Martha so that I can decide what I should do next. She is capable of being very destructive, and to tell you the truth, I think she is capable of a lot worse. She can throw things, supposing she throws something at you or Kitty? The consequences could be extremely serious. I have to understand fully why she is here, and why she's so angry and vengeful."

"I think the reason she has stayed here for all of these years is because she's too frightened to pass over to face whatever is waiting for her. She believed in judgement, retribution and the fires of hell and at the end of the day was too cowardly to accept the punishment for her sins, so she stayed here, making our lives difficult, while avoiding what she knew she had coming to her."

"There's one thing that I need to know. Why do you always tell me the story of the past in the children's room? Is it because, for some reason, you feel safe in here?"

Matilda smiled enigmatically. "That is correct. The children's room was the one place we could all escape to, knowing that Martha would not enter, and it has remained the same to this day. Martha may wander around the house, hiding in shadows and darkness, but she will not come in here. This little room is filled with love, memories and laughter. Martha was never welcome in here, and for that reason perhaps, she stays away."

# Chapter 15

## Meadowside 1921

The years passed by slowly. Matilda and Seraphina continued to do the best that they could for Kitty, while avoiding Martha. They didn't know what she did all day locked inside her bedroom, several days could pass with them not seeing her at all, but on the occasions that they did, they had noticed the change that had come over her. She had grown thinner, her skin paler, but her quick temper and razor-like tongue were every bit in evidence as they had always been.

Matilda wondered if Martha was ill, hoping that this wasn't the case as her sister had always been a demanding and an ungrateful patient, and Matilda really didn't believe that she had it in her to care for her, no matter how ill she might be.

"Of course, she is pale," Seraphina commented, "she never sets foot outside of the house, goodness knows how she manages to survive in that room twenty-four hours a day, if we didn't leave food outside her door, she would have starved to death months ago."

Matilda had come into contact with Martha earlier the same day in the hall. The sight of her wasn't expected, but it wasn't that which caused Matilda to gasp with surprise, it was the physical appearance of her sister. She noticed at once that Martha looked very unwell, that she had lost even more weight, but something else had also grabbed her attention, something that she couldn't immediately put her finger on.

"What are you staring at?" Martha growled, "you are looking at me as if you've never seen me before."

"You don't look well," Matilda stated with a dismissive shrug, "that is all."

"Of course, I don't look well," Martha said in a hushed tone, "I am not well."

Matilda breathed out an exasperated breath. "What is the matter with you now?"

Martha grabbed hold of Matilda's arm. "It's that gipsy girl, she is making me sick, she has infected the air that I breathe, the water that I drink, the food that I eat. It is a slow poisoning, Tilly, she wants to watch me suffer for as long as possible. I'm too afraid to eat or drink anything in case she had interfered with it."

Matilda had noticed that Martha's tray had often remained untouched, but she believed that she was probably helping herself to food in the kitchen when the girls were out of the house, or during the night.

"Please, Martha, not this again. Seraphina is not trying to kill you." She yanked her arm away from Martha's grasp. "What is wrong with you that makes you think these things? It's all in your head."

"That's what she wants you think, Tilly. She's clever, she wants you to believe that I'm imagining it all." Martha narrowed her eyes, "are you accusing me of being insane?"

Matilda stared boldly back at her. She did indeed look very ill, but as well as that there was a strange twitchiness about her, a hyperactive nervousness that hadn't been present before, as if her body was unable to be still. She repeatedly fiddled with her hair, that had now grown long and lank. Her thin fingers brushed constantly against the skin of her face, as if she had walked into a spiders web and was trying to brush it away. Her eyelids blinked rapidly, and her eyes darted anxiously all over the room.

"I am not accusing you of anything, Martha."

"You would rather see me dead than banish that girl? You would betray your own sister?"

"Seraphina has been more of a sister to me than you have ever been."

"I can't leave my room because of her. She is everywhere, everywhere that I look she is there. She shouldn't be here, she shouldn't, it's not right. She has turned you against me, make me a prisoner in my own home, she is making me sick, and still, you defend her."

"Nobody has turned me against you, Martha, you have done a very fine job of doing that all by yourself. It is you that has chosen not to eat and to spend all of your time in your room. You, Martha, nobody else. Anyway, if you're so worried about Seraphina poisoning you, then why don't you cook and prepare your own food? You are perfectly capable."

Martha sighed with irritation. "Because, Tilly, I am too sick to cook for myself." She tore at her hair and began pacing around the hall. "She is wicked, I tell you! Why can't you see what she is doing? Just look what has happened in this house since she arrived, our family has been decimated, destroyed, our lives ruined. She has cursed us, Tilly, put a jinx on us and Meadowside, and we will not know any peace until she's gone."

Matilda observed her sister with alarm. She was walking backwards and forwards across the hall, from one wall to another, wringing her hands and muttering beneath her breath.

"I think that Martha may be going insane," Matilda now said to Seraphina, as they sat side by side at the kitchen table preparing vegetables for the evening meal. "She's completely manic, and she keeps twitching and moving in a strange way. She still thinks that you're trying to kill her with a jinx or a curse. The reason that she's lost so much weight is that she thinks you're trying to poison her, and so won't eat anything."

"Oh dear," Seraphina laid down the knife she was using to peel potatoes. "Why can't she understand that I have no intention of harming her? If that had been my intention then wouldn't I have done it by now?"

"She believes that you are inflicting a long, slow death on her." Matilda allowed the cabbage she was chopping to fall out of her hands. "It's preposterous, and I am sick of walking on eggshells."

"We could leave," Seraphina dried her hands on a towel, "you are almost twenty years old, and I will be eighteen on my next birthday. I'm sure we would manage somehow."

"She wouldn't let us take Kitty, and she wouldn't take care of her if we left her here. I absolutely will not leave without Kitty."

"Perhaps if we took Kitty with us, she wouldn't care all that much, maybe she wouldn't even bother to try and find us. As you said she is sick and weak, so how would she be able to stop us?"

Matilda sat straighter in her chair, her brain taking in Seraphina's words.

"Where would we go?"

"I don't know," Seraphina shrugged, "Cambridge, or London, anywhere as long as we are away from Martha."

"How would we manage? What would we live on?"

"We would have to get jobs, you are good at so many things, Tilly, sewing, cooking, keeping house. I'm sure that we would both be able to get employment of some kind."

"It wouldn't be fair on Kitty," Matilda fretted, "she would be so confused and upset."

"She probably would be for a while, but for how long? The only things that Kitty really needs are us, and to be away from Martha. She is terrified of her, and you have to think about the damage that is being done to her. She may be upset in the short term, but in the longer term it would be much better for her."

Matilda slammed her fist onto the table in anger. "I shouldn't have to be even thinking about leaving Meadowside. It is our home just as much as it's Martha's. Why should we give it up because of her?"

"For happiness, Tilly, for the chance to build a peaceful and a happy life for us, and for Kitty. The only other way to solve this is if I were to leave on my own. Martha would be happy then, and you and Kitty would at least be able to live in peace."

Matilda stared at her with her mouth open. "Of course, we wouldn't be happy, Seraphina, we would be miserable without you. Promise me that you won't leave. Apart from Kitty, you are the only other person in the whole world that I care about, and if you left I don't know what I would do."

"I don't want to push you into anything, Tilly, but think about what I have said. We could leave and start a brand-new life. I know that we could do it together. Martha won't know where to begin looking for us, and we could be very far away from Meadowside before she even knows that we've gone."

"I will think about it," Matilda said quietly, "but I can't stand the thought of leaving Meadowside. You promise me that you won't leave on your own?"

Seraphina hesitated for a moment, and then said, "I won't leave without you, Tilly. I promise you."

Outside in the hall, shielded by the shadows, with her back pressed tightly against the wall, Martha listened to every word, her fury growing with every silent breath that she took. She then ran silently across the hall and up the stairs to her bedroom, barely able to prevent herself from screaming with anger.

Martha replayed the conversation that she had overheard, over and over again in her head. It was obvious to her that Seraphina was trying to coax Matilda away by promising her a happier life somewhere else. She had been very clever and devious in how she had gently encouraged Matilda to turn against her, never admitting that the reason that Martha was so difficult, and possibly dying, was all down to her. The calculating little sorceress had it all planned out. Having been so far unsuccessful in killing her, Seraphina had decided to take the only family that she had left away from her.

"We will see about that," Martha hissed through gritted teeth, knowing that she had to be every bit as clever as she believed Seraphina was being, every bit as cunning. She would play the long game, and when she acted, Seraphina would not know what had hit her. She stood up and went to the window, and gazing out over the garden, she began to make her plan.

*

The late summer turned swiftly to autumn, and inside Meadowside life became less tense. Martha had taken it into her head to start eating her meals in the kitchen with her two sisters and Seraphina. She had recently ceased to suspect that Seraphina was still trying to poison her, for she knew that the girl was far from stupid, and now that Seraphina knew that Matilda was aware of Martha's suspicions, she would not be silly enough to continue with her murderous plan.

Martha was working diligently and steadily towards creating a false sense of security within the house. She spent a short amount of time with the girls every day, careful not to do or say anything to cause distress or upset to anybody. She even managed to exchange benign words with Seraphina, even though it galled her, she knew it was for the greater good. Gradually, over time, the girls began to relax in her company, and to believe that at long last, Martha had accepted Seraphina as one of the family.

During this time, now eating healthily, Martha regained the weight she had lost and had taken to going out walking for hours at a time. Due to this she was looking healthy, and getting fitter, which was the most important thing if she was going to make her plan work.

Matilda believed that Martha had returned to her senses and had realised the stupidity of her accusations against Seraphina and was trying to make amends. Martha, in turn, was delighted with how the three younger girls had fallen for her pretence. She spent mealtimes with them at the kitchen table, speaking infrequently, but when she did, she was always friendly and respectful, and when she could no longer tolerate being in the company of Seraphina, she would leave them, returning to her room to make good her plan.

The atmosphere in the house became far more relaxed. Matilda was greatly relieved to see that Martha had stopped haranguing Seraphina, and her demeanour had completely changed. Gradually she integrated herself further into the house and the lives of her sisters and seemed to be transforming into a different person altogether. The girls, grateful for the lighter atmosphere and the relative peace, went out of their way to encourage this incredible transformation, including Martha in all of their conversations, inviting her to join them on their walks and activities, and even made her a cake for her birthday.

One morning Matilda commented, "I just can't believe the difference in Martha. I don't know what has come over her, but long may it continue."

Seraphina was standing at the range, breaking eggs into a saucepan. "Maybe she was getting lonely," she suggested, stirring the eggs with a wooden spoon. "Everybody needs company, so perhaps she grew bored spending all of her time alone in her room."

"Perhaps," Matilda was laying the table for breakfast, making a place for Martha at the far end. "At least she's stopped accusing you of trying to kill her, and she also seems to be much gentler with Kitty. It's like a miracle has occurred."

It was a day in early December when, yet again, life at Meadowside was turned upside down.

Martha was growing frustrated that she could never separate Seraphina from Matilda, the two were joined at the hip, always together, and then, one afternoon Matilda announced that she was going into the village to visit the wife of Jed carter who had been unwell.

"Do you want to come with me, Seraphina?"

Seraphina looked up from the task that had absorbed her since early that morning. On the kitchen table was a pile of winter greenery that she was using to show Kitty how to make a Christmas wreath for the front door.

"It will take me ages to clear this away, and Kitty is desperate to finish so we can place it on the front door. It will be hanging there by the time you get home, Tilly."

"I will look forward to seeing it." Matilda smiled, wrapping a scarf around neck and pulling on a pair of bright red gloves that had once belonged to Emma.

"How long will you be?" Martha had suddenly become interested in the activity taking place in the kitchen.

"Not long, just a couple of hours."

"Make sure that you are home before it gets dark, Tilly. I don't want you out in this freezing weather at night."

"I'll be home before four o'clock, Martha," she promised, pulling a woollen hat down over her ears and heading towards the door.

Martha nodded her head and smiled. Her plan was working, for there was no way that Matilda would have left Seraphina in the house without being there to protect her from Martha's temper, but now it was obvious that Matilda was under the fallacious impression that she no longer needed to worry about Seraphina.

As soon as Matilda left the house, Martha walked out of the kitchen and went to stand at her bedroom window. Already she could see the shadows gathering in the sky. It was close to the winter solstice, the darkest time of the year, the perfect time to bring to fruition the plan that had taken root and had been slowly growing and blooming in her mind.

Again, she looked at the sky, deciding that Matilda would be close to the village by now. She wouldn't stay long at the Carter's cottage, for she wouldn't want to be walking home alone in the darkness. Martha realised that if she wanted her plan to work perfectly, then she would need to act swiftly and with precision. She took her coat from the wardrobe and put it on and then returned to the window. She smiled with satisfaction at her own reflection in the glass, then turned and made her way to the kitchen.

\*

Matilda returned to the house shortly after four o'clock, surprised to see that there was no Christmas wreath hanging on the door. She removed her coat in the hall, hanging it on the stand in the corner. The house was unusually quiet, she heard no murmuring of voices, and nobody had thought to light the oil lamps, so the house was almost in complete darkness. She quickly lit the two lamps that stood on the bureau, and another that stood on a side table. She then turned and began to walk across the hall.

As she made her way to the kitchen, fully expecting to find Seraphina and Kitty still working on the Christmas wreath, she was stopped by a strange sound coming from the direction of the staircase. It was a strangled sob, closely followed by quiet weeping.

Kitty was sitting on a step halfway up the stairs, her head resting on her bent knees, sobbing as if her heart was breaking.

"Kitty?" Matilda sat beside her, "whatever is the matter?"

The girl became quickly hysterical, her entire body now shuddering and heaving with uncontrollable sobs, and then she began to scream, sounding exactly the same as when she used to wake up from a night terror when she was a much younger child.

"Stop it, Kitty!" Matilda yelled to be heard above the rasping cries of her sister. "Calm down and tell me what has happened."

Kitty lifted her head and looked at her, her face streaked with tears, her eyes wide with horror and fear.

"Kitty," Matilda placed an arm around her shoulders, "what has happened, where is Martha and Seraphina?"

"I...I tried to stop her, Tilly. I did, I tried as hard as I could, but she wouldn't listen to me. I kicked her and slapped her, but she just pushed me away. I was so scared, but I tried to stop her."

"Who did you try to stop?" Matilda felt a cold knot of terror contract in her stomach. "Where is Seraphina?"

"Martha took her away, Tilly. They were fighting, there was a lot of screaming, then Martha dragged her out of the house. Seraphina was yelling and kicking, and...and crying. Seraphina said that it didn't matter where Martha took her, for she would just come straight back to Meadowside, and Martha said...." Kitty started to wail again; her face contorted with anguish.

"It's alright, Kitty," Matilda soothed, "what did Martha say?"

"She said that there will be no coming back from where you're going. That is what she said to her."

Kitty wiped her eyes with the sleeve of her cardigan. "When Martha came back, Seraphina wasn't with her. I asked her where she was, and she said that I wasn't to give her a second thought for she won't be bothering us again."

Matilda felt her heart sink, her anger feeling like a white heat in her chest, radiating throughout her entire body.

"Tilly," Kitty sniffed, her eyes shrouded in fear. "Martha had blood on her, on her hands and all down the front of her coat."

For a moment Matilda thought that she was going to faint with shock, but then the fiery rage took hold of her again, feeding her with frenetic energy. She stood up shakily, ordered Kitty to wait in the hall, and then raced up the stairs. When she was at the top she screamed out Martha's name.

Martha came out of her room and slowly began to swagger towards Matilda, an arrogant smirk on her face.

"What have you done to Seraphina?" Matilda yelled furiously. "What have you done to her?"

Martha stood straight, perfectly controlled, her eyes cold and black. "Let's just say that she won't be coming back, not today, not tomorrow, not ever."

Matilda felt the air being knocked out of her lungs, as if she'd been physically winded. Martha stood so poised and self-assured, as if she had just achieved something that she was immensely proud of. She had a self-satisfied smirk on her face, and across the short distance between them, Matilda could see a strange excitement glittering in her eyes, as if whatever grizzly deed she had carried out, she had thoroughly enjoyed.

"Kitty said that you had blood on you. Was it Seraphina's blood?"

Martha stared at her for a long time, while Matilda waited with bated breath. Eventually Martha smiled coldly and said, "you can't make an omelette without breaking eggs, you know that Tilly."

Matilda caught her breath and barged past Martha, knocking her violently against the wall, and ran to the bedroom that she shared with Seraphina and Kitty. She sat on her bed for a couple of minutes, her breaths coming in agonising gasps.

Her eyes rested on Seraphina's neatly made bed, and then on her bedside cabinet where she had laid out her most precious possessions, a few silver bracelets and rings that had once belonged to her mother. She felt immediately distressed at the sight of them, but she quickly pulled herself together, she would have the rest of her life to mourn Seraphina, now wasn't the time.

She looked quickly around her and when her eyes fell on the heavy silver candlestick holder on her own bedside table, she picked it up, holding it in her hands for a few moments, feeling its weight and imagining the damage it could do.

From the other side of the closed bedroom door, she could hear Martha screaming at Kitty, telling her to shut up, that no amount of crying would bring Seraphina back, and that she should quickly get used to the fact that she was gone, and would never be returning.

"She got what she deserved, no more and no less. I was surprised that she didn't put up more of a fight to save herself, but it seems that, in the end, she was not as brave as you all believed her to be."

Matilda tightened her hands into fists as she gazed down at the heavily engraved candle sconce that was now laying on the bed beside her. She didn't even feel angry anymore as a strange numbness had taken over her. She stood up from the bed, and walked towards the door, the candlestick holder heavy and cold in her hand, concealed behind her back.

Martha was now standing at the top of the stairs, continuing to berate Kitty for her distress, calling her an imbecile, accusing her of stupidity and even lunacy.

"You will stop that interminable crying right now lest you want to join your unholy little friend out on the fen."

"Is that where you left her, Martha, out on the fen?"

Martha swung around, lifted her chin and sneered. "I warned you that I would get rid of her, Tilly. It is over now, she is gone, forever."

Matilda's anger returned, searingly hot inside of her. In her mind's eye she saw Seraphina, her smiling face, her deep blue eyes.

She saw her beautiful auburn hair falling in curls around her face and was overcome with the injustice of what had befallen her, that someone as kind and lovely as her could have their light snuffed out by someone so cold and evil.

Matilda walked expressionlessly to where Martha stood. For a second, she saw a shadow of fear pass over his sister's face, she saw her frown slightly, but then she smiled, a taunting sneer, opening her mouth as if to say something, but then she noticed something dangerous in Matilda's eyes, and closed her mouth into a thin line.

Matilda slowly advanced towards her, the candlestick still held behind her back. When she was just a few feet away from Martha, and without saying a single word, she lifted her arm high into the air, grasping the candlestick tightly, and using every ounce of strength that she possessed, she brought it down on the side of Martha's head.

Martha caught sight of the glittering object moments too late, she had no opportunity to move out of the way of its trajectory. Her eyes registered horror and shock, just before the object hit her with a resounding crack, fracturing her skull with a sound that could easily have been mistaken for a gunshot.

For a few shocking moments Martha stood completely still, her eyes fixed on Matilda's face. Matilda watched as the first trickle of blood seeped out of her hair, a streak of crimson against the impossible whiteness of her skin.

Martha then turned, as if trying to escape, but her legs would not support her weight, causing her to stumble down two steps, grasping hold of the banister to prevent herself from falling down the entire flight of stairs.

Matilda was greatly shocked as she heard an horrific bubbling sound coming from Martha's lungs. She thought that the weight of the candlestick would have killed her instantly, and now she was wondering if she should hit her again.

Martha was leaning with her back against the banisters, her legs half collapsed beneath her, her arms spread wide as they grasped the wood. Matilda walked slowly towards her, wondering what she should do now. She felt strangely disconnected, as if her body and her brain had somehow drifted apart and were no longer able to communicate with each other. She felt no emotion at all, just a grim determination to finish what she had started.

"I'm sorry, Tilly," Martha was sobbing, and Matilda was struck by the fact that this was the first time she had ever seen her sister cry. "I'm sorry about what I did to Seraphina."

"You are not sorry at all, Martha, the only thing that you are sorry about is the fact that I have the control now, the power. Seraphina is dead because of you, and I will not, as long as I live, forgive you."

Matilda stepped forwards, and fleetingly a glimmer of hope sparked in Martha's eyes that Matilda was going to help her, but she didn't. Instead, she placed her hand flat against her sisters chest and using the full weight of her body, she pushed her backwards over the bannisters, hearing the sickening thud as Martha hit the hard, tiled floor below.

For a very long time it felt that the world had stopped turning. The house was completely silent, as if shaken by what it had witnessed. It was freezing cold. It felt to Matilda as if she had ceased to exist, as if she was unreal, as if nothing was truly real. Her brain stopped thinking, as she stood, paralysed like a statue, halfway up the stairs.

After what could have been minutes, hours or days, Kitty suddenly started to scream again. The sound passed through Matilda's body like an electric current, as if it had brought her back to life. She breathed in a huge gulp of air, like a drowning swimmer at last reaching the waters surface.

Her body suddenly jerked into action, she ran down the stairs, her heart galloping in her chest.

Martha was lying on her back on the hall floor. Her head was tilted at an unnatural angle, and to Matilda's horror, her unseeing eyes were still open, staring directly at her, the look of terror still visible. Around her head was a dark halo of blood, and her arms were flung out to her sides, like the snow angels the children used to make in the garden all those long years ago.

Kitty had stopped screaming but had collapsed to the ground and was sobbing hysterically. The house around them grew darker, colder, more silent, as if the life force had been sucked out of it. One of the oil lamps on the bureau hissed, spluttered and then died, as she stood there, unaware of time passing, shivering violently, still without moving, as if she had forgotten that she could.

Suddenly a sound jolted her back to the present. Lifting her head, she saw Jed Carter walking towards her from the direction of the kitchen.

The old man stopped dead when he saw the scene before him. Matilda was standing over the body of her sister, a silver candlestick still held in her hand, blood dripping down her dress and onto the floor.

"Tilly," he whispered raspingly, hardly able to believe what he was seeing. "For the love of God, what have you done?"

It was then that the first wave of emotion hit her, it was fear and terror. What was going to happen to her now? For the first time she began to cry.

"She killed Seraphina," she sobbed brokenly. "She took her out onto the fen, and she killed her."

Jed stumbled towards one of the chairs that stood against the wall, put his head in his hands and tried to think. He knew what he ought to do, what any right-thinking person would do, he should go straight away to the police cottage in the village, but he knew that he couldn't do that, for that would see the girl that he loved like a granddaughter, hanged for murder. It would leave Kitty an orphan with no family, she would most likely end up being incarcerated in one institution or another.

After a very long time he stood up. Even though he was now very elderly, he was still wiry and strong, thanks to his years of hard labour. He thought carefully and quickly, eventually nodding his head, knowing that he would be physically capable of carrying out his plan.

"I will sort this out, Tilly," he said quietly, "stop crying now, I'll sort it out. Take Kitty away to one of the other rooms and when I have left the house, clean up this mess," he gesticulated towards the blood. "Clean it thoroughly. Give me that," he took the candlestick out of her hand, putting his free hand into his pocket. "I was bringing your gloves back, you left them at the cottage when you visited us this afternoon, and I knew that you would have been upset if you thought you had lost them, as they belonged to Emma."

"She deserved it, Jed, for what she has done."

Jed closed his eyes and nodded his head. "Take Kitty somewhere else while I move her," he jerked his head towards where Martha lay. "I will be back in a few hours."

Matilda took Kitty to the children's room, while Jed carried Martha's body out of the house, then transferred it into an old wheelbarrow that he kept in the barn, covering it with a couple of sacks that he found in the corner.

The huge black horsed snuffled and whinnied, as it watched Jed picking up a pick and a shovel that were leaning against the wall. Jed scratched the horse's nose and reaching into his pocket he pulled out a small carrot that he always carried with him for his own horses.

The horse lowered his head and nudged his shoulder. "God help me, Merlin," he whispered, "God help us all."

Jed took Martha's body far out onto the fen, where she was unceremoniously buried, using a pick and shovel from her father's barn, along with the weapon used to kill her.

\*

By the time that Jed returned to the house it was much later in the evening. The hard frost had made his gruesome task twice as difficult, and it had taken much more time than he had anticipated.

He found Matilda and Kitty in the children's room. The fire and oil lamps were unlit, and the room was dark and freezing cold. Despite this, young Kitty was fast asleep, lying curled up beneath a couple of blankets on the sofa, while Matilda sat staring into the empty fireplace, a shawl wrapped around her shoulders. Jed lit one of the lamps and then sat down opposite her.

"You understand what you have done, Tilly? You've committed

the greatest sin known to man, a mortal sin, and if it is ever discovered you will most likely hang for it." There was no point in sugar coating his words, for Matilda had to understand, in no uncertain terms, the gravity of the situation she had brought upon herself.

She stared at him with huge, frightened eyes and then nodded her head.

Jed leaned towards her, keeping his voice low, so as not to awaken Kitty. "I think it will be alright, Tilly. I have taken Martha very far away and have buried her in a place few people know about, let alone pass by. I have made her a good, deep grave, and I am as certain as I can be that she will never be discovered. Like I said, I think everything is going to be alright. Martha never was a great one for other people, I can count on one hand the number of times I have ever seen her in the village. She is not well known, and I don't believe that anyone will notice her absence. I don't think that anybody will come to the house to inquire after her, but if anyone ever does, you just tell them that she went away to make a life for herself somewhere else."

"She deserved it, Jed," Matilda reiterated the sentence she had spoken hours before. "She is dead, and she deserves to be, and try as I might, I can't be sorry for that."

Jed removed his cap and turned it over and over in his hands. "When you first learned of Seraphina's death, you should have come straight to me, and together we would have gone to the police cottage in the village and informed constable Davis. He would have come and taken her away, and one way or another, she would have ended up dead anyway."

"I lost my mind," Matilda uttered fretfully, tears coursing down her cheeks. "I couldn't bear what she had done to Seraphina. I couldn't stand the fact that she was free to carry on with her life while Seraphina was dead."

"You couldn't have been thinking straight, Tilly, and I know that you wouldn't have been capable of doing what you did to Martha if you'd been in your right mind."

"What am I going to do, Jed?"

Jed looked at her tearstained, terror-stricken face. "I will tell you exactly what you are going to do, Tilly. When I leave here tonight, you are going to lock all the doors behind me, and you are going to stay here, inside Meadowside. Don't go to the village, I will make sure that you have enough food and supplies, and don't wander too far from the house. Let time pass by, Tilly, let people's memories fade, and I reckon that in the space of a few years people will have forgotten all about Martha, and then you can just get on with your life as if nothing has happened."

Matilda wiped her tears away with the back of her hand. "Thank you, Jed," she cried miserably, "and I'm so sorry that you've had to be involved."

"Stop your crying now, Tilly." He turned his head and gazed at Kitty, still asleep on the sofa. "You have a job to do now, to take care of Kitty, make her safe and happy, God knows she deserves some peace and happiness in her life, and she only has you to depend on."

"I will look after her, Jed," Tilly promised solemnly. "I'll keep her safe and happy, here at Meadowside."

"Good girl," Jed stood up to leave and was halfway to the door when he stopped and turned around. "Bad things happen, Tilly, terrible things, but gradually, over time they tend to fade away. The human brain is a marvellous thing, it can choose what it remembers and what it forgets, remember the happy times, Tilly, and do whatever you need to do to make life bearable for yourself," again his eyes rested on Kitty, "and for her."

Jed Carter left Meadowside through the kitchen door, his heart heavy but believing that he had done a very wicked thing for a very good reason. He hoped that the God he so fervently believed in would see that when his judgement day came to pass, his only sin had been saving a young woman from the hangman, and in doing so had also saved the innocent Kitty, who surely would have suffered the most.

As soon as Jed left, Matilda went around the house and locked all of the doors, Kitty following closely behind her.

"We will stay at Meadowside, Kitty," Matilda said, "we will be safe here for the house will look after and protect us. One day, one day soon, we will be happy again, just you and me together, and I promise you this, Kitty, I promise you from the bottom of my heart, that I will never, ever, leave you here on your own."

Kitty blinked her tears away and smiled happily, for Matilda had spoken the very words that she needed to hear, and now her mind was settled and calm. She would forget that thing she thought she had witnessed in the hall; that horrible, violent act that could have, quite possibly, been nothing more than one of her bad dreams.

Matilda took hold of her hand and together they walked up the stairs. When they reached the landing Matilda suddenly stopped. In the darkness, right at the end of the corridor, she saw a strange movement. For all the world it looked like the shadows were moving, and then she saw the dark figure walking away from them. She held tighter to Kitty's hand, as she heard the opening of a door, and it being firmly closed.

She stood still, shocked to her core, her mind confused even though she knew very well what she had seen. It was Martha's ghost, making her way to her bedroom as she did every night around this time, letting Matilda know that she was still there, and the peace that Matilda craved, would be the last thing she would ever receive.

"We will sleep in Mother and Father's room tonight," she said, "we will be safe in there, and I will be nearby in case you need me in the night."

Before she entered the room that had once belonged to her parents she stopped and looked back down the corridor. The shadows were now still, the darkness silent and peaceful, but she made the decision there and then that from now on the far end of the corridor would be out of bounds, forever.

# Chapter 16

I sat completely still as Matilda finished speaking, unable, for a while, to find any words to say, and feeling utterly shocked by the knowledge, that the small, sick and fragile old lady that sat before me had, deliberately, and in cold blood, murdered her sister.

"Jed Carter was right, of course, I should have reported Seraphina's murder to the police, and let them deal with Martha as they saw fit, but at the time the thought didn't enter my head. I was hellbent on avenging Seraphina's death, and looking back, I don't think I was in my right mind, it was like a blind insanity came over me, a need to punish Martha, not just for Seraphina's terrible, lonely death, but for all of the years that went before."

A lone tear trickled down her cheek. "The grief that I felt over the loss of Seraphina was all-consuming, the loneliness of missing her has never truly left me. Kitty and I had been through so much, it was like my mind just fractured into a thousand pieces, and no matter how hard I tried, I couldn't fit the pieces back together again.

"Martha was so pleased with herself," Matilda continued with bitterness and condemnation in her voice. "She was actually gloating about what she had done, although, looking back, I think she did that to forge even more control over myself and Kitty, for if she had lived, I have no doubt that she would have threatened us with the same fate as Seraphina if we ever dared to challenge her or step out of line."

"I can't believe that you killed her, Matilda," I said eventually, "and in cold blood."

Matilda lifted her watery eyes to mine. "I did what I thought I had to do, to protect myself and Kitty from any further distress or harm at the hands of Martha." She bristled slightly and then sighed. "What I did was wrong, there is no doubt about that, but I was young and didn't know what to do."

After a long silence I leaned towards her, still reeling from the shock of what Matilda had done. I don't know how I was expecting her story to end, but this scenario had not occurred to me, until Nathaniel had suggested it.

"Matilda," I spoke gently, "was Martha really that bad? You are painting a picture of a psychopath, a cold-blooded criminal, who took a young girl out onto the fen and brutally murdered her."

"She was disturbed, consumed with superstition and fear. I think she really believed that Seraphina was trying to kill her and that she had supernatural powers, which I suppose, when you think about it, does not add up to a sane, clear thinking young woman. She was paranoid, Amber, and unable to listen to reason."

"So, that is why Martha haunts the house? Because you killed her, and she can't forgive you?"

"I think there are several reasons why she's still here, one of them is because I killed her, and if I can tell you one thing about Martha, it's that she could hold a grudge for years, and was slow to forgive. She was vengeful, spiteful and determined to get her own way, and in that respect, she hasn't changed." Matilda was silent for a while, her hands fiddling fractiously with her blanket. "I don't think I am the only reason that she's stayed here, I still strongly believe that she is here because she's terrified of what could be waiting for her if she passes over, Seraphina for a start, and hells fires and retribution. She is scared to go where she may be judged."

"What about you, Matilda? Are you scared to go where you may also be judged?"

Matilda straightened her back and gazed at me levelly. "I am prepared to face whatever I have waiting for me, Amber. I will face any retribution that I may have coming, but at the end of the day I did what I set out to do. I have protected Kitty and have done everything in my power to keep her safe and happy. I have cared for her for all these years, protecting her from a world that might frighten or reject her. Kitty has suffered more than enough heartache and grief, but all of that stopped on the day that Martha died, and I can't be sorry for that. I have sacrificed the life that I could have had, for her sake, and since that day eighty-two years ago, I have done everything right."

I slumped back in my chair, massaging my forehead to try and ease away the beginning of a headache. "You knew on the day that she died that Martha hadn't left the house, that her spirit remained?"

"I saw her creeping, dark shadow on the landing and heard her enter her bedroom. At that moment in time, the only thing that I wanted in life was some peace, peace within the house that had been in turmoil for so long, and peace of mind. Martha ensured that I didn't receive peace of any kind. I didn't want Kitty to be frightened by Martha's ghost, so I locked all of the rooms at the end of the landing to stop her going into them and inadvertently disturbing Martha."

"You have always said that Martha didn't cause you a lot of trouble, though?"

"No," she shook her head, "she hasn't, and in the strangest of ways, we have, all three of us lived here quite peaceably together. Over the passing of so many years I have grown used to Martha being here and have mostly managed to ignore her presence."

"Then I came along," I said quietly, "and disturbed and challenged her."

"She wouldn't have liked a stranger being in the house, and maybe that is how she viewed Seraphina, just as a stranger. It was Martha's distress and madness, I think, that made her accuse Seraphina of being a witch who had cursed Meadowside and my family."

"What did you think? Did you ever believe that Seraphina was capable of such things?"

Matilda laughed. "Seraphina would never have hurt a fly. She did say some strange things at times, she talked about being able to see the spirits of dead people, and she seemed to have an innate knowledge about life and nature, but I have never believed that she was capable of casting jinxes and curses. That was all just in Martha's head."

"You believed she could see dead people though, and look into the future?"

"Yes, I think that she could do those things, although I never did understand how."

"I don't understand how I can see Martha, but I can, or Issy in the meadow, and of course Kitty has always been able to see Issy."

"Yes, indeed," she concurred, "which makes me think that maybe spirits appear to people sensitive enough to open their eyes, or maybe even for people who have the desire to see them. All I wanted, all I ever wanted, was for Meadowside to be at peace and for the past to be over and done with, and I was certainly not interested in trying to resurrect the dead or the past as it used to be."

Matilda was growing tired again. I could see her eyelids growing heavy, and she yawned as she shuffled her weight in the chair.

"Do you know what Martha did to Seraphina, how she killed her?"

A shadow passed over Matilda's face. "Kitty said that Martha had blood all over her. It is my belief that Martha took a knife from the kitchen and used it to kill her."

Matilda became silent and closed her eyes. For a moment I thought that she had fallen asleep and was about to stand up and leave the room, but then she suddenly opened her eyes again.

"I walked out on the fen every day for months looking for Seraphina. Quite often Kitty and I would sit astride Merlin so that we could cover a further distance. I thought that Martha might not have succeeded in killing her, and could have just wounded her, leaving her out on the fen to starve and freeze to death.

"After several weeks my search changed, and I began to look for her body, but it was like looking for a needle in a haystack. She could have been anywhere, and Jed Carter believed that Martha had burned the body, for when he had taken Martha out on the fen to bury her, he searched her body for anything that might identify her, but the only thing that he found in her pockets was a box of matches. I wanted to search anyway, just to be sure, even though I knew deep inside me that Jed was probably right about Martha cremating the body. If she had managed to take Seraphina far enough out on the fen, then a small fire burning would not have been noticed in the village, and even if it was, people would have just thought it was a traveller making a camp for the night."

Matilda yawned again and turned her head towards the fireplace.

"I'll make us a cup of tea," I said, standing up, "and some biscuits, perhaps?"

"That would be nice, thank you Amber."

In the kitchen Nathaniel was sitting at the table with a newspaper spread out before him.

"Where's Kitty?" I asked as I filled the kettle at the sink.

"Beth has taken her to the supermarket, apparently it's her new favourite place."

While the kettle boiled I joined Nathaniel at the table, pushing the newspaper out of the way. "You were right, Nathaniel," I rubbed my eyes, suddenly feeling exhausted. "Martha took Seraphina out on to the fen and killed her. Apparently she stabbed her to death with a knife she had taken from the kitchen and then cremated her body."

"What?" He was frowning, his dark eyes registering his shock.

I laughed humourlessly. "That's not the half of it. When Matilda discovered what Martha had done, she completely lost all control and hit Martha over the head with a candlestick holder, then when that didn't kill her outright, she pushed her over the bannisters."

Hearing myself recounting what had occurred in the house, made the whole thing sound absurd. I stood up and made Matilda's tea, placing a few biscuits on a plate. I then returned to the children's room, allowing Nathaniel to take in the enormity of what I had told him.

I placed the tea and biscuits on a table at the side of Matilda's chair.

"Will you be alright here for a while, or would you rather go back to your room?"

"I'll be fine here, Amber. I will drink my tea and then I'll have a little sleep."

"Okay," I said, walking away. "I'll come back and check on you in an hour or so."

I returned to the kitchen and sat back down at the table. Nathaniel was still in shock, an incredulous expression on his face.

"I can't believe it," he said, running his fingers through his hair. "Why on Earth didn't she just report Seraphina's death to the police? What in God's name was she thinking of?"

"She wasn't thinking straight. She had just learned that after losing so many members of her family, she had now lost Seraphina too. It seems to me that it was the last straw and she just lost her mind."

"It's all making sense now," Nathaniel closed his eyes while he straightened out the facts in his head. "Matilda murdered Martha, which is why Martha's death was never registered, and why she doesn't have a grave in the churchyard, and the exact same scenario also applies to Seraphina." He frowned for a moment and shook his head. "If Martha took Seraphina out onto the fen alive, murdered her and then burnt her body, that makes sense, but what did Matilda do with Martha after she'd killed her?"

"Jed Carter, who was the gardener at Meadowside, walked in on the scene soon afterwards. To save Matilda, he took Martha's body out onto the fen and buried it."

Nathaniel threw his hands up in the air. "That is why Martha is here then, because she was murdered by Matilda and wants revenge?"

"I think so."

"Matilda should have reported Seraphina's death and allowed legal due course to take care of Martha, but then she had been pushed to the limit. It was a crime of passion, a heat of the moment thing, she discovered what Martha had done to Seraphina, lost her senses and lashed out at Martha, unfortunately killing her."

I gazed at him for a moment and then decided to speak the truth. "It didn't happen quite like that, Nathaniel, Matilda actually had to go and search for a weapon, she went to the girl's bedroom, decided that the candlestick would do the job and then attacked Martha with it, and don't forget, when that didn't work, she pushed her over the bannisters."

Nathanial slumped in his chair. "So, it was cold blooded, premeditated murder?"

"You have to remember that she was only nineteen years old, just a teenager, and what she had been through. I'm sure that the string of tragedies would have damaged someone so young. I am certain that she wasn't in her right mind." I looked at him pleadingly, suddenly feeling that it was important that he understood Matilda's actions and wouldn't condemn her. "She was also greatly burdened with the responsibility of Kitty, all she wanted was some peace and to protect Kitty from Martha."

"Does Kitty know what Matilda did?"

I lowered my eyes. "Kitty was there when it happened, she witnessed all of it, and was also on her own in the house when Martha returned, covered in blood and without Seraphina."

Nathaniel exhaled a long breath. "No wonder she's the way she is. How old was she when she witnessed one of her sisters kill the other?"

I shrugged, "I think she was about fourteen, maybe a bit younger even."

"Poor Kitty," he shook his head, "that must have been a terrible thing for her to see."

"Oh, Nathaniel," I cried in despair, "what an awful thing it was. It seems that everything spiralled out of control for Matilda."

I stood up and walked to the window, staring out beyond the garden to the fen. "It makes me shiver to think that two young women are lying out there, unknown about, undiscovered for all of this time."

"It's a tragedy," he came and stood beside me, resting his arm lightly around my shoulders, "but there is absolutely nothing we can do about it now."

I glanced up at him worriedly. "Should we inform someone? Are we obliged to?"

"What would be the point? Seraphina's body was burned, and Martha would be impossible to find. No, I just think it's best just to let the past rest in peace. The only thing we need to do now is to get Martha out of the house."

"Matilda was just telling me how she hasn't been too much of a problem over the years and how they have lived together here quite peaceably."

"That isn't the case now though, is it? All this moving things around, and throwing things at you, which is just plain dangerous. You know, Amber, maybe it's time we thought about getting some help, there are specialists in this kind of thing, maybe we could find someone who could do something to get her out of the house. I know that you haven't been keen on the idea before, but surely you can see that we have to do something."

I laughed scornfully. "Are you talking about an exorcist?"

He shrugged his shoulders and scowled at me. "Why not? These people only exist because other people have a need for their services." He rubbed his chin thoughtfully, and then looked at me with genuine worry in his eyes. "Have you ever seriously considered the possibility that Martha was insane? None of the behaviour that Matilda has described to you sounds like a well-balanced, mentally stable person to me. It sounds as if she were paranoid and had some kind of a weird fixation about Seraphina."

"Yes, I have considered it. Isn't mental illness sometimes caused by distressing events in one's early years? I must keep reminding myself that Martha went through a lot of what Matilda and Kitty did. I think that she was hugely impacted by Jack's death but was unable to express her grief. She may then have built barriers around herself, distancing herself from her family, protecting herself so that she would never feel that kind of pain again.

"You know, at the end of the day, I think it was Seraphina who understood Martha the best. I remember Matilda telling me that Seraphina believed that Martha had been affected by the deaths in the family far more than she let on, and her utter indifference towards everybody was just a form of self-protection."

"Seraphina sounds as if she was very tuned in for a person who was so young."

"Oh, she was, "I told him enthusiastically. "I think that the general consensus was that Seraphina was born with a special gift and had a deep empathy as well as an unusual understanding of human beings and animals."

"She sounds very special," Nathaniel said sadly, "what a shame she had to die in such a terrible way, and so young too."

"Yes," I sighed, feeling a heaviness in my heart. What had happened to Seraphina was playing on mind, it was such a needless tragedy, a senseless crime. "According to my calculations she was only sixteen or seventeen years old."

"What do you think about getting someone in to help with Martha?" Nathaniel pressed, obviously very keen on the idea himself.

"Let's just wait and see what happens now. I agree with you that Martha can't stay here, but it could be that now the truth of her death has been revealed, she might just leave of her own accord."

Nathaniel looked at my doubtfully. "Well, let's hope that you're right and that nothing else happens."

"I don't think that it will," I replied confidently. "I just have a feeling."

For several weeks it appeared that I may have been right. The house seemed to have come alive, and the oppressive atmosphere slowly lifted to be replaced with air of optimism and hope.

The darker nights set in, and winter arrived with a vengeance. Although Matilda remained physically weak, her health had slowly improved. She had gained a little bit of weight and was looking much better. During that time, we rarely spoke about Martha, or even Seraphina, and it seemed that in the telling of her story Matilda had managed to put the past to rest in her own mind. But then everything suddenly changed again.

It was a morning in late November. I awoke to the sound of the rain hammering against my bedroom window, and the eerie screeching of a high wind as it swept around the house.

It was still dark when I decided to get up. I was excited about bringing Christmas to Meadowside for the first time in several decades. According to Matilda the sisters hadn't celebrated at all, in fact, they barely acknowledged it. The last Christmas that Matilda could remember celebrating was back in 1913, just days before Jack died, and I was determined that Christmas 2003, was going to be special for them both.

Wearing thick, fleecy pyjamas, a dressing gown and slippers, I headed to the kitchen, made my first black coffee of the day, and sat at the table with a pen and note pad to make a list of what needed doing, and what needed buying. The weather forecast informed me that the rain was due to fade away by mid-morning, and I had plans to drive into Cambridge for some Christmas shopping.

I had written two or three items on the list, when I became aware of a strange noise. I stopped writing, glancing quickly around me to try and identify what had caused the sound. It was a quiet, scraping, and then I noticed that the chair at the table opposite me was slowly being pulled backwards, and was then rapidly spun around and hurled across the room.

The lights began to flicker, and I watched in horror as a tea towel that had been on the tabletop, drifted into the air, swirling around like a kite in the wind.

I stood up quickly as the large wooden dresser began to vibrate, the crockery and china inside jangling together, tinkling like an orchestra tuning up. Standing close to the table I watched, a little bit fascinated, but mostly terrified, as my coffee cup slid across the table, the contents spilling out of it, and was then thrown against the wall, the cup exploding into pieces onto the floor.

"Oh no," I uttered under my breath, backing towards the door, feeling the atmosphere growing sinister and dark as, at that moment, an empty vase standing at the end of the table, was lifted, hovering in the air for a few moments before it was violently thrown right at me. I ducked just in time and the vase hit the wall behind me.

I was now standing in the doorway of the kitchen, and then swung around and screamed in terror as I felt a hand touch me on the shoulder. Almost jumping clean out of my skin I turned to see Nathaniel, wearing a pair of tartan pyjama bottoms, and a long-sleeved tee-shirt.

As soon as he appeared, and as if by magic, the kitchen fell still and silent, the threatening atmosphere quickly fading away, the tea towel fluttered to the ground, and the rattling of crockery stopped dead.

"Nathaniel, she's back," I whispered bitterly.

"Evidently," he replied, his eyes skimming over the mess that had been created.

He led me to the front lounge, and we sat down in the armchairs. I felt thoroughly shaken, not least because I had stupidly believed that Martha had gone, that she had been placated by the fact that I now knew the circumstances of her death.

"Now what are we going to do?" Nathaniel asked despondently. "You could have been injured. You managed to dodge the flying objects, but what would have happened if it had been Kitty or Matilda in the kitchen?"

I frowned at him as I forced my brain to think. "I'm missing something," I uttered and then looked up at him. "The activity has never happened to Matilda, and apart from the night when Martha wrecked the kitchen, when Kitty was frightened by the noise and the flickering lights, it hasn't really happened to her either, in as much as neither of them are being targeted by Martha. It is me that she wants to get rid of, Nathaniel. Look what happened when you approached the kitchen, it all stopped dead. It is me she's trying to frighten out of Meadowside, and now I'm growing increasingly worried about how far she is willing to go."

"If that vase had hit you, Amber, it could have killed you." Nathaniel ran his fingers through his hair in exasperation and then fixed me with a solemn, determined gaze. "We need help, this has been getting out of hand for a long time now, and, in my opinion, it can only get worse, and most definitely is not going to go away on its own."

"I'm missing something," I reiterated, "Matilda has told me her story, I know everything that happened, and I truly believed that Martha had left. The house has been peaceful for weeks, why would she suddenly come back now?" I bit my thumb nail fretfully. "Perhaps Martha was just lulling us into a false sense of security, that was how she tricked Matilda into leaving Seraphina in the house the day that she was killed, she had set it up for weeks beforehand, pretending she had changed, that she had accepted Seraphina."

"Yes, Amber, and then she brutally killed her."

"Ghosts can't kill people, Nathaniel."

"You know that for certain, do you? She's dangerous, a maniac." He placed his head in his hands for a moment and then his eyes met mine. "Are you absolutely certain that Matilda has told you everything?"

"I believe that she has."

At that moment I heard the tinkling of a bell and immediately stood up.

"That's Matilda," I informed Nathaniel who had looked confused by the sound. "I gave her the little bell that was on the desk in the library and told her to ring it if she ever needed anything while I wasn't with her."

Nathaniel waited in the hall while I went into Matilda's bedroom to find out what she wanted. "Good morning, Matilda," I said brightly as I entered the room and walked towards the bed. "Is everything alright? You're not usually awake this early."

She had managed to sit herself up in the bed, but the pillows looked uncomfortable. I straightened them for her and sat in the bedside chair.

"I heard something," she said, her expression concerned. "Did you drop something in the kitchen?"

I hesitated for a moment but could find no reason not to tell her the truth. "It was Martha," I said, "I'm afraid she's back."

Matilda nodded her head. "I thought as much."

"Nathaniel is waiting outside; would you mind if he came in? He wants to hire some kind of help to deal with Martha, people who know about hauntings and how to get rid of ghosts and spirits. I can't say that I am too keen on the idea, simply because I can't see Martha leaving just because a priest, or whoever, tells her to."

"Let him come in," Matilda smiled, "let's hear what he has to say."

Nathaniel dragged the dressing table stool over to the bed and sat down.

"So, she's back?" Matilda laughed harshly; her eyes cold. "This is so much like Martha, making everyone think that she'd gone, and then suddenly returning when you least expect it."

"This can't go on, Matilda. I believe that Martha is dangerous and could seriously harm one of us." Nathaniel stared at the fragile old woman for a while before asking, "would you agree to me trying to find someone who could help us? I believe that the church has people who cleanse houses of spirits and suchlike."

Matilda was about to say something. It looked as if she was about to agree to Nathaniel's request, but I couldn't rid myself of the feeling that I had overlooked something; that there was something glaringly obvious that I just wasn't seeing.

"You have told me everything, haven't you, Matilda? You haven't forgotten something or withheld anything from me?"

Matilda removed her gaze from Nathaniel and focused on me. "I have told you everything, Amber, and I don't believe that I have forgotten anything of significance. There is nothing more to tell."

"So, Matilda, you are happy for me to try and find somebody to help?" Nathaniel quickly continued, pressing her for consent, while I, deep inside, knew that it wasn't the answer and was unlikely to work.

"It wasn't too bad when she wasn't causing any trouble. I knew that she was there, but all the time she was quiet, all the time that we stayed away from her, we could live with her." She turned her eyes to me. "I don't want this for you, Amber. After I have gone, I don't want for you to be still dealing with Martha and my past. I want you to live here and to be happy."

"Then I'll start to make some enquiries. I don't really know where to start, but I'll figure it out." He patted Matilda's hand comfortingly. "Don't worry any more about it, one way or another we will get it sorted."

I fiddled with a ring that I always wore, turning it around on my finger. It was a small diamond ring that my father gave to my mother on their first wedding anniversary, and on my sixteenth birthday my mother gave it to me, and I had worn it constantly ever since. I wondered about the information that my father had found that had somehow led him to Matilda all of those years ago, and not for the first time since arriving at Meadowside, I fervently wished that there was some way he could tell me exactly what that information was.

"I don't think that bringing someone to the house will work, in fact, I'm almost certain that it won't." I looked up at Nathaniel, "but I am happy to give it a try."

*

As it turned out the services of a psychic medium or a priest from the church, were not required. I spent the next few days busy with Christmas preparations, but every now and again I was increasingly convinced, that Matilda had forgotten a key element in her story, the missing link that would finally make everything fall into place. The feeling was one of pure frustration, and I went over everything that Matilda had related to me time and again but was no nearer discovering what the missing link could be.

Then, on the first day of December, I was with Kitty in the front lounge. I was writing Christmas cards, and she was busily absorbed in a jigsaw puzzle, depicting a cheery Christmas scene, and spread out on the coffee table.

As she concentrated on finding the last corner of the puzzle, she started humming to herself and then after a few moments she began to sing the words of the tune quietly, and then, as if I'd been hit by a sledgehammer, my blood turned to ice.

I stared at her covertly for a long time, trying to make sense of something that literally could not be explained.

"Kitty," I said, frowning as my heart fluttered in my chest like a butterfly trapped inside a glass jar. "How do you know that song?"

She moved her focus from the puzzle to me. "I learned it from Seraphina," she said after a full minute of deliberation. "She used to sing it to me when I was a little girl. I was always so frightened of storms, and she used to sit on the side of the bed and sing it to me until I went back to sleep."

"Are you completely sure, Kitty? Are you certain you learned the song from Seraphina?"

She looked at me with a mystified expression. "I am absolutely positive, Amber, it was definitely Seraphina who taught me the song. It was about a little gipsy boy who could change the weather by playing his fiddle. At harvest time he played for the sun to come out, and in stormy weather his music calmed the thunder and lightning."

"I see," my voice caught in my throat as I blinked away tears that were stinging the back of my eyes.

My thoughts were deeply confused, and I was unable to make sense of what had just occurred. I repeatedly told myself that it was impossible, but eventually, my brain, numb with shock, came up with the only solution that could possibly explain it.

I let out a gasp as the implications slowly dawned on me.

"Are you quite alright, Amber? You look awfully white. Are you sick?"

I shook my head, standing up. "I'm fine, Kitty; I just need to get some fresh air."

I left the room at a running pace, intending to go to my bedroom to calm myself and to properly figure out what had happened, but as I ran out into the hall, Nathaniel was coming out of the library and as soon as I set eyes on him, I burst into a fit of crying.

"Amber?" He came quickly to my side. "What on Earth has happened? You look as white as a sheet. Are you okay?"

I shook my head unable to speak. I was far from okay and was beginning to wonder if I would ever be okay again. I wanted to explain to him the cause of my distress, but I just couldn't stop crying.

"Nathaniel," I eventually managed to utter, "I want to go home."

"What?" He took hold of me by the shoulders and held me at arm's length. "You mean you want to go back to Cambridge?"

I nodded wretchedly. "Yes," I spluttered, "I want to go now, straight away."

He led me to one of the chairs positioned against the wall and pushed me into it.

"Stay here for a minute, Amber. I won't be long."

A few minutes later he returned to the hall, looking distracted and flustered. "I've phoned Beth and have asked her to come and sit with Matilda and Kitty. She's going to ask her parents to pick up the children from school and look after them." He gazed at me solemnly. "I had to tell her everything about Martha, how she murdered Seraphina, and how she was very active in the house recently. It is only fair that she knows the whole truth. She is going to bring her husband with her, so she won't be here alone."

I stood up shakily and walked towards him. "I don't think that Beth has to worry so much about Martha, I don't think any of us do."

He frowned. "Having a ghost in the house, Amber, is bad enough, having one who was a cold-blooded murderer is definitely something to worry about."

"That's just it," I sobbed, "I don't think that Martha murdered anybody."

"That's ridiculous," he replied sharply, "we know that she killed Seraphina, Matilda told you."

"I don't think that she did murder Seraphina, Nathaniel, in fact, I am almost certain that she didn't"

"Almost certain?" He looked at me as if I had lost my mind. "How can you know that? How can you be certain?"

"Because" I uttered, my stomach churning with nausea, "I think that Seraphina is still alive."

"What?" Nathaniel walked away from me, his hands on the top of his head as if he couldn't believe what I had just said. "How can she still be alive? Martha killed her, she took her out onto the fen and murdered her in cold blood? Why would Matilda tell you that if it hadn't happened?"

"I don't know," I cried, "I can't think straight, I can barely take it in myself."

"This is crazy Amber. I just don't understand how you have come to this conclusion."

At that moment Beth came bursting into the hall through the front door. She came straight over to me.

"Amber? What's going on? You look terrible and Nathaniel said that you want to go home?"

"Something has happened, Beth, and I need to go home to sort it out."

"You are coming back though?"

"Of course, I am, I'll be back later tonight."

"What is it, Amber? Are you ill? Is your Mother okay?"

"It's nothing like that. Look, Beth," I glanced behind me to see Nathaniel putting on his coat and searching through the pockets for his car keys. "I'll explain it all to you when I get back tonight. It's not making sense to me at the moment, but when I come home, I will know so much more."

"Okay," she nodded her head, resigned to the fact that she would have to wait to discover what had occurred to make me so upset. "Don't worry about anything here, Amber, my mum and dad were happy to pick the children up from school and will keep them until I collect them later or in the morning. Just go and do what you have to do."

"Thanks so much, Beth," I hugged her, "I don't know what I'd do without you. Did Stephen mind having to come over?"

At that moment Nathaniel and Beth's husband were chatting at the far end of the hall.

"He didn't mind at all. As long as he can watch the football, he'll be happy enough."

"Okay, thanks again Beth," I walked towards Nathaniel who was now standing at the open front door, waiting for me. "There's plenty of food, so help yourself to whatever you want. There's also beer and wine in the fridge, just have what you fancy, and I'll see you later on."

# Chapter 17

Nathaniel drove through the village, but it wasn't until we were on the main road, heading towards Cambridge, that he spoke.

"Do you think you could tell me what's going on now?" He pulled into an empty layby, took off his seatbelt and turned towards me. "I'm really confused as to why you think that Seraphina could still be alive, I mean, how could that thought have even entered your head after all that Matilda has told you."

I was feeling slightly better, calmer, but I was still stunned and emotional.

"I was in the front lounge with Kitty, she was doing a jigsaw puzzle, totally absorbed, and then she started humming a tune to herself, which I vaguely recognised, but nothing really registered with me at that point. Then she began to sing the words of the song, and I suddenly remembered that I had heard it before."

Nathaniel continued to look baffled. "I still don't understand."

"I asked Kitty how she knew the song. It's about a young gipsy boy who can influence the weather when he plays the fiddle, and Kitty said that it was Seraphina who used to sing it to her when she was little." I began to feel tearful again and dabbed at my face with a tissue.

"So," Nathaniel shrugged, "it was an old song from Kitty's childhood? Why has that made you want to go home? Why has it upset you so much?"

I sighed, placing my head in my hands, still unable to believe this incredible turn of events. "Because, when I was a young child, someone used to sing the same song to me, and that person told me that the song had been made up for her by her grandfather, that it had never been written down, it was a song specifically made up for her."

"Was it your mother who used to sing it to you?"

I looked away for a moment through the passenger window of the car and then slowly turned back to him. "It was my grandmother." The tears began to fall freely again, streaming down my face. "Her name is Sarah, Sarah Lewis, and years ago when she was a child, her grandfather made up a song that he used to sing to her every night, the same song as Kitty was singing today."

Nathaniel stared at me, frowning and mystified.

"Don't you see, Nathaniel, the only way that Kitty could know that song is if the person who sang it to her, and the person who sang it to me, were one and the same."

The car was silent while Nathaniel digested my words. I took a few deep breaths trying to calm the almost unbearable anxiety that I felt.

"She must have stopped using the name Seraphina and changed it to Sarah."

"So, this Sarah Lewis is your paternal grandmother?"

"Yes, and now I am thinking that my father might have found something that connected him to Matilda through Jack. I don't think I'm related to Matilda and Kitty through their uncle at all, I am related to them because Jack was my great grandfather."

Nathanial exhaled a long breath. "That's incredible. If this song was truly only known by Seraphina and her grandfather, and if she used to sing it to Kitty, then Seraphina must be your grandmother."

"Exactly, and you know what it also means?"

He looked at me blankly.

"Martha hated Seraphina. She could never believe that she was Jack's daughter and was convinced that she had cursed the house and the family and had no right to be living at Meadowside."

Again, I turned my head to the window. "Then I come along, Seraphina's granddaughter, of all people. No wonder Martha began to kick off, no wonder she's been trying to frighten me out of the house." I turned back to face him, feeling drained and exhausted, a sense of doom like a cold stone in my chest. "Martha was murdered because of Seraphina but, at the end of the day Seraphina had won. Martha died because of her."

"What are you going to do?" Nathaniel asked gravely.

"I want to go to my mother's house first and tell her what's been going on, and then I need to speak to Granny."

Nathaniel started the car engine and re-joined the sparse traffic on the road.

"What if I'm right, Nathaniel?" I started to cry again, hardly able to assimilate that such a thing could be true, but at the same time knowing that nobody else, apart from my grandmother could have known that song.

Nathaniel glanced at me quickly then focused on the road. "If you are right, Amber, then it explains everything about Martha and why she's still in the house, but not why Matilda told you that Seraphina was dead, and that Martha killed her."

I bit my lip distractedly. "Matilda truly believes that Seraphina was killed back in 1921 at the hands of Martha. She has spent all of these years grieving for Seraphina, believing her body to have been heartlessly cremated out on the fen."

"Why would Martha want to give Matilda the impression that Seraphina was dead if she wasn't, and more to the point, why would she want her to think that she had killed her?"

"I think she just wanted Matilda to believe that Seraphina was gone forever, and that there was no point in looking for her, and perhaps she also wanted to exercise control over Kitty and Matilda. Maybe she even wanted them to think that they were at risk of the same fate if they ever disobeyed her."

"She was so complex," Nathaniel said sadly, "if she had loved them, cared for them, and was pleasant to be around then neither Matilda nor Kitty would have wanted to leave."

For the first time I found myself feeling some compassion for Martha. She had obviously been a damaged person, vulnerable and afraid in her own way. "Somewhere along the way, she lost the ability to love her family. I think she was very hurt, angry and shocked by the deaths, and built up barriers around herself so that she couldn't be hurt like that again. In the end I think her grief drove her insane."

"What I can't understand is why she blamed Seraphina for the tragedies."

"Because, she had to blame someone, and maybe, deep down, she blamed herself. Emma had worn herself out caring firstly for Seraphina, and then for both of her parents, and Martha did nothing to help her. Matilda said that Emma's death would have been the one that affected her the most."

"She was probably terrified of catching it herself."

"Yes," I agreed, "she probably was, and she blamed Seraphina for bringing it into the house in the first place. She was the first to become ill and when she didn't die from it, but Emma and her parents did, it just gave her more ammunition to attack Seraphina with."

"What an absolute mess," Nathaniel declared as he took a turning off the main road and yet again, we pulled up at another set of traffic lights.

He placed his hands on his knees while he waited for the lights to change. "I don't envy you your job," he muttered quietly, "having to tell your grandmother all of this, and then having to tell Matilda that Seraphina is still alive and was not murdered by Martha."

At that moment, as the lights changed and the car headed for the city, I didn't know which outcome I was hoping for.

\*

My mother was delighted to see me and Nathaniel standing on her doorstep. She had met Nathaniel before, and she greeted us both warmly.

"What are you two doing here?" She smiled delightedly and then looked worried. "Is everything alright? It is the old lady at Meadowside?"

"Mum," I said tearfully, "I have to talk to you about Granny."

"Your Grandmother? She's fine, Amber, I was only at the home yesterday, and she was on top form."

We walked into the kitchen and my mother filled the kettle and switched it on.

"What's all of this about, Amber? You look upset." She sat opposite me at the small wooden table and took hold of both of my hands. "Have you been crying?"

"It's such a mess, Mum, I hardly know where to begin."

"Shall I make the tea, Mrs Lewis?" Nathaniel was hovering around, not quite sure what to do with himself.

"That would be helpful, thank you," she beamed up at him, "and please, call me Sally. The mugs are in the cupboard in the corner, and the teabags are just there on the worktop."

She turned her attention back to me. "What's going on then, Amber?"

"Well," I began, trying to organise my jumbled thoughts into some semblance of order, "as you know, Matilda has been telling me the story of her younger years at Meadowside. There has been a lot of tragedy and difficult times in her life. All of her family, apart from Kitty, died young."

"Unfortunately, that was very common in those days, thank goodness that things are better now."

"Yes," I agreed solemnly, "thank goodness. You remember that my dad wrote to Matilda because he had found something that had made him think they were related?"

"I do remember you telling me about it, but I can't recall your father ever telling me that he had written to Matilda."

"Well, Matilda always thought that we were related to her through her father's brother, but now I am beginning to doubt that is the case. Mum, did Granny ever tell you anything about her childhood?"

"Your dad didn't know much about that. He said that she was

orphaned as a young child, and then lived with a family for a few years, but it didn't work out and she left when she was about seventeen years old. Since your dad died, I have tried to talk to her about her past on a few occasions, but it seemed to upset her, and in the end, I stopped asking her about it."

I glanced quickly towards Nathaniel. He had turned from the worktop on hearing my mother's words and was now looking at me with his eyebrows raised. So far, everything was adding up.

"Mum, there's been quite a lot of disruption at Meadowside since I arrived."

She looked surprised. "You never told me about any disruptions in your phone calls. What sort of disruptions?"

"That's because I didn't want to worry you, and what I am about to tell you will come as a huge shock, but Meadowside is haunted."

"Haunted?" she repeated, her mouth falling open with shock. "Are you sure?"

Nathaniel brought the mugs of tea over to the table and sat down.

"We are absolutely certain. The ghost is Martha, who is the eldest sister of Kitty and Matilda, and she has been in the house ever since she died back in 1921."

"Martha is quite disruptive," Nathaniel added, "and now Amber thinks that she knows why."

"And it has to do with Granny."

"Your Grandmother, what could it have to do with her? I'm not understanding any of this."

"Before the first world war a young girl was left at Meadowside. Her name was Seraphina, and she was left there by her grandparents. Her mother had died, and they became too old and sick to take care of her. She came from a gipsy family, and her grandparents were of the very strong opinion that Jack Grey, Matilda's brother, was her father. Jack died in the winter of 1913, so there was no way that the family could ever be certain that Seraphina was Jack's daughter."

"Was she Jack's daughter?" My mother asked curiously.

"I think it is highly likely. Anyway," I continued, trying not to bombard my mother with too much detail, as the story was long and complicated and probably best saved for another time. My mother only needed to know how it pertained to my grandmother at that point. "This afternoon I was sitting with Kitty when she suddenly started to sing a song to herself. I thought nothing of it at first, but then I began to recognise the song. Mum, it was the song about the gipsy boy and his fiddle, the one that Granny used to sing to me as a child. Do you remember it?"

"Yes," my mother frowned. "I remember it very well, but Amber, that song was made up by her grandfather. She told me that the song was composed especially for her, so there's no way that Kitty could have been singing it."

"I asked Kitty how she knew the song and she told me that Seraphina used to sing to her when she was a little girl," I continued quickly.

"That's not possible," my mother insisted, "how could Seraphina have known it? The only people who knew that song was your Granny and her grandfather, and he's been dead for years. Like I said, there's no way that Seraphina could have sung it to Kitty."

"There is a way, Mum, but you are right, it does seem impossible that Kitty could have known that song, and sing it word for word," my voice faltered and for a moment I fought against the tears that were threatening to fall again, "Unless, the person who sang it to Kitty, and then years later sang it to me, were the same person."

My mother looked at me for a long time, a string of different emotions passing over her face. "What exactly are you trying to say, Amber? Are you trying to tell me that you think your grandmother is this Seraphina girl?"

"I think that she is. I think before she met Grandad, her name was Seraphina Grey, and at the age of seventeen, she left Meadowside and made a new life for herself in Cambridge and changed her name to Sarah. I think she did that so Matilda would never be able to find her."

"Why wouldn't she want Matilda to find her?"

I felt suddenly exhausted and emotional and asked Nathaniel to tell my mother the rest of the story.

"Mrs Lewis…Sally, "he quickly corrected himself with a half-smile. "Matilda and Kitty believe that Seraphina is dead. They believe that Martha took her out onto the fen and murdered her and then cremated her body. On the day that they believed that Seraphina had been killed, Matilda, distraught with grief and not in her right mind, killed Martha by hitting her over the head and then tossing her over the bannisters."

"Good grief!" My mother gasped. "Two murders, after they had already lost so many family members, it's unbelievable."

"Two murders if Seraphina is actually dead." Nathaniel clarified.

"You accept the fact that Kitty couldn't have known that song? It must have been Granny who taught it to her, there is no other explanation." I sighed wearily, wondering how this bizarre situation was going to end. "If Granny is indeed Seraphina, then it explains why Martha is causing havoc at Meadowside. If Seraphina is alive then Matilda killed Martha for nothing."

"What do you want to do, Amber?" She looked at me, her eyes troubled.

"I need to speak to Granny, Mum. I need to know if she is Seraphina Grey, and what happened on the night she left Meadowside. I also think that I may need to bring her back to the house, if she agrees to come with me."

"You want to take your grandmother to a haunted house? Amber, she's in her late nineties, I don't want her upset."

"I don't want her to be upset either, but Mum, I think that all that time ago Dad somehow found a link between Granny and Matilda; that is why he wrote to her. If Dad had lived he would have probably followed it through and eventually it would all have come out. I won't take Granny anywhere she doesn't want to go, but she loved Matilda and Kitty, she loved them all, apart from Martha. I need to know what happened when Martha took her out onto the fen, and the only way I can find out is by, unfortunately, upsetting Granny. But Mum," I leaned across the table and took hold of her hand, "I think that Granny needs to know the truth, she has the right to know. She must have been wondering for all these years what became of Matilda and Kitty. They were like sisters, Mum, they were so close."

"Alright, Amber, but go carefully with her. She is going through a good phase with her health, and I don't want anything setting her back."

"I'll be careful, Mum, and of course, you can be there."

My mother nodded, stood up and went to the phone to call the nursing home.

"She's having a good day," she said after hanging up. "I have told them that we're coming over for a visit and they're going to tell her that we are on our way and will take her to her room."

Nathaniel stood up. "I'll drive us," he said, picking up his car keys, "but I think I'll stay in the car while you have this conversation with your grandmother. The last thing she needs is someone she doesn't even know being there."

"Amber, I can't believe this is happening, it all feels so unreal." My mother zipped up the front of her coat and checked for her house keys in her handbag. "Ghosts and murders, and there was I thinking you had settled well into Meadowside and were having such a lovely time!"

"That's how I feel too, but hopefully we will be able to sort this all out for the good of everybody involved."

*

When we entered my grandmother's bedroom she was sitting in an armchair, her legs raised on a stool, her hands joined together in her lap, expectantly waiting for us to arrive. Her face lit up as soon as she saw me, and I wished that this was an ordinary visit and that I didn't have to confront her with something I was certain she would find distressing.

"Amber, how lovely to see you, it's been a long time."

I pulled up a wooden chair that was standing in the corner and placed it close to her.

"I'm sorry that I haven't been to see you, it's because I've been so busy." I sat down and held her hand as she happily smiled at me.

"I expect it's that new job of yours. I couldn't believe it when your mother told me that you were leaving the bookshop. I thought you'd be there forever, but I always thought that you were capable of so much more."

I decided that it would be best if I told her the reason behind my visit as soon as possible, while I still felt able to tell her.

"It is because of my job that I have come to see you today. I need to tell you something. I don't want you to be upset, but I have to warn you that you probably will be."

"Is everything alright, Amber? You're not ill or anything like that?"

I smiled gently, "it is nothing like that, I'm perfectly fit and well."

"Then, what is it?"

I glanced quickly towards my mother, who was sitting on the edge of the single bed, nodding her head, encouraging me to continue.

"As you know I am living in a house in the fens, looking after two elderly ladies," I began, my voice already thick with emotion. "Granny," I held her hand tighter as I fought to find the right words. "The house is called Meadowside," I watched her closely for any reaction. "The two old ladies who live there are called Matilda and Kitty Grey."

At first there was no change in her expression, but then, as my words slowly began to sink in, she lifted her head and stared at me incredulously.

"Meadowside?" She uttered, her voice quiet and breaking with emotion. She was then silent.

"Yes," I continued, "the house is called Meadowside, and it's situated all on its own on the edge of the fen. It has a wildflower meadow next to it, and the elderly ladies who live there are called Matilda, you might have known her as Tilly, and Kitty."

There was a long, tense silence. I looked worriedly towards my mother, who was leaning forwards, closely observing my grandmother, with bated breath.

"Meadowside," my grandmother whispered, tears misting her eyes. "I thought I would never hear that name again."

I felt my body slump in my chair and my eyes welled with tears.

"You know Meadowside, Granny?"

"Oh yes," she turned her head slightly towards me, her expression unreadable. "I know it well. I lived there when I was a child, right up until I was seventeen years old."

I placed my head in my hands for a few moments and thought carefully about what to say next. "And you remember Kitty and Matilda?"

"I have never forgotten them, and there hasn't been a single day in the past eighty-two years when I haven't thought about them. Are you telling me, Amber, that Matilda Grey is still alive, and Kitty?"

"Yes, Granny, they are both still alive. Matilda is extremely frail, and her health is not good. Kitty is fine and I imagine just the same as you remember her, just much older."

"Goodness, Amber, I don't know what to say. My years at Meadowside were both the best and the worst years of my life." Her eyes took on a faraway expression, "how I loved them, and how I have missed them. The months after I left Meadowside were so hard for me, my heart was broken, and for a while I thought I would never recover. I missed Meadowside, but most of all, I missed Matilda and Kitty, but I had to be brave, I had to put my love for them and Meadowside to one side. I left for their sakes, Amber, knowing that Matilda, especially, would have been devastated and would never know that I left to save her and Kitty from a life of misery."

"Because of Martha?"

"She hated me," a dark shadow passed over her face. "She was determined to be rid of me, or kill me, and I began to realise that the only way there was ever going to be peace at Meadowside was if I left, and never returned."

"You changed your name so that Matilda could never find you?"

"I did, but that wasn't the only reason. I wanted to draw a line underneath the past. I was from a gipsy family, Amber, and if there's one thing that Martha taught me it was how suspicious and bigoted people could be, how closed minded and judgemental, especially back in those days. I knew that I had to somehow live in the world, away from the culture I was born into, so I took on a brand-new identity. Seraphina Grey died on the day that I left Meadowside."

A shudder passed through me at her choice of words, as I tried to figure out how I was going to tell her how her leaving the house had set into motion a terrible, tragic chain of events.

"Granny, Matilda has been telling me all about her childhood at Meadowside, and the tragedies that the family had to endure, the deaths of Jack and then Issy."

"Issy," my grandmother gasped, "poor little Issy, such a beautiful, happy child. I loved her so much, we all did. Her death shattered the family, and I have carried the memories of that day with me for all these years. She fell out of a tree, you know?"

"Yes, Granny, I know, and then there were the deaths of Emma and Matilda's parents."

"That is right. Emma was the kindest, most caring, beautiful soul that I have ever met. She was completely selfless, and she loved us all so much. I never really got to know Eleanor Grey, like Martha she was suspicious of me, but Edward Grey, well, I loved him, Amber. He was a fine man, and over the years we built a special bond. He was nothing but gentle and kind to me."

Again, I took hold of her hand. "Do you remember the day that you left Meadowside? You and Kitty had been making a Christmas wreath, and Matilda had gone to see Jed Carter's wife who was unwell?"

Her bright blue eyes darkened with sadness. "I remember," she said flatly. "Matilda wanted me to go with her, and I would have done if I hadn't promised Kitty that I would show her how to make a wreath with holly and other greenery from the garden and the woods. Matilda left alone, and I stayed behind to finish the wreath with Kitty."

"Then what happened? Do you remember?"

She nodded her head, tears filling her eyes.

"Almost as soon as Matilda had left the house Martha came into the kitchen, she was wearing her coat and her outside boots. She grabbed hold of me and began dragging me across the kitchen floor towards the back door, screaming that she was going to get rid of me for once and for all. She was manic, like a wild animal. She had taken me by surprise, for she had been almost easy to live with for the preceding weeks, but that had just been a pretence, to make us feel safer in the house, to make us lower our guards. I couldn't fight against her, she was too strong, it was like she had gained superhuman strength."

"She took you out on the fen?"

"Yes, and at first I fought against her, but then, after a while I saw how futile it all was. If she didn't succeed in getting rid of me, another chance would always come along. She told me how life would be better for them all if I wasn't there, and I made a bargain with her. I told her that I would leave, that I would never return to Meadowside or try to contact Matilda, and in return she promised that she would treat her sisters kindly, that she would do better, and become a kinder person. I can only hope that is what happened?"

"Oh Granny," I cried, "Martha was never given the chance to do better or become a kinder person. Martha died on the day you left Meadowside."

My grandmother looked at me with confusion clouding her eyes. "She died? She was perfectly well when I left her. Did she have some kind of an accident on the way back to the house? I don't understand, Amber."

"Granny," I began quietly, "this is going to be very difficult for you to hear, and you need to prepare yourself for another shock." I swallowed hard and decided that I needed to get this over and done with as soon as possible. There was no point in drawing it out. "When Matilda came back to the house Kitty told her what had happened. She said that Martha had taken you out on the fen and had killed you."

"Oh, my goodness! How awful, although Martha did say that is what she intended to do, but I don't think she actually meant it."

"Kitty must have heard her when she threatened to kill you, and then when Martha returned to the house Kitty saw that she was covered in blood."

"Yes, she would have been, she badly cut her wrist on the rusty old gate that led on to the fen path. I told her to put a dock leaf on it, that it would help to stop the bleeding, but she wouldn't hear of it, and so bled profusely, all over her coat."

"Granny, both Matilda and Kitty believe that you are dead, that Martha murdered you."

She covered her face with her hands. "This is terrible," she uttered, "but why didn't Martha just tell them that I left of my own accord."

"I don't think Matilda would have believed that. You promised her that you wouldn't leave. Martha, it seems, didn't tell them that she had killed you in so many words. Kitty had seen the blood on her, had heard her threatening you, and Matilda assumed that she had killed you, and Martha, for reasons that I can't quite fathom, let her believe it. I think that she wanted to prevent Matilda trying to find you, by making cryptic comments, such as, you got what you deserved, and there was no coming back from where she had put you, things like that."

"I see," she took a tissue that had been stuffed down the side of her chair and dabbed her cheeks. "I thought that Martha would have told them that I had chosen to leave, that I had agreed never to return to Meadowside. Matilda would have been angry with me, she would have been furious, but she would have got over it, eventually. It never occurred to me, not for a second, that they would believe I was dead, or that Martha would have encouraged them to think that."

"It wasn't your fault, Granny. You did what you thought was for the best." My grandmother wasn't really listening to me, instead she was frowning and lost in her own thoughts.

"If Martha returned to the house alive, then how did she die?"

I hesitated for a moment, wishing fervently that I did have to tell her this, but knowing that I had no choice. "This is the hardest bit to tell you, but Matilda killed her."

"Matilda!" She was shaking her head in denial. "Matilda would not have been capable of killing anyone."

"She was so angry, Granny. She believed that you were dead, and that Martha had murdered you in cold blood. She wasn't thinking straight, she was distraught. She went to the bedroom that you shared together, she picked up a silver candlestick holder and she hit Martha with it, expecting it to kill her outright, but it didn't, so she then pushed Martha backwards over the bannisters and she was killed by the fall."

There followed a long, tense silence, during which my grandmother stared out of the darkening window, tears trickling down her face.

"Are you alright, Granny?" I asked her gently.

"How did you know that I was Seraphina?" She whispered.

"It was Kitty," I told her, "she suddenly started singing the song that your grandfather composed for you about the boy and his fiddle. She said that it was Seraphina who had taught it to her, and I knew then that the only way it could be true was if you were Seraphina."

"She used to be so frightened by thunderstorms. Tilly had little patience with her, but I knew that Kitty couldn't understand that it was just noise, light and rain. I used to sing her the song to calm her down and help her to go back to sleep. Fancy her remembering it after all of these years."

She fell into another long silence and I was concerned that she wasn't coping with the news, but after several minutes she suddenly grasped hold of both of my hands. "Take me to Meadowside, Amber," she cried, her eyes pleading with me. "I want to see Tilly and Kitty. I want to see Meadowside again."

"Are you absolutely sure that is what you want?" I moved to the edge of my chair so that I was closer to her. "There is one more thing that I have to tell you, it might make you change your mind about coming with me to Meadowside, but I think that you, more than anybody else, will understand this. Martha has never left the house, since the day she died she has been haunting Matilda, and now she is haunting me. She never went to the quiet places, Granny, she stayed in Meadowside."

"The quiet places," she laughed wistfully, "how well you know me now, Amber. The quiet places were a part of my other life, and as time passed on, I gradually lost my gift. Life was busy, and I had less time to spend in contemplation of days that had long gone, and my gift just slipped away from me."

She looked down at her hands for a while. "So, Martha has never left? In a way I am not surprised. She was murdered, and knowing Martha, she would want revenge."

"According to Matilda, Martha hasn't been too much of a problem for them, until I arrived. I think it is me being your granddaughter that has upset her, and she has tried her level best to drive me away from Meadowside."

"How very strange life is," she mused thoughtfully, "and what a trail of chaos we can leave in our wake without ever knowing. Poor Martha, she was so damaged, so angry, so utterly lost and shattered by the bereavements she went through. Her heart was broken, I think, but she couldn't cope, and in the end it all affected her mind. More than anything, I believe that Martha was sick, very sick indeed.

"The entire family were living such an enchanted life before Jack, my father, died. Meadowside was like a haven, full of innocence and happiness, they knew nothing but long summer days playing in the meadow. I think that they all believed that nothing bad could ever touch them. Emma was the strongest, the heart of the family, the one that kept them all together, and while Emma took on the responsibility of her parents, Martha just grew more bitter and disillusioned, and took her pain out on everyone around her. She knew no better, Amber."

I stood up and went to stand by the window. "Did you know that my dad wrote a letter to Matilda, saying that he believed he was related to her?"

"David did?" She looked shocked, "he never told me about that."

"It seems that he had been researching your side of the family, he knew so little about them and it must have made him curious."

"I never spoke about my past, about the fact that I was born into a gipsy family, not because I was ashamed, but because I didn't want to rake over history which seemed irrelevant to who I had become. I wonder how he made the connection to Matilda?"

"I wish that I knew," I shrugged, "he might have employed a professional to search for him. We searched for you in the records, but couldn't find a trace, no birth certificate, no marriage certificate, and of course, no death certificate either. He came very close to finding out all about your early life, I have no idea how, but unfortunately, Matilda never replied to his letter."

"I haven't got any of those things, Amber. My mother probably never registered my birth, and myself and your grandfather were never legally married, because you can't marry without a birth certificate. "

"So, you and Grandad were never married?"

She shook her head. "He was the only person that I ever talked to about my past, but it didn't matter to him at all. We just lived together as if we were married and were happy. In those days, Amber, people just assumed that if you lived in the same house and had a baby then you must have been married. It was never questioned. We really would have liked to have been married, but it was impossible."

"You are sure that you want to come back with me to Meadowside?"

"Oh yes, I want to go back. In a strange way, Meadowside has always been my home," she began to cry again, "and Matilda and Kitty, have always been my family. I thought they would both be dead, I certainly didn't think that I would ever have the opportunity to see them again, and Amber, I need to see them, I really do."

I left the room while my mother helped my grandmother to get ready for the journey back to Meadowside and informed the nursing home staff that we were taking her out for a few hours, warning them that she might not be back until late.

I walked along the corridor that led to the reception area and then out into the car park. Nathaniel had parked the car facing the nursing home entrance and got out as soon as he saw me.

"How did it go?" He asked as he approached me.

"Not too bad, definitely it wasn't as bad as I thought it would be. She was upset, of course, and shocked, but it all went better than I had expected." I looked up at him. "She wants to come back to Meadowside with us today, she is anxious to see Matilda and Kitty."

"That's great," Nathaniel grinned, but then his face fell. "This is going to be very difficult for Matilda, you'll have to handle it very carefully."

"I know," I sighed, dreading that particular conversation, "but at the end of the day, Matilda has the right to know what really happened to Seraphina."

"What about Martha? How will she react to Seraphina being back in the house?"

"I really have no idea, but at the moment Martha is the least of my worries." I bit my bottom lip anxiously. "Matilda will be alright, won't she?"

"Matilda has been through a lot in her life, and no matter how unexpected or difficult life has been for her, the one thing she has always been is alright. She has come through everything, even a dose of double pneumonia at the age of one-hundred and two, she will come through this as well."

Nathaniel looked over my head. "There's your Mother with your Grandmother now. Let's get Seraphina back to Meadowside and see how it goes, and Amber," he looked down at his feet for a couple of seconds, "you've handled all of this really well, not only this today, but all the rest of it too. You've done a brilliant job of looking after Matilda and Kitty, and you stayed, even when Martha was driving you to distraction, and not many people would have done that."

"Thank you, Nathaniel, that means a lot." I smiled up and him and turned to meet my Mother and Grandmother as they slowly walked across the car park.

*

As we made our way back to Meadowside, I planned in my head how I was going orchestrate this once we got back to the house, and how I was going to break the news to Matilda that not only was Seraphina very much alive, but she was also back at Meadowside and waiting to see her.

Beth was standing at the front door before Nathaniel had even switched off the car engine. I quickly got out of the car while Nathaniel and my mother helped my grandmother.

"Has everything been alright, Beth?" I hurried over to her and steered back through the front door and into the hall.

"Everything's fine here, but what about you? Are you okay?"

"Just about," I grimaced. "Where are Kitty and Matilda?"

"Kitty is in the front sitting room watching football with Stephen, can you believe? Matilda is in her room listening to the radio."

"Great. Look Beth, I need to tell you something, but I haven't got much time, so a more in-depth explanation will have to wait until later. The thing is, I have found out that Seraphina was never murdered by Martha; she is still alive and at this very moment is preparing to re-enter Meadowside for the first time in eighty-two years."

"What?" Beth's eyes were wide with surprise and her hands flew to the sides of her face in horror. "How? How can that be? Matilda told you what happened. How can she still be alive?"

As Nathaniel helped Seraphina over the threshold of the house, she suddenly stopped and looked around her. "It's just as I remember it," she said, "nothing has changed at all. It is like I have stepped back in time, as if the past and all of the people I have loved and lost, have come back to me."

"I'll explain it all later," I said to Beth, trying to imagine how emotional and strange this must be for my grandmother. "Can you take them to the big lounge, light the fire and perhaps give them something to eat? I need to go and explain all of this to Matilda."

Beth dumbly nodded her head, then went over to my mother and grandmother and led them into the lounge.

"Do you want me to be with you when you tell Matilda about all of this?" Nathaniel came to my side and rested his hand on my shoulder.

I wiped away a tear that was trickling down my cheek and shook my head. "I'll be okay," I whispered, feeling the nerves squirming in my stomach. "I think it would be best if I told her on my own."

Nathaniel went to join the others in the lounge. I took several deep breaths and composed myself as best as I could before walking across the hall to Matilda's room.

When I entered, I found her sitting in a chair next to the bed, listening to a classical music station. Her eyes were closed but I could tell that she wasn't asleep but just enjoying the music.

As I approached her chair she opened her eyes. "Amber!" She leaned forwards and seemed very relieved to see me. "I have been worried about you. Beth said that she didn't know where you'd gone, only that you had some personal business to attend to. Is everything alright?"

"Everything is going to be alright, Matilda. Everything is going to be fine, even though things are a bit surprising and difficult at the moment, it will all settle down." I pulled over a chair and sat opposite her. "I went to Cambridge to see my Mother and Grandmother."

"How lovely," she said, bewilderment in her eyes. "Are they both well?"

"They are both very well, but I went to see them for a specific reason. Look, Matilda, I don't want to upset you in any way, but there is something I need to tell you and it is going to be a huge shock for you."

"You are not leaving us and going back to Cambridge?"

I shook my head quickly. "No, it isn't anything like that."

"Then what is it?"

"I was with Kitty this afternoon," I began, finding it hard to believe that my realisation about Seraphina had only happened a few hours ago, when it felt to me as if days could have passed by. "She was singing a song, a song that my grandmother used to sing to me when I was a little girl. When I asked her Kitty told me that it was a song that Seraphina used to sing to her. The thing is, Matilda," I reached forward and took hold of her hand, "I knew that Kitty couldn't have known that song, for it was a made-up lullaby that my grandmother's grandfather composed just for her. It has never been recorded or written down in any way. So how could Kitty have known it?"

Matilda was frowning, the expression in her eyes utterly bemused. "I'm sure that I have no idea, Amber."

I took a breath, trying to still the rapid beating of my heart. "This afternoon I learned that Seraphina wasn't murdered by Martha. Martha took her out on the fen, but she didn't kill her."

Matilda looked at me as if I had lost my mind. She turned her head slightly towards me, a frown creasing her brow and I saw a flash of annoyance in her eyes.

"What are you saying, Amber? I told you what happened. Martha murdered her. Seraphina died back in 1921 and it was Martha who killed her."

I shook my head, tears springing to my eyes. "Martha didn't Kill her, because I know for a fact, that Seraphina is still alive."

"That can't be true, Amber. Martha killed her, she had blood on her hands, and anyway, if there is one thing that I know for certain is that Seraphina would never have left Meadowside, she would never have left me and Kitty. She promised me that."

"But she did leave you, Matilda."

"No!" She cried, "Seraphina died out on the fen. Who has been telling you these lies?"

"Please, Matilda, don't get upset."

"How can I not get upset? Seraphina is dead. She was barely seventeen years old and Martha murdered her out of pure spite. She would have contacted me if she had been alive. Whoever is telling you this, Amber, is lying. Seraphina has been dead for eighty-two years."

"Seraphina made a bargain with Martha." I continued, "she agreed to leave Meadowside in return for Martha being kinder to you and Kitty. She left of her own free will, hoping that it would mean that you and Kitty could live in peace. Martha did not kill her."

"This is ridiculous," she bristled angrily. "I have never heard such rubbish in my entire life. Martha killed her. I know that she did."

"You don't know for certain, Matilda. You only know what Kitty believed that she saw, and what Martha allowed you to believe. Did she ever actually tell you that she killed Seraphina?"

"She knew that is what I believed had happened, and she certainly didn't deny it. Anyway," she glowered at me, agitated and upset. "If Seraphina is still alive, where is she? Where has she been for all of these years?"

"She hasn't been far away; she's been living in Cambridge."

Matilda blinked her eyes rapidly and began to destructively pull at a loose thread in the blanket that covered her knees. "I don't know why you're telling me these lies, Amber, I really don't but it makes no sense. I know what I know, and Seraphina is definitely dead."

I leaned back in my chair, watching the old lady before me becoming increasingly angry and upset, but I had no choice, I had to continue.

"Like I said, I went to see my grandmother today. She lives in a nursing home in Cambridge. I told her all about you, Kitty and Meadowside. I told her because I suspected that my grandmother, now known as Sarah Lewis, was the person who sang that song to Kitty all those years ago. In fact, as soon as I recognised the song, I was convinced of it. My grandmother sang it to me, and Seraphina sang it to Kitty.

"When I told her about Meadowside she became upset because, when she was a young girl her grandparents brought her here. She knew all about her father, Jack, and Emma and Issy. She said that she didn't get on too well with your mother, but that she loved your father very much."

Matilda began to weep quietly. "Martha was covered in blood.

Kitty said that she had blood all over her."

"She badly cut her wrist on a gate, Matilda, when Seraphina was fighting against her. The blood wasn't Seraphina's, it was Martha's."

"So, you are telling me, expecting me to believe that after more than eighty years that Seraphina is alive, and is in fact, your grandmother, Sarah Lewis?"

"She changed her name when she arrived in Cambridge. She wanted to make a new start, and then she met my grandfather and had a son called David, and it is my belief that my dad discovered something that connected him, not to your uncle, but to Jack. If I am right, then that would make Jack my great-grandfather, and you and Kitty my great aunts."

She lifted her head slowly. "Jack and Emma looked so much alike. You, apart from your darker hair, resemble both."

"It's not unusual for a person to look like one of their great grandparents," I suggested and then reached into my handbag and handed her a photograph. "It's my father. I took it from grandmother's room today, with her permission, of course. He was about the same age as Jack in that photo."

Matilda gazed down at the photograph for a very long time and then sighed deeply. "It's like looking at Jack. The hair colour is the same and that mischievous grin."

I smiled, feeling a surge of relief, for this, perhaps more than anything proved that Jack was Seraphina's father, and that I was legitimately a part of the Grey family, and Meadowside.

"Is Seraphina well? Has she had a happy life?"

"Yes, she's had a very happy life and married a wonderful man, my grandfather. He died several years ago, but the thing that affected her the most was the death of my father, she took years to get over it, but generally she has had a good life."

"And you only made the connection between Seraphina and your grandmother when you heard Kitty singing one of her silly songs?"

"Yes," I laughed, feeling relieved that Matilda seemed to be accepting the truth about Seraphina. "If it wasn't for that, then perhaps we would have never found out."

"Does Seraphina want to see me?"

"Matilda," I smiled, taking her hand again. "She really does. She has missed you and Kitty so much, and still, even to this day, she thinks of you as her family."

"So, she will come back to Meadowside?"

"She is already here," I said gently, "at this moment she's in the drawing room with Beth, Nathaniel and my mother."

Matilda appeared taken aback. "I need some time," she muttered, "this has all been such a shock and I need time to take it in. I'm not quite ready to see Seraphina."

"That's fine, Matilda. Take all of the time that you need, and if you don't feel ready to see Seraphina tonight, then we can always bring her back to the house at another time."

"No," she straightened her back and lifted her chin. "I want to see her as soon as possible, but I just need to try and understand everything you've told me, to process it."

I stood up. "Just ring your bell when you're ready and I will bring her to you."

An hour later I heard the tinkling of Matilda's bell. I took my grandmother to her room, and the two of them stared at each other for several long moments.

"Tilly," my grandmother said, her voice cracking with emotion, "Tilly, how I have missed you."

Matilda kept her eyes fixed on my grandmother's face. I knew that in her mind she was remembering a young girl with vibrant eyes and fiery red hair, a girl of rare beauty. Now what stood before her was a very old lady, with hair as white as summer clouds, and faded eyes that had witnessed the passing of so many years.

"Seraphina?" Matilda leaned forwards as if trying to see her better.

"It is me, Tilly. It's Seraphina. I have come home."

# Chapter 18

My mother and grandmother stayed at Meadowside until almost ten o'clock, when Nathaniel, without a word of complaint, drove them back to Cambridge. Matilda and Seraphina had talked for a long time in private, and later Matilda told me that they had spoken about the day that Seraphina left the house back in 1921.

"Things would have been so different if she had stayed, but I now understand why she left, and between us, at long last, we have laid the past to rest, once and for all."

That night, while the house was peaceful and quiet, and before Nathaniel returned from Cambridge, I went to Martha's room and stood outside the door.

"Martha," I whispered into the wood, "I know that you didn't kill Seraphina, and I am truly sorry about what happened to you. It was a terrible thing, and it should never happened at all, but it was a very long time ago, and I know that there is peace for you somewhere, if only you would look for it. Please, Martha, leave here now, go and find the love and peace that you deserve. For your own sake, go and find Emma, Jack and your parents, they are there, somewhere, waiting for you."

I placed my hand flat against the door, knowing that she was there, listening to every word that I spoke. "I promise you this, Martha, I will never forget you or what happened to you, none of us will ever forget. Go now, be at peace, and God bless you."

My grandmother returned to Meadowside the following day, Nathaniel driving back to the city to collect her. It was obvious during that visit that Matilda and Seraphina wanted to spend as much time together as they could, and it was Nathaniel's idea that we ask my grandmother if she would like to move into the house.

"They want to be together," he said as we sat in the front sitting room, "and what difference will one more old lady make?"

"Quite a lot actually," I told him, my mind thinking ahead to when I could have three very elderly people all needing my attention at the same time. "My grandmother is used to living in a nursing home, she needs help in the mornings and the evenings, and so does Matilda, and if Kitty deteriorates, which one day she will, then I could have all three of them with numerous needs, all requiring assistance at the same time."

"I have thought of that," Nathaniel smiled knowingly. "Did you know that Beth used to be a carer and worked in a nursing home before she had the children? The long shifts and especially having to work nights and weekends didn't fit well with family life, so she left. We could ask her if she could take on some of the caring responsibilities and help you out in the mornings and evenings. What do you think?"

"That would work, especially as both Kitty and Matilda are so used to her."

"Beth's children are older now," Nathaniel continued persuasively, "and neither Kitty nor Matilda are early risers. Beth would have plenty of time to take the children to school and then come here, and if we ever needed to we could even employ another carer."

"You've thought of everything." I teased, "but where would we put my grandmother? Both she and Matilda need to be downstairs, her mobility is okay, but she would never manage the stairs."

"We can figure it out, Amber," he leaned towards me, his eyes shining with enthusiasm. "Neither Matilda or your grandmother have much time left. I know it's a difficult thing to think about, but it's undoubtedly the truth. Wouldn't it be lovely for them if they all spent their last month's together, here at Meadowside?"

"It would be wonderful," I agreed.

An hour later, after Nathaniel and I had talked through all the pros and cons, I phoned my mother to ask her how she would feel if I brought my grandmother to live at Meadowside.

"It sounds a lovely idea, Amber, but how would you cope having three elderly ladies all living with you? It would be a lot of work for you."

"Nathaniel and I thought about asking Beth if she would come in the mornings and evenings to help. She's already here a lot of the time anyway, and I'm sure she could do with the extra money."

"Okay," my mother seemed to be seriously considering the proposal, "it sounds like you've given it some thought."

"I think it could really work, Mum. Granny would save the nursing home fees, and she, Matilda and Kitty, would all be together again, which definitely seems what the three of them want. They have spent a lifetime apart, and if we can bring them back together again for their final years, or even months, then why wouldn't we?"

"At the end of the day, Amber, your grandmother is more than capable of making her own decisions, and always has been. If moving to Meadowside is what she wants to do, then I wouldn't dream of standing in her way."

"You can visit any time you want, stay over whenever you want."

"If this is what your grandmother wants, then I will fully support it. Poor old Nathaniel can't keep driving her backwards and forwards from Cambridge, so have a chat with her and see what she thinks of the idea."

"Thanks Mum," I could feel excitement rising within me, "I just wanted to run it by you before talking to Granny and Matilda."

"There's just one thing I wanted to ask you. What's going on with the ghost situation now?"

"I believe that Martha is still here in the house, but she's been very quiet and nothing out of the ordinary has occurred. The horrible atmosphere that was here before has completely gone, and I think she will remain quiet now that we all understand that she didn't kill Seraphina."

"It sends shivers down my spine just thinking about it."

"Well, I can feel that she hasn't left, but I think she's as happy as she can be and all the time she's not causing any trouble, then I think we'll just let things lie. I believe that, one day, when she is ready, she will leave, and the house will truly be at peace."

As soon I put the phone down, I went to the children's room and found my grandmother and Matilda laughing over some memory from their childhood. I had noticed that Matilda had become happier and laughed a lot more recently. Kitty and Nathaniel had gone for a walk to the village for a trip to the coffee shop and to pick up some bread and milk.

Kitty had been greatly confused by the reappearance of Seraphina, for a while not recognising her or understanding why she was coming to the house, but my grandmother had spent a lot of time with her, reminiscing about their life together as children. I think that my grandmother was very much the same with Kitty now as she had been all those years ago. She sang her songs and read to her and constantly reminded her of things they had done together as children, and gradually Kitty accepted her presence.

"We were just remembering Issy," Matilda said, as I sat down on one of the sofas, "she was always such a serious little girl, but she would say and do the funniest of things."

"She was always up to mischief, wasn't she, Matilda," my grandmother added with a smile, "do you remember the time she let all the chickens out of the coup, and we spent a fortnight trying to gather them in from all over the fen and the meadow?"

"I remember," Matilda replied wryly. "Emma tried to punish her by making her sit on the stairs, but, of course, Emma could not be angry with Issy for long, and soon gave in and in the end gave her a huge slice of cake to stop her from crying."

They both laughed together, and when the conversation dried up, I told them that I had something important that I wanted to discuss with them.

They both looked towards each other, and then at me.

"Nathaniel and I were wondering how you would feel, Granny, if you came here to live with us here, at Meadowside? We were thinking about how you have spent so many years apart, and how, maybe, you would like to be together all of the time now. What do you think?"

My grandmother was stunned at the proposal and it was Matilda who leaned towards her and said, "Seraphina, come home to Meadowside, properly. This is where you belong, where you have always belonged."

My grandmother removed her glasses and dabbed her eyes with a tissue.

"I will make sure that both of you, and Kitty, have all the care that you need. In fact, we were thinking of asking Beth if she could come and help. There's no pressure, Granny, have a think about it and see how you feel in a few days."

"Amber," she looked at me through misty eyes, "I don't have to think about it, or to see how I feel. I already know how I feel, and yes, I would like to move to Meadowside, I would like that very much indeed."

Matilda was delighted. "You could share my room, Seraphina. It's huge, far too big for a bedroom, really. You could have one side and I could have the other. Oh, Seraphina," she joined her hands together as if she were praying, her eyes alight with happiness. "It will be just like the old times."

*

It was my greatest wish to make Christmas as special as possible for all of us that year. Matilda told me that it would be the first year that the festive season had been properly celebrated since 1913, just days before Jack died.

Beth had readily agreed to adding to her work and hours and had already taken over some of the morning and evening duties from me, which I was grateful for when Christmas drew near and there was so much that needed to be done.

I wanted the house to look spectacular and Nathaniel and I worked tirelessly, decorating Christmas trees, hanging up holly and mistletoe, wrapping up presents and illuminating the entire house with twinkling lights.

"I can't thank you enough for your help," I told him, as we stood back and admired the tree that we had decorated in the drawing room. We had taken the huge dining table from the barn and had placed it at the back of the room by the windows, due to the dining room being out of use in the context of its original purpose and was now a bedroom for both my grandmother and Matilda.

"I have loved every minute of it," he grinned happily, "this could be the last Christmas for one or more of them, let's make it the best ever."

I hated the fact that Matilda, Kitty and my grandmother were so old, and more often of late I had found myself wishing that I had known them all in their prime, when they had all been young, beautiful and full of life. Time was a thief, and in the end, it was sure to have its way.

"It's going to be very special," I sighed with an edge of sorrow, "I just know it."

As it turned out, my belief that Christmas was going to be a magical time, was correct. My mother came on Christmas Eve morning and stayed until after the new year, helping with all the preparations and really throwing herself into the festive atmosphere.

At lunch time on Christmas day, we all sat around the table, the tree lights twinkling on the Christmas tree, candles burning on the table and a jovial, festive feeling in the room. Before the pudding was served Nathaniel stood up and made a short speech, toasting the year that had brought me to Meadowside, and had returned Seraphina to the family that she loved and the place she regarded as home.

"Happy Christmas, to each and every one of us." He finished, raising his glass high into the air.

A few minutes later Matilda also indicated that she wanted to say something. She remained seated as she looked at all the faces around the table. She thanked me for all the help and support I had given to her and Kitty, and for bringing Seraphina back to Meadowside.

"Christmas can be such a melancholy season, full of memories of the past, remembering those we have lost, but not this year, this year has been full of happiness and contentment, which I thank you for, Amber," she inclined her head towards me and took a sip from her small glass of wine. "Despite all the jollity and the celebrating, we cannot forget that the past happened." She struggled to her feet, and leaning heavily on the arm of her chair, she raised her glass. "To my family," she said, her voice now strong and determined to have its say, "who we remember especially fondly at Christmas time. The past is a funny thing, we remember it how we choose to, sometimes not realising that the past that we knew and lived, may have happened differently for other people." She breathed out a huge sigh, and once again lifted her glass. "At this special time of the year, I especially remember my sister, Martha."

Nathaniel and I glanced furtively at each other, surprise on both of our faces.

"I am sorry, Martha, that I couldn't understand you, and I am sorry for what happened between us. Lately, I have been thinking about how things could have been so much better between us if only we had taken the time to get to know each other better, in the way that all sisters should know each other. There was me with my quick temper and impatience, and then there was you with your aloofness and hidden pain. I made a mistake, Martha, a terrible mistake, and you made some too, but I understand now, and I forgive you, and hope that you can find it in yourself to forgive me too. The past is over, Martha, and I wish you nothing but everlasting peace."

She bowed her head for a moment and shakily raised her glass in the air again. "To family," she said, "past, present and future."

We all stood up then and toasted the very thing that Christmas was all about, family.

After lunch we sat around the fire, the table behind us still laden with empty plates and glasses.

"Seraphina," Kitty turned in her chair and faced my grandmother. "Do you remember Merlin?"

"Of course, I do," she smiled wistfully, "I remember him very well. It broke my heart to leave him behind, but I knew that I had to, and that you and Tilly would look after him for me."

"Oh, we did, didn't we, Tilly?"

"Yes, we certainly did." Matilda agreed, "we were out there at the crack of dawn every morning to feed him and to change his water, and to muck out his corner of the barn. He had a good, happy life, Seraphina, we made sure of that."

"Then, a very long time after you left, we went into the barn in the morning as usual, and he had died in the night. I was so upset and cried for days, but Tilly said that you had come to take him, so that you could be together again."

"I did say that" Matilda leant towards Kitty and patted her hand, "but now we know that Seraphina didn't die when we thought she did, so I expect it was one of the others who came to get him, perhaps Issy."

"Of course, over the years, I have often thought of Merlin, and when many years had passed, I knew that it was likely that he would have died." She glanced quickly towards Matilda, "I think it was your father who came to get him, Tilly, and whenever I think of Merlin I can picture him walking through a forest of trees, by your father's side."

In the evening, we listened to old time music, and my Grandmother, Matilda, and Kitty all sang along to the songs of their childhood. It was a wonderful, happy evening and I wanted to capture it forever.

"Where are you off to?" Nathaniel asked as I stood up to leave the room.

"I'm going to get my camera, it's in my room, I won't be a minute."

As I walked up the stairs, accompanied by the out of tune singing and the strains of an ancient song that I hadn't heard for years, I was thinking about what a lovely day it had been and how all the weeks of hard work had been well worth it. I found my camera in my dressing table drawer and stood for a moment on the landing, making sure that it was loaded with a full reel of film, and it was then that I noticed something subtly different about the landing space.

It was quiet, and when I turned my head I saw something that I had never seen before, something that I thought I may never see. The door to Martha's bedroom was standing wide open. It was in that instant that I knew it was over. Martha had chosen to leave.

As I walked back down the stairs I noticed how much lighter the atmosphere felt. I wondered if Martha had heeded Matilda's words and had decided to forgive, and to lay the past to rest. Whatever the reason for her departure, Martha had gone, and in all of the proceeding years that I lived in Meadowside, I never saw or heard her in the house again.

\*

Another summer came to Meadowside, and once again the meadow was ablaze with life and colour. All three of the elderly ladies had experienced a period of great happiness and good health, spending most of their time together, continuing to reminisce about their long-ago childhood days.

Often Nathaniel and I would take them to the meadow, my grandmother and Matilda in their wheelchairs, and Kitty, as if forever young, trotting behind us. We enjoyed picnics, and many blissful hours in the tranquillity and beauty that the meadow provided. Kitty and I often saw Issy, and the first time that my grandmother saw her, racing like the wind down the entire length of the meadow, leaping over the flowers like a young fawn, she cried.

"I can't understand why Matilda and Nathaniel can't see her. It doesn't make sense that some eyes can see something so beautiful, and others can't." I was sitting on the bench, while my grandmother was in her wheelchair beside me, at that very moment watching the shining vision of the little girl weaving in and out of the flowers, while Matilda and Nathaniel were chatting amongst themselves, not able to see her at all.

"I think I know the answer to that, Amber," she turned her head and smiled, an expression of pride in her eyes. "You are my granddaughter and have inherited the ability from me, my mother and my grandmother."

"Does that mean I will be able to see ghosts wherever I go?"

She laughed, "I doubt that, but you may be able to see the people you love, that's the way it was with me."

"The people in the quiet places?"

She laughed again. "When I was a very young child I noticed that I only saw them when I was alone, and when I was somewhere serene and peaceful. It was like, for however long I could see them, that I had stepped into their world, that was full of love and tranquillity. My grandmother used to say to me, 'where have you been, Seraphina?' and I used to tell her, 'I have been to the quiet places, Granny,' and she knew exactly what I meant and exactly what I had been doing.'

"What about Kitty? How can she see Issy?"

"Because she had never lost her innocent childlike eyes. She knew that Issy would come back to the meadow, and she waited for months. She expected it to happen, and in her mind it was a certainty. Let me tell you this, Amber, if you fully believe that there is no other option for something, other than for it to happen, then it surely will."

Both of us watched Kitty, standing among the flowers, shielding her eyes from the sun with her hand, as she watched her young sister running from one end of the meadow to the other.

"I just wanted to say something to you, Granny." I swallowed hard and tried to control my emotions. "I just want you to know how proud of you I am. I am proud of Seraphina, and Sarah Lewis, for the life that you have lived and for all of your wisdom. I am also proud of my gipsy heritage, of my grandmother, the young girl who fell in love with Jack." I turned my head and gazed at the house in the distance. "Look what you have all brought to me, if it wasn't for your mother and you, I would never have known about Meadowside, let alone lived here."

"Life is funny like that, Amber, we never know how people and events can affect us, change us, and mould the shape of our lives. We often don't know why things happen as they do, but we can be safe in the knowledge that there is always a reason."

*

It was a scorching hot day in August, a day that started the same as any other, but yet again, in the history of the house, it would be a day that would alter the fabric of Meadowside forever.

Early in the afternoon, Matilda had requested help to go back to bed for an hour or two, stating that the heat had made her unusually tired. This was nothing out of the ordinary, for she often had a short nap in the afternoon, but usually just in her reclining chair. I helped her to get on to the bed, made sure that her bell was next to her, drew the curtains against the garish summer sunshine, and left the room.

I spent an hour working with Nathaniel in the garden and had returned to the house to get us both a cold drink, when I encountered Kitty in a high state of excitement in the hall.

"You look very happy about something, Kitty," I observed.

She walked straight up to me, her eyes alight with exhilaration. She took hold of both of my hands. "She has never, ever, come inside the house before."

"Who hasn't," I asked, and then quickly realised who she was talking about, and a strange, uneasy feeling began to churn in the pit of my stomach. "Do you mean, Issy?"

"I left the front door open because it was so hot, and she just walked straight in."

"That's wonderful," I smiled, wondering if Issy had come into the house simply because she was aware that Martha was no longer there.

I took a few steps towards the kitchen and then turned back to Kitty. "Where did she go? Did she just go back out through the front door?"

"She went into Seraphina and Tilly's room. She wanted to see Tilly; I think."

"Do you know where Seraphina is at the moment?"

"She's in the front sitting room, reading a book."

"Why don't you go and sit with her for a while, perhaps she will read to you?"

Kitty turned obediently, wandering off across the hall, leaving me standing there with a sinking sensation in my chest. I could have been wrong, but deep inside, I knew what I was going to find even before I even opened the door to Matilda's room. She was lying on her back in the bed, her arms at her side, and the very first thing that I noticed was that she was holding a yellow flower in her hand, of the kind that were growing abundantly in the meadow.

I walked slowly to the side of the bed and sat down in Matilda's chair, knowing that she had gone, and needing this time alone with her before I broke the awful news to the other occupants of the house.

I don't know why I felt so devastated and shocked. Matilda, after all, was so old that I knew her life could not continue for much longer. I think the shock was due to the fact that she had been so well since Seraphina had returned, I had never seen her so lively and healthy, and above everything else, so happy and content. Issy, of course, had come to take her, and by the look of things, it was evident that Matilda had gone with her, peacefully and without struggle.

"I'm going to miss you, Matilda," I whispered into the silent air, "you have no idea how much." I stood and gazed down at her for a short while. "We are all going to miss you."

I left the room, silently closing the door behind me. From the front lounge I could hear my grandmother reading to Kitty. I went to the library and out through the doors that led to the garden.

Nathaniel was still at the flower border where I had left him, pulling up weeds. He straightened his back as I approached him, and straight away knew that something was wrong.

"It's Matilda," I uttered brokenly, wiping the tears from my eyes. "She has gone."

"Gone?" He repeated, throwing a handful of weeds onto the grass.

"She has died, Nathaniel, it looks like it happened in her sleep." I began to sob. "Kitty saw Issy inside the house, and as soon as she told me, I knew that she was there to take Matilda."

Nathaniel stepped forwards and put his arms around me.

"Amber," he whispered, "how lovely is that? She died peacefully, in a happy time in her life, and Issy came to get her."

I sobbed inconsolably against his chest, knowing that what he was saying would have been the absolute truth. Matilda wanted to die at Meadowside, in a quiet, peaceful way, and she had got her wish.

"Remember that this is how Matilda wanted it to be," he said, as if reading my mind. "She wouldn't have wanted to get ill again and to die in hospital, or anywhere else other than Meadowside. She was born here, and now she has died here. She has been blessed, Amber, and now all we have to do is to let her go."

"I have to tell Kitty and my grandmother. They are going to be devastated, and goodness knows how Kitty will take it, she depended on Matilda so much and for so long."

"I can help you to tell them, if you want, I can be there, at least?"

I nodded my head. "Thank you, Nathaniel, that would be good. I think this is going to be a difficult time for them both."

We walked slowly across the lawn and towards the house. Suddenly, Nathaniel stopped walking and turned to me. "You know what else this means?" He said gently, "you are now the new owner of Meadowside. How does that make you feel?"

I gazed up at the looming house, once again feeling the echoes of the past, the lives that were lived and taken too soon, the history and the drama that had taken place within the thick, protective walls.

"It's strange," I said, "I loved Matilda and wanted her to live forever, but she has gone, and I am so sad about it, but I am also happy. Meadowside is my future, my security, my life now, really. It's where I'm going to be, forever, and for that I feel happy, and so blessed."

Together we walked towards the house, and as we neared it I felt its sadness, as if it was letting go of a troubled history, for a brand-new era was on the horizon, and another story was just about to begin.

# Epilogue
## Meadowside 2023

Matilda's funeral was a small, quiet affair, attended just by me, Nathaniel, Beth and her husband, my mother, and, of course, Seraphina and Kitty, but it was deeply moving and beautiful. I believe that it was just how Matilda would have wanted it, simple with no fuss, just a wicker coffin covered with flowers we had gathered from the garden and the meadow. After a short but heartfelt service, the coffin was placed in the family plot, next to her parents and Emma.

The sun was still warm on that early September day, but all around the graveyard I could see the beginnings of yet another winter stealing across the sky. I returned to the grave in the early evening. Strewn with flowers it resembled the meadow itself. I had found it hard to walk away and leave Matilda there, even though my time at Meadowside had taught me that death was not the end, but rather the beginning of something new and different. In my heart I knew that Matilda wasn't there. I knew that she had gone with Issy, that she was safe, warm and loved.

My grandmother came with me to visit the grave and as we stood, looking down on it, I felt so cold and empty, so strangely alone.

"You know that she's not really there, don't you Amber?"

"I know," I brushed away a trickling tear. "It's just that I'm sad about the life she lived, all that energy and potential of her youth was all wasted. I can't help thinking what she would have become if her life had been different, where she would have travelled to, what she would have achieved."

"They say that life is what you make of it," my grandmother said, gazing down at the late summer flowers with a solemn expression in her eyes, "and Matilda built her life around Kitty, and I think the young Matilda would have wanted to travel far and wide, to experience everything life had to offer, but the older Matilda was happy with her lot. It was a simple life, Amber, a life of sacrifice, but in the end, I think that she lived it well, quietly and peacefully."

We fell silent as a shower of summer rain fell lightly upon the grave. I looked up at the sky, thinking that we really ought to get back to the house and to be there for Kitty. I was about to turn towards my grandmother when my eyes were drawn to something moving in the shadows of the old elm tree. My heart sank and a familiar feeling caused every muscle in my body to become taut and stiff.

"Granny," I whispered, nudging her, "look."

She glanced up at me then followed my gaze. "Martha?" She said with a small gasp.

She was standing beneath the tree, a tall, slender figure wearing a dark blue dress, with her hair falling loose and moving slightly in the breeze.

"What could she possibly want now?" I asked fractiously, "Matilda is dead, surely that has to be the end. What should we do?"

"We don't have to do anything," my grandmother said quietly, "just wait and see what happens."

We stood staring at each other, Martha and I. I was struck by her ethereal beauty and was then engulfed in a feeling of deep sorrow. Just like Matilda's, her life too had been wasted, whatever dreams that she had, all of her hopes for the future, were all taken from her far too soon.

We stood there, painfully still, our breath held in our lungs, too frightened to even breathe in case it caused something to escalate, but then, to my utter surprise, Martha smiled at me, and the gesture transformed her face from something stern and harsh, into something truly beautiful. She inclined her head slightly towards me, just a simple nod, that assured me that everything was going to be alright, that it really was all over. To my way of thinking, standing there beside the graves of her family, she was giving me peace, permission to be at Meadowside, and in some way, I felt that she had come to say goodbye, forever.

"It's over, Granny," I said with emotion, "it really is over." The strange thing was that I didn't know how to feel about it. I had only ever known Meadowside with the ghosts and story of the past, how different the house would be with Matilda and Martha gone.

The house was not the same after Matilda's passing, and neither were Kitty and my grandmother. Kitty missed her dreadfully and grew quiet and brooding, her grief all-consuming and heart-breaking to witness. Her health quickly deteriorated, and she passed away six weeks after Matilda, peacefully while sitting in the children's room. When I found her, she had a happy smile on her face, and in her lap lay a single white flower.

My grandmother lived until the spring of the following year. Her death was a bitter blow, even though I knew it was bound to happen, I still found it so difficult to let her go. She died in the middle of the night, in her sleep, and the single flower she held in her hand told me that, yet again, Issy had come to take her so that they could all be together again.

Nathaniel stayed on at Meadowside, and slowly our friendship flourished into love and romance and in the summer of 2005, we were married. Our twins were born the following year, two more little girls for Meadowside, who brought the house back to life and filled the rooms once more with laughter and noise. In a way they brought me back to life too.

I had found it so hard to live without Matilda, Kitty and Seraphina, and perversely I often found myself even missing Martha. There were no ghosts in Meadowside now, the house was hushed and felt hollow and bereft. Issy had vanished from the meadow, even though I looked for her, becoming more and more like Kitty, standing at the windows praying for a fleeting glance of her to brighten my day and dilute my sadness, but she never came.

Life became busy after the children were born, and the melancholy atmosphere lifted. We decorated the house from top to bottom, bought new sofas, carpets and curtains, but we made no drastic changes, and in many ways, Meadowside remains untouched and proudly reminiscent of the days when Matilda, Kitty and Seraphina were children. The little side room of the main lounge is still there and is still known as the children's room, especially as it became a playroom for our daughters.

As we gradually worked through the house we found a lot of memorabilia, in drawers and cupboards, things that would cause my heart to ache, transporting me far back in time to the warm summers before world war one. We discovered children's paintings, books given as birthday presents with inscriptions written inside, old dolls and toys, broken and discarded decades before.

The rooms at the far end of the landing were the last to be decorated. It was a task that I appreciated needed doing, but at the same time I was dreading it and procrastinated over it for years.

The rooms were just as their occupants had left them, clothes still hanging in the wardrobes, trinkets and ornaments still in place, shoes stored under the beds, hairbrushes on the dressing tables. Each room was inches thick in dust and swathed in cobwebs. All the objects that could be saved were placed in wooden boxes, the names of their owners written on top, for I could not throw their precious belongings away, and eventually the boxes were stored outside in the barn, where they remain to this day.

There was a stark difference between Emma and Martha's rooms. Emma's room was neat and tidy. The bed that she had died in was neatly made, the ragged curtains drawn across the filthy window, and on the wardrobe door, hanging by threads, was the remnants of a pale blue dress. The children's paintings adorned the walls, now faded into oblivion, and several handmade birthday cards were lined up on the dressing table. Unfortunately, the paintings and cards disintegrated as soon as they were touched, but we kept whatever we could.

Martha's room was the last to be cleared and decorated. There were no paintings or cards from the children, no ornaments or trinkets, no books, or keepsakes. Apart from the furniture the room was empty, and the wardrobe only contained drab, dark dresses, now thick with dust, and falling to pieces. As I swept the dust and cobwebs away I was very aware that I was removing the very last traces of Martha from the house, and by the time I had finished and the room completely decorated and refurnished, there was simply nothing of her left behind.

It was a relief to get the house fully cleared, decorated and freshened up, and it did go a long way to lifting my mood and the general feeling inside the house, but it was a day in 2008, when our daughters were coming up to two years old, when my heart was completely healed.

I was standing at the window of what had once been Kitty's room, and was now our children's nursery, looking out over the meadow, remembering Matilda, Kitty and Seraphina, with a heavy pain in my chest. I was just about to turn away and to get on with changing the bedding in the babies cots, when I suddenly became aware of a movement in the far distance. I thought at first it was a deer, for I had often seen them frolicking in the meadow, but this movement was slower and more deliberate.

What I could see was four young girls walking up the meadow, and my heart skipped a beat. I placed both of my hands on the windowsill, bowed my head, closing my eyes tightly, convincing myself that I hadn't seen what I thought I had seen, it had only been wishful thinking, a trick of the mind. I lifted my head, prepared for disappointment, but they were still there, closer to the house now and heading straight towards it.

I turned and ran to the door, yelling at the top of my lungs for Nathaniel to come. He soon appeared at the bottom of the stairs, gazing up at me in surprise.

"What's the matter? I was just doing the washing up."

"Never mind the washing up," I told him excitedly, my heart hammering in my chest. "There's something you're going to want to see. Hurry up!"

He ran up the stairs and I led him into the children's bedroom and towards the window. "What is it?" He asked.

"It is them, Nathaniel. They've come back to Meadowside."

He glanced down at me and then back out of the window, and I prayed fervently that he would be able to see them.

"Good God!" He exclaimed, his face draining of colour, but then a slow smile spread to his eyes, "I can see them, Amber," he said, his voice catching with emotion. "I can see them."

*

It is now 2023 and how quickly the time has flown. Our daughters are now grown up, both of them at university. Meadowside has been the perfect place to raise them, and their childhoods were full of happy summer days playing in the meadow.

The house has been at peace for twenty years and has been the happiest of homes, and neither Nathaniel or I will ever leave, the house is too much a part of who I am, of who I have always been.

The long, drab months of winter have passed, and it is early summer in the meadow. For two weeks Nathaniel and I have stood at the top of the mown path, hoping and waiting. On this particular day in June the sun is warm in a tranquil, airy sky and the flowers are blooming.

"Maybe tomorrow," Nathaniel says, slowly turning and walking back towards the house.

I continue to stand there anxiously, knowing that I was feeling exactly the same way that Kitty used to feel while waiting for Issy. Maybe, one of these years, they would simply stop coming to the meadow, it was my greatest fear, for I don't know how my heart could bear it, but then, in the distance I see them. Issy and Kitty, holding hands and running wildly towards me, and then Matilda and Seraphina catch sight of me waving, and they too begin to run towards me.

Nathaniel calls them the prettiest flowers of the meadow, but I call them family, and I always will.

THE END

# ABOUT THE AUTHOR

I live in Cambridgeshire with my husband, son, and delinquent dog. I have always been fascinated by old houses, and I love to imagine their past occupants and their lives. I am an avid reader of historical fiction, but I also enjoy other genres, and of course, I love a good, spooky ghost story.

Writing is my number one passion, and I particularly enjoy writing dual-timeline ghost stories with a bit of mystery and atmosphere. The stories I write are spooky but not full-blown horror, concentrating instead on creating exciting characters that readers can identify with and a ghost (or two) with a perfect reason for being there and for causing the havoc they inevitably do.

I also enjoy watercolour painting, cinema, theatre, country walks, and visiting historical buildings, which often inspire me.

Printed in Great Britain
by Amazon